Tess Thornton

An Angel
for the
Cowboy

 Walker Ranch Book 3

Copyright © 2022 by Tess Thornton

Paperback ISBN: 978-1-957082-05-9

To request permission, contact the publisher at: EagleCreekPressBooks@gmail.com

Library of Congress Number: Pending

Cover Art by: GetCovers

Photography and Graphics Courtesy Of: Shutterstock.com, Depositphotos.com, Twenty2 0.com, Elements.envato.com

Editing and Layout by: Eagle Creek Press, Inc.

Printed in the USA

Publisher: Eagle Creek Press,

EAGLE CREEK
PRESS

Contents

The Walker Ranch Series

For Baxter, Wylie, and C

Chapter 1

Dusty
October

I gulped when I saw the email pop up. *Stockman's Magazine* sent me a reply! It had been so long since I submitted I wasn't expecting an answer anymore. My fingers trembled as I opened the message.

> *Dear Sir,*
> *We have reviewed your submission...*

This was how rejection letters started. I'd seen enough of them to know. But I kept reading anyway, and... and it wasn't a rejection.

> *We will be proud to feature your poem, "The Cowboy's*
> *Call," in our December issue.*

I almost dropped my phone. I was barely awake anyway, and I thought at first it was a dream. But this was worth stumbling out of bed early for. I felt flushed all over. Published, at last! I wanted to whoop for joy, throw my hat in the air, and bark at the moon. I was going to be published! A real cowboy poet! I was no Waddie Mitchell or Baxter Black, but I'd cut my teeth on their writing. Maybe someday, someone would smile over my words the way I'd basked in theirs.

I should tell someone. I'd kept my poems under my hat for two years because, in my family, you didn't waste working hours on stuff that didn't put beef on someone's table. I solved that by writing at night, but I didn't expect anyone to get it. I couldn't stand my brothers' teasing or my dad's long, heavy look when he thought I wasn't pulling my weight. So, I'd kept quiet.

I read the email about ten times more, then celebrated by turning on my desk light and trying to capture the moment in a few lines in my journal. Once I was done, I pulled my clothes on and rolled out into the frozen dawn. I was about to bust inside, but stock still needed hay, and now I was running late. Luke would...

Oh, no. *Luke.*

How was I going to explain this? *No one* in my family poured all his feelings out on paper for strangers to read. No one spent good energy on something that didn't help pay the bills or take care of the animals. They'd think I was trying to be some kind of smart-aleck dandy, and that wasn't what made me want to write at all. I wrote because I couldn't *not* write.

I still wasn't sure what wild impulse led me to submit that poem to *Stockman's*. It wasn't like the fancy western periodicals that graced coffee tables in big country estates. I'd been turned down by all of those. *Stockman's*, on the other hand, was a working rancher's handbook. It was crammed full of market prices and sales reports and practical updates on horse and cattle veterinary research. Luke was always scanning it to look for the latest hot bloodline to augment our rope horse program, and Evan knew all the Angus stats by heart. My whole family read each issue cover to cover before the next one came out.

And I'd gone and sent my poem in.

Would it be too late to call the magazine and ask them to pull it? No, that was stupid. Besides, this was what I'd always wanted. At least I'd sent it in under a pen name—Wyatt Chandler. But since that was my middle name and my mom's maiden name, it wouldn't take half a second for my family to figure it out if they saw it. Maybe I could get hold of our copy the day it arrived and just... make that page disappear. It would be in the back. Maybe no one would notice.

It was Luke I was worried about most of all. I couldn't stand losing face in front of him. He wasn't just one of my brothers. He was kind of my hero.

Twelve years earlier

"Heads up!"

I ducked. In my family, if you heard that, someone was probably throwing a rope at you—especially when you're the youngest of four brothers. It was instinct by now to cover my head and get my arms where I could toss the rope off before someone could tighten it enough to trip me.

But I wasn't at home, and that hadn't been one of my brothers. Brody Egan, the Sophomore who somehow made Varsity, let out a belly laugh when his football beaned me in the head.

"Got you, Walker!" he laughed. His buddies from the football team slapped his back and joined him in pointing at me. "Why don't you go get yourself a calf to play with, little baby?"

It didn't do any good to tell him to stop. I was a puny eighth-grader whose voice had barely started to change, and Brody was even bigger than Luke, a Senior. And not a nice bone in his body. I just got up and started walking away.

"What's the matter, little Dust-ball?" he crooned as he got right up on my shoulder and followed me. "Are you gonna cry now? Go tell the teacher? You're her *favorite*, aren't you? Go on, tell the teacher!"

I balled my fists and kept walking, but my eyes were pricking with angry tears. I didn't cry anymore when the bigger kids picked on me, but there wasn't much I could do about the flush of hot embarrassment on my face. Brody always did this when the girls were watching.

And not just any girl. I risked a glance to my right, where a tight knot of ninth-grade girls were eating lunch. Sure enough, they'd stopped to stare, and right in the middle of them was Jess Thompkins. Her sky-blue eyes locked with mine, and they were filled with pity.

Pity was the last thing I wanted from Jess Thompkins. I looked away.

Brody shoved me in the shoulder, pushing me until I tripped. "Come on, Dust-ball! You got a spine? Say something!"

I thought about picking myself up, but what was the use? He'd just push me down again. I wasn't a coward, but I wasn't stupid, either. A guy my size had no chance against him and half the football team.

"Hey, Brody!" I heard from behind me. There was the heavy sound of a fist connecting with someone's jaw, then a savage, "Pick on someone your own size!" Even as he said it, Brody dropped beside me, groaning and holding his face.

My heart lifted, and I knew what I'd see when I looked up. Luke, the one who always saved me. He might not have been as big as Brody, but he was twice as tough. And he'd just decked my persecutor. I spat the dirt out of my mouth and got to my feet.

It wasn't just Luke who had come to my rescue this time. Marshall and Cody were flanking him, and the three of them were staring down the football team. I mustered what was left of my dignity and went to stand beside Marshall. Not behind him, like a little girl being protected. I was a Walker brother, and I'd stand with the rest.

After all, Jess was watching.

It all ended like these things always do—a teacher broke it up before we had to re-enact the Tombstone showdown. Luke never threw more than one punch, and he never started it, but he was always the one who ended up in the office. Since the teacher hadn't seen Brody push me, she didn't send him to the principal.

Luke got suspended for a week over it. But he still drove us all to school and home every day, because he was the only one with a truck and a license. On the second day of his sentence, Marshall and Cody had to stay after school for being tardy to class. I figured I'd just be sitting on the park benches waiting for everyone else, but when I came outside, there was Luke, honking his horn at me.

"Hey, little brother! Wanna go get some ice cream?"

That was how it was with Luke. He was a lazy student and a lack-luster athlete—the football team had cut him after the first week—but he was fiercely devoted to the family. Mostly to me. He was four years older, and our personalities couldn't have been more opposite, but we'd been almost inseparable since I got my first pair of boots. I was his sidekick, his roping partner. I did his homework half the time, and

I helped him get a date for his Senior Prom when Minnie Stephens dumped him. "Brains and Brawn, and Walker through and through" was what Dad always called us—two sides of the same coin.

That was why it was such a slap in the face when, twelve years later, Luke asked Jess Thompkins out.

Luke wouldn't know what to do with a nice girl if she gave him an instruction manual.

Marshall wasn't much better, but at least he knew how to keep a girl talking to him once he got started. Why had I suggested coming to town tonight? I didn't want to see this—any of it. But I couldn't stay away, either. Marshall was over in the corner fight-flirting with Kelli Mason, and Luke was more interested in watching the game over the bar counter than talking to the goddess at his table. The whole night was humiliating, and I was here to watch it all.

"Why shouldn't I ask her out?" Luke had harrumphed when he first told me. "She's single. I'm single. She's hot, and I'm—"

"A horse's behind," I'd shot back. "You really only asked her out because she's single and beautiful?"

"Isn't that enough? Calm down, little brother. You'd think I was gonna elope with her the way you're carrying on. It's just nachos at the diner."

Nachos. He really ordered nachos. I buried my face in my palms. Jess was way too good for him. Too innocent and gentle and far too intelligent. Not that he could see that. Luke was my favorite brother, but he'd gone too far this time, asking out the most amazing girl in town and thinking she was no different from all the rest.

Except she didn't seem to mind Luke's less-than-polished ways In fact, it looked like they were having scads of fun, sitting close to each other, laughing and bumping elbows over their nachos. My stomach twisted, and it had nothing to do with my meal.

Somehow through the evening, I found myself snared into a long conversation with Austen Conrad, the guy who'd just bought the ranch off High Line Road. He seemed like a nice enough guy, and I was able to answer some of his questions. I was glad for the distraction because I was stuck at the diner until Marshall decided to quit arguing with Kelli Mason and drive home. We burned up half an hour talking feed conversion and bull stats and keeping my mind off Jess Thompkins. Mostly.

Eventually, Austen paid his tab and left, and then there was nothing more for me to do but wait. I sat back to finish my drink and scrolled on my phone for a while. It was better than looking up and seeing what I'd probably see. That was when Jess passed by me on her way to the restrooms.

I looked over at Luke, but he was walking the other way, leaving their coats and even Jess's purse hanging on the backs of their chairs. It was a small town. People did that.

But it gave me an idea.

I fingered the printout of the poem in my pocket. *The* poem, the one that was going to be published. I wasn't sure what had made me print it and bring it tonight, as if I could find a chance to show it to someone. There was only one person in the room who would probably like it, and her coat was hanging right there.

I didn't need to claim it as mine. She could just read it and hopefully enjoy it. Would she find it creepy having a poem show up in her pocket? I prayed not. I had never worked up the courage to ask her out, but maybe I could do this one small thing. Before I could talk myself out of it, I was on my feet, the slip of paper concealed in my hand.

And it was done.

Chapter 2

Jess

"Good night, Jerry! 'Night, Tucker!" I waved at the guys in the paint booth as I walked out of the shop, keys jingling in my hand. They both stopped cleaning their sprayers long enough to wave back. My dad's office was next, and I found him at his desk, squinting over his glasses and typing up the day's invoices.

"I can do those in the morning if you want," I offered.

He looked up and took off his glasses. "Oh, hey, sweetie. Thanks, but I have to get Jed Watts's total sent to his insurance company this evening. You heading home?"

"Yeah. I need to get chores done early and get cleaned up. I sort of have a date."

"Oh? Who's the lucky guy?"

I laughed and shook my head. "Luke Walker. I can't believe I agreed to go out with him."

Dad replaced his glasses. "Neither can I. I wouldn't have thought he'd be your type."

"Not really, but he's not a bad guy. I've been out with worse," I said with a teasing wink.

He snorted. "That's not saying much. Have you ever thought of going out with Will? I think he likes you."

"Our Will? Dad, I'm not dating a co-worker. It would make things too weird."

"But you don't exactly work *with* him. You have the whole back mechanic shop to yourself, and he's up front in body repair."

"Still too close. Don't worry about it! I'm not getting serious about Luke Walker. He flirts with everything that walks, and that's not for me, but he's fun to dance with. You're always after me to get my nose out of the book and get out more."

He sighed. "Well, have a good time, then. See you later."

I walked over to kiss him on the cheek. "Bye, Dad."

The motion lights came to life when I pulled into the darkened driveway. I parked in front of the barn and zipped my coat as I got out. I only had one horse now, but Kelli had just moved her new horse in a couple of weeks ago, so old Nash had a friend again. Two horses made for a little more work, but Nash was happier now that he had another horse to talk to over the bars. It was good for everyone.

I switched into my mud boots in the tack room and walked out to the stalls. Both horses were already fed, with fresh bedding and topped-off water buckets. I shouldn't have been surprised. Kelli had been beating me here lately, and I had hardly picked a stall since she'd brought Joy home. I just reached through the door frame and stroked Nash's forelock. "Good night, sweet boy. See you in the morning." He nudged my hand, then went back to his hay.

I got back in my car and drove around to the house. It was weird living back at home after being on my own for five years. Even weirder with Mom gone. But Dad needed me more than he'd admit, and it was just the change I'd needed. My time in Oklahoma had left a hole in my heart that I was just now discovering. I didn't know what the cure was, but somehow I felt like it had to be here.

I sent a text to Kelli, thanking her for doing my chores again. It meant I'd have more time for a proper shower, which was definitely in order. I wasn't exactly trying to impress Luke, but a girl just didn't go out to dinner with automotive grease under her fingernails. I untangled the grimy handkerchief from my hair, grabbed the bottle of heavy-duty hand soap, and got to work.

If I hurried, I'd have time to pick up my book for a few minutes before Luke showed up.

"Hey there, sweet thing." Luke leaned against the porch railing, giving me a cheesy wink when I opened the door. And suddenly, I wasn't sure this was a good idea.

"Let me get my coat," was all I said. He gestured that he'd wait and stuck his hands in his pockets like he was looking for a can of chew that wasn't there.

"I thought you quit that."

He froze—caught like a little kid. "Huh?"

I pointed to his pocket, where a faded ring in his jeans testified to his old habit. "Chewing. I heard you talking about it at Morgan and Cody's wedding. You said you'd quit because your dad and Dusty finally nagged you into it."

"Oh. Yeah." He pulled his empty hand out with a sheepish grin. "Once in a while, I forget it's not there anymore."

"Well, I hope you don't start again. I saw a cowboy once who had a hole rotted all the way through his gums."

Luke's face went slack. "Nuh-uh."

"Scout's honor. Besides, you'll have better luck with the ladies if you don't have brown stains on your teeth and on your breath."

That cocky grin returned. "So, you're saying I have a chance with you?"

I patted his cheek with a sweet smile. "Hell would freeze over first. Ready to go eat?"

He just shrugged. "Sure. Where do you wanna go?"

I gave him a confused look as I locked the front door. "I thought you had something planned."

"Oh, I did, but it just came to mind that maybe you'd like somethin' fancy."

"Like the steakhouse? That would be fine. Were you thinking of something else?"

"Nachos are on special at the pub."

I blew out a sigh. I should have known not to expect anything too nice. This was Luke Walker, after all. "Fine."

We got to the pub and made our order, and then we just looked at each other across the table. "So," I said after an awkward silence.

He nodded. "Yup." Some conversationalist.

"How, uh... How are things at the ranch?"

"Oh, can't complain. Dozer scored me some clean practice runs this week. The ol' man's still got it."

I narrowed my eyes. "And Dozer is?"

"My heading horse. Gettin' a little stoved up, though. Think I might need to retire him. Oh, hey, the game's on."

"Oh, I'm sorry to hear about Dozer. Doc Burns gave me this great supplement for Nash because he gets a little... Luke?"

Luke's eyes had already glazed over, his attention centered about six feet above my head. Good grief. "Hey, Luke!" I mock-shouted, just loud enough to get his attention.

"Huh? Oh, right. Sorry." He folded his hands on the table and twiddled his thumbs, the strain of not looking at the TV twitching all over his face. He forced a smile that looked like something out of a cartoon for how pained it was. "Wha'd you want to talk about?"

"Anything. How about what you like to do in your spare time?"

"What do you mean?" His eyes flicked helplessly to the TV.

"You know. Movies, books. Do you have a workshop you like to tinker in?"

"Workshop? Heck yeah, we have a workshop. We all have to weld and stuff like when the mower..." His forehead wrinkled, and his gaze tightened when the TV announcer got all worked up about a play. Luke was obviously trying to be polite, but he lost the battle. He jumped to his feet to watch the quarterback streaking across the screen. "Get him! Run, you butterfingers! Aw, man. What's wrong with you? Is that ref blind? For crying out..."

When it went to a commercial break, he sat down with an apologetic look. "Sorry."

I just hiked a thumb over my shoulder at that all-pervasive screen. "Who's playing?"

"Broncos."

"Denver?"

Luke scoffed. "Heck, no. College ball, Boise State. Buddy of mine used to play for them. What were you saying?"

I had to think about it. "Oh, you said you had a shop of some kind. I was asking what you used it for."

He lifted a shoulder. "We fix stuff. Me and Dusty had to put a new head on my truck a while back. Didn't it sound good?"

"Oh. Um, yes, it did," I said as politely as possible. "I was thinking more like a wood shop. Crafts, projects, that kind of thing. Do you have any hobbies?"

He grabbed a handful of peanuts and stuffed them in his mouth. Then he talked around them. "What for?"

I refused to cringe. If I'd been interested in Luke as more than just a friend, I'd have cared, but as it was, I just sighed and arched a brow. "Just something to do. Everyone has to have some kind of outlet."

"Not us Walkers. We work." He grabbed another handful of peanuts.

"What about when you take a break? You're a pretty good dancer," I remembered.

He grinned. "That's right, I am. I'm a better roper, though. Pretty good at tyin' things up."

It took me a second to realize he was making some kind of innuendo. I probably turned about six shades of scarlet, but Luke didn't notice. The game was back on.

"Go! Catch him, you filthy varmint! What the heck are they paying you guys so much for if you can't take down—"

"Luke... Luke! You know they can't hear you, right? And didn't you say this was college ball? They're not professionals."

"Half the fun of watching the game, yelling at the quarterback. So, where were we? Oh! Nachos are here."

That was when I gave up trying to fight it. What was the use? Luke would never be the kind of man I was looking for, and I'd told him that straight up. Why not just enjoy him for what he was?—a decent guy I could kid around with like a brother. I scooted my chair around the table to watch the game with him. Luke grinned his appreciation and slid the nacho plate a little closer to me. Then all his attention was on the TV. And that was fine with me.

I did have fun. Once I truly let go of any hope that Luke was the kind of guy I could have a sweet, romantic dinner with, I started cheering and whooping at the game with him—and half the other cowboys in the bar. We banged glasses, we yelled at the home team by name, and we joined in a round when our team won. It had been a long time since I'd had that much fun on a date.

Luke mopped up the last of the nachos and brandished that famous Walker grin at me. "Wanna dance?"

I actually thought about it for a minute. "You know, I think I'll pass tonight. Do you mind?"

His jaw shifted to the side, and he shook his head. "Naw. You ready, then?"

I stood up. "Just a minute. I need to visit the powder room."

The whole drive home, I was trying to figure out how to end the evening. I didn't want to hurt his feelings. I never could find it in me to be mean, but I couldn't have him thinking I'd be his go-to girl whenever he wanted to watch a game and eat nachos. Not that I hadn't had a great time, but...

We pulled into my driveway, and Luke put the truck in park. "Reckon we're not the dancing kind of friends, huh?"

My chest sagged in relief when Luke said it first. "Not really." I turned to smile at him in the darkened cab. "I'm sorry. Are you okay with just being regular old friends?"

"Aw, heck, we had us a good time. Friends is fine. It was better than sittin' at home watching Evan read the paper."

I snickered. "Well, thank you for asking me. I did have fun."

He squinted at me from under his hat. Even in the dark, those Walker eyes were enough to take a girl's breath away. "But you don't want me to ask again, right?"

"You know, Luke, some girl is going to count herself very lucky someday to be yours. I'm just not the girl."

He scratched his ear and crunched his face up like he was trying to decipher my words. "So... does that mean no necking by the porch light?"

I laughed. "Good night, Luke."

"Good night."

I slipped into the house and sagged against the door. We'd ended things the way we should have, but I couldn't help feeling disappointed. A friend was great, but it wasn't a friend I was looking for. I wanted to lose my head and heart over someone and stay there the rest of my life. I wanted the kind of romance people write books and make movies about.

Did that kind of man even exist in the real world? It wasn't like I hadn't had options, but none were even close to my silly old fantasies. There was Colby, whose mother still ironed his drawers. Porter, who thought the way to woo a girl was to put his hands *everywhere*. Tanner... Tanner didn't count because I'd turned him down when he spat out a stream of tobacco immediately after asking me out. Rafe, Ryan, Robert, Sam, Steve, Stu... all good-looking losers who thought primarily with their little brains.

There had to be a few left who didn't paw a girl for attention and could act like a grown-up. Maybe even some who thought about more than football and how good his truck sounded. Just not in this town.

And there was the rub because as much as I needed to be here at home, in the place I loved where I was free just to be myself, I needed something else more. Something to hold on to, a dream to chase, and maybe even someone to build a life with. Because right now, my life was stagnant, boring, and lonely. So lonely that the best time I'd had in months was shouting at a television in a crowded bar with a cowboy I could never fall in love with.

I sighed and pulled off my gloves to stuff them in my coat pockets. And that was when I found it. A sheet of paper, crisply folded into perfect quarters. That hadn't been there earlier, had it? I unfolded and scanned it. It was a poem, but no poem I'd ever read. In just a few lines, it pulled me into someone else's world.

The Cowboy's Call

Mist over the mountains, golden grains in the valley
The rocks and the trees, dotted with danger.
Born of the land, dust and sweat on his brow
He's a cowboy, formed for his work.
Life in the saddle, taut sinew on his bones
The bawl of a calf, creaking leather in his ear.
His horse lunges right, the slip of the rope
The dance begins, music of his earth.
Silence crackles around him, his heart is afire
Galloping over open spaces, the gold of dawn.
He'd ride through a storm, the ice and snow
By iron-shod feet, toward the keeper of his flame.
Born of the land, tamed by her
The glow of her smile, the key to his joy.
She is his air, his hope, his love,
He is her cowboy, hers alone.

I turned the paper over a couple of times. No author, no address. Just a folded poem stuck in my pocket. Had I picked it up somewhere? Surely, I'd have remembered. I only wore my nice coat for going to town, but I'd worn it to church on Sunday. I couldn't have forgotten something like this in that little time.

I reread the poem more slowly. Whoever wrote it had a gentle way with words and an expressive turn of mind. The way they described the hardships and glories of the life they loved was like a tender challenge to live, fully live, the moment one was given. It made me choke up a bit. I couldn't know who had written it, of course, but it seemed to speak into my soul with the voice of a man. A man who knew honor and love and beauty and sacrifice.

And, apparently, a man who had to be from around here. I carried the page to my room to spread it on my dresser, where I could read it over and over again. But who wrote it?

Chapter 3

Dusty

"Snow's really comin' down now," Luke announced as the door of my barn office slammed behind him. It created a gust that picked up and swirled my stack of feed invoices to the floor, and I jumped up to catch them.

"Darn it, Luke, I just got those sorted! Can you close the outside door next time before you come in?"

"Sorry." He bent to help me collect the papers, but he wasn't much help because the pile he handed me was rumpled and entirely out of order. It would have been easier for me to pick them up neatly, one at a time.

I still wasn't sure if I wanted to talk to Luke. I'd had nightmares for a week about him and... I couldn't even think of her name in the same sentence as his. Obviously, though, Luke didn't notice my sour mood, and he wasn't going to give me much choice in talking to him. I just sighed. "Thanks. Where are you coming back from?"

"Hardware store."

"Oh, yeah?" I slid my laptop aside and wetted my finger to flip through the pages. "I hope you kept the receipt for me. What broke this time?"

"Nothin'. Just hangin' out with the Langton boys. Gage has a new truck."

"Don't get any ideas. Yours is only two years old."

"Yeah, but it's got sixty thousand miles on it."

I set the re-sorted stack of invoices down on my desk and deliberately placed a rock in the middle of them that I kept in my office for just that purpose—in case of Luke. "It's your money, I guess. So, is Dad looking for me or something?"

Luke's face crunched. "No. Why?"

"Why'd you come up here?"

"Oh! That. Wanted you to look at a horse I'd like to buy." He pulled his phone out, touched the screen a few times, turned it sideways, and passed it to me.

I shouldn't encourage him. I was still annoyed with him, and Luke had too many horses. But I never could stay mad at Luke, and when I saw the picture on his phone, I whistled in surprise. "Wow."

"I know, right? She's a beaut."

"Gorgeous." I tapped through the pictures, zooming and turning the phone with the angles of the photos to get a better view. It was a silvery gray mare, nearly white but for a chiseled black muzzle and large, liquid brown eyes. "Seven years old, fifteen-three hands. Where is she?"

"California. Been some guy's wife's trail horse, but he says she was originally trained as a header."

I clicked away from the pictures and scanned the mare's pedigree. "All good lines. Some world champions up close here. Huh. How much is he asking?"

"Too much. That's how you know it's a good one, right?"

I snorted as I passed his phone back. "I wish it worked that way. What do you need another heading horse for? You have three in various stages of training already, and we have fifty out there you could pick from when you're ready to retire Dozer and start a new one."

"We don't have any of these lines. Figure I can breed her to Bud Wilkins' nice stud someday and get us some fresh blood."

"Do what you want, I guess. Has she been vetted?"

"No."

"Any videos of her working?"

"No."

I shook my head and laughed. "So you could be buying a lame bronc for all you know?"

"I'll have a vet check done before she gets on the trailer. I'm not that stupid."

"But you don't know if she can do the job. The guy really has no videos of her?"

"Naw. His wife just died, and he's selling everything off. He's got the mare boarded like fifty miles from his house and just needs to get her homed."

"So, it's a charity buy—assuming he's telling the truth. I don't know, Luke. You're paying top dollar for a horse you can't be sure of unless you ride her."

"Well, I hope she works out. I already gave the guy a deposit."

I dropped my head on my desk. "It's a good thing I do the ranch books and not you. You'd have us all driving new trucks and behind on the bills."

He shrugged. "At least I know it. You about ready to wrap up?"

"I would be if you hadn't blown in here to interrupt me." I closed my laptop and turned off the desk light. "Heck with it. Let's go get some food cooking."

"Now you're talking."

I pulled my coat on, and we came out into the barn's balcony together. The big roll-up door was open at the end of the aisle, and it was starting to get dark outside, save for the thick white carpet of snow that had fallen while I was in working.

"Boy, you weren't kidding," I said when we got to the bottom of the stairs. "We might be snowed in by tomorrow."

"Yeah. Hey, you know what? We should go out the back door."

"Why?"

Luke stuck his arm out in front of me and jerked his head toward the window that looked out into the arena. There was someone out there, and it wasn't Cody on one of the show horses.

"What the... is that Marshall and Kelli Mason?"

"Search me. I couldn't see either of their faces when I walked by before."

I leaned a little closer to the window. "Saturday night, they were bickering like a couple of toddlers. And now they're... well, what do you call that?"

"Interesting is what I'd call it. Wish a woman would kiss me like that."

I swallowed and kept my gaze low. "You didn't get a kiss on your date the other night?"

"Me? Bro, I'm not talkin'. You know the rules."

I'd been holding my breath, and I let it out slowly. So, he'd kissed her and probably held her and run his fingers through that flaxen hair. Luke and the girl I'd been dreaming about since middle school. My heart squeezed so hard I had to pound on my chest. "You... you had a nice date, then?" I choked.

"Sure. Hey, speaking of which, nachos sound good again tonight, too. How 'bout you?"

My mouth tasted like sawdust. "I don't care." How could I think about food? Luke wasn't known for getting serious about women, so either he'd break her heart, or... or worst of all, she would be the one woman to change him. And I'd have to watch. My head was swimming so much I could hardly see straight.

Luke laughed and nudged me with his elbow as we turned around and walked the other way. "Check it out! Marshall's horse wandered off. Think we should go catch him before we head in?"

"Marshall's a big boy." And a happy one, too, from the looks of it. What would that feel like?

It was more than just a question. Deep down, I wanted to *know* and be able to explain, from my very marrow, what it was to fall in love and be loved back. Like Mom and Dad. Like Cody and Morgan. Like what Marshall was feeling right now.

I was a writer. Whatever else I was, I'd finally given up fighting that one. I made things up, and I made words happen. I made people feel things, and I put ideas in their heads.

Well, not many heads. So far, just an online group of other would-be writers, all of them too scared to actually pour their hearts out in public—like me. But, as someone in the group said, just because I didn't have an audience, it didn't mean I was any less of a writer. And writers are supposed to know what love feels like. I could watch, and I had an imagination, but it wasn't the same. What I wanted...

Well, I wanted to *feel*, and I wanted to give of myself like that... but I wanted it to be with the girl who'd owned my heart for years. If my idiot brother hadn't gone and beaten me to it.

Jess

"So, are we snowed in?" I came out of my bedroom at six, still tucking my hair into a knot and fumbling into my favorite oversized flannel shirt. Dakota, my Australian Shepherd, trotted behind me. His shoulder bumped my leg with every other step as he stared at me, hoping I had something to throw.

Dad was standing at the window, looking out into the blackened yard with a cup of coffee in his hand. "Looks like it. I already called the guys to tell them to take the day off."

I came up behind him to rest my hands on his shoulders. "Well, I know someone who will be happy about that."

"Hmm?"

"Didn't you notice that Kelli didn't bring her horse home last night? She got snowed in up at Walker Ranch and had to stay in the bunkhouse."

"Oh?" He turned around with a funny smile. "And what was she doing up there?"

"You mean 'Which brother was she with,' right?"

"It's a valid question. Four single cowboys up there? It's like one-stop shopping."

I laughed. "It was Marshall, and I'm dying to talk to her when she gets home. Sounds like they had an interesting afternoon."

"You never told me how your date with Luke went. I assume since you didn't get snowed in at the ranch with Kelli...?"

"Oh, no, I'm in no danger of that! Kelli can have the whole Walker family if she wants them."

Dad sipped his coffee and smiled over the rim. "Sounds like she's picked one out already. By my math, there are still two more of them. Not worth your notice?"

"Oh, Dad, I don't know. I think I'm through with guys for a while. It seems all I ever do is give one after another a chance, and then I'm sorry I wasted all that time on them. Maybe I need to not date for a while because it's just been such a merry-go-round of duds."

I chewed on my lower lip and sighed in frustration. Why did this seem so easy for everyone else? I didn't think I was that picky, but I was so used to going through them like the ticker on a slot machine that I wouldn't even be able to spot the right kind of guy if he was standing in front of me.

Dad frowned. "Well, I never figured dating for a recreational sport anyway. Too much at stake. You deserve the kind of man who thinks you hung the moon."

"I'd settle for one who could spell it! Is there more coffee?"

He gestured toward the pot in the kitchen. "Lots. Guess it's just you and me today. Any plans?"

I poured my cup and then got some creamer out of the fridge to drizzle on top. "We could tinker with the hot rod."

"Nah. We work on cars all week."

That was the first time I'd heard my dad say something like that. He loved his hot rod, and he loved it even more when we worked on it together. "Well..." I blew the steam off the top of my cup and took a sip. "We could do a puzzle."

"The last time we did that, my eyes hurt for hours. Too many tree leaves to tell apart. Do we have any with better color contrast?"

I sank into the couch. "I don't think so. I could bring some saddles in to clean, and we could watch a movie while we work."

He shrugged. "Maybe this evening. I don't want to watch movies all day. I'll go bonkers. What do the other girls do on days like this?"

I frowned. "What other girls?"

"You know, your friends. They probably don't work on hot rods or clean their tack in the house."

"I don't know. I'm sure Kelli's getting cozy with a cowboy, and Morgan... well, same thing, probably. I haven't seen Britney for a while, and Nikki just had a kid."

"Is that all?"

"Around here, yeah. Most of my friends left town as soon as possible and never came back." It would get even more lonely if Kelli took up with Marshall Walker. I'd been the popular girl in high school, with more friends than I knew what to do with. But now, it was hard to find anyone to hang out with at all.

Maybe Audrey, Kat Tracy's sister. I liked spending time with her, but she was always so busy helping Kat and Lizzy that I'd never gotten a chance to know her well. There just really wasn't anyone who could fill that gap.

Dad looked down into his coffee cup, gave it a swirl, and drained the rest. "Well, think I'll go shovel the walk."

I watched him go, then tucked my feet on the couch and gave the cushion beside me a pat. Dakota hopped up and snuggled against my leg, laying his head on my knee and staring at me with his mismatched eyes full of anticipation.

"You wanna go play in the snow?" I asked, tugging on his silky ear. His muscles tensed, but he didn't move.

"Let me finish my coffee, then we'll feed Nash, and I'll throw the ball for you."

That did it. He dashed down from the couch, ran to the door, and returned with the ball and the thrower in his mouth. His whole body was alive with wiggles, and he whined in excitement.

"Okay, okay! Maybe we can set your agility course up in the yard this afternoon. That will be fun to play in the snow, huh? Go get my boots."

Dakota dropped the ball thrower and ran to the mud room to pack my boots, one at a time. He even went back a third time to drag my heavy chore coat off the hook and through the house. Then I had to carry them all back to the door to put them on, but it didn't matter. This was our game, and he loved to show off what he could do.

That was what I'd do today—teach Dakota a new trick. I'd just have to think of one because he knew everything I'd dreamed up so far. But when he was the best company around, what else was I supposed to do? We'd play for a while, and then I'd curl up in front of the fire with him next to me. I'd get a big furry blanket and a hot tea and bury my nose in a book about romantic heroes and the kind of love stories that span the ages.

I could think of worse ways to spend my day.

Chapter 4

Dusty

Monday morning, we were snowed in. We could've gotten to town if we'd really needed to—we all had chains, and Luke could drive through anything with that souped-up truck of his. But we had our hands full just taking care of stock after a hard snow, and there was no shortage of problems that came with the weather. Like the door of my work truck being frozen shut at five in the morning, and all the water troughs having six inches of ice floating on top.

Evan took a tractor out to scrape the driveway. Then he putted down the road to help some neighbors. There was one older couple who couldn't get out to feed their goats when it snowed like this, so he went and checked on them while Luke and I covered his chores. He was out most of the morning, clearing what he could and making sure the folks who lived around us were okay.

By about nine, some of our ranch help who lived nearby were able to get through on their ATVs. We'd have asked a couple of the guys to stay in Cody's old bunkhouse last night, but Marshall had already claimed it for Kelli. So, we just had to make do, short-handed and overworked, until the county got our road plowed in the early afternoon.

By the time I finally got up to my office in the barn, it was too late to start on any real paperwork. I'd just have to put it away in a few minutes, but I could update the ranch's webpage, check on a few neighbors, and purge my emails. First, though, I scrolled down to that one from *Stockman's Magazine.* It was still real.

Had Jess found the poem I slipped in her pocket? The longer I thought about it, the more I cringed. That had been a stupid idea. What would she say if she found out it was me? She'd think I was a creep or something. I should have just waited for a better opportunity. How could I explain that one? "Gee, sorry, I didn't realize that was *your* coat. I thought it was Luke's." Stupid.

But I still wanted her to know it was me. That maybe we shared something she didn't even realize, and that could be everything. And I wanted more than anything to talk to her about... well, all of it. Life and feelings—not even romance, really, just how to roll along in the world, always trying to reach something exquisite and wondering if there was more. The things you can talk about with someone who has a soul like your own.

And I'd gone and stuffed a poem in her pocket like a fifth-grader. I was an idiot.

But it didn't matter anyway. She was seeing Luke for now, and I could never—*would* never, even if I could—step in and mess that up for him. I might wring his neck, but I wouldn't try to steal his girl. *My* girl.

I scowled and gave my mouse wheel a quick flip, just checking one last time for new messages before I closed it down to head out to feed. Just as I was reaching for the off button, a message came from Austen Conrad.

Hey, Dusty,

*I forgot to get your text number the other night. You said
you handle all the ranch emails, so I figured you'd get
this.*

*I was hoping to ask you to come to check out my herd and
go over some ideas I had for next season. You know your
stuff, and I'd be grateful for the help. Just let me know
when you're free.*

Thanks,

Austen

Well, that was pretty flattering. Austen seemed like a smart enough
guy and not one to waste his time. It felt good to have someone ask
for my help because that meant he trusted me to know my stuff and
knew I'd be straight-up honest with him. I replied that I could be free
anytime the roads were clear, gave him a number to call or text me on,
and shut the computer off to finish chores.

Kelli had gone home by the time I got down to start feeding. That
left Marshall to rejoin life, with stars in his eyes and a spring in his
step and the whole bit. He looked about like Cody had last summer,
smiling nonstop and whistling everywhere he went. I wouldn't say I
was jealous, but I wasn't in the mood to watch. Not when I was so
inept at love and showed no signs of improving anytime soon.

He took over the rest of my chores before I could even get to them.
Maybe that was his way of apologizing for slacking on work earlier in
the day, although no one had complained. I just checked everything,
found there wasn't much left to do, and went in the house to start
cooking a huge pot of baked beans to go with whatever Marshall had

on the grill. That would taste good to everyone after a cold, nasty day. Plus, I didn't have to babysit dinner once I got it in the kettle. I slipped back to my bedroom and turned on my desk light.

Maybe I should write something to Jess. Just in case things didn't work out with Luke, I told myself. I was good on paper, and the words were clattering around in my head, banging to get out. I'd capture them now while they were bottled up, and I knew them by heart, and maybe someday, I'd have a chance to give them to her. Just not as a cryptic note stuffed in her coat pocket. Only a moron would do something like that. I pounded my forehead with my fist.

I'd just write her a little note of explanation. Simple and honest, clear the air. I swirled my pen over the page, waiting for the first word to take shape in my mind, and then let the ink flow.

Dear Jess,

I'm sorry for imposing on you the other day, and I hope I haven't made you uncomfortable. I'm kind of new at this. I have wanted to talk to you for so long, but I never knew how. I should have just approached you like a normal person! I'd really like to get to know you better, but right now, I don't even know how I will work up the courage to give you this.

If you do find this note in your hand someday, know that I won't intrude where I'm not wanted. I just had to ask. If you're willing to take a chance on me, I'll trust you to show me somehow. I don't know what would happen if we were to spend some time together. Maybe nothing. Maybe everything. I just know you're the sweetest, kindest woman I have ever met, and no matter what you decide, I wish you happiness.

My pen stopped. Should I sign it? What should I say, "With love?" While true, that reeked of serious stalker vibes.

When was I planning to give her this? Not while she was dating Luke, not even if it killed me. But Luke went through girls like water, so maybe they wouldn't last. I could only hope.

What then? It wasn't like I never saw her in town. She went to the feed store pretty often, and there were only two grocery stores in town. I'd waved at her just last week at the hardware store. I could find a chance to slip it into her hand. She'd know it came from me this time, and if she didn't want it, she could throw it away.

My pen pressed into the spot where I would put a signature. I could just write my name. Simple and honest. But I kept trying to envision actually giving this to her, and the more I thought of it, the less plausible the idea seemed. I'd have to know where she and Luke stood first. After that, it would be easy.

I just had to work up the guts to talk to her.

Jess

We only had one day of deep snow. It was still cold, but the frozen stuff came in small flurries rather than heavy storms. Thanksgiving came and went, then there was a solid week of the most glorious blue skies and sheet white glare from the snowy landscape. Beautiful, but the auto body business always picked up on weeks like this. People would get blinded by the winter white or hit a patch of black ice, and then we'd get a call.

I was running the office more than I was fixing engines lately. It wasn't like Thompkins Auto Body was the first place people thought of when they needed their injectors replaced. I'd known I wouldn't have a lot of work when Dad offered me his back shop, but I didn't know I'd be spending so much time at a desk. I breathed a long sigh as I clicked through the screen of vehicle damage estimates. All these needed to be sent over to insurance companies for approval or payment—a job Dad hated doing. I could get it done in half the time he could, so I cracked open a soda can and got to work.

I'd been clicking away for maybe an hour when someone knocked at my office door. "Yeah?" I said, not really looking at him. The guys always came to talk when I was working.

A man cleared his throat. I squinted one last time at the line of figures I was entering, then shifted my gaze. It wasn't one of the shop guys.

"Hello," he said, with a smile as wide as Texas and sweet as honey. "Jess Thompkins, I believe?"

"Yes, sir. Can I help you?"

"They say you're the mechanic?"

"Only one we've got."

He took his hat off and entered the office to draw up a chair. "My name is Austen Conrad. I think we've met before."

I didn't remember his name, but he did look a little familiar. Most guys had started to look alike to me, and it was a sad realization. I'd gotten so jaded that I didn't even notice them anymore. "Oh. Nice to meet you again."

He kept smiling. Friendly smile, but to be perfectly honest, I didn't care for it. Jerks smiled just as much as nice guys. I'd learned that the hard way.

"Well, I'll start at the beginning. I bought the old Finney Ranch up on High Line Road last fall. It's Silver Falls Ranch now, but that's not the point."

I was nodding and checking the stack of invoices in front of me. I'd have them all done by lunch. "Go on," I said.

"I inherited Finney's equipment, and some of it's been giving me problems. I have this old twenty-five-horse Kubota that stalls every time I try to use it."

I shuffled the finished paper estimates into the file folder. "Probably blocked fuel lines."

"Wow, you *are* good! You can tell that just from what I told you?"

"Pretty common problem with old diesels, actually. Especially tractors."

"Great! Well, what do you do about it?"

"Clean or replace the lines. Shouldn't be too hard if you have the tools. How long since it was serviced?"

Conrad shook his head and laughed. "Finney didn't exactly 'service' his equipment. It ran, or it sat. No in-between. Something is going on with the bucket hydraulics, too."

"Sounds like it needs a thorough going-over, then."

"I'm sure it does. So, should I drop the trailer? Or would it be better to unload the tractor and leave just that here?"

I squinted. "Leave it...? Oh, I don't service tractors."

He looked crestfallen. "You don't?"

"No, you need someone with tractor experience, especially if the hydraulics are messed up. You probably have other problems you don't even know about yet. Bobby Eckhart is your guy. Here, I have his card... somewhere." I rummaged around in the desk until I found the clutch of business cards Dad kept in there for things like this. They were all scattered and out of order, so it took me a second to find the right one. "There, give him a call."

He took the card and frowned at it. "You sure you can't just clean the fuel lines?"

"I probably could, but I'd get in there and find a lot more that I can't fix for you, and then you'd have a disassembled tractor to haul to Bobby. You're better off just taking it to him before I crack it open and mess something up."

He sighed. "Well, you're probably right. Thanks for your time."

"Sure thing."

Conrad got up, and I returned my attention to my billing screen. He was halfway out the door when he stopped. "Is that your dog?"

I glanced down at Dakota, curled in his bed behind my chair. His ears flattened, and his stumpy tail wiggled when I made eye contact with him. "Yeah. He goes everywhere with me."

"Beautiful dog. Blue merle Australian Shepherd?"

"Thanks, and yes, exactly."

"Where did you get him, if you don't mind?"

"I brought him back from Oklahoma. He knows all kinds of tricks."

He smiled. Again, with the big smile. "Like what?"

I looked at my dog. "Dakota, turn off the light."

Dakota jumped up and dashed to the switch, stretching his furry little body to reach it. He slapped at it several times, and the lights went out.

"Wow! What else can he do? Can he turn it back on?"

I got out of my chair. "He can, but it's harder for him, and he scratches the heck out of the wall." I came over to the door, bringing me to Conrad's range. He smelled nice—Stetson unless I missed my guess. Who wore cologne to drop his tractor off with a mechanic? Obviously new around here. I flicked the switch and went back to my chair.

"That's... that's quite a dog." He fumbled with his hat.

"Thank you. He's my buddy. Have a nice day!" I set my fingers back on the keyboard. I'd never get my work done if this guy didn't take the hint.

"I, uh... I'm looking for a couple of dogs. To work cattle."

"Oh."

"Know anyone around here who raises or trains them?"

I sighed and dropped my hands from the desk. This guy wasn't leaving. "A few. Border Collie or Heeler?"

"Huh?"

"What kind of cow dog do you need? They do different jobs."

"Well, I don't know. Maybe one of each. What do you think?"

"I think you should go talk to the Walkers. They're the only ones I know off the top of my head who breed both. They could tell you where to start, and they might even have some pups coming up." I deliberately bent down to stroke Dakota's ear, then turned back to my desk.

"Oh, that's good to know. Dusty's supposed to come out to the ranch tomorrow. I'll talk to him."

"He'd be the one to ask. Good luck to you."

Austen stood a few more seconds in the doorway. I glanced up once to offer a quick, neighborly smile, and he finally put his hat back on. "Thanks for your help."

"Anytime." I sagged back in my chair and sighed again when he finally walked out. What was with that guy?

I mean, I *knew*. It wasn't like I was stupid. Guys always tried to hit on me, and it made it hard to get anywhere in a conversation. It would be different if all the guys who flirted with me were ones I'd be interested in flirting back with. But half the ones who acted like that were married, too old, or just plain gross, and I'd mostly learned to ignore them. The colder, more business-like I was, the sooner they started figuring out how to talk like regular people.

Dad popped his head into the office, his painting respirator dangling around his neck. "Who was that?"

"Name's Austen Conrad. He came to see if I'd work on his tractor. I sent him to Bobby."

Dad's eyebrows crunched together. "He hauled his tractor all the way into town without calling first to see if you could even work on it?"

I shrugged.

He snorted and shook his head. "City folk."

I laughed. "Pretty much. Are you taking a break? I might as well stop for lunch now since I'm not getting all these done as fast as I hoped."

"Yeah. Hey..." He leaned a little farther through the door and lowered his voice. "Will asked me a bit ago if I thought you'd have dinner with him sometime. I told him I didn't know. He might ask you when he gets in the break room."

"Argh." I groaned. "You know what? I think I'll stay here and try to finish these."

Dad gave me a sympathetic smile. "Want me to bring your sandwich over from the fridge?"

"Please."

Chapter 5

Dusty

"So, what do you think?"

I crossed my arms in front of my chest and nodded toward the red Angus calves in Austen Conrad's corral. "They're in good condition but not growing as well as I'd have expected for their age. It hasn't been that cold yet, so that shouldn't be slowing them down. Did they get all their shots?"

"I don't know. They were five or six months old by the time I got the ranch."

"That might be part of it. Finney was getting up there. Maybe he got a little careless this last year or so. It's a lot to stay on top of. We should also have Doc Burns check your parasite load, but I'm betting that's not the problem."

"Okay. Got it." Austen tapped some notes into his phone. "What else?"

"Let's go take a look at your yearling heifers."

We got back into his ranch truck, and Austen drove slowly past the weanling pen and up a gravel drive to a rusty gate. "I had to put a bunch of new fence posts in when I got the place," he said. "That gate was held on to a rotten post with baling wire."

"I believe it." I got out to open the gate, and he drove through, then I closed it.

There were about twenty heifers with their heads buried in piles of hay, and they didn't pay much attention to us as we wandered among them. I checked each one over, poked through the feed, and then walked around the herd again. "They're plump and just right for their age. Your hay looks good, too."

"It's not too tough and stemmy? It was all I could get by the time I got here. Finney hadn't bought enough hay for the winter, and all the better stuff was gone."

"Who told you that?"

He shoved his hands in his coat pockets. "Oh, I see. Good old boys ripping on the new guy, huh?"

"Probably. This was a bad year for hay, but there's still good stuff around to buy, and there's nothing wrong with yours. It's not the best I've ever seen, but it's fine. I swear sometimes cows can digest barbed wire."

"That's good, but that's the last time I buy hay from Morris."

I laughed. "We sell quite a bit every year. I'll put a word in for you with Evan."

"Thanks."

"Anything else? I don't see anything to be worried about with your heifers. What were you thinking?"

"Well, I thought they were fine, but I thought a lot of things were fine until I found out they weren't."

"Right." We walked back to the truck. "How's your new bull settling in?"

"Fat. He's pretty friendly, actually. I didn't expect that."

"They can be, but don't take it for granted," I warned. "He's still a bull."

"Wouldn't be much good to me if he wasn't. So, where to next?"

"Did you want me to take a look at your records? Maybe we can spot some trends."

"You don't mind? I'll order a pizza if you can stay that long."

"I'm up for pizza. I'll get the gate."

"So, what brought you here, of all places?" I kicked back in the chair at Austen's kitchen table and crunched down the last pizza crust.

Austen had a glass of milk and finished a long chug of it before answering me. "Wanted to get out of the city, mostly. I grew up in northern California—beautiful scenery, lots of horses and cows, and farming. Always missed it after I left."

"To go where? I heard Silicon Valley."

"That's right. I spent my career in San Jose developing and selling software. Wrote a lot of apps, got lucky a couple of times, grew tired of the smog and the traffic, and cashed out. I got enough for my house alone to buy the land here." He shook his head. "Amazing. Anyway, I was looking all over the country for ranches, but when I saw this one and visited the area, I decided this was where I wanted to land."

"What made you want to get into ranching? You could've just bought a view property in the wilderness."

He smiled. "Call it a little boy's dream. Always wanted to be a cowboy. People laughed and told me you have to be born into that kind of thing, but I wanted to prove them wrong. Not doing a very good job of it so far."

"Well, for one thing, they're wrong. And for another, you've done a lot here in just a couple of months. It's a pretty steep learning curve, but you're on top of it."

"Thanks to a few guys like you, who've taken the time to help me out. I really appreciate it. You're great at this."

I shrugged and looked down. I never knew what to do with praise. "You will be, too, once you've done it for a few years."

Austen finished his glass of milk and set it down. "But you know what's still weird to me? Where I come from, you're always in competition. Sure, people will 'help' you, but you have to be careful not to let them know too much, or they'll turn around and use it to get ahead of you."

"And how exactly would I do that? We all sell beef to the same market."

"Yeah, but if yours are fatter than mine..."

I waved a hand. "Doesn't help me at all if my neighbors aren't thriving. We all depend on each other. Branding season, everyone turns out and helps everyone else by turn—you, included. We'll all come up and make a day of it, sorting calves, giving shots, and doing ear tags."

"Really?" He let out a sigh of relief. "I was going to ask you how that worked. With the neighbors, I mean. I have a small bunch, so I just assumed I was on my own. Figured I'd hire a few kids from town who know how to rope and flub my way through it."

"Nope. It'll be a quick day at your place, but we'll get a few guys. Speaking of which, you still look short-handed here."

"Yeah. I was having trouble finding anyone who knew what they were doing and didn't already work for someone else."

I nodded. "I know some guys you could check out for your foreman. And some kids, too—we always have some high school kids working for us part-time, learning the job and stuff. This is too much to tackle without hiring good help."

"Tell me about it! Oh, that's another thing I was going to ask you. I heard you raise dogs."

"Not at the moment, but we have in the past. You could really use a good Border Collie. It would be like having an extra cowboy at your right hand. I have a one-year-old male I was training this summer I could let go. Unless Evan decides he needs him—guess I need to check on that."

"Already trained? That would be great if you could sell him to me. You know, I'm kind of jealous of you guys, having a whole family to keep things running."

"It's nice. Most of the time." I toyed with my empty plate for a second. My family was everything, even when they frustrated me. I wouldn't have it any other way. "You haven't said much about family. Got any?"

Austen shrugged. "Not much worth talking about. I was an only child, and my parents were divorced. My mom died a few years ago, and I never got along with my old man." His brow clouded, and he stared at his empty glass. "And then... well, like I said, it's not worth talking about. What about you?"

I squinted. "Well... you know, three brothers, plus Cody. He just got married, but the rest of us are single. I guess Marshall's not... I'm not sure what Marshall is."

Austen chuckled. "The girl from the pub? The one with the long dark hair?"

I snorted. "How'd you guess?"

"He wouldn't stop staring at her until he got over to her table. I hope it works out for him."

"Yeah," I mused softly. "Me too."

"But no one special for you, huh?"

I frowned at my plate. Special? Jess was more than special to me. She was that tender place beside my heart that ached whenever I saw beauty, or truth, or something worth writing down. She was the words that flowed from my pen, and she was the feelings that were too big for words. But she wasn't mine, and there didn't seem to be anything I could do to change that. I hesitated, then just shook my head. "No."

"Yeah," Austen sighed. "Not for me anymore, either. I did meet someone, though."

"Really?"

His face softened, and he got a huge, sentimental smile. "She's... she's incredible. I've never met anyone like her. Beautiful and smart and... and so *different* from other girls. I don't even know how to put it into words."

"Well, congratulations. Have you asked her out?"

He shook his head, and his smile dropped. "No. She barely gave me the time of day. I talked to her for a while, but she was all business, no matter what I tried."

"Too bad. Maybe you need to step it up a little."

"You think? Like, what, flowers?"

I laughed and held my hands up. "I'm not the person to ask. You don't see women hanging around me all the time, do you?"

"They would if you were in California. Good-looking guy like you, friendly and helpful, and wearing a cowboy hat? You bet you wouldn't be lonely."

"Well, I'm not in California."

"Yeah," he sighed. He got up to get the milk jug from the fridge and topped off both our glasses. "Maybe I'll try flowers. At least there's no way to treat that like a business conversation, is there?"

"Not unless she's a florist."

He chuckled. "You're pretty good with the one-liners. I'll let you know how the flowers go. If they flop, maybe I'll have to ask you for help with more than just my cows."

"Hah. I'm not much help, but I'm here." I downed the glass he'd just poured me and stood up. "I'd better get back to the ranch. Thanks for the pizza."

He stuck his hand out to shake mine. "No, thank you. I appreciate it."

I went to the door to slide into my coat and grabbed my hat. "Anytime."

And I meant it. Family was family—they were the blood in my veins. But Conrad had no claims on me; neither of us owed the other anything, and I'd been able to help him. It had been a long time since I'd felt needed and appreciated like that.

Jess

"Hey, lady, how about a ride?"

I was in the barn, grooming Nash when Kelli led Joy in from the pasture.

"Where?" I asked. "It's going to be dark soon."

"Just the round pen. I've *got* to work on some things, so I don't fall off again!"

I stopped brushing to actually look at her. She'd been limping since last weekend when she rode in the hills with Marshall and her horse spooked. But a little limp didn't slow Kelli down. "How's your ankle? Still swollen?"

"Yeah, but don't tell anyone. Marshall will say I should sell my horse, but I won't do it. I'm going to prove him wrong about her."

I turned back to Nash but sighed when my face was hidden. I agreed with her boyfriend on this one, but if Marshall wasn't getting anywhere with that argument, I wouldn't either. I might as well try to help her wherever I could. "This old guy could use some exercise. We'll lope around with you for a few minutes."

"Yes! Race you with the saddle!"

I chuckled and went to get my stuff. I hadn't been riding much this last year. It wasn't that I didn't enjoy it anymore, but riding alone on an easygoing, push-button horse like Nash had gotten pretty boring. There was no spice or excitement anymore, just like with everything else. Having Kelli at the barn was the first time I'd had someone else there since Mom, and it was nice to have the company. In fact, seeing her working so hard with Joy almost made me want to get a colt to train again. Almost.

I'd trained Nash for my mom. He didn't have quite enough speed and pizazz to be my rodeo horse, but he was steady and respectable, and he took care of his rider. Mom used to joke that he was the ideal man. Maybe she was right, and I'd been chasing after the wrong kind all these years.

As life changed, I had sold all my other horses one by one. They were out there now somewhere, breaking arena records and making other girls' dreams come true. But I hung on to Nash, and it was fun to have a reason to enjoy him again. I spent almost an hour fooling around in the round pen with Kelli. I gave Nash some refresher lessons, more to show Kelli some pointers than anything else, and then we just walked around for a long time, cooling the horses out.

"I thought this would be so much easier," Kelli sighed in frustration. "What am I doing wrong?"

"Nothing, really. She's just not an easy girl."

She stuck her lower lip out in thought. "People say that about me, too."

I burst out laughing. "I'm sure they mean it in the nicest way!"

"Pretty sure they don't, but whatever. So, do you have any tips on making things click better? I'm just not sure what to do with her, and I really, *really* want this to work out."

I watched her horse walking along, champing at the bit and swishing her tail at Nash every few strides. "Nothing earth-shattering. Time and patience, I suppose. And chemistry."

"Like pharmaceutical chemistry or romance-type chemistry?"

"The second!" I laughed. "Horses connect just like people do; sometimes, it's hard to explain. You just feel it."

"Like how?"

I thought for a minute. "Remember Knightley, that gray horse I used to run barrels on?"

"Yeah, you always beat me."

I blinked. "Oh. I'm sorry."

"I'm kidding! You think I expect you to apologize for being good?"

"No." I squirmed a little in the saddle. "I just never felt comfortable with standing out."

"But you can't help it. It's who you are."

I was frowning down at Nash's head. Kelli was right—I always stood out, no matter what I did. I didn't try. It just happened. And I didn't like it.

She sighed and waved a hand. "Oh, never mind. No need to get all serious about it. What about Knightley?"

"Well, it was like that with him. We could feel each other's thoughts. He was greener than my other horse, but we got along better. The minute I touched him, I just *knew* he was special."

"Wow," Kelli breathed. "Okay, another one."

"Another horse story?"

"No. You said romance chemistry, and now I'm thinking about a certain cowboy. I think we have 'it,' but I guess I'm not sure. Any ideas for me?"

"I wish." I frowned and fixed my eyes on Nash's ears, bobbing and twisting as he picked up our conversation. "I don't think I've ever had 'it,' as you say, with any guy. I don't know. Maybe it's not even that important, and I'm making too big of a deal out of it."

"No way. I *need* this to be true, or my Hallmark-loving heart will just break. Come on, you really never felt like *any* guy was special? Even after you got a chance to know him some?"

"I should. I dated enough... but... no. Not really." I shrugged. "They all just felt the same."

Kelli heaved a dramatic sigh. "Well, if even *you* can't find Mr. Right, what hope does that leave for the rest of us?"

I squinted at her. "What is that supposed to mean?"

"I mean, you're the girl we all want to be. I tried hating you for it, but you were too nice to me, so I couldn't even get that right."

My ears burned hot. *This* was exactly the sort of talk that always made me uncomfortable. "Come on. I'm not—"

"Yes, you are. Like it or not, Jess Thompkins, you're gorgeous, inside and out. You're smart, you're sweet and tough and graceful. I still haven't figured out how to walk like you do."

"But Kelli, it's nothing—"

"Hang on, I'm not finished. How is it that you, of all people, never 'clicked' with any guy? It seems like you could have something special with just about anyone because you're so easy to be around. You don't have my bad temper or Morgan's stubbornness. And you're smart enough that you have something to talk about with just about anybody. You're just... kind of perfect."

I stared at Nash's ears again, my stomach knotting. Was this the way people saw me? Just easy-going Jess, never causing a ripple and always saying and doing the right thing? A pretty face with a perma-smile? They didn't know me at all!

"Kelli, I don't know where you're getting any of this," I mumbled uncomfortably. "Really. I'm *not* always nice, and you're much more interesting than I am. I don't have all that many friends, and I'm a big screw-up when it comes to relationships."

She turned to me with that quirked brow and kinked her lips to the side. "We'll see about that, Jess Thompkins. I'll bet there are at least five guys who dream about you at night and are just waiting for you to notice them. Who knows? Maybe one of them is your knight in shining armor."

I snorted. "There are maybe five single guys in this whole valley."

"See? And all you need is one of them."

"I don't think so," I said with a laugh and a sigh. "But you're sweet to say it. I think, for now, I'll just live vicariously through you and Marshall. So, got any good stories you can share?"

"Do I ever. Hope you're not cold because I'm not going to shut up for a while."

"Chat away!"

She did. For over an hour, while we did chores and went inside for a mug of tea. But I didn't mind. I was much happier listening to Kelli's romantic tangles than explaining why I didn't have anything to talk about.

"Down, Dakota." I walked into the living room, balancing a monster bowl of popcorn, another fresh mug of Earl Grey tea, and my favorite book under my arm. Dakota was bouncing backward, trying to see into the popcorn bowl and probably trying to trip me so I'd spill some of it for him. He was freaky smart that way.

I dropped into the couch and pulled my furry throw over my feet, then settled the popcorn bowl in my lap. "There, have some," I said, tossing him a handful. "That's all."

He gobbled down my offering, then proceeded to stare at me with his mournful gaze. I gave him a stern look, and he finally heaved a sigh and turned his back on me. I patted his head, then lost myself in my hardcover copy of *Emma*.

My mom loved this book. I remembered her reading it to me when I was so little I could barely understand it, and it was such a long book that it took months of bedtime stories for us to get through it. And when we finished it, she started it over. We wore out two hardcovers that way, and I was well on my way to turning the third into a rag.

In my teens, we'd have popcorn and movie nights with one screen adaptation or another. I'd even named my favorite queening horse

Knightley because he was such a dreamy guy. He was the stuff of *my* dreams, anyway. I still regretted selling him, even though I'd thought it was a good idea at the time. Things change.

I never got to say goodbye to Mom. In the last phone conversation I had with her, she was putting away groceries in the kitchen, and I could hear the miniseries playing in the background. She probably just had it on because it reminded her of me and all the cozy evenings we had spent watching it.

Mom died when I was on a tour in Texas, working for the Miss Rodeo organization. It was so sudden that Dad didn't even have time to call for help. She'd been pruning the roses and just collapsed from a heart attack. Dad was so broken when he called me that he never even got the words out. I just knew I needed to come home.

So, I did. For good.

And just like Mom, I somehow always returned to our favorite old story to remember her when I was feeling lonely. Watching the movie alone made me cry, so I usually read the book. I had a stack of others like it, too. I'd learned to love Georgette Heyer, Elizabeth Gaskell, and the Brontës. If it involved sprawling old estates and deliciously outdated customs, ladies in scrumptious gowns who flirted with the boundaries of propriety, and gentlemen who sacrificed everything to gallop in on a white horse and save the day... yeah, I was a sucker for all of it.

Maybe that was why I was still single. I'd never met the guy who would give up his time or his job or whatever else might have lain in his path just to be with me. It sounded selfish to say it like that, but all I'd ever known were guys who wanted me for what I could do for them. Guys who expected me to be the one to give up everything to be their arm candy, and I was over it.

That was what I should have said to Kelli earlier. Maybe there *were* still guys out there who were interested in me, but could they be what *I* was looking for? Just once, I wanted to find the guy who would put me first, ahead of all his other ambitions. And I'd do the same for him because that was what love was to me.

I guess they just didn't make real life that beautiful.

Chapter 6

Dusty

-Can you come out to the yard?

I picked up my phone to read the text from Luke. Why would he be asking that? He knew I was trying to get the bills paid before the end of the week, and he usually didn't bother me unless it was an emergency. But if it was an emergency, he wouldn't have phrased it so politely. He was up to something again, and I wasn't sure I wanted to be a part of it. I still wasn't sure I wanted to talk to him right now. I frowned and texted back.

-I'm busy.

His answer was almost instantaneous.

-Dude, this is worth it. I need you.

I cast my head back and scowled at the ceiling for a minute. Somehow, I had to find a way to deal with Luke, even through this. I swallowed and sent him a reply.

-On my way

When I got outside, there was an enormous horse hauler with California plates backing into the driveway. Luke was spotting for the driver, wearing a huge grin. "Five more feet," he called. "You have lots of room!"

I came beside him and hooked my thumbs on my belt. "You bought her."

Luke glanced at me and shifted something around in his cheek. "'Course I did."

"And you're chewing again. I thought you quit that."

"It's gum. See?" He hung his mouth open to give me a view.

"I don't want to see your stupid gum." But I couldn't help smiling, just a little. Luke would always be Luke, goofy stunts and all. As frustrated as I was with him, I loved him more.

"Suit yourself. That's far enough! Crank it a bit now and then back up off the driveway," he yelled at the driver. To me, he said, "Don't want to make her step off on slick pavement, you know?"

"Since when do you care about that?"

"Since I emptied my bank account buying her."

I rolled my eyes. "I just hope she's half as nice as you think she is."

"She will be. Okay, that's good! I'll get the door!"

I followed Luke around to the back of the semi-trailer. The hauler was supposed to unload the horse, but Luke beat him. He was already inside, unfastening the dividers and banging around before the driver even got out of the truck. We heard some thumping, a horse sneeze, and Luke's voice soothing the mare. Then hooves sounded on the matted floorboards as he backed her out.

"Well, what do you think?" he demanded proudly.

"She's wearing a blanket. I can't even see her."

"We'll fix that. I'll get her all gussied up and lookin' fancy. Here, hold her while I tip the driver."

I took the lead rope and studied the mare's face as Luke reached for his wallet and walked off with the horse hauler. Judging by what I could see of her, the pictures hadn't done her justice. Her head was broad and flat between dark, intelligent eyes, with a slight dish to her profile that made her look delicate. But offsetting that delicacy were wide, powerful jowls and a toned, muscular neck. Her long mane was white, with slight waves that would probably tangle into fairy knots if Luke didn't keep it braided. She was only seven, but she must have turned gray early because the remaining dapples on her neck were a vague silver, almost invisible. She'd be pure white in a couple of years.

"Hello, pretty lady," I said as her paper-thin nostrils drank in the scent of my coat sleeve. "Do I smell like dinner? Don't worry. It's coming soon. I'm sure Luke is going to feed you like a queen."

Her ears, shorter than most mares', swiveled at my voice. One of the geldings in the paddock whinnied at the new arrival, and she gave a low whicker in reply. Luke came back right about then.

"Alright, all settled. Don't you go gettin' sweet on my mare, now. I'll take her in."

I chuckled and gave Luke his lead rope. "So, what did you pay for her?"

"You don't want to know." Luke walked away, whistling Woody Guthrie's *I Ain't Got No Home*. "Come on," he called when I didn't follow. "This mare ain't gonna brush herself, and you need something useful to do."

"I *had* something useful to do. You made me stop." But I went after him anyway because that was what I always did. Luke came up with a hare-brained idea, and I followed.

He clipped her into the cross-ties in the middle of the barn aisle, stripped her blanket off and gave a low whistle. "I think I got what I paid for."

I ran a hand over the mare's wither and down her broad back. She had so much "shape," as the old horsemen say, that she might have been set in marble. Perfectly exquisite. "You sure might have. Hope she rides as good as she looks."

"Oh, yeah. She'll put us in the money next summer, little brother. You wait and see. And in a few years, I'll have me a string of handsome gray colts that everyone from here to Wyoming is gonna be chasing after me to buy."

We both stepped back, sweeping our eyes over her conformation. Her legs were clean and straight, all her angles and proportions were just about perfect, and she looked in the bloom of health. "A touch on the heavy side," I said. "That's about all I can see wrong with her."

"She's been standing around for six months. We'll get you in shape, huh, old girl?"

"What are you naming her?"

"Gal who had her called her Pinkie."

"That's awful."

"Yeah. Her papers say Royal Diamonds or something like that. Any ideas? You're the creative one."

I scratched my chin. "It's not very creative, but she looks to me like a 'Duchess.' Classy, regal girl like her? That's what I'd call her."

"Works for me. She cost enough to be named Duchess, that's for sure. You know what she needs, though? Some of that purple shampoo they use on the sheep to make them all sparkly white."

"Luke, it's December. She doesn't need a bath."

"Just her tail. I wanna show her off to Bud Wilkins next weekend, and that tail needs some love."

I blew out a sigh and rolled my eyes again. I did that a lot when I was with Luke. "I was going to make a run to the feed store soon. I guess I could pick some up for you."

"Good, because you still owe me for that cup of coffee I bought you last week. I'll be here when you get back."

"I'm going right now?"

"Unless you want to help feed and bed her down."

I shook my head. "Guess I'll be back in a while."

Jess

"That will be thirty-two fifty," the cashier said.

I pulled my wallet out of my purse. "Did feed go up again? I thought this grain was only twenty-nine a bag last month."

"Yeah, fuel prices. Sorry," the girl replied with a shrug. "Manager said it will go up again before spring."

"Good thing I'm only feeding one horse," I said with a chuckle. "I'd go broke if I had a whole ranch full!"

The girl behind the counter faked a smile, but I could tell she wasn't all that interested in my joke. She probably just wanted to get her shift over with. I sobered and pushed my card into the chip reader. People didn't seem as friendly as they used to. Had the town changed that much? Or was it me?

I hadn't been able to stop thinking about what Kelli said. I'd lost sleep over it. I knew she meant it kindly, but it really bothered me. Did people actually see me the way she claimed they did? The "best" at everything, "graceful" and "smart" and... and bland as old dried toast? Intimidating to get close to and no fun once you did? I wouldn't even want to be around someone like that. It wasn't a nice feeling to find out that *I* was that person.

"Have a nice day," the girl said as she ripped off my receipt. Her smile was plastic, and her eyes cut away from mine as soon as possible without being rude. I sighed as I stuffed the receipt in my purse. Maybe she was just shy. That was probably it. But she wasn't the only one.

I hefted the grain bag over my shoulder and headed outside, Dakota trotting at my heels. He loved going to the feed store, but this time no one had offered him a treat, and he was nudging my pant leg as if to remind me that he was supposed to get a cookie at the register. "Sorry, buddy," I told him. "Maybe next time."

As we went through the door, I passed a short, older lady who gawked at me through her thick glasses like I was some kind of weirdo for not using the cart. I hadn't even thought about it. This was how I always did it, so I didn't have to return the cart. Apparently, I'd accidentally found another way not to blend in. I pulled my sunglasses down with my free hand and avoided looking at anyone.

I threw the feed in the trunk, then opened the door for Dakota. He jumped in, then turned and waited for me. As he did, I caught a glimpse of his old collar. It was getting pretty ragged, and I'd been meaning to replace it. And it wasn't like I had anywhere to be... or anyone waiting for me. I frowned.

"You know what, buddy? Let's go back in and find you another collar while I'm thinking about it. Maybe you'll even get a treat this time through."

We went back in, and I took my time, threading my way through the store. It was nice to be away from work and out of the house, where real people lurked from time to time. I didn't miss being in Oklahoma, where the busyness and rush of my job and the people I kept up with had threatened to overwhelm me. But plunging back into small-town life, with a job that didn't put me in touch with many people, was a lot to get used to again. Once in a while, it was nice to see some fresh faces.

"Jess?"

I turned around. It was Dusty Walker, just leaving the horse grooming aisle carrying a basket full of bottles. I smiled. "Hey, Dusty."

He smiled back and shifted the basket to his other hand. "Hey. Uh ... hi." He drew a breath and looked like he was going to say something else, but then gave up and offered another tight smile as Dakota sniffed his hand.

Dusty bent down to stroke my dog's ears. "Hey, buddy. What's his name?"

"Dakota."

Dusty glanced up at me, then back to my dog as he rubbed the scruff of his neck and chest. "Hi, Dakota. You're a lovely fellow, aren't you?"

Dakota whimpered and licked Dusty's hand, and Dusty found the magic scratching place under his chin. That was it for Dakota. His whole body broke into Aussie "talk" and happy squirms. I tilted my head and watched them, acting like the best of buds when they'd just met. Dakota didn't take to just anyone, but he was a sucker for good scratches once he let them get started. They could go on like this all day.

"So, uh…" I interrupted.

Dusty affectionately tussled Dakota's head one last time, then straightened. "Sorry. Dogs, you know. They know a dog person."

"Yeah." I gestured to his shopping basket. "Getting some horses ready to show?"

"Hmm?" He squinted like he didn't understand, then remembered the stuff in his hand. "Oh, this? No, just picking some stuff up for Luke. He just bought a gray horse, so now he's got this idea about purple shampoo and… well, you know Luke. Can't tell him anything."

I laughed. "Yeah, I know. He asked me to watch the game with him on Wednesday night, but then he said he was going to show up at the tavern wearing blue and orange face paint. He didn't understand why I wouldn't love that idea."

Something changed in Dusty's expression, but I couldn't put my finger on it. He looked… almost angry. At least sad. What could I have said? His eyes dropped, and he wouldn't look back up again, which was a shame because of all the Walkers, I always thought Dusty had the most striking blue eyes. And that was saying something.

"Yeah," he mumbled, shifting the basket from one hand to the other. "Luke does get some pretty horrible ideas sometimes. I'd better go."

That was abrupt. I wouldn't have minded talking to him for a few minutes, but I guess not. "Well, see you around? Come on, Dakota."

He nodded and started to wave goodbye, then stiffened. "Wait, Jess?"

I stopped. "Yeah?"

His mouth moved, but no words were coming out. I narrowed my eyes. "Come again?"

Dusty blinked. "I was... just wondering how things are going with Kelli's horse. At your house."

"Oh. Fine, I guess. Kelli's been coming out and working with her every day. If the round pen isn't frozen, Kelli's riding. She's pretty determined to make it work, you know?"

"Yeah. Well, that's good." Suddenly, he reached for his pocket, as if he was looking for something, but didn't find it. His hand dropped, and he sighed.

I shook my head. Talking to Dusty was usually a little awkward. I couldn't decide if he was just shy or if he didn't like me and was forcing himself to be polite. Whatever it was, he wasn't very good at it. "Well, I won't keep you. We're looking for a new collar, aren't we, Dakota?"

Dusty stepped back. "Okay. Have a nice day."

"See you."

As I walked away, I kept pondering the mystery of Dusty Walker. How was it I'd never really spent any time with him? He seemed like a sweet guy, and everyone in town said he was probably the most likable of all the Walker brothers. He was usually the first one to figure out when someone needed help, and people respected him.

Dusty *was* really nice, but for me, he was almost painful to talk to. What was it about him? He seemed comfortable enough talking to my dog, but he shut down the minute he had to look at me.

I didn't know what to make of it, except it didn't feel good. According to Kelli, people either found me intimidating or boring. I'd never thought I was either one, but when I reflected on the last two years, with all the failed friendships and relationships that never got off the ground, it was starting to make sense. I was the ice queen, and I never even knew it.

What could I do about that? Was I supposed to change who I was? Even if I could, I wouldn't even know how. Should I find some clothes that didn't fit as well? Cut my hair and dye it brown instead of blonde? What would that prove? I twisted my hands on the steering wheel as I drove home, trying to wring the answer from the road.

I wished I could ask my mom. She'd know what to tell me. And even if she didn't, she'd at least bake me some cookies and promise it would all work out okay. That at least one person in this world understood and accepted me just as I was.

I pulled into the driveway and yanked the gearshift into park. And for the first time in at least six months, I just bowed my head over my steering wheel and cried for my mom.

Dusty

I blew it.

More than blew it. Jess probably thought I was some kind of a goofball. I had a perfect opportunity to talk to her, and what did I do? I petted her dog!

He was a really nice dog, though.

I closed my eyes and pounded my forehead on the truck's steering wheel. Idiot, idiot, idiot! Now that she wasn't there, all the things I wanted to say came rushing to my head. I'd ask her about her dad and how the shop was doing. I'd ask her how she liked being back in town and if she'd been up to Morgan and Cody's new place yet. I'd even ask her what kinds of books she'd been reading lately and... well, if she hadn't mentioned Luke, I'd have gone out on a limb and just asked if she wanted to have dinner sometime. It wasn't a crime to ask, was it? Maybe she wasn't serious about him.

Other guys would have managed it. Heck, even Luke could get the words out, and Luke had almost flunked out of school. Words weren't his strong point. Why was it so easy for everyone else to just say what they wanted to say? "Hello, Jess, nice to see you. Oh, what a nice dog. By the way, are you busy Friday?" How hard was that?

Too much for me, obviously, especially after she mentioned my brother. I'd just stood there, gasping like a kid called to the blackboard after he didn't do his homework. I was almost twenty-five years old, and I couldn't talk to the woman I'd adored since middle school. What was wrong with me?

What I would have given to know what she really thought of Luke! She couldn't be serious about him, could she? If I'd had even the faintest clue about that, I'd have given her the note I had folded in my wallet. Or maybe I didn't need to give her the paper, if I could just repeat the words I'd written. But I couldn't manage to choke them out. Not when I didn't know what I needed to know.

Somehow, I had to find a way to learn the truth. I couldn't ask her because that would be meddling. And Luke wouldn't tell—talking details about girls we were dating was against the family code. And anyway, Luke was thick enough that he might not even know Jess's feelings. Could I somehow find a way to be around Jess enough to learn the truth without actually asking?

I could get lucky and run into her again this week. But I should find a way to go to her. What if I tagged along with Marshall sometime when he went to see Kelli and her horse? Except, last I heard, that horse was a sore spot between them. I didn't need to be in the middle of that kind of drama. Should I drop by her work? That would be weird.

Weird or not, it might be the only chance I'd have for a while.

Chapter 7

Jess

I finally had some work.

One of Dad's customers had smashed his car into a tree in the last snowstorm. He was fine, but his car was a total loss. Instead of using the insurance money to buy a new car, he decided to fix his old truck, including a complete engine tune-up. Replacing seals, checking valves, cleaning the heads, all of it. And once I was done with his truck, he said he'd bring in his wife's Excursion for new plugs and an oil change.

That was gravy work, and I was glad to have it. Dad paid me by the hour when I filled in with office jobs, but it wasn't as good as working on engines. I'd had no savings left when I came back a year and a half ago, and I was trying to turn that around.

Besides, I genuinely loved the challenge of picking things apart and trying to find out what was wrong. It was like a puzzle, and for some reason nobody could explain, I was good at it. There were few things more satisfying than turning the key and listening to an engine purr after I'd tweaked and fiddled and made everything new again.

This would be a particularly gratifying job because I was working on one of my favorite older engines—one of the kinds that kept on chugging long after the vehicle had started to fall apart around it. I rolled the truck up on the hoist and pulled the switch to lift it so that I could get to the underside. I tugged on some gloves and was just pulling the drain plug on the oil pan when I heard Tucker's voice calling me from the front shop.

"Jess? Hey, Jess, you have a visitor!"

He startled me, and when I jumped, I dropped the plug into the drain pan. Crap! Used engine oil was pouring out, and I'd have to fish the plug out of that mess.

"Jess!"

I growled a little as the plug vanished in the puddle of black ooze. All because someone decided he had to come chit-chat when I was working. "Five minutes!" I shouted back.

I had to wait till the oil was done dripping before I could duck under there. Then I grabbed a hook and a rag and fished around in the pan. *There.* I pinned it against the side of the pan and just about had it dragged up to the surface when...

"Hello?"

I dropped it again. "Argh!" I bit my lip against the bad-tempered words brewing on my tongue, scrunched my face into a frustrated scowl, then took a deep breath. By the time I climbed out from under the truck and straightened, I hoped I didn't look like I was trying not to swear.

It was that same guy from a few days ago, Austen Conrad—the one with the tractor. And he was holding a bouquet of crimson and white mums. Good grief, what now?

His eyes widened when I stood up, and his gaze fastened on my cheek. Suddenly self-conscious, I swiped it with the rag in my hand,

and it came away black. Of course, I'd have a smear of grease on my face.

"Sorry to bother you," he said with that same broad smile.

"Oh, it's no bother," I lied. "What can I do for you?"

"Well, I... here." He extended the bouquet. "I wanted to thank you for your help the other day."

I took the flowers hesitantly. "Thank you, but I didn't really do anything."

"You took your time to talk to me. That's something, right?"

I narrowed my eyes. "Right."

Conrad looped his thumbs in his coat pockets. "And anyway, I'm trying to get to know all the neighbors. Nice to hear recommendations, word-of-mouth type stuff."

"I guess it would be. But really, you didn't need to bring flowers. It wasn't a big deal." They *were* pretty. Festive and cheerful and creatively arranged with a wintry silver ribbon. I could never turn down flowers, but... why?

"I thought it was a big deal."

I lifted my eyes slowly. Conrad was staring at my face, still smiling, and he'd come a step closer. And his breathing had gotten a little irregular.

Oh. So that was what it was.

Okay, sure. It was always a little flattering to be noticed that way, and Conrad seemed like a nice enough guy. Definitely not a creep, or at least I didn't get that impression.

But flowers, the second time we ever talked? This guy was trying way too hard, and in my experience, that never ended well. I wouldn't go all mushy just because he gave me some Christmas mums, that was for sure. I'd pay attention from now on, but I wasn't going on any more desperation dates after that pointless dinner with Luke.

"Well, thank you," I said, trying to sound business-like. "I'll put these in the break room. We didn't put any Christmas decorations out, so these will cheer up the place."

"Great," he echoed, but his voice was flat. "So, do you work here every day?"

"Nine to five, Monday through Friday."

"Huh. Interesting job for a..."

"For a girl?" I guessed.

His hands twitched in his coat. "I wasn't going to say that, but yeah."

"It pays the bills. When I have work, which I do right now."

His face was blank for a second, and then he seemed to realize what I meant. "Oh. Right. I should let you get back, then."

I nodded. "Yeah, I have to have this done before the weekend." Then, as an afterthought, I pulled off my greasy gloves and put my hand out. "Thanks for the flowers."

His smile returned, and he took my hand, cradling just the tips of my fingers in a light touch. Not a great handshake at *all*, but he was a Californian. I guess I couldn't expect him to know how to shake a girl's hand proper in Idaho.

"You're welcome," he said. "See you around."

I waited until he left before I walked to the break room to set the flowers in a tin can on the table. I probably should take them home, but... well, they looked nice there, where everyone could enjoy them. That was it.

Then I pulled out a pair of fresh nitrile gloves and went back to fish that plug out of the drain pan.

Dusty

"You ready?" Luke asked.

I glanced over at him, parked on my left, aboard his new gray. I shook out a loop and nodded. "Just about. You, Austen?"

It was Saturday, and Luke wanted to score some practice runs on his mare to see how she handled. I'd invited Austen over to watch. He said he wanted to "get better" at roping, but I found out he didn't even know the basics.

Rather than embarrass him by giving him lessons in front of Luke, I just asked him to drag the hot heels with the four-wheeler for a bit, and then I'd show him some stuff later. Marshall was off somewhere with Kelli, and we needed someone to pull the roping dummy anyway.

Austen gave us the thumbs up, and Luke nodded. "Okay!"

Luke's job was to run up on the left side and get a loop over the cow's head. He and his horse would then "switch" the cow, pulling it forward and to the left, so it kicked its heels out to the right for me to rope. A cow roped safely and efficiently in the branding pen couldn't hurt itself or anyone else, and Luke and I were usually figured to be about the best team in the valley for getting the job done without roughing up the stock. Everyone always asked us to rope, anyway, and that was something to be a little proud of.

Austen gunned the engine, and the practice dummy shot forward. I was off my mark, and my horse was in a great position, but Luke was fighting with Duchess. She should have been right up on the dummy, but she was too far back, dead even with me. "You're behind!" I yelled.

"You think I don't bloomin' know that? Gee up there, mare!" Luke tried urging Duchess up for about three more strides. Then we were going to run out of room. "Doggone it! Stop." He pulled his horse down and backed her up.

"What was that?" I asked.

"Just hesitated. I told you, she's rusty."

"How rusty? Do you think you should school her a little before roping off her?"

"She's fine. Let's give it another try."

I shrugged. "Okay." We jogged back and waited for Austen to get lined up again.

"Ready when you are," Austen said. "Set?"

Luke raised his loop and gritted his teeth. He was ready to jump hard this time. "Go!"

Our horses leaped into action, Luke's gray mare powering up and closing in faster than before. He was still fighting to keep her where he needed her, pushing her up farther than she wanted to be, but she did respond. Three quick twists of Luke's wrist and the loop snaked into place, just as pretty as a picture.

I had my loop in motion, and my hand had just dropped in the release when Luke's rope went slack. Instead of running ahead of the dummy and holding tension on her end, Duchess dug her heels into the dirt and cut hard to the right, almost colliding with my gelding. She ran over both ropes, and it was only some quick handling on Luke's part that kept her from getting tangled in them.

"What in blazes?" Luke hollered. "What happened?"

"Your horse tried to plow me over, that's what happened!"

"You were too close."

I snapped. All the frustration of the last couple of weeks, my irritation with Luke, and my own failure to act when I'd had the chance—it all boiled over. "I was right where I was supposed to be! Your horse screwed up."

Austen stopped and turned off the quad's engine to turn around and watch.

"It wasn't her fault. Something didn't feel right, and she called me on it," Luke said as he coiled his rope.

"Now you're just making up excuses. You sure that trick knee of yours didn't act up? Maybe you jerked the bit or kicked her this way."

"It wasn't my knee," Luke growled. "Let's just reset."

I choked down my temper and coiled my rope, trotting my horse in a little circle while Austen looped around with the roping dummy. "You ready this time?" Luke called.

"I was ready last time."

"Like heck you were. Don't cross-fire it this time. You threw too soon."

"I *didn't* cross-fire," I snarled. "You never switched it!"

"I jolly well did. I was dragging the whole dummy sideways for a second."

"Just keep your horse lined out this time, okay?"

"I'll keep *you* in line," Luke grumbled as he shook out his loop.

Austen was still turned around on the quad, and he flashed a grin. "Do you guys always bicker like this when you're roping?"

"Naw," Luke said. "Usually, we get mad. Ready?"

Austen glanced at me. I was steaming, but I swallowed it and gave him the nod. "Let 'er rip!" he shouted over the engine.

Luke's catch was smooth and perfect, but I was watching his dally this time instead of dropping my heel loop. I had an idea...

Luke did everything just right. But the second he had the rope fast, that mare slammed on the brakes and veered toward me again. He turned her head back to the left and tried to urge her on, but she wasn't having it. She twisted her body and kept going right until she hit the end of her slack, then she turned to face and got in a tug-of-war with the quad.

"Of all the... You never even threw!" Luke cried.

"Yeah, you know why? Because you didn't buy a heading horse. You bought a heeler, and your horse is trying to do *my* horse's job!"

Luke's jaw went slack. "Did not."

"Betcha? Okay, you go saddle Dozer and let me run Duchess. Fifty bucks if I'm wrong."

He growled as he swung a leg over and went to fetch his rope off the dummy. "You'd better be wrong. I can't fix a horse that's been trained on the wrong side."

Luke stalked off, leaving Duchess ground-tied where she stood. White ears swiveled, and she watched her rider leave. Then, she fastened her expressive black eyes on me since I was the closest person, and she waited to be told what to do. Someone, somewhere, had put a lot of time into training this horse. Just not the kind of training Luke thought.

"What's the problem with her being trained on the wrong side?" Austen asked.

I stepped off my horse and led him to the rail to tie him up. "She's been taught to rate the cow differently, back off the hip instead of running up on the shoulder. And you saw how she kept stopping and pulling to the right. A header is supposed to run ahead and to the left."

"So? Why can't he fix that?"

I grabbed my rope off my saddle and walked over to Duchess to adjust the stirrups. Luke was two inches taller than I was. "He could, but it's not easy and maybe not worth it. You don't ruin a good heeler to make them a mediocre header."

"Huh. That's wild. I never heard any of this stuff before."

I checked Duchess's cinch and put my foot in the stirrup. "Stick around. You'll hear all kinds of stuff. Some of it's even true."

The minute I settled in the saddle, I felt something click. Some horses just feel *right* the second you touch them. Others become a fit for you with time, and some never do. But something about getting on Duchess was like coming home. She was soft and elastic, and her responses were almost a mirror of my own thoughts.

I loped her around a couple of times, learning how her stride felt and how she responded. Luke hadn't said anything about how well-tuned she was, but she was like driving a sports car—all smooth power, ready to answer at the slightest touch. If I was right about her, it would be a crying shame for Luke, but she was still about the nicest horse I'd ever swung a leg over.

Luke came back in the arena leading Dozer, the horse he'd won the most money on. "Okay, little brother. Fifty bucks says you're wrong."

I grinned. "I don't know why I bothered betting you. Didn't you say you're broke?"

"Not for long."

We took up our positions, and Luke gave Austen the nod. And I didn't even have to think about it. The mighty gray mare put me exactly where I needed to be, hanging just off the right hip of the dummy as we waited for Luke. His loop dropped clean and crisp like it always did, and I threw mine for a solid catch and a quick dally. Then, like a machine, Duchess sat down, took up the slack, and faced the dummy. Perfect.

Luke yanked the dally off his horn and threw his rope, followed by a string of cussing. Austen was laughing silently and shaking his head as he watched. I just released my rope and stepped down. And for the first time in the last couple of weeks, I honestly felt bad for my brother.

"Sorry, Luke. For what it's worth, she's the smoothest heel horse I've ever been on."

Luke scowled and rubbed his jaw as he walked over. His forehead creased, and his eyes shone the sharpest disappointment I'd ever read there. "Dad-blast it!" He sighed and stroked Duchess's silver neck. "Looks like you got yourself a horse, little brother."

"Hold on, there. I never said I was stealing your horse."

"I sure as heck can't use her. I'm too old to re-learn how to rope the south end of a north-bound cow."

"Bull. You're younger than Evan, and he can catch both ends."

Luke's cheek flinched. "Evan doesn't have a bum left knee."

I sobered. Luke always joked about his bad knee, but maybe it gave him more trouble than he'd let on. "How would that matter? You ride everywhere else just fine."

He shook his head and shrugged. "Something about how you have to twist to make your catch. I've tried it, and it's no good, especially if I want to be competitive. Guess I'll have to sell her." He dragged his rein off Dozer's neck and walked toward the gate, his shoulders drooping.

Sick pity twisted in my stomach. I'd been so hung up on what I thought Luke might be up to with Jess that I'd missed the sheer hope he'd hung on this horse—the dream he'd just lost. I knew what that felt like. "Why not just breed her in the spring?" I called. "That's what you wanted to do in the first place, anyway."

He turned, a thoughtful look on his face. "I wanted to rack up some winnings at the jackpots on her first, so the foals would be worth more, but... how 'bout a partnership? You run her for two seasons, and I'll get the foals."

I stroked Duchess's neck. I'd never been on anything like her, and I'd give my right arm to do it again. But... "I don't need another horse."

"Neither did I. Deal?"

I frowned and cocked an eyebrow. This was stupid. I should just tell Luke to sell the horse and move on. But my brother had wanted this so badly. If I could help him hang on to his scheme somehow, turn a disappointment into a triumph, then didn't I owe him that? Something in my chest tightened, and I knew there was only one thing I could say. "Deal, I guess."

Luke nodded and led his horse out of the arena.

"So..." Austen asked from behind me. "I guess you're the broke one now?"

I laughed. "Looks like it. You interested in paying for some roping lessons? Something tells me I'm going to need the cash."

Chapter 8

Jess

"Ho, ho, ho, Merry Christmas!"

I pushed into the crowded tack room at White Pines Therapeutic Riding Center. Morgan had asked me to stop by this afternoon for their Christmas party, and the guys at the shop had pitched in for some Secret Santa gifts for the kids. The room was completely packed.

It was a good thing that next year, they'd be at the new facility and it wouldn't be so crammed. Kids were lined up down the barn aisle, each waiting for a turn to talk to "Santa." I chuckled. Cody didn't look too bad in the red suit and beard.

"Hey, Jess. You made it!" a warm voice greeted me. "Can I get you some hot chocolate?"

I turned and found Katherine Tracy's sister, Audrey Livingstone. She was manning the beverages, which meant it was her job to keep rowdy kids from tipping over the cups or hogging all the marshmallows. She held up a steaming insulated paper cup.

I hefted the plastic bag of gifts I had slung over my shoulder. "I'll take you up on that. Just let me set these down. Where should I put them?"

Audrey pointed, but before she could complete the gesture, Dusty Walker was at my side. "I can get those. That was right nice of you guys."

"Of course. They were all happy to help out."

Dusty's fingers brushed mine as his hand closed over the bag, and I released it. He hesitated, and sky-blue eyes flashed to me for an instant. He looked like he was going to say something but then smoothed it over with a smile. "Thanks. I'll give these to Santa's Elf."

"You mean Morgan?"

Dusty's face split into an easy grin. "Hey, you're not supposed to guess! You'll ruin the fun."

"Well, it was either her or Kelli, and since I happened to pass Kelli and Marshall driving somewhere in his truck, it wasn't that hard to figure out."

He tossed the bag over his shoulder. "I guess there you have it. Be back in a few." Dusty disappeared around the corner, and I turned to Audrey to accept that hot chocolate.

"You look like you need this," she said.

I blew the steam off my cup. "Mmm. Oh, wow. This tastes like one of Kelli's concoctions."

Audrey leaned over the table a little. "Probably because it is. She was here earlier. You should have seen the fit she threw when Morgan tried to serve the packet cocoa."

"I can only imagine! This is going to stick right to my hips."

She shrugged. "Probably, but Christmas is one time I make an exception to my sugar rule. I've already had three cups."

"You?" I teased. "Aren't you the sweets police in town? All those kids will be in your office next week with toothaches."

"The reputation comes with the territory, but I'm not always a stickler. I can turn down candy any day, but give me something hot and rich and sweet like this? I'm a sucker."

I took another innocent sip of my cocoa. "Are you still talking about the hot chocolate?"

She laughed. I think I'd only heard Audrey laugh maybe half a dozen times since I'd known her. "Unfortunately, yes. So, what's new?"

"Nothing much. You probably don't care much about the cylinder heads I replaced this week."

"And I doubt you're very interested in how many cavities I filled," she countered. "We need a life, do you know that?"

I laughed and held up my cup in a salute. "Indeed, we do."

"So?" Audrey picked up what had to be her fourth cup of cocoa and sipped it demurely. "How does one do that?"

"Snag yourself a cowboy and have some fun, I guess. Seems to be working for Morgan and Kelli."

Her lip curled. "No, thank you. Well, anyway, it's not for me, the cowboy thing. I don't understand it."

"Maybe you just haven't met the right one," I challenged with a grin. "What's your type? Tall and muscular?"

"Intelligent and able to communicate in more than grunts and monosyllables." She drew another long pull of her cocoa. "I haven't met many men around here who seem overburdened with those qualities."

"Well," I sighed, "they're out there. They have to be."

"Just not in this town. That Dusty Walker might be an exception," she said, gesturing to the cowboy passing out Christmas boxes with Morgan. "Not my type, but he seems pretty nice."

"He is," I admitted. "I just never figured him out. Not much of a talker."

"Better than one who talks too much, especially about himself."

"I can't argue with that. So you've been in town what, about a year? And none of our local cowboys have ever interested you?"

She frowned and shook her head. "But that's okay. I don't plan on being here forever. Someday, when Kat's doing better, I'll get back home to…" Her voice trailed off as she lifted her paper cup to her lips once more, then her gaze sharpened, and her body went rigid. "What in the world? Excuse me."

Without a word of explanation, Audrey slammed her cup down and marched off. A moment later, she was dragging her niece Lizzy toward the door. I didn't see what had precipitated that swift action, but I heard her scolding Lizzy on the way out to the car. "I don't care if Dustin was taking too long to open his gift. You may *not* rip it out of his hands and shake it over his head!"

I chuckled and finished my cup. The remaining kids were still sorting through the wrapped gifts, trying to be the first to grab the one they thought would be the best. I watched with a sort of detached fascination.

I'd never had siblings, never experienced that kind of frantic scramble to get what I wanted. Poor Dusty Walker was trying to supervise the bunch, and I wondered how he would manage. Most people would blow a gasket or at least raise their voices. Or they'd just throw up their hands and let the chaos reign.

But Dusty didn't do any of that. He gave one loud whistle with his fingers, drawing even the most reluctant eyes to him, and then silently passed a gift to Dustin, the kid who had been shoved to the back of the bunch. He didn't need to say another word. The rest of them looked shamefaced and settled down to open their presents with less noise and better manners. Dusty scooped up the one box that remained untouched and headed straight for me.

"Did Lizzy have to leave?"

"Sounded like it."

His face tugged into a shy, crooked grin. "Well, I'll set this aside. Maybe I'll drop it by the house for her if her aunt approves."

"That's a nice thought. Lizzy seems like a good kid, really. Just... energetic."

"She knows what she wants out of life." His grin deepened for an instant, then vanished. He shifted the box under his arm and looked away, watching the kids. "Uh... how's your dad?"

The shift of topic sobered me. Mom had been gone for a while, and by now, most people had moved on. They'd stopped asking how we were holding up and maybe even forgotten all about her. But apparently, not Dusty. "Fine, I guess. It's still hard."

"Yeah," he replied, the lines around his eyes softening. "It nearly killed my dad to lose Mom."

I crossed my arms and blinked back the sheen threatening my own eyes. How could I have forgotten? I was just as bad as the people who forgot my mom because it hadn't even occurred to me that Dusty knew exactly what that was like. Marci Walker had been a saint, but she hardly came to my mind after three years. I forced some air into my lungs so my voice would steady and made myself look him in the eye. "I'm sorry, Dusty."

Dusty's lips thinned to a tight smile. "Thanks. Dad's starting to do better now. He keeps occupied, and that helps. We don't even know where he is half the time."

"I'm glad to hear it. I wish my dad would find a hobby or something to keep him busy. He has too much time on his hands."

"Really?" Dusty looked thoughtful. "Hmm."

I studied his face for a few seconds. He was watching Cody in the Santa outfit, the kids with their gifts, glancing down at his boots—anything but looking at me. He really was a good-looking cowboy. His blue eyes were so bright they almost looked like contacts, and he had a soft mouth that usually turned up just a little, unless he was lost in thought. He shared the Walker trait of that devastating lopsided smile and the hint of a dimple, but the resemblance to the others ended there.

His older brothers all boasted strong jaws and smoldering gazes, even when they weren't trying. Dusty's face was more refined, with high-set cheeks and a clear, direct gaze when he looked at someone. A pity he never looked at me, because he had the kind of eyes a girl could get lost in. And he was quiet. Thoughtful. I liked that about him.

If only he didn't act like he was in pain every time I talked to him.

"Can I have some more hot chocolate?"

I snapped from my musings over Dusty Walker and stared down at the threesome of youngsters gathered at my feet. They each clutched a horse-themed Christmas present from the pile—a stuffed animal for one, a t-shirt for another, and a brand new grooming brush for the third. "Miss Morgan said we could have as much as we wanted," the first kid reminded me.

"Right. I guess I'm on duty since Audrey left." I blew out a breath and grabbed a cup to fill. "Nice seeing you, Dusty."

He lifted his free hand and walked off. Half a minute later, he was swallowed in the crowd of parents coming to collect their kids, and I didn't see him again.

Dusty

"Thanks for dropping this by. Lizzy will be excited—that is, after she finishes her chores." Audrey leaned against the door frame and crossed her arms, glancing over her shoulder. "I told her she had to do the dishes after that scene at the Christmas party. Poor Dustin!"

"Aw, don't go too hard on her. She just got excited." I passed over the gift. "Dustin didn't seem to be too bothered by it."

"Well, that's a relief. Ah, look, I'd invite you in for a minute, but Katherine's sleeping, or trying to."

I shook my head quickly. I didn't want Audrey to get the idea that this was anything more than a gift delivery. "Oh, no, I have somewhere to be. I just thought I'd leave this on my way by."

She stepped back, waving through the doorway. "Thank you, then. I..." A clatter from the kitchen made her jump. "Elizabeth Marie Tracy! What in heaven's name?" She spun around, and the door slammed. I chuckled and walked out to my truck. Audrey had her hands full, caring for a sick sister and a boisterous child on her own.

But Audrey wasn't the one I had come into town to see. Jess had given me an idea—another way to see more of her without actually stepping on Luke's toes. And maybe I could also be a source of cheer to a man I'd always liked. I pulled out on the road and drove half a mile south, to an older white house on a modest five-acre farm.

Jed Thompkins was parking his tractor and lowering the bucket when I pulled up to the driveway. He squinted and walked over to the gate, still clearly uncertain who I was, until I stepped down from the truck. When he recognized me, his face broke into a pleased grin. "Well, Dusty. I just saw your dad in town this morning."

"Really? He's been disappearing every morning at about ten. We haven't been able to put together what the old coot's up to."

Jed leaned on the gate and chuckled. "Imagine he'll tell you when he feels like it."

I laughed. "You're no help at all."

"'Fraid not. Are you looking for Jess?"

My heart flipped, and I gulped. His casual assumption scared the spit out of me. How many guys still showed up at this man's house looking for his daughter? "Uh, no. I... I was driving by and thought I'd stop in. Haven't said hello for a while."

He pushed the gate open for me. "Well, you'd better come in and have something to drink."

He led me to the garage instead of the house—fitting for a guy who had worked on cars all his life. And anyway, it was no ordinary garage. The interior was all finished and gleaming, with a sealed concrete floor, an overhead track for lifting car parts, and high-end LED lighting. A black vintage refrigerator stood beside a massive tool chest, and he cracked it open to let me have my pick of his glass soda stash.

"Thanks." I gestured to his hot rod, a red Ford Coupe with a scoop on the front and chrome sparkling from every corner. "I haven't seen that in a long time. You used to drive it in all the parades."

He shrugged. "Haven't felt much like it lately. I've got the back end torn apart right now for new shocks."

"Oh?" I sipped my coke and walked around the car. "How long will that take?"

Jed scratched his chin. "Another six years at the rate I'm going."

I glanced over at him. "Do you want some help?"

He pursed his lips and tilted his head. "Well... why not? I'm not doing anything important this afternoon. You're not too busy?"

"Not at the moment." I set my bottle on the work table. "Where do we start?"

I'd never been much good when it came to fixing cars. That was Luke's department, with his tricked-out truck and his insatiable desire to add extra horsepower to everything, even our lawn tractor. But I was good at one thing; handing over tools.

Jed Thompkins was under the car, twisting away at his wrench and occasionally asking about our cows or the prices of hay or whatever else came to his mind. Once in a while, he'd stick his hand out and ask for a different tool, but I never did actually touch the car. For a long time I was feeling pretty useless.

And then it dawned on me; he didn't need help with the car. He could have wrapped this up by himself in an hour if he'd wanted to. He just needed someone to talk to while he worked, and I was a good listener.

"That should about do it for this side. All I need is..." The dolly scooted farther under the car. "Will you hand me that 7/16"? And the 1/2" too."

I scraped up the requested socket wrenches and placed them in his hand. He grunted a thank you, and I heard the ratcheting sounds of him twisting the nuts in place.

"Jess is bound to be pleased," he said at length. "She's been after me to finish this thing for months. Keeps trying to drag me out here to work on it. Not that I didn't want to get it finished, but..." His voice trailed off.

I squatted down so I could see his face better. "She likes helping you with it, doesn't she?"

He grunted again. "She does, but I don't like to see her wasting her life under a car. There are better ways for her to spend her time."

I narrowed my eyes. *That was it.* Jed Thompkins wasn't aimless and depressed. He was keeping away from his hobby to give his daughter a push into doing something else.

"Like what?" I asked, trying not to sound like my life hung on his answer.

"Anything but work. Something with people to talk to." He rolled out from under the car, and I reached down to give him a hand up off his dolly. "Thanks."

"You know," I mused, "I told Cody and Morgan I'd volunteer at the therapy program this winter. She ran my background check already, and I'm all set, but other than today's party, I haven't had much time yet. I mean to get over there more."

"See? Something like that. Good for the soul, doing something to help someone else. And you never know." He winked. "You must just meet someone special in the process."

He knew. Saintly bovines, *he knew.*

Well, what if he did? It wasn't like I was expected to be blind, and if I was reading him correctly, he didn't seem to care if I was interested in his daughter. Maybe he was even encouraging me. I swallowed the great knot in my throat. If I was going to make something of this, there was no time like the present to start.

"You might be right. I was thinking about heading over there this week. Cody says that right now, they're the most short-handed on Tuesdays and Thursdays, starting from about two o'clock."

Jed Thompkins broke into a slow smile and clapped me on the shoulder. "You do that, son. You never know. Might just be the best thing you ever did. Cold one for the road?"

I couldn't help grinning at him. Oh, yes, he knew, and he was on my side. "Much obliged, sir."

Chapter 9

Dusty

I hopped in the side-by-side and drove out to the road so I could pounce on the mailbox as soon as the little white truck drove away. Today should be the day!

My palms had been sweaty, and my heart was in my throat all morning. When I opened the box, the stack of bills and junk mail went into the seat of the side-by-side. What I cared about was rolled innocently at the bottom of the box—the December issue of *Stockman's Magazine*.

I flipped to the table of contents and found the section devoted to "Cowboy Sayings," the reader submissions page. That was where my poem would be. The slick pages melted away from my fingers, and I held my breath. Almost...

That was when my phone rang.

My hand twitched like a kid caught in the cookie jar, and the pages slipped. I'd have let it ring if it was one of my brothers or anyone else. But it was my dad's ringtone. I sighed and tossed the magazine in the side-by-side as I hit the answer button.

"Hi, Dad."

He sounded like he was in a restaurant or somewhere busy. There were lots of voices in the background. "Are you headed to town today?"

"I was planning on it. Need something?"

"Yeah, can you pick up some teriyaki sauce? I'm going to make another batch of jerky."

I frowned. "Sure, but why now? You should have like five pounds of it."

"Gave it all away, need to make more. You're going today, right?"

"You sound like you're already in town. You could get it faster than I could."

"Tied up till later, won't have time to stop. You sure you can?"

I squinted at the horizon. Dad was acting weird lately—hardly ever home, and on his phone all the time when he was. Like a teenager. "I guess, but that's a lot of jerky. Who did you give it to?"

"Tell you later. Oh, pick up some Worcestershire, too. Gotta go!" And he hung up.

That left me staring at my blank screen. I *had* been planning to go to town, it was true, but it wasn't to run ranch errands. I promised I'd stop by Austen's place this afternoon, but first, I wanted to see Jess. Talking to her dad had inspired me to take a chance, to throw caution to the wind. I was going to ask Jess if I could ever have a chance with her.

I'd put it off for two days. Whenever I thought of it, my skin broke out with goosebumps, and I got dizzy. What if she wasn't interested? What if other people saw me getting shot down? *What if she had already fallen for Luke?*

But what if I did nothing?

I'd been brave enough to send my poem out into the world. Granted, I didn't plan on letting my family see it. I'd be tearing the back out of that magazine as soon as I got half a chance. *Maybe.*

I swallowed and looked at the page. My fingers itched to tear it out, but what if I waited? What if I just let someone find it? My family would finally know the truth.

It was time for me to tell Jess the truth, too.

"Jess? She's out this morning. Her dog had a vet checkup or something." The guy at the body shop was wearing a pair of coveralls with "Will" on the chest. He and about three others had dropped what they were doing to stare at me the second I said her name.

I swallowed. Of course, I picked the one day all week when she wasn't there. And now I looked like a disappointed idiot, asking where she was in front of a bunch of guys who had probably seen a dozen men walk into that shop looking for her.

"I see. Do you know when she'll be back?"

Will shook his head. "Maybe later. Maybe tomorrow. You could ask the boss," he said, gesturing to the office.

"Thanks."

I wandered to the office and looked through the glass at Jed Thompkins, sitting at the desk. His back was turned, and he was adjusting a pair of reading glasses as he held up a sheet of paper, squinting by turns at it, then his computer screen. Occasionally, he'd tap some numbers in with his index finger, then recheck the paper.

I knocked on the window, and he swiveled around and pulled off his glasses. "Dusty! Come on in."

I inched my way through the door. "Morning, sir."

He surveyed me under bushy eyebrows. "You're not going to tell me you came here looking for me again, are you?"

"Uh..." I cleared my throat. "I guess not."

His gaze softened. "She'll be back after lunch. If you're not in a hurry, you could wait."

I shuffled my feet. "I can't stay long. I wouldn't want to make anything awkward."

"Just what is so awkward about a fella waiting for his girl? No one will care."

My ears were starting to burn like firecrackers. "I'm not... exactly... you see, she's not my g..." I couldn't help clearing my throat again. "She's kind of seeing Luke, so I wouldn't want to... you know."

Jed Thompkins squinted, tilted his head like he wasn't sure his ears were working, and then he started laughing.

I backed away. "I'm sorry if I wasn't supposed to say that. I thought you knew."

He pinched the bridge of his nose and replaced his glasses. "What, er, gives you that idea, son?"

"Well, they went out. And Luke implied..." I gestured helplessly, wondering at the blank look on his face. "I guess he didn't really imply. That is, we don't talk about women. Like, ever. It's the rule."

"Ah." Thompkins sighed, then gently shook his head. "I don't know what Luke did or didn't say, but Jess is definitely not seeing him. She told me they parted over a handshake, and that was that."

My heart picked up rhythm. "She said that?"

"She did. And then she said she wanted to find a new hobby, so she'd never be bored enough to accept if he ever asked again."

I laughed weakly at his joke, but my mind had already leaped miles ahead. It was like music swelling in my ears, all the possibilities opening up before me again. My feet might have even left the ground.

"Dusty? Hey! You alright, son?"

I snapped back to focus. "Yeah. Yes! I'm good—great! She's really not dating anyone?"

"Oh, well, I couldn't say that for sure. I know she's not dating Luke, but I assumed you two had something of an understanding. Isn't that why you came over the other day?"

"Not exactly. I just..." I sighed and confessed. "It sounds really bad when I say it out loud, but I guess I wanted to try to be next in line."

He chuckled. "The early bird, huh? Well, you just stay here and wait if you like. I'm running out to do some estimates shortly, but she'll be back in about forty-five minutes."

Forty-five minutes? I checked my watch, and my heart sank. There was no way I could justify sitting in town that long. I had work to finish, and I'd promised Austen I'd help him, too. Besides, I'd look like the chief moron, sitting there alone in the office for forty-five minutes just to pounce on her when she walked in the door. "It's not that important," I decided, my disappointment as keen as my joy had been a moment ago. "I'll just have to catch her another time."

He shrugged. "Suit yourself. You could leave her a note if you want, and I'll see she gets it."

A note. Of course! My hand swept to my wallet, where I'd stuffed that sentimental rambling I'd written out for her. Well, why not? If it came through her dad, she'd surely read it. And she'd know I was serious, right? A guy who just wanted a little fun wasn't going to get friendly with a girl's father.

"I, uh... I have something here," I stammered and pulled the rumpled paper out. "It's not much."

He took it with a dubious look. Then his gaze returned to my face, and his smile warmed. "I'm sure it's enough."

That was all I needed to hear. I should have talked to her father years ago! Who knew her better than he did? And he seemed to like me, too, or at least, he hadn't tried to run me off. Maybe he would encourage her to give me a chance.

Anyway, if she wasn't interested, it would save us both the embarrassment of a rejection. I just didn't think I could bear it, gazing into her sea-blue eyes and hoping for hope, then only finding disappointment. And I didn't think she would enjoy saying it, either. Yes, it was definitely better this way.

I tipped my hat to Jed Thompkins as I went out. "Thank you again, sir."

"You're welcome. Best of luck to you, son."

Jess

"Well, big guy, you look pretty good." Doc Burns ruffled the top of Dakota's head. "You can let him down off the table now, Jess."

I picked him up and set him on the floor, and Dakota, who had been frozen in terror on the stainless steel examination table, suddenly came back to life with his usual happy squirms.

"I wouldn't worry about his teeth. Just watch his weight. Looks to me like he hasn't been running enough lately."

I grinned sheepishly. "Not as much. He and Nash are both putting on the padding this winter."

Doc Burns chuckled. "Sounds like you need to get them out for some exercise. But look at me. I don't have any room to talk," he said, patting his middle. "I'll get you that heartworm treatment, and you're all set."

I scratched Dakota's ears, and he groaned, leaning into my hand like it was the only comfort he'd had for hours. The big clown. He always hated coming to the vet's office.

"You survived, buddy. Ready to go back to work? I still need to finish that truck." He grunted and moaned at me in his typical Aussie talk as I grabbed my purse, and we headed to the front of the office to pay the bill.

When I returned to the shop, I went straight to the break room to grab my sandwich from the fridge. The guys were busy painting in the booth, and Dad was nowhere to be found. Dakota curled up in his customary spot under my chair, and I dug into my turkey on wheat. Boring and flavorless, but it did the job.

I sighed and let my gaze rove the white brick walls of the break room. Everything in my life was boring lately. Audrey Livingstone had nailed it: I needed to get out more.

Dad had said something to me last night that might be worth thinking about. We'd been cleaning up after supper when he asked about Morgan and the new White Pines facility. "Don't they need some extra help right about now, what with all the building and expanding?"

I'd turned off the faucet so he could hear me better—Dad always had trouble hearing over background noise these days. "I'm sure they do. Kelli said something the other day about trying to dig up more volunteers."

"Well, how about it?" he asked.

I blinked and stared at him. "But they need the help during the weekdays. I'm working."

Dad just shrugged and turned the faucet back on to rinse a plate. "We're not that busy lately, especially for mechanic jobs. I could spare you a couple of afternoons a week. What do you think of maybe taking off Tuesdays and Thursdays after lunch?"

I frowned and thought about it as he stacked the plates in the dish drainer. "Are you sure you don't need me in the office?"

Dad chuckled and shut off the faucet, then tossed me a towel. "I got along fine without you doing all the billing. Why don't you go help out with the kids and the horses? Seems like something you'd love doing."

"Well... I'll think about it," I'd promised.

I hadn't been able to *stop* thinking about it since last night, and the idea had taken seed. Why not? It would get me out around people more, and I'd be back to doing something I believed in.

Deep in thought, I chewed the rest of my sandwich, and finally, something flicked in my head. This was the best idea I'd heard in a long time. I'd taken the morning off today, so I couldn't start volunteering until next week. Maybe I would talk to Morgan after I got off.

But first, I had to finish that truck.

I polished off my flavorless lunch, put my things away, and then walked by the office to stash my purse in the desk drawer. I tied my hair back up and covered it in a scarf to keep the grease out of it, and I was headed for the back shop when I passed my box on the wall.

There was a paper sticking out of it. That was where people always left the important stuff they wanted me to find. I pulled it out, and my heart stopped. It was... a wonderful question is what it was.

I had a secret admirer. One who was too shy to ask me out to my face, but one who seemed to want to hear my heart. Sweet and kind, he called me... but he didn't say I was beautiful.

That was refreshing. Usually, the first words out of any guy's mouth were about my looks and nothing else. This one seemed to think I might be human on the inside, too. And he wrote like maybe we shared something special, but he was letting me make the choice of finding it out.

I'd never heard anything like this. From *anyone*.

Who *was* this mystery guy? It had to be the same person who left the poem in my pocket. The handwriting was the same because I'd memorized it. At least now I knew *why*. But *who*?

I folded the note, my pulse pounding. I had to know who this was! Dad was out doing an estimate this afternoon, but I walked back up front to ask the guys in the paint booth. The only one I saw was Tucker putting the finishing touches on a body repair job.

"Hey!" I called over his grinder. He stopped, pointed at his chest, and I nodded.

He lifted his face shield. "What's up?"

"Did anyone come here looking for me earlier?"

He shrugged. "I saw a couple of guys come in, but I didn't talk to either of them."

"Do you know what they looked like?"

"They were both wearing cowboy hats. I didn't pay too much attention. They walked up to the office and then left."

Cowboy hats. I knew it. "They came together?"

"No, one was about ten, and the other right before I went to lunch."

I frowned. "And you don't know who they were at all? Did they talk to anyone?"

"Sorry, no idea. The first one was pretty tall, and I'd guess the second guy was about my height if that helps."

"Better than nothing. Thanks, Tucker."

I chewed the inside of my lip as I wandered back to the mechanic shop, re-reading that note. Which cowboy was I looking for? And why wouldn't he sign his note, if he wanted me to respond somehow? There was a dot of ink there like he had almost put down his name and then changed his mind.

If it was the same person who'd dropped the poem in my pocket, he had to have been in the tavern the night I went out with Luke. I sifted through my memory, trying to recall the faces I'd seen there. I remembered a few. And surely, I'd run across this guy since that night, too—maybe he'd been trying to get my attention in other ways, and it hadn't worked.

I slipped the note into my pocket and went back to work, my mind churning. That was one thing I liked about my job—I could work, and my thoughts could wander as far as they liked. But the more they wandered, the more they came back to the same place. And I had a pretty good idea of where I should start looking for my cowboy.

Dusty

"So, if you sell this bunch now..." I tapped on the spreadsheet program on Austen's laptop. "At current market prices, you'll recoup your increased repair costs, save hay through the winter, and have enough left over to buy a bunch of bred heifers to replenish your numbers by spring."

Austen shook his head with a relieved smile. "The numbers work?"

"Sort of. You'll still be down a couple of dozen head, but with your new bull and the fresh batch of breeding cows, you'll be in business for real by next year."

He stuck his hand out to shake mine. "Awesome. This is great news! I really appreciate it."

"You're welcome. And Evan did agree to sell you some one-ton bales when you run low. I figure you'll need some before spring."

Austen nodded and blew out a sigh. "Dusty, I don't know what I'd have done without your help. Everyone else I've talked to basically told me I'd figure things out, and then they just sat back to watch."

I grinned as I packed up my phone and notebook. "The old guard. They don't say much. I think they mostly figure it's respect, letting a guy work it out on his own. Don't take it personal."

"Oh, I don't, but still. You've saved me a pile of time and money, I'll tell you."

"Good. You can buy me dinner since I've probably missed it at home. I hope I have, anyway."

Austen grabbed his coat. "What's that?"

I made a face. "I think it's Luke's turn to cook tonight."

He laughed. "The pub it is, then."

We had mopped our plates clean and sat back, polishing off our drinks before heading home. I didn't want to be out too late—after all, the morning feeding came early. But I enjoyed hanging out with Austen, and it was a nice change from being with just my brothers. Luke was horse shopping again and would probably want me to approve of another wild idea. Marshall could be smiling and chipper, or in a rotten mood, depending on how things were going today with his girlfriend. Dad was... Dad, and Evan didn't really talk at all anymore.

Had any of them picked up the *Stockman's Magazine*? I'd left it on the end table by the couch. Probably not. I was starting to wonder if they'd ever notice unless I shoved it under their noses. My brothers weren't exactly the type to read cowboy poetry.

I'd almost shown it to Austen. I was so over the moon that Jess wasn't seeing Luke that I'd have shouted all my secret thoughts from the rooftops if anybody would have cared. Austen had a copy of this month's issue on his dining room table when I got to his house, but... I don't know why, the words stuck to the roof of my mouth like peanut butter. Then we were talking about livestock and business and it just never came back around to anything else.

Maybe it never would. Once I opened that door, there was no way to close it. How well would I have to know someone to feel comfortable opening up about my little hobby? And why was I so darned private about it? It wasn't like I was doing something wrong, so why was I scared to show anyone? I didn't have the answer to that.

"Well," Austen said, in the tone of voice that usually precedes a farewell. "Probably should get moving."

"Yup." I swallowed the last of my glass and reached into my coat pocket for my keys. "I guess I'll see you..."

He stiffened suddenly, his eyes on the door. "Hold that."

"Hmm?" I turned around.

Jess was walking in.

She had her hair loose this evening—long and shimmery-soft with curls tipping just the ends, making it look alive. She was wearing her usual black coat with a red wool scarf, denim leggings that hugged her shape, and knee-high western dress boots that I was sure were left over from her rodeo queening days. But it didn't matter what she wore. To me, she was always classy and just right. Tonight, though, it looked like she'd spent a little extra time on her looks, and it was a treat to see.

She paused just inside the door, slipping her scarf from around her neck as she glanced around the room. Then her eyes settled on me. And she smiled.

I swallowed. She was walking toward me! My pulse was galloping in my ears, and I had to force myself to breathe before my eyes crossed and my mouth malfunctioned. She must have read my note! I'd been aching to know about it all afternoon, but I hadn't expected such a quick answer. Was this a yes? Could it really be?

"Hey, guys!" she said brightly as she arrived at our table.

My muscles were frozen for an instant, then jerked to life. "Uh... hi, Jess." I lurched out of my seat and grabbed my hat off the back of my chair. Austen was slower than I was—I guess no one ever taught him you don't sit when a lady is standing, but he got the hint.

"Hello," Austen said. "Good to see you again, Miss Thompkins. Would you like to join us?" I reached for the chair closest to her to pull it out, but Austen beat me to it.

She smiled and eased into the seat, and Austen pushed it in for her. "Thank you. I was hoping I'd run into you this evening."

Austen and I glanced at each other, and I felt my cheeks getting hot. She wanted to see me! But... but she was looking at him. And he was smiling, too.

"You were?" he asked, his face starting to glow. "Well, that's nice to hear. To what do I owe the pleasure?"

She wetted her lips and toyed with the spare fork in front of her. "I thought about what you said, and..." she sighed and turned her beautiful eyes to me. And then she stomped on my heart.

"Dusty, would it be okay if I talked to Austen alone?"

I just sat there, blinking stupidly. "A... alone?" I stammered.

She caught her lower lip in her teeth. "I don't mean to be rude if you guys were in the middle of dinner or something."

"We just finished," Austen piped up—a little too quickly. "Dusty was just about to head out, weren't you, Dusty?"

I couldn't answer. My mouth just wouldn't move. She came here to see *him?* What about me? Did she get my note, or didn't she?

"Oh, good," Jess said, still looking at Austen like he was a sugar cookie. "I'm glad I caught you."

"Sure, sure. Hey, Dusty, thanks for all your help today. I'll get the tab, no worries." He sat down, tugging his chair closer to the corner of the table. Closer to *her.*

I was still standing there, holding my hat, watching them get cozy around the table. What was I supposed to do? There was only one thing I knew how to do. I closed my eyes, fisted my hand around the keys in my pocket, and turned away.

And I left, alone, while the woman of my heart and my new best friend bent their heads together and laughed.

Chapter 10

Jess

Austen Conrad was actually a pretty funny guy. Who knew? I guess it serves me right for pushing nice guys away before giving them a chance. I found out he didn't really have any family, had a terrible weakness for sweets, and that underneath his cowboy hat, he was a brainiac with computers. I liked that—there was more to him than met the eye.

He ordered a giant slice of chocolate cake for us to share, and we picked at it and talked for almost an hour. He was open about his struggles with getting started at his ranch, and he kept me laughing at the frustrating things that kept happening to him. How his boots had gotten sucked off his feet in the corrals after the first week of hard rain in October, his first experience chasing loose cows back into their pen, and how every single vehicle and piece of equipment that had come with the ranch had broken down at least once in the last two months. But he told it all in a way that made it sound comical rather than discouraging.

"But thank goodness I've had a little turn of luck," he said as we pried apart the last few bites of cake.

I loaded my fork and slid the chocolate into my mouth. "What kind of luck?"

"Well, the tractor is back, and it seems to be running fine. I finally hired a guy named Danny to live in the bunkhouse and keep things maintained. Oh, and I got a good stock dog. That's been a big help this week."

"Oh, great! Did Dusty hook you up?"

Austen nodded and swiped the last bite of cake up with his fork. "Yeah, with pretty near everything. Nice neighbors in these parts."

I grinned. "You're starting to talk like them."

"Am I?" His smile widened. "Is that a compliment?"

"Why not?"

He folded his napkin and tossed it on the table. "Where I come from, it's... well, it's different. Some of the smartest people I've met here would be seen as no-account rednecks down there."

"Good thing you're here, then."

Austen hitched forward, leaning his elbow on the corner of the table closest to me. "I think so. Even with all the annoying things that have been happening, I'm glad to be here."

I rested my chin on my hand and smiled. "By 'here,' are you still talking about the town?"

"I was kind of referring to this table, right now." His eyes wandered over my face, and his expression warmed. "I was starting to think you'd never give me the time of day. What made you come over tonight?"

"I guess I decided..." I tilted my head and quoted that note, the one I had already memorized. "... maybe it was time to take that chance."

His brows lowered, and he smiled politely. "Which chance?"

"Well..." I gestured between us. "You said you wouldn't intrude, so it was up to me to say something."

Austen's gaze grew misty, and he nodded slowly. "I don't recall saying that, but…"

"In your note. The one in my box."

"Ah! The note! That's right." He frowned and looked thoughtful. "I sort of forgot what it said."

"I didn't. It was the sweetest thing anyone's ever given me."

Austen leaned back in his chair. "Better even than flowers?"

"*Much* better than flowers. It was sincere and beautiful and…" I took a sip of my ice water and thought for a second. "And it made me realize how much I'd missed. I've probably dated too many deadbeats because I'd gotten to the point that nothing impressed me anymore. But your note did."

His expression had turned somehow fragile, curious, and maybe even bemused, and he sighed a gentle, "Oh."

"So, I guess that's it. Everyone has their thing. I didn't realize it, but apparently, I'm all about pretty notes and poems and fanciful ideas of old-time romance. You know, the fairy tale bit."

"Knights in shining armor," he supplied.

I gave him a half smile. "I guess so. Does that make me cheesy?"

"It makes you beautiful." He held out his hand in the space between us, his fingers curled to catch mine. When I cautiously rested my hand on his, he lifted it to his lips. "I hope you give me a chance to saddle that white horse for you, Jess Thompkins."

My heart started beating faster. "You don't need a white horse. Just speak to me from your heart like you did in that note. That's all I really want."

His hand clasped mine. "Can I see you again tomorrow?"

"Yes."

Dusty

"I need help. Bad."

I sighed at Austen's voice on the phone, but I rubbed my eyes and tried to keep the impatience out of my voice. He wasn't my favorite person this morning. "What's going on today?"

"Dude. It's Jess."

Cold fever swept through me. *Not Jess. Please, not Jess.* I'd waited too long one time too many, and now when I'd finally worked up the nerve to ask for her love, she'd gone and fallen for Austen. I swallowed and drew a shaky breath. "What about her?"

"It's so wild. So, after you left last night, she stayed for a while, right? We talked a lot, and I really *really* like her."

I felt dizzy. Numbly, I reached back to feel for a hay bale and dropped shakily onto it. He couldn't be after Jess. Not her! I'd help him with anything he wanted. I'd spend all my spare time helping him get his ranch into shape and get a good start. But I couldn't just watch him sweep in and steal her.

"Dusty, you there? Did I lose you?"

"No," I said, my voice cracking. "I'm here."

"Well, anyway, like I was saying, she's pretty amazing. You know her fairly well, right?"

"Y..." I cleared my throat. "Yes."

"So, here's my problem. She's not like other girls. I think I was doing everything wrong to make a good impression on her, you know?"

I closed my eyes and rapped the back of my head on the wood of the barn wall. "I know what that's like."

"Yeah, but I think I finally found something that will work. Trouble is, I have no idea how to do it."

"Look, Austen, I don't—"

"No, Dusty, please! I mean it, I really need help, and you seem like a guy who knows this kind of stuff."

I was going to be sick, right there on the barn floor. "If I knew this kind of stuff, I wouldn't be single," I bit out.

The line went quiet for a second. "Well, at least hear me out. Please, I don't know who else to ask."

I ground my teeth and glared at the roof, chewing on all kinds of bitter words I'd have liked to spit at him. "Fine. What is it?"

"See, she doesn't care about flowers. Compliments and buying her stuff won't work. I don't think she's the kind who wants big shopping trips or fancy dinners. She's different."

"Of course she is. She's had to put up walls because of all the guys chasing her for her whole life."

I heard Austen gasp on the other end. "Holy smokes, you're right! I knew you were the right guy to ask."

My stomach twisted. "No, I'm not. Really, I can't help."

"You may be the only one who can! See, she's kind of old-fashioned. Do you know what I think she'd like?"

I sagged against the wall, my fingers kneading my pounding forehead. "Books. Letters. Poetry. Something that speaks to her heart, not superficials."

"Exactly! Except I have no idea about any of that stuff."

"Why don't you just ask her?" I grumbled. I was a fine one to talk.

"Because she thinks I already know! I gotta get up to speed, and fast. She wants the hero type, you know, saves the damsel. What do you give a girl who wants a... a Cassanova?"

"Trust me, she does *not* want a Cassanova. That's the last thing she's interested in. I think you mean an Ivanhoe."

"I don't know the difference."

"Well, I don't know what to tell you. You can't just pretend to like what she likes. She'll see through anything fake." *Please, oh please, let her see through...*

"I'm not talking about being fake. I just want to show her that I'll find what's important to her and try to be that guy."

I bit my lips together and closed my eyes. They stung like I'd rubbed sunscreen into them. "Austen, I don't know."

"How about a book? I was never much of a reader. How do I know where to start? Can I get like Cliff's notes or something?"

"That seems a lot like being fake," I barked.

"You know what I need? I need to write her something, just for her from me. But what?"

"Well, you're a smart guy," I said, my voice dripping with sarcasm. "I'm sure you'll figure it out."

"That's the problem. You'd be better at this than me."

"Then maybe you're not the guy for her! Ever think of that?"

"No," he replied thoughtfully—and totally missing the frustration in my voice. "I don't think that's it. She's not easy to get to warm up, you know? She's kind of terrifying, really. A woman who looks like her, who can fix a guy's truck for him, and who's so smart? She's got her head full of like old hero-type characters, super high standards. What does she need a guy like me for?"

"Good question."

Austen laughed. "She's scary, isn't she? But now she's finally talking to me, and I need to keep it that way. If I can just get her to know me a little, let her take the time to read me…"

"Then write her a stinking letter!" I shot back, my hackles raising. How dare he ask me for help wooing the woman I was in love with?

"Sure, that's the thing to do. Can you come over this afternoon? I really want your advice on this."

I chewed the inside of my cheek and almost threw my phone. How could he be so dense? Couldn't he tell I wanted nothing to do with this? I'd love to watch her shoot him out of the skies.

But I wouldn't sabotage him any more than I could have kicked Luke in the teeth. I couldn't sink that low, not for anybody. And I still liked him, even if I could have busted him in the kneecaps right then.

Maybe if I agreed to "help," I could keep my finger on the pulse of what was happening. Turn this ship around before he got too carried away and she lost her heart to the wrong guy. Because *I* was the right guy for her. Wasn't I?

"Fine. I'll be over after I get the morning feeding done."

Jess

"So, are we cooking turkey in the oven or smoking it for Christmas? I'd better get to the store." Dad was poking his head in the pantry, rummaging through what we had on hand. "Potatoes and gravy? Stuffing? Green bean casserole?" He pulled a can of green beans out and stared at it, his shoulders sagging. He sniffed faintly.

I set my book aside and got up from the couch to walk over and take the can. I knew what he was thinking.

His fingers were trembling as he let me take it. He was quiet for a few seconds, and I just waited. "Nobody made green bean casserole like your mom. Or stuffing."

I shook my head. "Nobody."

He sighed and scrubbed his face, probably trying to hide the fact that his eyes had gotten misty. "But we should still try. It's just not Christmas dinner without green bean casserole and stuffing."

"We could do something different this year," I offered softly. "Maybe pick up a honey-smoked ham?"

He was looking down. "That would be easy. And some scalloped potatoes or something."

"Another of Mom's specialties," I reminded him.

"I guess so. She sure could cook." Dad gave a half smile and took the green beans back to stare at the can some more. "You know, it's not that I miss the food. But I sure miss seeing her in the kitchen, singing like she used to do when she chopped vegetables. And when she would decorate the house all beautiful for every holiday, remember that? I never cared much about that, you know. Figured it was still a house, it looked fine with or without decorations, but she made it..." He cleared his throat. "You know."

"Yeah." I put my hand on his shoulder. "I know."

"Ahem, well, anyway." He put the can back. "Let's try the ham this year. I'll go to the store later. Can you write me a shopping list?"

"Mind if I text it to you?" I walked over to pick up my phone from the living room to start putting things down while I was thinking about it.

"Fine. Hey, where did you get that book?" He pointed at the one I'd left on the couch. "I don't remember it."

I picked up the antique leather-bound and gold-embossed copy of *Emma* I'd been reading. "Kelli found it and gave it to me for Christmas. Beautiful, isn't it?"

He admired it when I handed it to him. "It is. Kelli gave it to you? Hmm."

I laughed as I took it back. "What do you mean, 'Hmm'?"

"Oh, nothing. I was just hoping some young man had finally figured out how to get your attention. That's how I asked your mom out, you know."

I tilted my head. "I thought it was over a flat tire. You stopped and helped her."

Dad chuckled. "That was when *I* noticed *her*. It took me a while to impress her with the fact that I wanted to do more than fix her tire."

I slid my book back on the couch and sat down. "Like how long?"

Dad sank into his recliner and scratched his ear thoughtfully. "Couple of months. I'd talk to her whenever I saw her at school, and she was sweet to me, but no more. It wasn't like she forgot that I helped her, but she didn't act like she noticed me. Finally, I discovered that she would sneak off to the school library during lunch every day, so I started doing the same. Took me about two weeks of sitting at the same table before she caught on. Finally, one day I got there before her and checked out the book I knew she would want to read." He pointed at my book. "Jane Austen. When she got there and started looking on the shelves, I handed it to her and told her she could have it if I could take her to a movie sometime."

I laughed. "It took all that? How could she be that oblivious?"

Dad raised his eyebrows and gave me a look. "I have no idea."

"Oh, wait, we're talking about me now?"

"Well, you're just like your mom in all the best ways. But maybe you have one or two of her faults, too," he said with a tender grin.

"I don't call it a fault not to go crazy over every guy I meet."

"Not at all." He picked up a magazine and started to leaf through it. He wasn't fooling me. He couldn't read that small print without his glasses on. "So, did I hear a rumor about someone trying to get your attention?"

There it was. I smiled and tucked my feet up on the cushion. "Austen Conrad."

Dad's magazine dropped, and his smile faded. "The tractor guy?"

"That's the one."

He rubbed his chin and stared at the wall, sighing. "That's... ahem. Not what I was expecting. How did that happen?"

"I saw him in town last night, and we talked for a while. He's a great guy. I think you'd like him."

Dad was frowning and fumbling with his magazine. "Oh. Oh, yes, I'm sure I would. That's... that's all that happened yesterday?"

"Well, I guess so. What else could there be?"

He kept stroking his jaw. "Nothing. I just thought there was something else."

"Not that I know of," I laughed. "So... I'm going out with Austen this evening. Just dinner, that's all. There's still spaghetti in the fridge if you don't want to cook, or I can make you something before I go."

He shook his head and picked the magazine up again. "I'll be fine. You just go and have a good time."

Chapter 11

Dusty

I was going to strangle him. Slowly. I ground my fingers into my eyes again and threw my hand in the air.

"Look, just... just talk to her! You don't need to bone up on nineteenth-century literature. She's smart and kind, and she'll be right there at the table listening to you. What's the problem?"

"I told you. She looks sweet and all, but she's a tough nut to crack. You know her, don't you? She's like talking to an airline ticketing agent."

"What in the world is that supposed to mean?"

"Friendly, smooth, even-tempered, never ruffled. She doesn't get mad, she doesn't get sad. She just plays all her cards close and doesn't let anything bother her."

I sighed and rubbed my chin in thought. "Okay, maybe. She's pretty easy-going."

"And nothing gets to her, right? Not even the good stuff. Now, I finally found a crack in the wall, and I need to figure out what's behind it. So, what do I say?"

"I don't know. What's so wrong with just being yourself? If regular old 'you' wasn't good enough to catch her attention before, what makes you think you'll be able to keep it when she gets to know you?"

"I told you, I just need to widen that crack a bit. See if there's something there. Dude!" He slapped the table. "I know what I need. I'll give her a poem or something."

I snorted and shook my head, but deep down, my soul was breaking. Giving her poems was *my* play. *My* idea. How dare he steal it? I rolled my eyes and slumped unhappily in my chair, staring out Austen's kitchen window. "Why are you so set on her? You've only met her a couple of times."

"Because she's... she's peaceful. Honest. There's something just pure about her, you know? I've never met anyone like that. You wouldn't believe the drama, the narcissism, and the pettiness I've dealt with."

"Oh, come on, they can't all be bad."

"You'd be surprised." He blew out a long breath and swiped a hand over his face like the memory had suddenly made him sweat. "I've been punched and spit on by women I cared about. Had my bank account drained, my dog stolen, my car... I won't even tell you what one woman did to my car. I didn't even call HAZMAT. I just scrapped it. My house wasn't as lucky, though."

"Holy guacamole," I breathed.

"That's just the stuff I called the cops about. The stuff that hurt the worst was right here." He poked a thumb at his chest. "Ever hear of gaslighting? My last girlfriend had me convinced I was going crazy—like, my doctor was even writing me some hard-core scripts, but it was her all along. The one before that was manic, or whatever the word is these days. She needed medical help, not a boyfriend. And the one before that..." he sighed. "She left me for my best friend."

I could hear my heart thudding in my ears. How miserable! Could a string of failures like that all be bad luck? "You sure can pick 'em."

"I guess so." He drummed his fingers on the table, and his eyes took on a haunted look I'd never seen there before. "I've been looking for so long to find someone I could trust, let my guard down with. Someone who would stick around. I could spend the rest of my life with someone like that. I just want to be able to make her happy and finally be the good guy for the right kind of woman."

I stifled a groan and looked out the kitchen window again. It served me right. I *had* to become best buddies with the new guy in town, and now, I felt sorry for him. But did I feel sorry enough to not only walk away from all my hopes, but to help him chase after *my* happiness?

One thing he said kept ringing back to me. I'd had years to turn Jess's head and never managed it. Austen had done it in just a few weeks. What hope did I have that she could ever fall for me if even a rich, tall, handsome, and interesting guy like Austen had only barely caught her notice?

She really was out of my league. But maybe if I worked a little behind the scenes, I could help two people I cared about find a little of their own happiness. Even if it killed me.

"Fine," I mumbled. "I have an idea for you."

Jess

Austen picked me up in his truck, a brand new silver Chevy with velvety leather, LED floor lighting, and about every bell and whistle you could put on a truck. It even had a seat massager built in. I felt bad just getting into it because in the middle of winter, there was no way to keep from getting at least a little mud on my shoes between our front door and the driveway.

"Oh, that's okay," he said as I tried to swipe my feet in a patch of snow. "It's a work truck."

"Doesn't look much like one."

He held the door for me and grinned. "See? Rubber floor pans. Good to go."

I climbed in and glanced around at the interior as Austen walked to the driver's door. The thing was beautiful. Way too beautiful to be a ranch truck. But Austen was new at all this and hadn't yet found out just how fast something like this would get trashed.

He closed the door on his side and reached for the ignition button. "Dusty said Beaufort's would be the place to go. Are they any good?"

"Very." I was still ogling the truck, admiring the purr of the sleek new engine, and the soft glow of all the interior features. I was turning around from checking out the back seat when I caught Austen smiling. "What?"

He chuckled. "I've had women admire my sports cars, but I never thought a girl would drool over a pickup."

"You have sports cars?"

"Not anymore. Sold them when I bought this."

I grinned. "Good trade."

"You really do like trucks, don't you? I gotta ask; what got you into being a mechanic? And don't say it was just your dad because I'll be disappointed."

I let my finger trail along the perfectly stitched leather armrest. "Well, I guess you'll have to be disappointed. Dad has this hotrod, a '33 Ford Coupe he bought right after he and my mom got married, but he never had a son to work on it with. So, he taught me. We spent a lot of nights and weekends huddled around that thing."

"That's all? Really?"

"Not totally. I used to think I wanted to be a television news reporter, but the more I saw of living 'on stage,' as I used to call it when I was queening, the less I wanted it. And I guess I got tired of everyone telling me what they thought I should do, what was expected."

"So you went and did the opposite?"

I shrugged. "Pretty much. After my tour was up, I was homesick, so I did what seemed like going home. Besides, there's good money in it if you know what you're doing."

"Huh. I had it figured for something different."

I leaned forward so I could see his face better. "Such as?"

"Oh, you know. Ex-boyfriend broke your heart but left you with a passion for working on engines or something."

"Nope. That would be why I left Oklahoma."

He flicked his eyes to me. "You just said you were homesick."

"No... well, yes. I meant the second time I left. I was working my first mechanic job after school when I reconnected with Owen. He was the son of someone high up, you know how that goes, and he got them to offer me a job with the Miss Rodeo organization. It was a great job. Lots of opportunities for advancement, and it paid well. My parents encouraged me to take it."

"There's a 'but' in there, isn't there?"

"Yeah. Owen wanted a piece of arm candy that didn't think or talk for herself. And he wasn't too choosy, either. One was as good as another." I rested my chin on my fist and gazed out the window.

"When he got mixed up and came to pick me up for an event he hadn't invited me to, I got a clue. And then Mom... You know, I'm sorry. I didn't mean to unload all my woes on you."

"No, keep talking. I like hearing about you. And for the record, Owen is a loser."

"Oh, believe me, I'm with you. Best move I ever made was leaving Oklahoma when I did."

He nodded. "That's how I'm starting to feel about California."

"Yeah? Why?"

His mouth worked, and then he squinted at me. "Not much to tell. I just like it better here."

I watched his face for a few seconds, then looked away. I'd hoped to learn a little about him—where he'd grown up, why he chose to settle in our town, what he wanted out of life. I guessed that would have to wait till he got more comfortable. I went back to admiring the truck just to take my eyes off him, and something caught my notice.

"Hey, what's this?" I asked. A worn leather-bound journal was stuffed in a side pocket, right where it could be picked up easily. I figured it was ranch stats or mileage records or something, but the broken-in look, so different from everything else in that sparkling truck, made me glance at it twice. It had been used a lot, and the leather only looked warmer and richer for it.

"Oh, that?" Austen grinned. "Just a few thoughts, musings. Notes about life. You can look at it if you like."

I slipped the journal out of the pocket and caressed the smooth cover. I could see the marks where it had been held the most; stains of sweat and probably dust ground into the leather. It was bound up with a narrow string of latigo, and the edges of the pages were feathered and soft, like it had been read and written in a thousand times. "You're sure you don't mind?"

"Help yourself."

At last, a chance to learn a little about Austen Conrad. I untwined the binding and let the pages fall open on their own.

Dusty

I shouldn't be here.

I kept thinking that over and over, but I couldn't make my feet move.

Why in the world had Austen asked me to be here tonight? The last thing I wanted was to look across the restaurant and watch the two of them getting cozy over the table. They weren't exactly holding hands or kissing, but from the way things looked, it was only a matter of time.

Jess was doing most of the talking. Austen was just listening, with a stupid grin on his face. I rolled my eyes and turned deliberately away. I'd probably have an even dumber look on my face if I got to sit across from Jess and smile at her while she talked to me. But I'd never have that chance now, would I? All because I'd felt sorry for Austen.

Had I done the right thing? I risked another look. Jess looked relaxed. Animated. Happier than she'd looked in a year.

Well, that was what I'd wanted for her, wasn't it? Deep down, beyond even what I wanted for myself. I could live with it if I knew she, at least, would have what she needed and wanted most. I just wished it could have been me sitting at that table.

I downed another drink and was ready to call it a night and leave, despite Austen's begging, when Jess got up. My head swung around—I couldn't help it—and I gazed hungrily after her as she walked toward the hall. Why was watching her so intoxicating? It wasn't that she moved seductively or tried to attract attention. Maybe it was because she *didn't* try.

My phone buzzed, and I looked down. Of course, it was Austen. I sent a glance over at his table, but he was acting nonchalant, avoiding my gaze. I sighed and looked at the message.

 -I'm out of ideas.

I frowned.

 -Looks like you're doing fine.

 -Dude, she's way smart.

Oh, good grief.

 -You're not exactly dumb. You're supposed to be a software genius, right?

 -That's different. I don't understand what she's talking about half the time.

I looked over at him again, this time in annoyance. How could he be such a blockhead? She was giving him her undivided attention! Wasn't that enough? I typed another message.

-Then don't pretend you do.

-Seriously, what do I say? I read that book you gave me, and I didn't get anything from it.

I blew out a sigh. Of course, he wouldn't get it. Those were *my* poems, *my* thoughts in that journal. I couldn't surgically transplant them into his head. But he'd been so frantic about what to say to a woman who loved books and relished the simple life that I didn't know what else to do but let him read my poetry journal to see if it gave him any inspiration. He'd been awed by it at first, but I doubt he read more than a handful of pages because his eyes glossed over before I even left his house.

-Just talk about your ranch. She'll appreciate that.

-I already did.

-Then tell her about yourself! She deserves to know who she's eating with.

I watched Austen read that last message. His face dropped into a frown, and he was holding his phone like he was ready to type, but nothing was happening. Finally, his fingers moved, and a message popped up on my screen.

-I can't. Not yet.

That was it. I typed one last message.

-Then I can't help you. I'm out.

I chucked some bills on the table and grabbed my hat off the back of my chair. Austen could dang well figure it out on his own if he was going to act like a helpless teenager when the most incredible woman in town was his date. I was through watching.

I was halfway to the door when Jess returned from the restrooms, and I almost ran into her. Literally. She jerked to a stop to keep from slamming into me but still found a smile. "Oh, hi, Dusty! I didn't know you were here."

I was too exasperated with Austen to remember my usual nervousness around her. I dipped my hat and smiled tightly. "I was just leaving."

"Too bad. How did that shampoo work out?"

I squinted. "Huh?"

"For Luke. A while back, when I bumped into you, you were buying special shampoo for Luke's horse."

"Oh." I laughed. "The shampoo worked out great. The horse, not so much."

"That's a shame."

I shrugged. "For Luke. She turned out perfect for me. Best heeler I've ever been on."

"Isn't it funny how that works? Sometimes one person's bad fit can be another person's dream come true."

I stared into her eyes, the crystal white centers with deep blue flecks around the edges, and all I could do was grunt a soft, "Yeah. Funny."

"Well, I shouldn't keep you. I'm here with Austen."

I nodded. "I saw."

"Oh! Right. He told me you recommended this place. You guys have gotten to be pretty good friends, huh? You should come over and say hello."

I glanced over my shoulder at Austen, who was watching us with curiosity mixed with a touch of... was that jealousy? "I just talked to him. Sorry to run, Jess, but I have something I need to do."

She folded her hands over her purse and smiled one more time. "Of course. The ranch sure keeps you busy. Well, Merry Christmas if I don't see you around." She walked past me, back to Austen's table, leaving me looking after her.

"Merry Christmas," I murmured.

Chapter 12

Jess

Austen let me keep his journal. I hadn't meant to ask, but he could see how curious I was about it. I said something about how I wished I had more time to look at it, and then I started to put it back where I'd found it. He stopped me.

"Did you want to take it now?" He looked uncomfortable offering.

"Oh, no. That's okay. I'll read it again sometime if you don't mind."

"Well, I... I don't carry it with me all the time. I usually... uh... usually it's at home."

I wanted to take it, but he didn't seem very confident about offering. "Really, it's fine. I don't want to steal your journal."

"I don't need it for a day or two, though. Just..." His hand dropped from mine like he was forcing himself to be calm. "I'll need it back in a few days. After Christmas. Is that okay?"

I slid the journal back into my lap, caressing the cover like a pet. "Of course. I'll keep it safe, and I won't share it with anyone."

"I know it will be safe with you." He was leaning toward me like he wanted to say something. Or kiss me. But something inside held me back. He was a nice guy, and I'd had a great time. But I didn't know him very well yet, and he hadn't been very forthcoming. Maybe he was modest. That was why the journal was such a treasure, and his letting me read his private scribblings was a tremendous gift.

"Well," I said after a moment. "Guess this is goodnight."

He smiled. "Guess so."

I hesitated. Should I kiss him? What if he moved and I didn't feel right about it? Would I have to pull back and embarrass him, or would I just let him kiss me anyway?

I knew the answer. I'd probably be too afraid to hurt his feelings, like always. So, I took matters into my own hands and leaned over swiftly to kiss him on the cheek. Simple, and affectionate, but it set a boundary. For tonight, anyway.

I'd obviously surprised him, because he didn't get another word out until I had my hand on the door handle. "Good night," I said.

He blinked. "Good night. I had a great time."

"Me too." I paused on the step of the truck. "Hey, what are you doing for Christmas?" He was probably all alone. And it was just Dad and me at our house. Maybe…

"Oh. Christmas." He tugged at his ear. "Danny's watching the ranch, and I'm flying back to California for two days. Some old friends wanted me to come."

I shrugged. "Next time, maybe. Have a safe trip."

"I will. See you when I get back?"

"It's a date." I hopped down, closed the truck's door, and then stood back. Austen threw it in reverse and backed out of the driveway, waving one last time when his tires reached the road. I held the journal to my chest, drank in one last gulp of the biting winter air, and then went into the house.

Dad was still up. He switched off the TV and took his glasses off when I came in. "You're back earlier than I expected." He paused and looked behind me. "Well?"

"Well, what?"

"Where is he?"

"On his way home, probably. Why?"

Dad whistled and put the remote down. "It went that badly, huh?"

"No! What do you mean by that?"

"I mean, I figured he'd walk you to the door. Don't guys still do that?"

"Not for a hundred years, Dad. Maybe some of them, but it's not expected anymore." I took my coat off and hung it in the closet. "What did you do tonight?"

"Nice try. We both know I sat on my duff and channel-surfed. So? Where did you two go? What's he like?"

"Beaufort's." I dropped onto the couch, still clutching the journal. "He's nice. I'm still trying to figure out what he's all about, but I like him. Planning to see him again after Christmas."

"Well, that's good to hear. I'm off to bed."

I put my hand up to pat him on the arm as he walked by. "Good night. Love you, Dad."

"Mmm," he grunted. "Love you, too."

I waited for his door to close, then looked down and sighed. I hadn't gotten very far in that journal earlier this evening, but I meant to soak in it now that I had it all to myself. I smoothed my hand over the cover once more—the buttery soft leather that told of sweat and toil, of being thrown in a truck or a saddle bag or being folded over backward and then stuffed into a coat pocket. This was the man's heartbeat.

I don't know what I expected. An accounting of his days, maybe, or a record of the work he'd done on the ranch since he bought it. But it was nothing like that.

The yellowed pages were filled with funny little quips—anecdotes of his day on the ranch. They ranged from short stories to one-line thoughts. Some were sparse and incomplete ideas, while others flowed onto the page with the eloquence of a bard.

It was simple things set artfully into the light and examined with care and fascination. Cheerful yellow weeds waving among the alfalfa stalks in a July thunderstorm, the particular curl of hair on a special bull's nose that made him look playful, the way the sun broke over the mountains after a snowfall. He could make the mundane inspiring, and he saw beauty in things others never noticed.

The back of my neck was tingling as I flipped page after page. I had found my poet.

Dusty

"Pull!"

Dad released the catch on the clay pigeon shooter, and Luke tracked the orange target with the muzzle of his twelve gauge. One quick blast, and it shattered.

"That's another for Luke. Evan, your turn."

My oldest brother stepped forward and lifted his shotgun. "Pull." Evan knocked the clay out of the sky and grunted in satisfaction. "That makes ten total for Luke and me. You guys are up."

I gave the barrel of my shotgun a quick wipe-down and walked up to the line. This was our Christmas Eve tradition—a team trap shooting game we had invented when we were kids. We'd draw straws for teams, and each shoot six rounds, then swap, kind of like a baseball game, and the losing team did the other team's chores. Except this year, Cody was married, and Marshall was out having dinner with Kelli's family, so Dad stepped in to be my partner.

"Ready?"

I nodded, and Luke sent the orange pottery winging through the icy blue skies. I led the path, getting ahead of its arc, and pressed the trigger.

"That's a miss."

I lowered my shotgun and scowled. I hadn't hit one all day. Dad took his turn, and like always, he nailed it. "Bit off your form today, Dusty," he said as he stepped back. "Feeling okay?"

"Not really. Pull."

I didn't miss this time, but it was such a grazing hit it almost didn't count. What was wrong with me? I caught my brothers muttering something from the corner of my eye, but they hushed up when I looked at them.

I wasn't blind. They'd all been whispering lately, saying something was up with me, but I wasn't in the mood to talk about it. How could I? It would require confessing a bunch of my private thoughts all at once, and that was just too much.

Dad and I finished our round, with him hitting every one and me missing most. Once I got a bad start, it was hard to get right again. My head just wasn't in it, to say nothing for my heart.

"Well," Luke said at the end, "that's a win for us. Looks like you two are cleaning stalls tonight." He and Evan high-fived, and we started packing away our gear.

"I'll take care of chores," I told Dad. "You go on in."

"Nah, fair's fair. We lost."

"*I* lost. Your back's still bothering you, isn't it?"

Dad snorted. "Only because you all won't let me do the heavy work anymore. Bit of exercise'll do me good."

"I mean it." I shoved my gear bag into his hands. "I'll do stalls."

He didn't argue. Just took my stuff, loaded it in the side-by-side, and drove off.

I didn't mind cleaning stalls. I didn't do it that much anymore because we had enough hired help to handle most of the mundane chores, except around the holidays. Dad liked to give everyone a day off for Christmas Eve or Christmas Day—everyone, that is, except for us.

But I enjoyed a little time in the barn. Quiet, meditative time, alone with my thoughts and the animals. It was times like this when I could let my thoughts meander and wind their way to clarity—when I could make sense of things.

And life didn't make sense today.

I guess that's natural when you've just watched your greatest hope disappear in a puff of smoke. What do you do next? I hefted one forkful after another into the wheelbarrow, waiting for that flicker of inspiration, but nothing came to me. All I could think and feel was that this wasn't how it was supposed to be. That I'd sabotaged my future, and that Jess was meant to be with me.

I felt sick and weary when I finally got back to the house. I found Luke where I thought I'd find him—shopping for horses on his phone, his stockinged feet propped up on one of Mom's old cushions. He looked up when I came in. "Hey, little brother. What do you think of this one?"

He showed me his phone, and I gave him a half-hearted thumbs-up. "Nice."

"I thought he was a lot more than 'nice.' He's already got ten thousand in earnings, for Pete's sake! What's up with you?"

"Nothing." I grabbed the *Stockman's Magazine* and automatically flipped through the pages. I'd lost track of how many times I'd looked for my poem; it was like muscle memory now. I always picked it up when I was frustrated because it was the only proof I had that I'd done something right lately. My eyes found the familiar lines, and I took a deep breath.

That was when Luke swiped it out of my hands.

"Hey!" I cried. "What's the idea?"

He rolled it up and tossed it aside. "Tryin' to figure what's been eatin' you this month. Evan thinks it's stomach trouble, blames my cooking. Can you believe that?"

"Unbelievable," I deadpanned, bending over to scoop up the magazine again.

"That's what I told him! I say it's a woman what's buggin' you. So, who's right?"

What was the use? He was going to find out anyway. I rubbed my forehead and blew out a sigh. "You are."

"I *knew* it!" he crowed. "What's her name?"

I stared at him.

"Come on, I won't tell. Hey, promise. Swear on my new horse!"

"What new horse? You made me buy her."

Luke clenched his fists in front of him and looked like he was in genuine agony. "You're killing me! I tell you who I'm dating, don't I?"

"But I'm not actually dating her." I almost smiled as I watched him writhe and contort into the best begging face I'd ever seen on him. Rarely did I get a chance to give Luke a hard time—usually, it went the other way.

"What, do you think I'm going to blab to everyone? I wouldn't do that!"

I raised my eyebrow. "Just like you wouldn't spill the beans about that crush I had on Mandy Perkins in third grade?"

He put his hands up. "Okay, but this time I really, *really* won't. Come on, you have the memory of an elephant. With Cody moved out and Marshall losing his mind, and Dad… wherever Dad goes lately, you're the last good person around here to talk to. If you go bats, too, I'll have no choice but to get married or something."

I rubbed my face and gave a low, reluctant chuckle. "Like any woman would have you."

"I don't know. I thought Jess Thompkins was kind of fun to hang w… wait a minute." He slid forward on his chair and pointed a trembling finger. "That's *it!* You've got a thing for Jess! I might'a known!"

I couldn't even deny it. I could feel my face betraying me; with the flush of heat and cold, it must have changed colors a dozen times. "What gave it away?"

"You, hangin' around the restaurant like a lost puppy when I took her out, that's what."

"I was not! I was with Marshall!"

"And you wouldn't even look over at us. I kept trying to make goofy faces at you when she wasn't watching, and you never even saw. You were as bad as Marshall, pretending not to notice Kelli Mason. Dude, how come you didn't say something?"

I let out a weary sigh. "What good would that have done?"

"Well, for starters, I'd have never gone out with her if I knew you were sweet on her."

"You'd already asked her out by then."

"So? I'd have canceled it or even pushed you into it somehow. You don't go out with your brother's woman. That's one of the rules."

I shook my head. "She's not mine. Never has been and never will be."

"You don't know that."

"I'm afraid I do." My hands tightened around the rolled-up magazine like I was trying to choke it. "I waited too long, and now she's dating Austen Conrad."

Luke even turned pale at that. He sat back and gave a low whistle. "Not good." He rubbed his jaw. "Not good at all. Half the women in town are after him."

"I know."

"Isn't he your buddy, though?"

"Yeah, and I basically helped him get her."

Luke stared, his jaw slack. "Dude. That's messed up."

"Tell me about it."

Jess

Dad and I didn't do much for Christmas. It felt weird to put on our traditional celebration without Mom, and anyway, how much food could two people really eat? So, we spent the morning watching movies in our pajamas, nibbling on crackers and cheese and salami for lunch while the ham baked. Dakota pestered me until I threw his ball in the house, and when our last movie ended, I curled up with that delightful cowboy poetry journal again. It was a quiet, peaceful, no-fuss kind of Christmas, and it was perfect.

I was going out to the garage refrigerator to get the potatoes when I happened to glance at the hotrod. I had been thinking it would be fun to tinker with it that afternoon, but something different caught my eye. It wasn't up on the jack anymore. Odd. The rear end had been disassembled for months over what should have been a quick job, and Dad just hadn't been in the mood to finish it.

"Hey," I said when I got back inside, "when did you finish the shocks?"

Dad's expression changed from blank confusion to warm pride. "A week or so ago. Looks good, doesn't it?"

"Yeah, but I thought you wanted some help with that. I was ready whenever you were."

"Oh, no, it was simple. I had a friend stop by, and we shot the breeze and got it done."

"Oh." I dumped the potatoes in the sink to rinse them. "Which friend?"

His mouth twitched, and for a second, I wasn't sure he was going to answer. "One of the Walkers."

"Blake? He's such a good guy."

Dad's cheek flickered, and he looked away. "They're all good guys. Salt of the earth, always willing to lend a hand. Honest and friendly and just decent folks."

I laughed. "You're starting to sound like a matchmaker. I think Blake might be spoken for."

"I wasn't just talking about Blake. And what do you mean, he's spoken for?"

"Oh, it's just that every time I drive by the bank lately, he's sitting in his truck having coffee with Meryl Justice."

Dad chuckled. "Better keep that to yourself. I think everyone in town knows, except for his boys."

I plopped the first few potatoes on the cutting board and reached for the peeler. "Why wouldn't they know?"

He wandered in from the living room and stopped at the kitchen counter to load another cracker with cheese, but he didn't eat it right away. "I think some folks like to let their feelings grow without a lot of interference, even from the people they care about the most. Maybe Blake's just private. Couple of his boys are like that, too."

I tossed the first potato into the pot. "I could see that. Not about Luke, but maybe Evan. He's almost a hermit since he lost his wife."

Dad nodded and crunched on his cracker. "And there's Dusty."

I turned a quizzical look on him. "What about Dusty?"

He shrugged. "Seems like a guy who thinks a lot more than he talks, that's all."

I frowned as I peeled and chopped. "Maybe. I always thought he just wasn't very sociable."

"Maybe you never took the time to find out."

I swept the last of the chopped potatoes from the cutting board into the pot. "I'm not sure how I'm supposed to do that. He never really says anything when I run into him in town. In fact, he usually acts like he can't get away from me fast enough."

"He could just be shy."

"He doesn't seem like that with other people. And anyway, I'm seeing Austen right now, so it would probably look bad for me to try to solve all the mysteries of one cowboy named Dusty Walker."

"Hmm." Dad grunted and helped himself to another cracker. "I guess it would."

Austen got home early on the twenty-seventh and picked me up from work to grab lunch at Burger Shack. And then, after milkshakes and curly fries, he drove me out to see his ranch.

I hadn't been out there since I was a teenager and came up to watch a branding. The place had gone downhill since then, but here and there, I could see where Austen was already fixing things back to what they should be. Old gates that would need to be replaced soon swung from new posts. There were sections where the barn siding had obviously been repaired, and a patch of new steel had been welded into the feed silo where it had probably rusted through.

"Lots of stuff still to do," he apologized as he shifted the truck into park. "For now, it's like plugging holes in the dike until the floodwaters recede and I can fix things right."

"I'm sure." I pushed open the door of the truck, and Dakota, who had tagged along, hopped out behind me. He started sniffing everything in the path until we got to the front porch, where a shifty-eyed Border Collie sat waiting for us. The dogs squared off for a few seconds, taking their measure of one another, then Dakota sneezed and turned away to nudge my hand.

"Meet Shep," Austen said. "He and I are still getting to know each other, and he's giving me the silent treatment for leaving town." He chuckled and reached down to pat Shep's head. He was right—the dog gave Austen a suspicious look before permitting him to stroke his ears.

"You had someone watching the ranch, though, didn't you?" I asked as I extended my hand for Shep to sniff. He hesitated, then cautiously licked my fingers.

"Danny was here, so he was well taken care of. But you'd think I was cheating on him or something by the way he's acting today. I'm not sure why he's so funny about it."

"Give it time. He's just figuring you out, and these working dogs are like Velcro. They really bond to their handler, and it upsets them to be alone."

"I guess so. Well, shall I give you the ten-cent tour before you have to get back to work?"

"Sure! Only I'm not going back to work today. I'm starting to volunteer out at White Pines a couple of afternoons a week."

He looked mystified. "The horse therapy program? But you're not a therapist. What can you do there?"

"Oh, lots of stuff, now that they have the funding to expand. Morgan always needs volunteers, even if it's just for stall cleaning and feeding. You should stop by if you have time."

"I doubt I will. One thing I'm learning about being a rancher is you don't get spare time. Unless..." He slipped an arm behind me and tugged me closer.

"Unless what?" I asked in a whisper. I let my hand rest on his chest as prickles raced over my skin.

"Unless something is really worth investing in." He pulled his hat off and leaned down. I met him halfway.

He was nice to kiss. Gentle and considerate, and he smelled like aftershave. I didn't let it carry on too long, but I wasn't sorry. I'd seen a bit of his soul in his words, and so far, I liked what I saw.

Austen drew back. "Well, I guess we'd better hurry up if you have somewhere to be. What would you like to see?"

"How about the horses?"

"Sorry to disappoint you. I've been ranching on a four-wheeler. Danny's trying to set me right, though. He claims I'll get some things done in half the time on a horse."

"He's probably right. A four-wheeler can't react nearly as well as a horse. It would save you a lot of time and trouble."

Austen shrugged and grinned. "Only if a fellow knows how to ride. I mean, beyond the basics of staying on. Dusty started teaching me how to rope, though."

"Really? He and Luke are some of the best around, everyone always says. You should see if he'll sell you a horse while you're at it."

"Yeah. Hey—" His expression changed, the flirtiness vanishing and the businessman returning. "I just remembered that journal. Do you still have it? I sort of need it back."

"Ah, yes." I fished around in the deep pockets of my coat and produced it. "Thanks for letting me read it. It was... it was really special." I let myself drift, my balance swaying toward him as my hand slid up his shoulder again. I wouldn't mind kissing him one more time, just to show him how much I meant it. I loved seeing the person behind the mask.

But for once, Austen wasn't looking at me. He thanked me for the journal, tossed it on a chair just inside the house door, and reached for his hat. "Better get going, huh?"

I fell back to flat feet. "Sure."

Chapter 13

Dusty

"Thanks for coming to help out, Dusty!" Morgan called over her shoulder. "I'm sorry, I have to run!"

"No problem," I replied, though I didn't think she could hear me. She was already halfway out to the arena, slightly out of breath and more than a little harried. She was trying to do the jobs of three people today since one of her usual volunteers had taken a part-time job on Tuesdays and Thursdays, and another had called in sick. I thought she would kiss my feet when I showed up and asked her to put me to work.

I expected to be given a pitchfork and an aisle of stalls to clean or some hay bales to buck. I was fine with hard work; the heavier, the better. It took my mind off Jess Thompkins.

The job Morgan gave me, however, was going to be a heck of a lot harder. Darn near impossible. I blew out a breath and set my hands on my hips.

Five fresh young faces stared back at me, eyes wide and trusting and cheeks rosy from the nip in the air. These were the test pilots, the first of a new breed of client for White Pines: the after-school program.

I was in over my head.

The program was a brilliant idea, birthed out of the sudden growth White Pines had seen since their benefit auction. Morgan felt there was a need for something fun and constructive for latch-key kids to do in those hours before their parents got home, and she felt like White Pines had a lot to offer. In exchange, the program found another source of funds to cover feed expenses for the horses. This week, between Christmas and New Year's, was all part of a test to gather feedback from families before Morgan opened it up to the general public. And somehow, I'd been tagged with the job of making it work this afternoon.

By myself.

I clapped my hands together and rubbed them as if eager to get to it. "Okay, has anyone ever brushed a horse before?"

Five pairs of eyes blinked and looked around at each other. Finally, one little girl in the back cautiously slipped her hand up, just even with her ears. "Mister Dusty, we all did that yesterday."

I nodded. "Right. Morgan said this was your second day here, huh?"

"Not me!" piped up a boy in the back. "My mom just heard about it today and signed me up. I wanted to play video games with Connor, but she said I had to come here. Are we going to ride a bronco?"

"I'm afraid not. What's your name, son?"

He crossed his arms. "Aedyn, and I'm not your son."

"Everyone is someone's son, and don't forget it. Now, let's—"

"Are you Miss Morgan's son?"

I squinted and tried to find the source of this question. "Am I what?"

Another boy in the front was digging at his nose, then he sniffed and asked earnestly, "Is Miss Morgan your mom?"

I had to fight the urge to chuckle. I mean, the kid was so *cute*, and his question so beguiling. But he was being serious, so I owed him that courtesy in return.

"No, she's not my mom. In fact, Miss Morgan and I are about the same age. Just like you guys. How old are you..." I had to turn my head upside-down to read his name tag. "...Billy?"

"I'm five, but on January first, I'll be six," he answered smartly.

"No, you won't," retorted a girl who looked suspiciously similar to Billy. His sister, I guessed. "Your birthday's not 'til April."

"But Miss Morgan said everyone gets older on January first, no matter when their birthday is," he insisted. "Because she said, Duke is sixteen, and he'll be seventeen on January first, even though she didn't know his real birthday."

This time, I couldn't help a small chuckle. "Billy, you're absolutely right, but that's when we're talking about horses, not people. We do things kind of funny with them, don't we?"

He looked frustrated. "I still think it counts."

"Maybe, Billy, maybe. Okay, gang, let's get started. What did you do yesterday?"

"I wasn't here yesterday," Aedyn reminded me.

"Okay... Morgan said she has some coloring books to start on that teach you about the different types of tack and stuff. Shall we get started on those?"

"I don't like coloring," one of the girls said primly. "I just want to ride."

I bit the inside of my cheek and counted to three. "We won't be riding today. We can learn to groom the horses, though."

"Do I have to shovel stinky stuff?" Billy asked in his most serious voice. "Because I get sick." He grabbed his stomach and made a gagging sound to demonstrate.

I rolled my neck and grimaced. How in the world was I supposed to point all these kids in the same direction? Just when I didn't know what to say or do next, my salvation arrived. I heard a car door closing outside, and Morgan's voice drifted in toward us. "Oh, I'm so glad you could make it! Would you mind helping Dusty with the kids? You're a life-saver!"

I didn't know who had just shown up, but with them helping me, we'd do a whole lot better than I was doing on my own. I was watching the door when a familiar Australian Shepherd dog trotted inside, assessing the surroundings. He made one pass around the room, sniffing boots, fingers, and coats and eliciting squeals from all the kids. Finally, he came to me, wagged his tail, and sat. Then he barked like he was expecting me to give him a treat.

"Dakota, come!"

The dog sprang up when he heard the voice that made my heart stop. *Jess.* She had come, after all. My eyes were glued to the doorway until her figure darkened the entry.

The late afternoon sun made a halo in the sweep of her flaxen hair, and for an instant, I almost could have fancied an angel had come down from heaven. She hung her coat on the wall and strolled into the barn aisle, smiling at each of the kids as she passed them. Then she stopped and smiled at me.

"Hello, Dusty."

I was tingling all the way to my toes, and it took me a couple of attempts to get the words out.

"H-hello, Jess."

"So remember, never wrap the lead rope around your wrist. Hold it like this, instead." Jess was crouching beside a girl named Karli, coaching her on how to lead Duke up and down the barn aisle safely. The other girls clustered around, eagerly waiting for their turns.

I had pulled the two boys aside to teach them how to throw a rope at a dummy. They weren't doing much more than swinging it around their heads and occasionally at each other. That was probably my fault; I was watching Jess a lot more than I was watching them. But they seemed to be having fun, even Aedyn. I bounced back to reality when one of them shot a loop at my heels and almost tripped me.

I turned around, shaking my head and spreading my hands as they dissolved into whoops and belly laughs.

"Whoa, guys, don't bite off more than you can chew," I said. "Let's catch the calf head a few more times before you try to step up to heeling. Try this." I took Billy's rope, coiled it up for him, and then showed him how to shake out a loop again. "Got that? Now, try swinging it."

He was an eager student—too eager, from the looks of it, because he made an enthusiastic toss that landed the loop right over Aedyn's head. I sighed. "Good energy, Billy, but let's work on your aim."

"That's right where I was aiming."

I heard a laugh at my shoulder, and I turned to find Jess. She was leaning on the nearest stall and smiling. "Boys, that's a wrap for today. Your parents are starting to show up."

Billy let out another whoop and ran off. Aedyn carefully coiled his rope the way I had shown him, and he brought it to me. "Can I practice tonight?"

"I don't see a problem with that. You can take the rope home and bring it back tomorrow. Had fun today, huh?"

He shrugged one shoulder. "It's okay. I'm gonna rope Billy tomorrow. Fair's fair."

Jess sputtered in laughter and had to hide behind her hand, but I almost managed to keep it together. I crouched down to get eye level with him, and he met me with stone-cold seriousness. "We'll see about that. Just don't practice on any cats or dogs, okay?"

Aedyn's face fell. "So much for that idea," he muttered. His mom was at the door to collect him, so he slung the rope over his shoulder and yelled, "Bye!" He trudged off, scuffing the heels of his shoes on the floor and walking bow-legged, just like a rodeo cowboy.

"You sure changed his tune today," Jess observed. "I thought he would be cross all day until you broke out the ropes."

I straightened. "Sometimes it takes just the right thing to catch someone's interest. I got lucky."

Her smile warmed. "I guess so. You got Dakota's interest, anyway."

I glanced down at the Aussie. He had been following me all afternoon, bumping my hand, nudging my leg, whatever it took to make me look at him. And whenever I did look at him, he would grunt and moan in his little Aussie Shepherd language about how happy he was that I noticed him. He was doing it again now. I stroked his ears, and he flopped on the floor to show me his belly.

"You're a friendly little fellow, aren't you? And pretty determined, too."

"He knows how to get what he wants."

"I wish I had that talent." The words slipped out of my mouth before I realized I'd thought them. I swallowed and looked away, hoping Jess hadn't noticed what I said.

"What is it you want, Dusty?"

I closed my eyes and groaned silently. Slowly, I risked looking at her face. "I guess what everyone wants. To see a little bit of beauty in this life and to leave a little behind me when I go."

A fine crease appeared between her brows, and her mouth drew into a thoughtful bow. That was the expression right there—the one that stabbed me to the quick and robbed me of breath. It was the look she got when something broke through that smooth surface and plumbed to her heart.

"So simple," she murmured. "Yet you said it all, in just a few words. Thank you, Dusty. I'm going to remember that."

"But I should be thanking you. I was way out of my depth with those kids until you got here. I'm... I'm really glad you came today."

Her smile touched her eyes, and my heart melted like butter. No one could smile like Jess when she really meant it. "Are you coming back Thursday?"

"I told Morgan I would. And Saturday for the New Year's Eve work party. You?"

She nodded. "I had a great time. I'll definitely be back."

Warmth spread through my chest. I'd get to spend the afternoon with her again! I was probably smiling like a goon, but I didn't even care. "Well, I guess I'll see you on Thursday."

Jess

Thursday morning couldn't pass quickly enough. I'd finished my last job by ten, so that left me behind the desk typing up invoices until lunch. Except I wasn't working very fast.

Something was nagging at the back of my thoughts, but I never could put my finger on what it was—except that it had something to do with my afternoon plans. I was just excited to work with the kids again, probably, but it felt like something bigger. Like something was staring me in the face, and I hadn't figured it out yet. Maybe I was meant to be a teacher and not a mechanic.

"Penny for your thoughts?"

"What?" I looked up at my dad, leaning on the office door. He was sipping at a cup of coffee and had one foot crossed over the other like he'd been standing there for a while.

"You look like you're wrestling with something a bit heavier than those invoices, that's all. Everything okay?"

I clicked off the screen and closed the computer down. "Fine. I was just thinking about something." I got up from the desk and shuffled the remaining papers into the file folder. "I'm headed out to White Pines this afternoon."

Dad nodded, but he didn't move from the doorway. "Figured you would be. Sounds like you enjoyed volunteering the other day?"

"Even more than I thought I would. The kids are great! I know it's not always rewarding, but giving my time like that was pretty special. I felt like I could actually make a difference to someone, you know?"

He nodded slowly, a distant smile in his eyes. "I have an inkling. Was, uh, anyone else there?"

I grabbed my coat. "Dusty Walker was. It's a good thing, too, because they were really short-handed." I slipped my arms into the sleeves and picked up my keys. "You know, it's funny. I've known Dusty for years, but I think I heard him talk more to those kids on Tuesday than I've ever heard in my life."

"Some fellas aren't talkers. There's more to them than that. You just have to look a little deeper."

I tilted my head. "Maybe you're right. I guess I'll get my chance today, because he's supposed to be back. Austen said he'd try to come, too."

Dad looked down into his cup. "Still seeing him?"

"What is that supposed to mean?" I laughed. "I like Austen. He's smart and funny and easy to talk to. And he knows what it's like to be the odd duck in the crowd. Oh! I invited him over for New Year's Eve." I pointed at his chest. "Be nice. Don't show him your shotgun."

"What? There goes all my fun."

I shook my head and laughed, then kissed him on the cheek. "Bye, Dad."

Dusty wasn't there yet when I arrived. I found Morgan, who looked only somewhat less frazzled than she had on Tuesday. She heaved an enormous sigh of relief. "Oh, Jess, thank you a million times for coming!"

"I said I would. Do people often say they'll come and then not show up?"

"You have no idea. Especially this time of year, no one wants to leave their house if they can help it. I was worried I'd have to call Cody down. He and Marshall are getting the electrical finished up at the new place this afternoon so we can sheetrock on Saturday, and if they don't get it done..." She blew out a long sigh. "Well, I guess it wouldn't be the end of the world, but we'd be behind. I don't know what I was thinking, taking on this after-school program right now."

"It'll be fine! How's it been going so far?"

She shrugged, her face awash in wonder. "I don't know how or why, but it sounds like a ringing success. All the parents say they love it, and the kids all seem excited to come. I think it must be a miracle! I talked to the school district and if we meet their qualifications—which we will—they're willing to charter a bus out here. I only pray we can keep it staffed."

"Well, you can count on me."

Morgan nodded toward the window, where a truck was pulling into the driveway. "And Dusty. I wish I could have you two working together every afternoon. You balance each other perfectly."

I cocked her a funny grin. "We do?"

"Oh, absolutely. It makes the class so much smoother if the teachers have some chemistry together. Shoot!" She snatched a glance at her watch. "I have to be in a session in five minutes. Are you good? The kids will be showing up any minute."

"I'm good," I echoed. I watched her go, then crossed my arms and leaned on the counter. *Chemistry*, she had said. Dusty and me? I laughed. *Really?*

But three seconds later, my laughter died in my chest. The door opened, and a quiet, blue-eyed cowboy walked in and doffed his hat. And then, he smiled at me.

Maybe Morgan was on to something.

"Sorry I couldn't make it today," Austen apologized when I opened the door to him that evening. "Danny and I were fixing fence, and I forgot to check the time."

"That's alright. Come on in." I held the door. "I'm sure you guys get pretty busy trying to keep things running."

"It's a lot of work, and I won't deny it." He glanced around the living room with a wide grin. "Home sweet home, huh? I always like seeing where someone lives for the first time."

I chuckled as I led him through to the kitchen. "Why is that?"

"Gives you an idea of who they are. Except I hope you didn't judge me by the ranch house. I haven't had a chance to do anything to it yet."

I opened the fridge. "No judgment. Can I get you something to drink? We have... milk and water." I frowned. "I think we have more stuff in the garage."

"That's okay. I really just wanted to come by and say hello to my favorite girl." He came behind me and gently closed the door of the refrigerator, and then his arms slid around me. "So? How was your day?"

I let him nuzzle my neck, my pulse skittering wildly. Was this too fast? "Amazing," I managed shakily. "Yours?"

"Better now." He leaned back to look me in the eyes. The man really knew how to work that smile, and it curled my toes. I needed to find a way to tap the brakes on things, or they would speed ahead before I had a chance to figure out which way we were going.

"How did it go with the rescue thing?"

My brain started to clear a little. "Oh, I wasn't working with the rescue horses. You'll never believe it! I'm working with a bunch of kids. They're just testing things out right now, but hopefully, it will be part of a new after-school program. I'll get to teach them about horses and animal care and lots of crafting and farm skills. It's such a great opportunity for them!"

"Huh. That's cool. Who's normally supposed to be teaching it?"

"Well, for now, I am. There are others, but we all have certain days we can come. That's kind of how it works with volunteers."

"You mean you're planning to keep doing it? I thought it was just an occasional thing. You know, write off the shop hours on your taxes, that kind of deal."

"Oh, no, I plan to go out as much as I can. I haven't enjoyed anything that much in longer than I can remember. The girls are so sweet, and the boys! I thought I'd die laughing when Aedyn roped Dusty's hat!"

Austen's brow furrowed. "Dusty was there?"

"Yeah, he's volunteering, too. He's terrific with the kids."

"Huh." He blinked, his gaze drifting past me. "You know, it sounds like a pretty cool experience. Think I'll come with you to that work party on Saturday."

My whole body warmed right to my toes. Did he really want to come with me? I couldn't think of a better way to spend time together. "You will? You'll love it, I promise!" I stood on my toes to kiss his cheek.

"I'll love it even more if you kiss me proper."

I laughed. "Deal." He leaned down, and I sank into his arms, wrapping my own around his shoulders. His hat was in the way, but we figured it out.

Until my dad cleared his throat.

I jumped, but Austen didn't pull back that quickly. He lingered, his hands only slipping reluctantly away when I took a breath and put on a smile. "Hi, Dad. This is Austen."

He raised his eyebrows, but that was all. Dad had always been good at not embarrassing me, but I could tell he was just as uncomfortable as I was. He put his hand out. "Ahem. Nice to meet you, young man."

Austen remembered to take his hat off before he shook my dad's hand. "Likewise. Jed, isn't it?"

Dad's eye twitched. "That it is. I hear you're joining us Saturday evening for our wild night of puzzles and pizza."

Austen glanced at me. "I hope that's okay. If I'm messing with any family traditions..."

"No, no, that's fine. Hey, since you're here, I could use a hand in the garage. Do you have a minute?"

"What did you need, Dad?" I asked. "Is it the hotrod? I brought a new oil filter home. We can work on it later."

Dad shook his head. "This will only take a minute. I need someone tall to get that extra hood scoop down that's hanging on the wall." He winked at me, then gestured to Austen. "Well, come on, young man, I promise I won't keep you too long."

Austen followed my dad out to the garage, glancing questioningly over his shoulder at me as he went. I just lifted my arms. I had no idea what my dad was up to because he'd never dragged any of my boyfriends to the garage before. I guess he really just needed someone tall.

Chapter 14

Dusty

"Forty-nine, ninety-nine... seventy-six, ninety-five... twenty-eight..." The door opened behind me, but I didn't stop tabulating. If I broke concentration, I'd forget where I was on the week's expenses and have to start all over again. Besides, it was probably Luke, and he'd wait.

"Sixty-four, ninety-f—" Something heavy plopped on my desk. I stopped, the figures long lost, and turned around.

Austen Conrad pointed at the leather-bound book he'd dropped beside my elbow. "I brought your journal back."

"You could have knocked."

"Would you have answered?"

My hand was smoothing over that familiar cover, caressing the worn leather, but I looked up in surprise at the accusation in his voice. "Why wouldn't I?"

Austen stuck his hands in his pockets. "You tell me. Maybe you're not the nice guy I thought you were."

I swiveled my chair around and got to my feet. "Just what is that supposed to mean?"

"I think you know exactly what that means. It means you knew all about me wanting to get together with Jess, and you moved in to get in the middle. You're trying to screw me over, and I'm calling you on it."

The blood started pounding in my ears. "*What?* You think I'm trying to *sabotage* you? I've done everything I could to help you!"

"Only because you couldn't get her attention any other way. I guess you figured you'd just watch my moves and jump in when you saw the chance?"

Shivers of rage shot down the back of my neck and my fist balled. *Nobody* made accusations like that around here. Nobody dared.

"You've got some nerve," I said through clenched teeth. "Where are you even getting these crazy ideas?"

"How about the restaurant when I saw you talking to Jess on your way out?"

"Oh, for crying out loud. Now I can't even talk to someone when I'm passing them?"

"It's the *way* you were talking. You looked like you would have kissed her right there if I hadn't been watching. And what about volunteering at White Pines, conveniently at the same times she is?"

"I don't control her schedule. I didn't even know she was coming."

"Oh! Then it's just a coincidence. Sorry, I wasn't born yesterday. I trusted you, Dusty, and you went behind my back!"

I lunged across the room, my fist cocked and my dander up, but I checked myself just before grabbing him by the collar and throwing a punch that would have left him counting his teeth. Austen flinched, his eyes wide, but he didn't back down.

"How dare you?" I hissed. "You barge into my office and throw down like this, you'd better have something better than your own insecurities to back it up!"

Austen's pupils were dilated, his breathing unsteady, but to his credit, he didn't cower. Nor did he provoke me. Slowly, I lowered my fist.

"You know, I thought you were different. I told you that before, how I was amazed that you would bend over backward to help me out. I said how strange it felt because everyone else I'd known would use the opportunity to take advantage of me. And you say that's not what you're doing? Sure doesn't look that way from where I sit."

"Then you're hopeless, and you'll never understand what it is to be a neighbor in these parts. I gave my word, and I *never* break it."

His jaw muscles trembled, and he twisted his mouth into a seething scowl. "Then you tell me, Dusty. What am I supposed to think when I watch you watching Jess, and I see the look of a starving man? What am I supposed to think when I remember everything you said about who she is and what she wants? You've spent years watching her, haven't you?"

I stepped back and spun my chair around to drop into it spraddle-legged. I leaned over the back of it and scrubbed my face as my blood cooled to a normal temperature. "I've known her since we were kids. If anything could have ever happened between Jess and me, it would have already happened."

"Things change."

"You're right. They do. She's dating you, and that's that."

"'That's that,' huh? Spoken like a man who has given up? Or just wants me to think he has."

I leveled a heavy, exhausted stare at him. "Jealousy isn't a good look, Conrad. Especially not on the one who came out on top. I told you before I'd help you, and I've done nothing against you. My personal feelings don't matter. I gave my word."

He crossed his arms and shot one eyebrow up as he stuck his tongue in his cheek. "I'll be coming to that work party tomorrow."

I shrugged. "I'm sure they could use you."

Austen snorted. "You mean to tell me you weren't planning to use it as a chance to get close to her?"

"Intentionally? Never, not in that way. And it wouldn't do me any good even if I did try because she doesn't see me like that. I've known her for too long, and it will never be any different."

"Really. You, the guy who's so amazing at working with kids, according to her?"

I blinked. "She said that?"

"Sounds to me like you did find a way to get her to see you differently, huh?"

"Look, none of that was my idea. It just happened because Morgan was even more short-handed than I realized."

Austen narrowed his eyes and frowned. "Okay. You say you didn't plan any of that, and you'd never go behind my back. Prove it. Don't show up tomorrow."

My hackles went up, and I inhaled sharply. I'll never know how, but I managed to count to three before slowly letting it out, and then I answered with a deadly growl. "I gave Morgan and Cody my word. You don't just bail on a work party. They've already assigned the jobs and bought the materials. Around here, you show up and help someone if you can."

"I'll do your jobs, then. You say you don't want to step on my toes? Don't."

I pushed out of my chair, my lip curling as I stalked toward him. Austen couldn't know how close he was to a good old-fashioned Walker Roundhouse punch to the jaw.

"You're the one stepping on toes. You really don't know how it works, do you? I. Gave. My. Word. You can go ahead and come tomorrow, but I promised to help Cody and Morgan, and I'll be buggered if I don't show up. And the same goes for next week. You think you can't trust your girlfriend around me? That sounds like your problem, not mine."

Austen's nostrils flared, and his throat bobbed. "*My* girlfriend. That's right, she is. Stay in your lane, Walker." He pivoted on his heel and slammed the door behind him.

I was shaking, my vision blackened with a temper I hadn't unleashed since I was a little kid, and my muscles screamed out to bash something. Anything! Austen's face would do. I whirled around and grabbed the first thing in my reach—my journal. With a snarl of rage, I hurled it against the door of my office with every ounce of pent-up fury I possessed.

And then my senses slowed with frightening clarity. Like feather-soft petals, I saw the yellowed pages exploding apart, then floating gently to the floor. One after another, they drifted apart, then slid into scattered disarray as they touched down.

All my thoughts, my dreams, every whimsical notion and beautiful idea that had ever come to me—blown to bits, each and every one of them. Over a jealous tantrum, more befitting a toddler than a grown man!

I don't know what I was expecting to happen, but that wasn't it. My knees gave out, and I just crumpled there amid the strewn pages. Alone, still, and with no idea of what to do now.

Jess

"Hey, guys! Thanks for coming!" Morgan greeted us brightly on Saturday morning.

Austen closed the door behind us, and I got my first look at the new White Pines office. It was enormous compared to the makeshift welcome room in their old barn. It was open enough for wheelchair access everywhere, and it would let in a lot of natural light. I whistled. "Wow, Morgan, you weren't kidding. This is going to be a game-changer for you guys. You've done amazing work here."

She cracked a huge smile, and then Cody walked up to put his arm around her and kiss her on the cheek. "You're looking at the brains of the outfit right here," he informed us, giving her a little squeeze. "She did all the layout and design. I just lift the heavy things. Hey, sweetheart, you got any more donuts I can take to the guys? Marshall looks like he could use one right about now."

He gave her a significant look when he said it as if they both knew some secret about Marshall. I didn't have to ask—I'd been talking to Kelli, and it wasn't much of a secret by now that they were sort of on the outs. Kelli even planned to sell her horse, even though Morgan and I had both tried to talk her out of it. I didn't doubt that Marshall would be in a foul mood today.

"I hid the donuts behind the counter," she said, patting her husband on the cheek. "I wanted some to be left by the time everyone arrived."

"No wonder I couldn't find them earlier! See what I put up with?" he chuckled as he stuck his hand out. "Austen, good to see you again. Appreciate the help today."

"Cody." Austen shook his hand. "Any idea where you need us?"

"Morgan?" Cody asked. "I've got Marshall hanging drywall in the back hall and Dusty's cutting the pre-measured sheet rock and trim boards out in the lean-to. Walter said he'd like to stain the trim board. You've got a fleet of mudders and painters coming in, but we could use a good team to put the drywall up in this room."

Morgan nodded. "Can you guys do that? It sounds terrible, but I can't trust just anyone with certain jobs if you know what I mean."

"Understood," I said with a smile. "Did you say Dusty's already cutting our drywall pieces outside? We can bring them in now and get started."

"I'll go," Austen volunteered. He rested a hand at the small of my back. "It's going to snow like crazy all morning. You might as well stay warm and dry while I run out there."

As he walked away, Morgan was wiggling her eyebrows at me. I caught her eye, and she puckered her lips to tease me. "You've got yourself quite a gallant gentleman there."

I sighed, my cheeks and ears heating up even as my heart turned to putty. "Sure seems like it."

Disaster has a funny way of sneaking up on you.

We'd worked quickly, slapping up the drywall pieces in rapid-fire order. By eleven, Austen and I, and a few others, had both the front office and the break room ready for the finish work. I was rolling my neck, trying to un-kink the knots that had worked their way in from lifting sheetrock over my head all morning. And then, gentle fingers probed their way into the sore places, finding and releasing the tension I'd locked in there by trying to work as fast as the guys did.

I opened my eyes and smiled at Austen. "Thanks."

He grinned back, but his fingers didn't stop. They dug deeper, and I winced. "Breathe through it," he suggested. "It will help."

It did, but I was hissing between my teeth, and my eyes were scrunched tight in pain for a few seconds. Then, magically, the tightness began to melt, and I rocked my head back and forth. "That's so much better."

"Good. Another minute and you'll be good as new."

My shoulders dropped in weary relief, and I could relax enough through his ministrations to look around the room. Everyone was getting ready to start the next job, most of them wandering around and waiting to be told what to do. Then, Dusty walked through the door, his Carhartt work coat soaked with melted snow and his face red with the cold of working outside all morning. He stepped aside as a couple of kids careened by him, then stopped dead, his eyes locked on me.

And suddenly, it didn't feel right to let Austen give me a neck massage right there in the middle of the room.

I couldn't say why. Maybe it was because he was the first person to actually look at me, sitting there on the receiving end of some pampering while everyone else was getting ready to start working. Or maybe it was that strange spark in his eye, something I'd never seen there before. I squirmed and moved away from Austen's touch.

"Thanks," I mumbled, not wanting anyone to overhear me. "That's probably good for now." I rubbed my hand over the sore spots as I stood up.

"Anytime." Austen straightened, and I saw his gaze land on Dusty. For a second, I thought I saw a flintiness pass between them. But then it vanished, and Austen was smiling. "Hey, Dusty!"

Dusty had started to walk away, but he halted and slid a funny look to Austen. He didn't say anything, but his eyes flicked to me for an instant. I saw his jaw clench, and he lifted his chin in the barest greeting before moving off.

I turned to Austen. "What's the matter with Dusty today? Has he said anything?"

Austen shrugged. "No idea. He's probably just cold."

"Well, I'm going to go talk to him. I had some ideas about class on Tuesday anyway, and—"

"Guys?" Marshall Walker's voice carried over the room's chatter, the clattering of tools, and the echo of feet on the unfinished floor. "Has anyone seen that kid that was here earlier?"

Everyone turned to look at each other, but nobody had any more than a blank stare for an answer. "What kid?" I asked.

"Dustin? Eleven or twelve years old, I guess. The one who was helping me back here. I sent him out to put a horse away half an hour ago, and he never came back."

The hair on the back of my neck prickled. I knew that kid. He was autistic and had his own way of dealing with the world. For one thing, he refused to wear coats. If he had been out in a snowstorm for that long in just a t-shirt...

Cody burst through the door. "His tracks disappear at the corral. I think he's on a horse."

He didn't have to say anything else. It was in a look—a look only brothers could know. In a heartbeat, Cody, Marshall, and Dusty were almost scrambling over each other to get outside, with Cody shouting directions to people they passed in the hall. I was close to a window, and I saw Morgan and Dustin's mom beating a path for the woods to look for him.

I didn't have to think. You don't, in times like that. I was pulling on my coat and gloves to join the search party when Austen tugged at my arm. "Wait, where are you going?"

I lifted my hands. "Out there? Come on, they need all the help they can get!"

"But you heard Cody. If the kid's on a horse, we won't find him around here. You'll have to let someone on an ATV go after him."

"That doesn't mean he couldn't have doubled back or gotten dumped or something. What do you want to do, sit here and wait?"

"Well, it seems to make the most sense. Don't you think? Of course, I hope the kid is found, and soon. I just don't see how we can do anything but get in the way. A whole bunch of people who don't know their way around, making more tracks in the snow isn't going to help them find his any better, now is it?"

I swallowed and glared at the floor. He was making sense. But he was also making me angry. It just didn't feel right, doing nothing. I swiped at my mouth with my gloved hand. "I don't know, but I'm at least going outside."

Austen rolled his eyes and went back for his coat, lying on the counter. "Fine. I'll come with you, but I really don't see what—"

His voice was cut off by the sound of the ATV engines firing up outside. I pushed the door open just in time to see Cody tearing up the hillside, with Dusty's quad kicking up a plume of snow behind him. I closed my eyes, drank in the crisp mountain air, and breathed a prayer of hope that Dustin would be found safe and sound. He would be. He *had* to be.

But I'd never wanted to hitch a ride on the back of an ATV so much in my life.

Chapter 15

Dusty

"He'll be fine," I assured Meg Truman, Dustin's mother. "I don't even think he has a scratch on him. We just need to get him warmed up."

She nodded, her eyes never leaving her son. The poor woman was still pale with fright, but she was a whole lot more composed than I would have been under the circumstances. "Thank you, Dusty," she said, and I thought I detected a faint waver in her voice. "I don't know what I would do without you guys. You've been good to him. He hasn't known many men who were kind to him."

I didn't know what to say to that. I didn't know Meg all that well, except that she seemed to be made of iron. Looking at her right now, I decided that maybe she wasn't. I rested my hand on hers, then went over to talk to Dustin again.

Morgan was busy piling blankets around him in front of a space heater. The poor kid was a popsicle, but he'd come through his ordeal well enough. Physically, anyway. It might be a long time before he got over the terror I'd seen in his eyes when we'd found him—lost and alone and freezing in that white wilderness.

Cody had gone back out to search for Marshall, who had high-tailed it up the mountain after us on a horse. Someone said Kelli had come, too, and was also out there looking for him, but neither of them had come back yet.

I checked my watch. It was almost three o'clock. My stomach grumbled, but I'd missed the pizzas Kelli had brought for our lunch. There were only a couple of pieces left when we returned with Dustin, and we made sure he ate them.

Most of the volunteers had dispersed after Dustin was found. We'd planned to get a lot more work done this afternoon, but we'd lost the rhythm now. Walter Perkins, an Army veteran with a titanium leg, had stayed behind because Walter was the kind of guy who would wait all day just for the honor of fetching someone a cup of coffee. A few others had lingered, too—mostly just to talk to each other. I scuffled my muddy boots on the plywood floor. There wasn't much for me to do now, except maybe start putting tools away.

"Hey. Did you ever get warm?"

A shiver of pleasure spread through my chest when I heard Jess's voice at my side. I hadn't talked to her all day—but, to my credit, I had managed to avoid punching Austen, so it wasn't all a fail. I sent an apprehensive glance around the room, but I didn't see him anywhere. Only then could I smile at her and answer.

"Mostly. I just need some dry jeans. I wasn't expecting a joy ride in the mountains today, and these aren't exactly waterproof."

That delicious mouth curved softly. "I'm afraid my pants wouldn't fit you, but how about this?" She held out her hand, and her fingers uncurled to reveal a protein bar. "I always keep a couple in the car, and I don't think you got anything to eat, did you?"

"I didn't, but you don't need to do that. Thank you, though."

Her smile quirked to the side, and she gave me a suspicious look. "Are you turning it down because you don't like chocolate peanut butter or because you're trying to be polite?"

"Well..." I let my eyes rove over her face. She was so... so perfect. Like an angel, but flesh-and-blood-real, and I never could get enough of looking at her. It wasn't just her alabaster skin or those sculpted cheekbones or the lips that looked like they'd been crafted out of rose petals.

It was those crystal blue eyes that could speak; the gentleness and intelligence in them, the patience and humor, and something else I couldn't define. I'd always felt like if I ever got the chance to really open up to her, we'd find that our stories were penned by the same author.

Jess reached for my hand and pressed the protein bar into it. "You can say yes, Dusty. It's okay to accept things for yourself once in a while."

I allowed a slow smile and tore the wrapper open. "I'd rather share things than have them all to myself." I broke off the end and offered it to her. "Did you get anything to eat?"

She chuckled. "Some." But she did accept my offer. And then she smiled, her eyes twinkling at me as she chewed. That tasted better to me than any protein bar ever could.

"Dusty, there you are. I think we're going to take off."

Austen had come up behind Jess, and I'd been so lost in watching her that I hadn't even noticed him. He didn't look angry today, and I couldn't figure it out. How does a guy flip a switch like that? He even smiled and put his hand out to shake mine.

My Adam's apple bobbed in my throat as I hesitated. I couldn't refuse because then *I'd* look like the jerk. I thinned my lips and shook his hand. "Drive safely," I mumbled.

"You too. Roads are getting icy. I promised Jess's dad I'd have her home in time for puzzle night. Right, angel?"

Even Jess blinked at that. She raised her eyebrows at him, and an ironic laugh escaped before she caught herself. "Oh, I don't think I'm any kind of an angel, but yes, we should probably go. Take care, Dusty. I hope they find Marshall quickly, and that the roads don't get too bad before you guys leave."

A yawning pit of lava was slowly engulfing my stomach. I could feel it—the bitterness, the jealousy, the indignation of it all—and the mortification of having to smile at them while they ripped my guts out. How was I still breathing? But I grunted some kind of answer about how Marshall was just fine, and we'd head home as soon as he got back. And then Jess gave me a small wave as Austen led her away.

Angel. That was *my* word for her! Had Austen managed to steal everything of mine? My words, my thoughts, and even my heart. And I was probably the only one who'd caught a glimpse of the other side of him, but no one would believe me if I said anything.

Well. My family would. But that wasn't much help right now.

"Call an ambulance!"

The words split through my thoughts, and I whirled around to see where they'd come from. Morgan was on her feet, too, and we plunged out the door together into a snowstorm. A lone horse was walking up the little slope to the barn, carrying two people. One was Kelli Mason—the reins in one hand while the other arm wrapped around...

"Marshall!" I bolted out the door and ran to meet them.

Marshall was practically lying on Kelli, his head rocking on her shoulder and his eyes glazed over. But despite the bruises and blood all over his face, he was wearing the most ridiculous smile.

"What happened?" I demanded. I started to reach for him to pull him down.

"Silly cowboy decided to belly flop onto some rocks," Kelli replied. "Be careful. I think he broke some things."

"What? What did he break?"

"All of it," Kelli grunted. "Come on, cowboy. You have to let go of me."

Marshall already looked drugged. "'S awright shugar," he slurred. "Gimme 'nother kiss an' ah'll be jes fine."

"He's in shock," Morgan said. "Meg! Call 911! Somebody get some blankets out here!"

"Naw, I'm not in sh... sh..." Marshall rolled his head around and smiled at Kelli. "I'm in luff." His forehead wrinkled, and he winced in agony as Kelli tried to shift him. "Oof. Luff hurts."

As I tried to wrestle my brother down from that horse, a million thoughts were wrestling in my head. But the one that stuck there the rest of the night and through the next few months, was that Marshall was dead right about one thing.

Love hurts.

Jess

"Yes, you heard me right. Marshall and I got married this morning!"

Kelli's voice echoed through the soap bubbles coating my phone speaker. My whole phone was dripping because I'd dropped it in the sink when she first made her announcement. All the blood felt like it had drained from my face, and the only response I could manage was a gasp and a gulp. "Whhaaa... How? Why??? Weren't you guys fighting, like, two days ago?"

"That's called 'miscommunicating,' we decided. I'm sure we'll have some bumps in the road, but... Honey! Get back to bed! What do you think you're doing trying to... Hang on."

The phone muffled, and I could hear Marshall and Kelli bickering cheerfully in the background. Kelli was scolding her... I guess he was her husband, to stay off his feet, but it sounded like he had no intentions of going back to bed without her.

"Oh, for mercy's sake," I sighed. "I don't need to listen to this!" I called loudly enough that she had to be able to hear me. I was about to hang up when Kelli's voice came back on.

"Sorry about that. Cowboys! You know how they are."

"I have an inkling."

"So, anyway, I figured I'd better let you know the news!"

I laughed. "Uh, yeah! I can't believe you didn't invite me to the wedding. Did you just go to the courthouse?"

"We sort of got it up in a hurry. It was just my family and his there, but hey, we got what we went there for! We'll have a big party when he's feeling better. So, that leads me to the next thing. Joy."

"Uh-huh. I thought you'd come around to this. I assume you're keeping her after all, and you'll be moving her up to Walker Ranch now?"

"Well..." Kelli's voice sounded hushed like she was trying not to be overheard. "Yes. Marshall made a big deal about living at my place in town to start with. We haven't figured out anything else yet, but he'll still be going to the ranch daily to work once he's feeling better. It doesn't make any sense to keep Joy somewhere else. I'll sure miss riding with you, though."

"I understand. You'd already moved her out anyway to sell her. Doesn't really change anything for me at this point."

"I know, but I wanted to explain what was going on. You deserve that. I'd have never survived these past couple of months if you hadn't been helping me with her."

I smiled into the phone. "I enjoyed having you here. You lit a fire under my britches to get out and ride more."

"Oh, I'll light a different kind of fire under you, just give me half a chance. Once Marshall's all healed up, you and that handsome rancher of yours are all mine. Coffee isn't the only thing I'm good at mixing up, you know."

"I'll take your word for it. But I think I'll just take my time with this one, Kel. I'm not in any rush to get married."

"Don't knock it till you've tried it!" she giggled. "Okay, I'd better go. Mom's calling again. She told me she was making a huge chicken soup for Marshall and if I don't answer, she'll be over here spoon-feeding it to him in ten minutes. I don't think she understands what I meant when I said 'Wedding night.'"

"I don't understand why you're still on the phone. Sounds like you have better things to do."

"Whoo-eeee!" she whooped. "Later, Jess!"

My screen went dark, and I pushed the phone across the counter so I could finish rinsing the dishes. I chewed my bottom lip as I tried to take in the shock of it. *Kelli married.*

I heartily wished her and Marshall the best, and I couldn't imagine either of them with anyone else. But there went another couple, paired off and starting their own life together. It wasn't like it was a race or anything, but I was beginning to feel more and more left behind in the dust.

How does a person know, really *know,* when they've found the one for them? Where is that feeling that flicks on? Is it an instantaneous thing or something that grows in fits and starts? Morgan had told me once that she knew Cody was special by the end of their first date. But my mom had taken months to make up her mind about my dad, so when was I supposed to know? And was Austen *it* for me?

I dried my hands, tossed the towel on the hook, and wandered into the living room. I'd worked in a cold auto shop all day, finished my chores, cleaned up after dinner, and now I wanted to curl up under a fuzzy blanket on the couch with a syrupy romance. After Kelli's news, I was in the mood for a happily-ever-after to feed my soul this evening, but when I thumbed through the stack of books on the end table, none sparked my interest. I was tired of all of them, and I'd never felt like that before.

Something new sounded good. Maybe there were still some holiday specials on; the cheesy ones I couldn't help adoring. I reached for the remote, realizing only then that Dakota had snuck up beside me on the couch. I let my arm rest on his back as I flicked through the channels.

Stupid. Already saw it. Boring. Old. And who thought *that* was a good plot? I sighed and clicked off the TV after half an hour of nothing. How could I be so hungry for a good story when absolutely nothing sounded interesting?

It was a pity I'd given Austen back his journal. A little bit of his poetry and ramblings would be fun to read right now. Light and entertaining, but thoughtful enough to make me smile and camp on them for a while.

Maybe I should just call him. Except the man I would talk to on the phone wasn't very much like the man in the journal. When would he show me that side of himself? There had to be more under the surface that he hadn't let me see. I guessed it would take time. That was why

I'd told Kelli I was in no hurry. You didn't rush the kind of love I was looking for.

I started thumbing through my phone, scrolling through social media, and after a minute, my thumb stopped on an ad that popped up. It was for an article in the *Stockman's Journal*, a magazine many of the local ranchers subscribed to. "Eight ways to get kids excited about ranching," was the tagline.

Okay, I admit it. I'd maybe googled a few ideas to try for the kids at the White Pines class, and now it seemed like the whole Internet was conspiring to give me tips. I needed them. Morgan had said things were a go for this week, and we'd probably have some new kids signing up. That meant I had to bring my "A" Game.

We, actually. Because I'd never survive that two-hour class without Dusty's help. He might be the quiet type, but he was steady, cheerful, and always there when you needed him. And the kids really responded to him.

I clicked on the article from *Stockman's* and read through it. Most of the ideas were either impractical for our situation or things we'd already done, but one was pretty cool. It was about teaching kids to groundwork a horse, progressing from basic handling skills through higher level maneuvers and even Liberty work. The idea was to give them a course to run, goals to achieve, and a way to mark their progress.

That actually gelled pretty well with White Pines' mission of connecting people with horses, and it was something we could accomplish. Plus, it would be fun. Those kids didn't come to the after-school program to get better at coloring pictures. They wanted to handle the horses more.

Pleased with my new idea, I scrolled through my phone contacts. Did I even have Dusty in here? Ah, yes. Under Walker Ranch, probably because Dusty handled the books. The last message thread was over a year old, when I'd ordered some hay. But I knew this was his personal phone number because he'd mentioned which Walker I was talking to.

I clicked the link for the article and forwarded it to him, then typed out a message of explanation.

> *-Hey, this is Jess. Came across this article. What do you think of the idea in the last paragraph? Could we do that tomorrow?*

I didn't expect an answer right away, but I'd scarcely pressed send before the message showed that it had been read. Almost immediately, he sent a reply.

> *-I was reading this same article yesterday. Do you get Stockman's?*

I stuck the tip of my tongue out as I typed.

> *-No, I just saw the link and read it online.*

> *-They have articles like this every month. One of the editors is an FFA and 4-H leader, so there are always things for youth.*

-Maybe I should subscribe, then! Do you think we could manage this? Would Morgan let us?

The reply field blinked for a few seconds.

-I'm sure she would. I'll ask if we can use Biz tomorrow. Hang on.

I waited a little while, playing with Dakota's floppy ears as I thought. How could we manage doing this with, say, ten kids? Would we need two horses? How were we supposed to keep the others entertained when one was taking a turn? My phone dinged while I was mulling over my ideas.

-Morgan says all her therapy horses are booked tomorrow for multiple sessions.

I frowned.

-Well, there goes that idea. Maybe when the arena's open.

-It's not a space problem. She says we can use the indoor ring if I bring one or two of my horses. Some of the program horses are already moved up to the new ranch, and she doesn't want to wear out the ones that are still here.

Excitement tingled again through my fingers. We could make this work, after all! Hurriedly, I sent a reply.

-I can bring Nash. He loves kids.

-I have a good one to bring, too. Want me to pick up your horse? It's on the way for me, and that way, we don't have to haul two trailers.

I grinned as I typed.

-Deal. See you tomorrow.

Chapter 16

Dusty

"So, that's how it's going to be."

Those words had sent a second set of shock waves through the house this week. First, Marshall up and married Kelli on about a thirty-six-hour notice. Just dragged her off to the courthouse—actually, she might have been the one doing the dragging—and then he was gone, moved into her house on Main Street in town. His socks were still on the floor of his bedroom, for crying out loud, but his chair at the table sat empty.

But somewhere between Marshall's announcement of his engagement on Sunday morning, and his actual wedding on Monday, there was Dad's bombshell. He gathered all of us together, including Cody, and told us that he was seeing Meryl Justice, and had been for months.

And none of us had ever figured it out.

To be fair, he had been pretty sneaky about it. It made sense now—the way he'd gulp down the one cup of coffee I poured for him in the morning, then turn up at Kelli's Coffee Wagon every morning at about ten so he could pick up something for Meryl. The way he would slip off upstairs whenever there was no work to do so that he could talk to her on the phone. All the beef jerky vanishing before the rest of us got it, because he was taking it to her 4-H meetings and passing it around for the kids. The quick way he'd reach for his texts lately and the random chuckles we would hear from behind his closed bedroom door.

My dad was in love again.

I couldn't quite decide how I felt about that. Meryl was an amazing person—everyone would tell you that. Not many people enjoyed the kind of respect she commanded in town, and she had a kind heart. How many people spent thirty years volunteering as a 4-H leader when they'd never even had their own kids? If Dad was going to be seeing someone, Meryl Justice was as good as it got.

But dating? My *dad?*

No one expected him to spend the rest of his life alone, but I don't think we had considered what it would be like if he ever found someone else. Someone who wasn't Mom. She'd been gone for more than three years, and I could hardly remember what her voice sounded like until I dug up old videos of her on my phone. Then, it was like she'd never left. Was I ready to see someone else by my dad's side?

But I couldn't process all that right now. I couldn't worry about Marshall's hasty marriage, and I didn't have time to fret about Dad maybe following in his footsteps. I couldn't possibly think of anything but that I was supposed to pick up Jess in an hour.

It's nothing, I kept reminding myself. *Not a date.* She wasn't getting in my truck because she liked me, or because I'd finally said what was on my heart. It was just luck, a matter of convenience. Just a couple of volunteers who found a way to do their job better together.

But I couldn't stop my heart from pounding all day.

She was standing by the gate when I pulled up, grinning and waving. And it was just... *oh.* She was so cheerful and radiant; pure as gold, like the shining hair curling round her shoulders, and warm as the rosy cheeks that glowed against the winter snow. And she had no idea how amazing she was.

I rolled down the window as I drove through the gate she'd opened, and the words stopped in my throat. *"Good afternoon,"* seemed way too formal. *"Hey,"* was too... too kitschy or something. Maybe if she was my girlfriend, but she wasn't. I just swallowed and blurted out, "Hi."

Her smile got even brighter. "Hi, Dusty! Just pull in. There's room to turn around. I'll grab Nash."

I parked the truck and moved to open the door, but before I did, I thought of something. This was a work truck, but it was just fancy enough to have heated seats. I'd never met a lady who didn't rave over them in the middle of winter. I reached over and turned her side on to warm up while we got her horse loaded.

Five minutes later, her gentle old roan gelding was standing in the trailer beside my Duchess, and Dakota was in the back seat greeting Daisy the Border Collie, who'd begged to tag along. And Jess was beside me.

She glanced down as she got in and smiled at me. "Thanks for the seat warmer. Feels good on a day like today."

I just returned her smile and nodded. There was probably a smooth answer to that, but I didn't know what it was.

"So, I hear congratulations are in order," she said. "New sister-in-law, huh?"

I chuckled. "That's not the half of it. My dad is... well, I guess he's dating someone. Want to guess who?"

"Meryl Justice," she replied with a smug grin. When I looked over in surprise, she just laughed. "I think everyone knew but you guys."

"What? How?"

Jess leaned back and traced her fingers over the window ledge. "You probably didn't want to know. Don't tell me the signs weren't there."

I shrugged. "They were. You're right."

"So, how do you feel about it?" Her voice was gentle but probing.

"I don't think it matters how I feel about it. It's his life."

"But it affects you. Just like Marshall and Cody getting married and leaving the ranch. Of course, you're going to have feelings about it."

I frowned and adjusted the visor. The afternoon sun was already hanging low enough to shine the glare off the snow. "I really don't know yet," I finally admitted. "It will take some getting used to."

"How did your brothers feel?"

"Hah. Luke is all for it, and so is Marshall—I guess because he doesn't have any room to complain. Cody loves Meryl because she was practically a mom to Morgan. And Evan said she'd be good for Dad. Didn't talk about his own feelings, though."

"And what did you say?"

I permitted a slow smile. "About the same thing I said to Marshall that morning. That it wasn't something you rush into. Not that that's going to stop either of them."

Jess laughed. "I wouldn't expect it would."

"Well, how would you feel? Say it was your dad? Neither of you will ever stop missing your mom, but you want him to be happy. You want the best for him. He's got a lot of life to live still, and you don't want to see him lonely. Especially if…" I stopped and swallowed. I didn't like the last thing I'd almost said.

"If…?"

I blew out a sigh. She had to be thinking it already, anyway. "If… say, you leave someday. Maybe… I don't know. Get a job somewhere or… or get married." I turned to gaze at her, probably looking like a forlorn lost dog or something, but I had to know.

Her eyes narrowed, and her shoulders rose and fell as she rested her arm on the center console. So close to mine. "I've wondered about that a few times. I really don't know, you know? He's still in love with my mom and always will be. I don't know if anyone will ever be able to catch his attention, but a week ago, you'd have said that about your dad, too."

I nodded.

She turned to look at me, the low sunlight making those blue eyes blaze in a way I'd never seen before, and it was breathtaking. "I'd probably feel like you do. Happy for him, but apprehensive about all the changes it will bring."

"You nailed it. That's exactly how I feel."

She smiled, and it was a smile that lit my whole world. "I guess I'll saddle that pony when it shows up. For now, I'm just taking life a day at a time. And today—" She pointed at the driveway we were about to turn into— "Today, let's just have some fun."

Today. I could live with that. Because today, at least for a couple of hours, Jess was all mine.

Jess

"One, two, three... go!" Dusty counted.

Kylie and Bree, both giggling riotously, launched from the start cone, each dragging a horse by the halter toward our little obstacle course. Dusty's mare, Duchess, handled like a Showmanship horse, matching her strides to Bree's and responding at the lightest of touches. We made sure the most timid kids got to handle her because she was so easy and fluid.

Nash was a good old sport, working up a dutiful trot as his lower lip flopped lazily. Kylie didn't seem to mind that he was slow, which was good. He'd never go any faster, but he acted like he was enjoying the attention.

"Remember, it's not a race," Dusty reminded the kids. "Precision and good horsemanship are what count! Jess will be scoring you based on how you handle your animal. Pay attention to your cues!"

Both girls had rounded their end cone and were heading for home. Duchess was in the lead, of course. But I was watching the kids and the care they were giving to their charges, and one stood out. They trotted over the chalk line we'd laid out for the finish, and I held up my arms. "The point goes to Kylie for taking extra time with her horse on the circles and trot poles."

"But Bree was faster," Aedyn pointed out. "That's not fair."

"Bree's *horse* was faster," Dusty reminded him. "It's not about who can make their horse do things faster. It's about being considerate to your horse and asking them to respond with gentleness and patience. Jess, where are we on team scores now?"

I made a mark on my clipboard and added up the totals. "Team A, the Longhorns, have six, and Team B, the Corrientes, also have six."

"Tiebreaker!" Billy shouted. "I wanna take the dogs through the cones!"

Dusty and I shared a bewildered glance, and he walked over to me. "We could do that. Will Dakota mind?" he asked in a low voice.

"Mind? He'll think it's the best thing that happened to him all week. He's an agility addict. What about your dog?"

He grinned. "Daisy will probably try to herd the kids into a corner, but it will be fun to watch." He turned back to Billy and clapped. "Okay, Billy, since it was your idea, you get to handle Daisy. Pick a challenger from the other team."

I called Dakota and clipped a leash to his collar. Aedyn had his hand up, so I gestured to him to come over. "Okay, I'll show you his signals. To ask him to heel, you do this."

We spent about five minutes giving the boys a crash course on dog obedience. Then I walked them through the same obstacles we'd used for the horses, but with adjustments made for the dogs. And then, Dusty and I stood back to watch.

Dakota took over for Aedyn, shoulder-checking the kid into place when they rounded cones or crossed little hurdles. Billy didn't fare as well with Daisy. She had no idea why she was supposed to be going around cones or jumping over logs, and she kept ducking under things or stopping to creep along on her belly and look for a loose cow that wasn't there. Every time Billy yelped in surprise over something she did, she'd screech to a halt and cock her head at him like he was speaking a foreign language. It didn't work to drag her forward—she seemed sure there was a cow somewhere she was supposed to herd, and she couldn't figure out why it wasn't showing up.

It's not nice to laugh at kids, but I couldn't help giggling. Just a little. But I couldn't let the boys think I was making fun of them, so I tried to hide behind Dusty. His shoulders were shaking in laughter, too, but somehow he kept his face straight. "We need more to judge!" he decided. "Go through one more time!" And then he snickered almost silently.

"You're so mean!" I whispered over his shoulder.

"Just trying to make it a fair contest," he reasoned, but he was trying to choke back a belly laugh. "Besides, we have ten more minutes to kill. Might as well enjoy it."

Everything looked like it was going smoother on the second pass through until Dakota bumped Aedyn one time too many. He knew how you were supposed to go around an obstacle, and he was losing patience with Aedyn dragging behind and getting in his way. "That's it!" he grumbled and threw down the leash. "I'm done with this dog!"

That was all the freedom Dakota wanted. Like a wild thing, he dashed for the next barrel—apparently, he'd already memorized the pattern. But it wasn't enough to run full speed through the obstacles with his tongue lolling. He had to stop and nip at Daisy's heels on his way by.

Daisy was a tough little herding dog—wiry and stubborn, and she didn't take that kind of treatment lying down. Lickety-split, she was after Dakota like a stray calf. Billy kept up for about three frantic strides, then the leash ripped out of his hand, and he toppled forward in the dirt. And the dogs didn't stop.

Dakota was rounding the barrels with his eyes wide like a gleeful savage, and Daisy was after him with the snarl of a frustrated cow dog when the stock won't mind. All the kids started squealing and yelling, egging the dogs on and cheering for the one they wanted to win the impromptu race.

I was dying. I couldn't help a little shriek of laughter, and Dusty wasn't holding it together much better. He couldn't speak, and his face was turning red, his eyes filling with tears as he tried to hold back. It was all I could do to stay upright, and I grabbed his arm to hide my face behind his shoulder. He swayed a little and looked around, and for a second, his eyes held mine. And he wasn't laughing anymore.

I saw his throat bob. His smile changed in an instant from mirth to something softer. It was that crooked Walker grin that had been breaking hearts all over the valley for years, and mine did a little flip.

I'd never touched Dusty before. Odd, how that suddenly sprang to mind. I don't think I'd ever even shaken his hand... no, that wasn't right. He'd touched my hand when we were giving the kids Christmas presents. And I still remembered how his fingers felt.

Still, there wasn't much precedent, but it had seemed so natural to reach for him like a friend sharing a good laugh. Had I gone too far? That smile told me I hadn't, but I'd changed something, even if only for a moment. I let my hand slide down his arm, wondering how to retreat from this. Or if I should try.

Dusty rested a hand on mine—a friendly squeeze before I dropped it, that was all—and turned his attention back to the kids. "All right, settle down!" he called. "I think we have to proclaim Billy's team the winners of today's stock handling challenge because he didn't quit trying. We'll mix it up and try again on Thursday."

There was a chorus of cheers from the winners and "Awe, man!" from the losers, but Dusty put his hands up. "And remember, next week we'll start holding class up at the new facility. Make sure you have a pair of mud boots because you'll need them!"

It wasn't long before all the kids had been picked up, and Dusty and I began loading our horses up to take them home. "I wonder if Morgan will hear any complaints about kids getting plowed down by wild dogs," I said as Dusty secured the back of the trailer.

His face split into a wide grin. "Probably. I think I've decided it was worth it."

"Think we'll get fired for that little stunt?"

He chuckled as he fished the truck keys out of his pocket. "You can't fire volunteers. No, I think it's more likely that we'll have an audience of parents next time, trying to catch the show." He walked around to the truck's passenger side and opened the door for me. "We should totally bring the dogs again."

I paused before I got in and smiled up at him, with his hat rimmed in the early evening darkness by the lights of the barn, and the fog rising from his breath. There was something there that I'd missed, all those years. I'd always thought Dusty was unsociable, even awkward.

But now that we had something in common, something to talk about, being with him was like slipping on a favorite pair of boots. Not flashy or sensational in any way, but comfortable and work-worn and dependable. He offered his hand to help me step up into the truck, and I took it.

We didn't talk much on the way back to my house, but it was a space that didn't seem like it needed to be filled. Dusty had a gentle, relaxed smile, and occasionally he would turn my way to share it with me. He didn't demand anything from me or act like he wanted my attention. He just seemed content to be there, in that warm truck cab with the headlights cutting through the darkness toward home.

He got out when we arrived and helped me get Nash all settled in for the night. There wasn't much to do, just buckling his blanket back on and checking his water, but I didn't have to do it alone. Once I rolled the stall door closed, Dusty stepped back, his hands fumbling for his pockets. "Guess I'll head out." He flicked his wrist over as if remembering something. "Good grief, is it only five-thirty? It feels like a lot later."

"Yeah, it does. I get home just in time for dinner on Tuesdays, but it feels like eight."

His face fell. "I wish it were. It's Luke's turn to cook again. Don't ever let him talk you into trying his cabbage stew."

I laughed. "Oh, don't worry. I already learned my lesson about having dinner with Luke. I don't love football *that* much."

Dusty's cheek twitched. "Hah. Yeah. Uh..." He winced and rubbed the back of his neck. "You wouldn't want to... that is, sometime. Maybe some evening, after..."

I squinted, trying to make out what he was saying, but a pair of headlights sliced through the yard behind him. And then I remembered—I had somewhere I was supposed to be tonight.

"Hang on, Dusty, I'm sorry." I held my hand up. "I think that's Austen pulling in. I almost forgot that we were supposed to go out for Taco Tuesday at the diner, and I'm still wearing muddy jeans. I'd better go!"

He put his hands back in his coat pocket and stepped back. "Oh. Yeah, sure. You don't want to keep him waiting."

"Thank you for understanding!" I started to walk out of the barn ahead of him but stopped. "Thanks for the ride today, though."

He was looking down, but his eyes lifted for just a second, and he gave a tight-lipped smile. "Anytime, Jess."

Chapter 17

Dusty

I was counting down the hours until Thursday.

We'd gotten permission from Morgan to bring our horses again, and I assumed I'd pick Jess up. It made the most sense since it kept the small driveway from being overcrowded, and Jess's house was on my way. And she seemed to have fun before.

I wasn't trying to steal her heart. Truly, that was not what I'd meant to do. Jess wasn't the kind of girl to cheat, and I wouldn't want to put her in that position, no matter what my present thoughts were about the guy she was dating.

But there'd been a few times that day when I'd catch her eye, or she'd say something in a certain way, or when she touched me. I found out just how weak I was. Had Austen not pulled up in the driveway that night to take her to dinner, I'd have asked to take her myself. And I didn't think she would have refused.

Today, I'd have another chance. I'd laugh with her in the truck, work by her side with the kids, and then ask for a few more minutes when I took her home. And maybe in that few minutes, the whole world could change.

After all, it wasn't like she and Austen were serious. They'd gone out a few times, and I didn't want to know what else. But he didn't own her heart yet. I didn't even have to ask—I knew, because she would never have let herself get that friendly with me otherwise. And so, I'd decided it was time to stop pulling my punches. I'd just be honest, and maybe I'd find out if there was really something there worth fighting for.

Half an hour before I needed to leave, I slung Duchess's halter over my shoulder and walked into her stall. "Hello, beautiful," I murmured as the silver nose touched my hand. I stroked the fine bridge of her nose, the delicate curve of her ears, and slipped the halter on. I had told myself I wasn't going to fall in love with this mare, but it was already too late.

I knew the ranching life by now. You didn't get sentimental, and you didn't get attached. Horses are the job. They're a tool to get the work done, and the good ones are money in the bank when they're sold—always right when they're really at their best, and you'd like to keep them, too. We didn't have the luxury of holding on to our favorites. We just counted ourselves fortunate to have a ranch full of good ones, with talented horses walking through our barn like a revolving door.

But Duchess's story would be different. She would join the ranks of horses like Five Iron and Maserati, who took their turn in the show pen or the rodeo arena, then retired to mint little copies of themselves to keep the ranch deep in good horses for another generation. And I was the lucky bloke who got to enjoy her until then.

"Are you ready, pretty lady?" I tugged the blanket off, and she stood like a queen, all statuesque and gorgeous, while I groomed her. Jess had loved her. I smiled at the thought as I brushed out Duchess's tail. I should offer to let Jess ride her some time.

They were a bit alike, these two ladies who had staked their claims on my heart. Stunning to look at, sweet to be in company with, but easy to underestimate. And too often misunderstood. Very little rippled the surface, and if you weren't careful, you'd be fooled into thinking they were quiet, simple, and uncomplicated. But deep waves swelled underneath.

Maybe that was what appealed to me about them both.

I tossed my brush aside and slid the stall door open to lead Duchess to the trailer. A few minutes more, and the afternoon would be just right. Jess would climb into my truck, smile at me, and I'd do everything in my power to make her want to stay there forever. But just as I was closing the horse trailer door, she sent me a text.

-I'll have to meet you at White Pines. I won't make it home in time for you to pick me up. See you there.

I sagged against the trailer. So she was running late. That was no big deal, but what about the horse? Wasn't she bringing him today, after all? That changed all my plans. I took off my leather gloves and just typed back a quick acknowledgment. She'd probably tell me all about it later.

"Dusty! Good to see you!" Austen Conrad strolled toward me with his hand out as I opened the door of my truck.

My fist tightened on the door handle, and my jaw clenched before I could compose myself. It wouldn't do to create a scene. Not here—it wasn't my turf, and Morgan didn't need a couple of idiot stags locking horns in the parking lot of her therapy program. I forced a tight-lipped smile, but I picked up a stack of used lariats from the back seat so I'd have an excuse not to shake his hand. My dad would have had my hide for that stunt, but I didn't care. "Conrad," I grunted.

"I heard you were volunteering out here a couple of times a week. Came out to see what it's all about."

"It's about kids. Helping someone besides yourself. You should try it," I growled as I walked toward the barn with the ropes. Jess's truck and trailer were already here, which meant she was inside somewhere with Nash.

He followed me. "Actually, I wanted to ask you about that. They help kids with disabilities here? And they put them on horses?"

"Some of them. They do lots of things here."

"Like what? I met the guy who's missing a leg. What else do they do?"

"All kinds of stuff, but I just work with the after-school program. You need to talk to Morgan."

"I ask because I'd really like to try it, or donate, or something. You see, I... Seriously, can you stop walking so fast?"

My shoulders sagged, and I turned around. "Fine. What do you want?"

His mouth shifted, and he held my gaze for a few seconds, then dropped his eyes. "I wanted to apologize. I was out of line the last time we spoke. I'm sorry."

That was the last thing I expected. I blinked, swallowed, and just nodded. Then I walked off.

"For real, Dusty," he said as he fell in behind me again. "You were nothing but a good friend to me, and I bit your head off. I was stupid. Jealous. That wasn't cool."

I slapped the ropes down on a bench inside the barn and turned around. "No, it wasn't cool. You don't snap off like that and expect no one will judge your character for it."

"I know. I know. But that's not the guy I am, and I'd like to make it up to you."

"You can't just make something like that up. That's what you don't seem to get. It takes time and a lot of goodwill. No one cares what you say if you don't follow through with your actions."

He sniffed and shoved his hands in his jeans pockets. "Okay. How do I start that? I hope I can still call you a friend."

I scrubbed my jaw with my hand, turned around, and headed back for the trailer. I didn't have an answer for him. "I gotta get the horse unloaded," I muttered.

"I'll help."

"I don't need help unloading a trained horse, but there's probably something else you could do. That's all it is, Austen. You just show up. Pitch in where you can, and don't be a jerk."

He nodded, and the look on his face was, I'll admit, perfect contrition. "Okay. Whatever it is, I'll do it."

"Fine." He was still following me. I rolled my eyes and reached for the latch on the horse trailer. "So what are you doing here today, anyway? Did you talk to Morgan?"

"No, it was Jess. She didn't have much work today, so she took the morning off and came over to help me with my new horse. She and Danny are showing me the ropes—get it?—of moving the cattle from horseback."

My fingers fumbled on the latch. She was giving him riding lessons now? I swallowed. Lots of guys had captured their lady love from the back of a horse. There was just something romantic about it, the power and the freedom and the beauty, shared with one special person. Austen was no dummy.

"That's why she was running late. She had her horse over at my place first, so when she needed to leave, I just rode over here to watch today."

So much for that perfect afternoon I'd been dreaming about. "Sounds peachy," I said through gritted teeth. "I need to get ready for class, so..."

"Hi, Dusty!"

An electric jolt shot through me at Jess's voice. I was inside the trailer reaching for Duchess's halter, but I froze and turned back. Her voice could call me from the grave, I was pretty sure of it. She had walked up outside the trailer, and Austen put his arm around her, then kissed her on the cheek with a smarmy, "Hello, darlin'." She beamed up at him like he was the butter on her biscuit, then turned to look at me like I was supposed to be smiling, too.

And I think I died a little.

Jess

"This is just amazing. You guys knocked it out of the park." Morgan set her hands on her hips and scanned the indoor ring, where the after-school kids were racing through a new obstacle circuit Dusty had set up.

At one station, they practiced tying a bowline knot, a clove hitch, and a quick-release. At another, they had to rope the horns on a practice steer head and then dally from a saddle sitting on a nearby straw bale. When they got to Duchess, they had to lead her both forward and backward through two cones in a figure eight pattern, and then when they got to Nash, they had to practice putting a saddle on safely. It was keeping them busy, which was the whole point of an after-school program, but more importantly, it was sparking new ideas and interests in kids who wouldn't have had these opportunities otherwise.

I was just as in awe as Morgan, and I couldn't tear my eyes off the guy who'd invented this course. Dusty was roving from station to station, helping every kid who asked for it and patiently watching the ones who didn't. Occasionally, he'd glance up and accidentally catch my eye, and I'd give him a smile or a thumbs-up. He'd just tip his hat and get back to helping the kids.

"I'm glad you brought Austen today," Morgan murmured behind her hand. She nodded toward my boyfriend, who was goofing off with one of the lariats. He'd managed to rope himself again, and Aedyn was busting a gut laughing at him.

"Why are you glad? So you can recruit more slaves?" I chuckled.

"You know me! We always need help, the more the merrier. And a guy who can get kids to laugh with him is worth his weight in gold around here. The boys especially love it when a man spends time with them. And I love having the kind of help that can heft hay bales."

I rolled my eyes. "I don't know if Austen is planning to come back. He's buried up to his neck, trying to run his place. It just worked out today, but I'm glad he at least got to come and see what this is all about. It's important to me, you know?"

Morgan nodded, her eyes a little misty. "I know all about that. It's what keeps us going here, and it's pretty special when you find someone who wants to dive in alongside you."

"That's a good way to put it. Or at least someone who will support you, even if they can't join you."

"Hmm. I guess we all need the supportive type just as much as we need team mates. Hey—" She tipped her head toward me with the air of a conspirator. "What do you think of Dusty?"

"Dusty? He's a great guy. I mean, just look at what he did here today. None of that was my idea."

She nodded, her finger thoughtfully tapping her lips. "Cody and I were talking about him last night. I'd really like to see..." She drew a long sigh and frowned. "You know, when I first met the Walkers, I took an instant liking to Dusty. He's probably my favorite 'brother-in-law,' even though I love them all. He's just so kind and modest. But doesn't it seem like he's the only one who hasn't found his purpose?"

I narrowed my eyes. "I never thought of it like that."

"I didn't until lately. But I stole some peeks in here on Tuesday, and I don't think I'd ever seen him more alive. And watching him with the kids today, I think I put it together."

"Put what together?" I watched Morgan's face as a mischievous grin brewed. "What?" I laughed. "Now you've got me all curious."

"Oh, maybe it's just me and a bit of wishful thinking." She patted her stomach and arched her eyebrows at me.

My mouth fell open. "No. You're..." I broke off, looked around, then whispered. "You're *pregnant?*"

She giggled. "Not yet. I'm still trying to convince Cody that it's a good idea, but once that bug got in my head, it's like a disease. I see babies and kids and families everywhere, and I'm dying to start my own. Oh, Jess, it's terrible! I can't look at anyone without assuming they're in the same boat. And you know something? I'm watching Dusty, and it occurs to me that he'll be an amazing dad someday. If he ever gets the chance. Don't you think?"

I turned back to see what she was seeing. Dusty was kneeling beside Alyssa, who was trying to hold back frustrated tears because she couldn't get Duchess to back up without hitting the cone. I couldn't hear his voice, it was so low, but I could see its effect. Alyssa was still wiping her eyes, but she was nodding. He'd talked her into trying again.

"Yeah, you might be right. What about Austen? You say you've got these baby glasses on, so do you see any little cherubs circling his cowboy hat, too?"

Morgan stuck her lip out and nodded slowly as she watched Austen. He was laughing at Billy blowing raspberries and taking turns making funny faces. Morgan shrugged. "Sure."

"You don't sound very sure."

"Well, I guess I'm not. I don't know Austen very well. He seems like the kind of guy who could grow into those boots. But Dusty—" She smiled as she watched the guy she'd claimed as her honorary brother-in-law. "He's already filling them."

"You sure you don't want to come with us?" Austen called through the window. I turned the truck ignition over. "We're getting something to eat before Jess drops me off at the ranch."

Dusty tugged his kerchief over his mouth and shrugged deeper into his coat. "No, thanks. I have a lot of chores when I get home." He was standing by my window, already shivering against the snow blowing up under his hat and starting to pelt his eyelashes. He did have some really long lashes for a guy.

"I have chores too, but I have to eat, even if it's just a burger. Offer's open if you change your mind, my treat," Austen said.

Dusty didn't answer, but his eyes flashed quickly over Austen, then back to me, where they lingered for a moment. "I'll have to pass. Looks like we're getting a good storm tonight, so I'd best not dally."

"See you Tuesday, if not sooner?" I asked. "First time up at the new ranch, huh? I'm almost bummed about that since we won't need to bring our own horses from now on. I think Nash was enjoying himself."

I couldn't see his mouth, but his eyes looked like he might have smiled for an instant. Then the warmth faded, and he stepped back. "Tuesday. See you then."

Dusty's dark figure in the swirling snow fell away as I pulled the truck forward. I stuck my arm out to wave at him one last time, and watched the mirror until he lifted his gloved hand in reply. He hadn't moved from where he was standing.

"Brr!" Austen said. "Man, it got cold quick." He cupped his hands over his mouth and blew to warm his fingers.

I took the hint and rolled the window up, then cranked the heater. "Welcome to winter in the high country. This is nothing. Usually, we have drifts higher than my truck on the mountain roads."

"I thought that was just rancher talk. You know, how fishermen's hands get farther apart every time they describe their catch?"

"Hah. No, this is for real. It's been a mild winter so far."

"Geez. Maybe I should rethink living here. What do you think?" He shot that wide grin at me.

"I think lots of people love it here in the summer, but they don't last a whole year," I replied with a sweet smile.

"Maybe they just don't find what they're looking for. It has to take something pretty special to keep them here. Don't you agree?" He reached over for my hand, and I let him take it. He toyed with my fingers, teasing and playing with them until I couldn't help glancing down at them. I should feel something more when a man caresses my fingers, shouldn't I? Shivers and tingles and a swell of longing that makes my chest ache. But this just seemed... strange.

"Hey, you know what sounds great on a cold evening after a long day?" he asked. "A hot toddy and a movie. Best way to wind down on a winter's night. It's even better with a beautiful girl on the couch next to you."

I raised a brow with a knowing smile. "Except you have animals to feed."

"That won't take long. You just drive the truck and pitch some hay."

"And break the ice in the water tanks, and check your mama cows, and give the fences a once-over, and clean your horse's stall, and make sure the block heaters on your vehicles are all plugged in with the wipers pulled out, and..."

"Okay, okay!" he laughed. "It feels like a lot of work when you have to do it, but it sounds even worse when you list it out. So is that a no on the movie night?"

I shrugged and pulled my hand back to drive with it. "Maybe not tonight. I'm going in to work early tomorrow because I was gone today. I don't remember the last time I skipped out for the whole day."

"Well, I, for one, am grateful. It meant a lot to me, you coming up to show me some stuff on the horse. I know it cost you a day of work, what with going to White Pines right after, but I appreciate it."

I looked over at him with a light smile. "It was worth it. All of it."

"Good. So, what's it going to take to get you to hang out with me some evening? We've been seeing each other for a little while, right? I'm not going to bite, Jess. I just want to spend time with you when no one else is around."

I drew a careful sigh, wetting my lips as my eyes fixed on the road. "I guess I'm just a slow kind of girl."

"I can deal with that. How about I just cook you dinner sometime? Call it an early night? No pressure."

My fingers drummed on the wheel. "You know what I'd really like? I'd like to warm up by a crackling fireplace and hear more of your poetry."

"My poetry?" He went quiet. "Why would you want that?"

"Why not? It's beautiful. It's what caught my notice about you."

"But I'm here! Right now. You and me, together in the same truck. We..." He huffed. "I don't get why that's important. This is what matters."

"I just like it. What's wrong with that? I get to see things from your imagination that people don't talk about. Things that aren't easy to say or show, but I can feel them in your writing."

He shook his head. "I'm not comfortable with that." He cleared his throat and adjusted his hat. "Kind of private, you know?"

"Oh." I glanced in my mirrors, then stared back at the road. "I'm sorry. You let me read them before, so I thought..."

"I'd rather not bring them up again." He frowned, scratched his chin, and lifted his shoulders. "A guy just doesn't read that stuff out loud, and... I'd rather not."

"I see."

"No hard feelings, though, huh?"

I made up a smile. I was good at that. "No. Of course not." Except that was pretty much my idea of a perfect evening with the kind of man I wanted to spend the rest of my life with. Put in a hard day of work, side by side if possible, and then while away those last precious minutes of the day dreaming together. But Austen didn't seem to get that.

I stared straight forward as the truck cut through the streaks of falling snow. The flakes were getting heavier now, big clumpy things that powdered the windshield and caught the glare of my headlights. I didn't even get out of the truck to kiss Austen good night when I stopped at his house. All I wanted to do was get home.

Chapter 18

Dusty

My face was numb, and my ears were aching with cold by the time I stumbled into the house that evening. Work didn't stop just because I'd taken a few hours away, and I had a long list of things to do when I got home. I plowed through my chores, not even going in the house to grab something to eat first. There'd be leftovers, and I wasn't feeling very sociable yet.

What could an intelligent woman like Jess see in that pretender? I'll admit it; I was fooled at first, too. For me to buy that apology of his today, I'd have to see a lot more behind it. Time, like I told him. And I was just willing to bet that he couldn't play it straight long enough to change my mind.

But that didn't matter anyway. Who cared what I thought of Austen Conrad? Precisely nobody. Except for Luke, who had decided to hate him for me out of solidarity. I'd never even told him about Austen's change of face—it was enough that Austen was dating the woman I loved, and Luke decided the guy was no good. He was a great brother that way.

"There's stew in the fridge," Luke called when I hung my hat at the door.

My lip curled but I managed to hide it. "Thanks." Toast sounded good. "Where's Dad?"

Luke pointed to the den. "He and Evan are talking business. Might get something in your belly before you beard the lions."

"Huh." I rummaged around in the fridge, scraped up fixings for a roast beef sandwich, then plunked down at the table to scroll through my phone. I hadn't checked my emails all day.

"Things go good today at the therapy program?" Luke asked.

I didn't look up. If he saw my eyes, he'd know. I just nodded as I chewed.

"How'd my mare do?"

This time I did glance at him with a sideways grin. "My mare, you mean?"

"Like fun, she is. Remember who found her. We gotta get some practice runs in, or we'll never clean up next season. Been kind of busy with Marshall out."

"I know, and me being gone two afternoons a week isn't helping, either."

Luke shrugged. "We'll manage. You got a good reason to be there."

Not much of a reason anymore, but I didn't tell him that. If Austen was going to start coming, there wasn't much point. Except for the kids. I sighed. I really did like working with the kids.

Luke didn't say any more, leaving me to finish my sandwich and scroll my emails in peace. I dragged my thumb down the screen, looking for anything that wasn't spam. Most of it was junk coupons or something, but then one caught my eye. It was from the editor of Stockman's Journal.

Dear Mr. Chandler,

I am reaching out in response to your poem, The Cowboy's Call, which was published in our December issue. We have received tremendous reader feedback on the piece, and have decided to dedicate a section every month to similar works.

Our January issue goes to press next week, but I have reserved a space if you would like to contribute another piece. It should be no more than 200 words for the space allotted. I understand the short notice might make it impossible, but if you have something you would like to send in, and if you could email it by Friday evening, I'll make sure it gets printed.

Thank you for your interest in our publication.

The email closed with the editor's signature and contact information. My mouth was hanging open—I'd forgotten to chew. They wanted more? By gum, I'd send them something! I didn't even have to think about it. I knew just the poem I'd send. I even had it saved in the notes on my phone because I'd written it in the cab of my truck on Tuesday. Right after driving Jess home.

I opened the poem and read through it again. Usually, I change a word or two every time I review my writing, but this one seemed just right as it was. It was the work of a few seconds to copy it and send it back to the editor.

What a turn of luck! My writing was where I went to stave off discouragement or to pour out the hope that seemed to build up and try to burst free. I couldn't think of a better way to lift my mood tonight than someone asking for more of it. Maybe I'd managed to touch someone, and that felt pretty good.

I put my dishes away, glanced at the editor's email one more time with a smile, and slipped my phone into my pocket. Then I went to say hi to Dad and Evan before turning in for the night. They both stopped talking and looked up when I opened the door to the den.

"Look what the cat drug in," Dad said.

I flopped into the nearest chair. "Hi, Dad. Evan. Busy day?"

Evan nodded and steepled his fingers. Then he slid a questioning glance to Dad. And suddenly, I had an idea that they weren't just gabbing. They'd been talking about me.

"Yeah," Dad said, fumbling with his Farmer's Almanac. He rolled it up and twisted it a couple of times, and my stomach sank like a rock. This didn't look good.

It couldn't be the ranch finances because I knew exactly where we were. Not rolling in profit, but secure for now. Stock disease? I'd admit, I hadn't seen the yearlings since Monday, and… oh.

"Look, Dusty," Evan began, glancing at Dad. "This just isn't working."

I blinked. I knew what he was talking about, but I was too stubborn to just heave over. "What isn't working?"

Dad huffed a sigh. "I'm sorry, son, but we just can't have you gone two afternoons a week. I know you're doing good work, but with Marshall busted up, and all of us trying to keep on top of things, we can't spare you right now."

I felt like I'd swallowed hot coals. My face was on fire, and my insides were all twisted up. "But I got my stuff done this evening," I protested. "I'm gone for maybe three, four hours, and that's not something I can't make up."

"I know, I know. It's just that we have a lot more to do right now. We're in survival mode at the moment when we ought to be staying ahead of things. We're barely keeping our noses above the water line, and that's not where we need to be. You know that."

Luke chose that moment to stick his head through the door. By the look in his eye, I knew he'd been listening in. "I'll pick up Dusty's stuff," he offered.

Evan uncrossed his boots, lifted an eyebrow at Dad, and waited for the nod to go ahead. "It's just not enough, Luke. Today, we had a couple of cows miscarry. Doc Burns came out to inspect the fetuses, and I had to dig through all the files to find proof that we'd vaccinated those cows for brucellosis. That's typically Dusty's department."

My shoulders drooped. "Yeah, it is."

"Oh, come on. What are the odds that'd happen when he was away?" Luke cried. "It's just a fluke. We said we'd support White Pines however we could, didn't we? I don't see what's wrong with Dusty—"

"There's nothing wrong with it," Dad cut in. "I'm all for it, but it's too much right now. Maybe in a month, when Marshall's back to work."

"Then we hire someone else like we did when Brandon broke his arm," Luke suggested.

All eyes turned to me, and I lowered my head. I knew the answer to that better than anyone. "We kept Brandon on the payroll when he was hurt, and hiring someone to cover for him dropped our savings. Market prices were down last fall, but county taxes were up. And the biggest thing is that we, uh…" I gulped. "We made some pretty huge donations to White Pines. We can't justify hiring someone else right now just so I can go volunteer."

"Whaddaya mean? Are you saying we can't afford it? We have money to campaign the show horses, don't we? We have hay sitting in that barn to sell, don't we? We're not exactly eating rice and beans. I don't see why y'all can't let Dusty have a few hours a week."

"I don't want us surviving on rice and beans," Dad said, finality in his tone. "We get through the hard times because we tighten our belts before we're starving, not after. And right now, we need everyone. It's only for a little while, Dusty. A month—six weeks at the most."

I was staring at the floor, my teeth grinding. I knew what that meant, even if Dad wouldn't say it. Tax season was upon us, and that was my job. We'd be hot in the middle of calving season by the time Marshall got back to full strength, and that meant every man on deck around the clock. Then it would be branding season, when we ran our fool heads off helping everyone get their calves vaccinated and tagged before turning them out on summer pastures. Realistically, it would be May before I'd be able to take a breath. And by then, Luke and I would be trying to win some money at the ropings, and I couldn't let Luke down.

I'd never have this opportunity again; that was what it boiled down to.

"I'm sorry, Dusty," Evan said.

I looked up and swallowed. I was a grown man now, and my eyes didn't sting like they did when I was a kid. At least, I wouldn't show it. "It's alright. I'm going to bed. Night, all."

Dad and Evan grunted their good-nights, but Luke followed me down the hall. "Man! Why wouldn't you just tell them the truth?"

I turned around. "Because there's nothing to tell, Luke."

"Sure as shootin', there is. Don't tell me you weren't puttin' some moves on when you were working with Jess. Dude! Chicks dig a guy who loves kids. You've probably got her wrapped around your pinky by now!"

"Not so as you could tell it." I shook my head. "She brought Austen today."

Luke hissed and sagged against the opposite wall. "That sucks."

I lifted a shoulder, trying to act philosophical. "Some things just aren't meant to be. You know the old saying about the Lord closing a door."

"Ain't He supposed to open a window? That's a load of bull crap. You got to kick that door open yourself."

I gave a rueful laugh and shook my head. "It's no good. She's made her choice. I might as well learn to live with it sooner or later."

"Yeah, well, they ain't hitched yet. Don't give up till the writing's on the wall, little brother."

I tried to smile and failed. I just pounded a fist on my big brother's shoulder. "Thanks. Night, Luke."

Jess

"No Dusty today?" I stood on my toes to scan through the windows, over the tops of the kids' heads. No gray truck had pulled into the driveway, and no blue-eyed cowboy had shown up to greet the kids like they were the most important people in the world.

Morgan shook her head. "No. I guess they're short-handed at the ranch. He called me the other day. He didn't say anything to you?"

My forehead creased, and I felt my lower lip quiver just a bit. "No, he didn't. I would have thought he would."

"He thought he'd be back in a couple of months, but you know how it is for the ranchers. One day at a time." She pointed at the window. "But I have good news! Audrey said she'd help, and here she is now."

I looked outside and saw the black Lexus rolling up and turning off its lights. "I thought she'd have her hands full, too."

"Well, she keeps dentist hours," Morgan chuckled. "And she spends most afternoons trying to keep Lizzy out of trouble anyway, so she figured she might as well bring her up here. I told her you'd show her the ropes." She checked her watch. "Whew, okay. I've got a Zoom call with someone who's thinking about sponsoring us, so are you good? Biz and Markum, one of the retired show horses that came up from Oklahoma, are both waiting in the indoor ring for you to use. Do you need anything else?"

"We should be fine." My voice sounded a little hollow, even to my own ears.

"Great. Sorry to race off. Thank you a million, once again!" Morgan blew me a kiss and power-walked off to her new office.

I let my gaze wander around the reception room. It still wasn't finished. Neither was the arena, which didn't have sand or siding walls yet. But the place was serviceable, at least. To its clients and volunteers, it was a labor of love, and people are more forgiving of works in progress when the heart is invested, too.

I couldn't help remembering the work party two weeks ago—before Dustin got lost and Marshall got hurt. Everyone had such a great time pitching in together. There'd been joking and teasing, laughter and a spirit of camaraderie with all of us working for the same goal. I could almost hear the echo of voices still, and see the faces that bustled around the room with huge smiles.

But one was missing.

Dusty had worked as hard as anyone—maybe harder than most. But he'd been outside with the table saw, missing out on the joy and fun we were having indoors. We couldn't have done anything without him feeding us the cut materials, and he managed to stay ahead of three different work crews, all needing something from him. He'd just worked out there all morning, head down, probably freezing, but never complaining, just doing what needed to be done.

And no one ever thanked him.

The world needed more guys like Dusty Walker, I decided. Just decent men. Not flashy or ostentatious. Maybe not even charismatic or funny—although, once you got to know Dusty, he could be both. He was kind of like my dad in that way. A quiet sort of man who gives to everyone but saves his best for the people closest to him. I was lucky to have him as a friend, and I was going to miss working with him.

The door jingled, and Audrey stepped inside, pulling off her chic winter hat and leather driving gloves and shepherding her niece Lizzy ahead of her. "Jess! I hear we get to work together today."

That did sound like fun. A girl needed girl time too, right? I grinned. "That's the rumor. Ready to get started?"

"No! But I'm game to learn. Just promise me I don't have to handle any horses. They scare me."

"Well, some of the kids scare me, so we're even."

Audrey laughed. "If we survive the day, I say we go out to that little Italian bistro off Main. My treat. Deal?"

"Deal."

"Well. We survived." I held up my water glass in a salute.

Audrey groaned and struggled to sit upright. "You call that surviving? My ears are still ringing. And I think I might have a black eye." She fished a compact out of her purse and flipped it open to inspect the damage.

"Billy can be dangerous with that rope. Let me see." I leaned close to get a better look. "Looks okay for now. Tomorrow might be another story."

"Oh, well." She clapped the case shut and put it away. "Nobody will see it behind my mask and visor at work, and it's not like I'm trying to impress anyone outside of there. Not my scene around here anyway."

"I guess not." I toyed with my spaghetti. "So, is it still your plan to get back to New York?"

"Eventually. I just need Kat to get better." Audrey's voice sounded cheerful, but her face was a study in dejection.

"How is she doing?" I asked quietly.

Audrey swallowed a long gulp from her glass, then shook her head. "It's not good, Jess." She sniffed and rested her chin on her hand, avoiding me with her eyes. "She talks like she'll be back to normal in a week or a month, but we both know that's just for Lizzy's benefit. The truth…" She dropped her hand and stared at the table. "The truth is, it will take a miracle for her to see Lizzy's next birthday, and I think she's running low on those."

"Oh, Audrey! I didn't know it was that bad. Poor Kat!"

"Don't tell anyone, will you? She doesn't want it going around town, but it feels good to share with someone rather than keep it all to myself."

"Of course. Is there anything I can do? Should I be visiting her? I can take her to the doctor or something for you."

Audrey shook her head. "She usually doesn't feel up to visitors, and I have all her appointments scheduled around my work. I just worry about Lizzy. She's been getting in more and more trouble at school, and I don't feel like I know how to help her."

"What about her dad?"

"Hah. No. He's no help." Audrey finished her ice water, then pasted on a smile. "But really, that's enough. If I wanted to fret about my troubles, I'd have gone home. I want to hear all the dish about your new boyfriend. Everyone is curious about him."

"What do you want to know?"

Audrey's eyes widened, and she leaned forward. "Let's start with all of it? What's he like? Is he a secret millionaire, or does he have a former wife locked away in the attic? Is he a CIA operative? Son of a congressman? Is he going to buy up all the ranches around here and turn them into a shopping mall?"

I chuckled. "Rumor mill must be working overtime, huh?"

"People either know facts, or they make up their own. So, who's the real Austen Conrad?"

"He's a nice guy. Smart, practical, funny, easy to get along with, good with kids."

"Romantic?"

"In his own way."

"And what way is that? Come on, details!"

I shrugged, laughing. "I don't know! He's always trying to do something nice for me. How about that?"

"Good, but tell me more. What kinds of nice things?"

"Well… he offered to cook me dinner. Brings me flowers at work. And he gave me the sweetest poem." I frowned. "But just once."

I still hadn't figured out why he'd changed so suddenly on that. He slips a poem in my pocket, writes me the most endearing note ever, lets me read his journal, then says he's not comfortable sharing his writing? I wanted to ask why, but it didn't even seem like I could ask.

Audrey gestured for me to keep going. "And? What else?"

I gave a little huff and held up my hands. "I'm still getting to know the guy. Cut me some slack. I think he's a little slow to open up."

"Oh, I get it. One of those. Say no more." She put up a hand to me and reached for the water pitcher to refill her glass.

"Wait, what? What are you talking about?"

She batted her thick eyelashes and gave me a sly grin. "I call that type 'The Sleeper.' Seems nice and civilized, and then whoosh! Before you know it, you've got yourself a real heartbreaker."

"I don't… I don't want a heartbreaker."

"Yes, you do! There is, in fact, a good way to get your heart broken. Think of this." She pantomimed a video screen with her hands, her eyes animated. "You walk in the door, say you've been gone all day or something. You're tired. So tired your knuckles are dragging, and you can't see straight. What do you want to come home to? Option a: A bower of roses and a half-naked cowboy holding a champagne bottle."

I giggled. "That would wake me up."

Audrey quirked a brow. "Option b: His mother making dinner for him in your kitchen and complaining that you buy cheap cookware."

"Ew! Where did you even come up with that one?"

"That was just to see if you're paying attention. Now there's option c: He's got dinner on, the kids are asleep, and when you collapse like a rag doll on the couch, he slips behind you and rubs your shoulders. Then, when you're nice and relaxed, he carries you to bed, snuggles you against his chest, and just holds you until you drift to sleep." She finished with a wicked smile and a nod.

"Um… Let me wipe the drool off my chin." I picked up my napkin to fan myself. "You weren't kidding."

"Mmm-hmm," Audrey sighed, pretending to dash a little perspiration off her brow. "That, my friend, is how a guy shatters a girl in all the best ways. He'll make you cry, but they'll be happy tears. You'll be worried every time he leaves the house, but it'll be because you're praying he comes home safely, not that he'll be faithful. You hold out for the guy who can break your heart like that, and when you find him, trust him enough to let him do it."

She chugged more from her glass, then held a finger up as she swallowed. "Oh. And find out if he has a brother because I'm in the market for one of those, too."

"Hah! I thought you didn't like cowboys."

"I don't. But didn't you say Austen is a California guy?" She lifted her shoulders daintily. "West coast men are practically all savages, but I might be able to make that work."

I laughed and tossed my napkin on my plate. "I can't imagine there could be two of those floating around, but if they're out there, maybe we'll get lucky. I mean, why not us, right?"

"Exactly. Why not us?"

I thought about what Audrey had said the whole way home, and the rest of the night. I thought about it for weeks, actually. I didn't know where she'd learned this wisdom about men, but she made perfect sense. That was the kind of man I could love for my whole life.

Was Austen that man? He'd rubbed my sore muscles at the work party, which had been really sweet, like he was trying to look out for me and make me comfortable. But the rest of it… actually, the roses and champagne guy sounded more like Austen. No doubt about it—he'd be the one with the huge bouquet and maybe the expensive gifts and the promise of a fun night on the town or something more… exotic at home.

That would be exciting, but I liked the idea of the guy who'd just take care of his woman—no fuss, no demands, and no need to make a show of it. Just a quiet, gentle hero who wanted a partner to wade through life with. One who thought romance was more about what you did than what you said or what you bought. And the only face that kept coming to mind belonged to Dusty Walker.

But he didn't seem to like me like that. There had been that one moment when we were laughing together over the kids and I touched his arm, when I thought I read tenderness and promise in those blue eyes of his. But that was all I could be sure of. Like Morgan had said, he was sweet and kind to everyone, and his reputation in town bore that out. He didn't treat me any differently… did he?

Maybe I should try to find out. I was bundled in bed, with Dakota curled up at my feet. He liked to hog the bottom of the bed, and he'd get mad if I tried to get up. Crazy dog. It was late, but I wouldn't be able to sleep unless I at least reached out to Dusty. Could I do that without sounding stupid? Or desperate?

I bit my lower lip and whispered, "Come on, girl. He doesn't bite." I picked up my phone and typed. Maybe I'd just send a shot over his bow, so to speak. Just something to start the conversation.

> -Morgan said you were buried at the ranch.
> Sorry you couldn't make it today.

I didn't expect a reply until morning, but ten seconds later, he answered.

> -Bad luck, I know. We'll be slammed for a while with Marshall out.

I thought for a second, then typed again.

> -Well, the kids missed you, especially the boys.
> Any idea when you'll be back?

Was that enough? Should I say that I'd missed him, too? That might be coming on too strong. Dusty was a shy kind of guy. I'd wait to see what he said.

> -I really can't say. Maybe a couple months.
> Maybe not till late summer.

Oh. That didn't sound promising at all, and I couldn't tell if he was sorry about not having an answer. Maybe he didn't want to come back, anyway, from how he phrased it. He was too nice to come out and say it, but how many grown men wanted to spend two afternoons a week wrangling a bunch of kids? For free?

But when else would I have a chance to see him? If he was that slammed at the ranch, he wouldn't get away very often, unless he needed his truck fixed or happened to be in the store when I was. It could be weeks. Or months.

I'd lived in a ranching town long enough to know about early spring calving season. Those guys would all but disappear for over a month, and when they showed their faces again, they'd be like walking phantoms—blood-shot eyes and ten pounds lighter. What could I say to let him know I'd be looking for him but not sound too clingy?

> -I guess I'll see you around town. Maybe I'll
> bump into you in the horse shampoo aisle.

That sounded cute, I thought. Something to make him smile and remind him that I was here, whenever he wanted to find me.

But he never answered it.

Chapter 19

Dusty

I t had been over three weeks since I'd seen Jess.

She texted me that first day I didn't show up at White Pines. It was just a simple message, saying she was sorry I couldn't make it, and the kids had missed me. She didn't say anything about missing me herself, but still, at least she knew I was alive. I hadn't been able to bring myself to respond with more than a short thanks. If I'd sent her something saying I'd be back soon or was crushed with disappointment that I couldn't come, it would spiral into wishful thinking and things that couldn't be.

I saw her dad a couple of times, though, just passing him on the highway. He waved and honked. He even called me once because he wanted to stock his freezer with some beef. I sold him a quarter, but I was out feeding calves when he came to pick it up. I would have liked to talk to him, but it was probably just as well that I didn't. He couldn't have anything to say that I'd want to hear.

Marshall was limping around a little better. Kelli had lost the battle of trying to keep him home to heal, so finally, she gave up and drove over with him every day. She'd ride her horse while Marshall just got in the way. He wanted to work but couldn't do anything without someone else stopping whatever they were doing to help him. Finally, I'd had enough one day, and I dragged him upstairs to teach him how to do payroll for the ranch hands. Then I made him learn how to pay the bills. I've never heard him complain and moan so much, but at least he couldn't hurt himself in the office, and it freed me up to do other stuff.

The last weekend of January, Luke and I decided we needed to get a lot more serious about shaving down our roping times if we hoped to be competitive this year. We talked Kelli into dragging the practice sled for us, with Marshall running the clock. Duchess was on fire, and she was starting to really eat up her job. If we weren't up to our top speed yet, it wasn't her fault—it was mine.

"Set… go!" Luke called to Kelli. The woman was a devil on that ATV. With a hoot of delight, she put the hammer down so hard that the thing popped a wheelie as it broke free. If I knew Marshall, he was probably cringing and praying she wouldn't flip it, but she got the heavy utility quad lined out and was streaking for the far side of the arena as our horses jumped out of the chutes.

Luke was on the loop in just a couple of strides, then he dropped his dally and set me up for the heel catch. I wasn't quite that fast, but it was me, not the horse. Duchess was like a freight train. She'd been flabby and soft when we got her, but with all the legging up I'd done on her this winter, she was coming on strong, and she was getting fast.

With every practice run, she got sharper. I didn't even have to correct her much anymore—she knew her job, and her great white haunches were like bellows pumping hot steamy snorts into the air with each stride. But she'd taken too many of those strides already, and I was hesitating. I gritted my teeth. A few quick twists of my wrist, and I had the heels.

"Great catch, little brother!" Luke crowed. "What's the time, Marshall?"

"10.8 seconds."

"That's bull! Check your timing eye. You sure you got that thing set right?"

"It's set right!" Marshall shot back. "You're just slow, you old geezer!"

Luke poked a finger in the air. "Say that one more time to my face, you busted up cripple."

"Okay," Marshall said with a smug grin. "You're slower than mooollllaaaasssssesssss. You're so slow, you couldn't catch my mother-in-law's fat old cat. You rope like a sloth groping around in the dark. Vultures will start circling your head before you find that cow."

Luke growled and gestured wildly at Kelli. "You better get him outta here before I break somethin' else on him!"

I'd hopped off Duchess to collect my rope and reset the chute barriers, laughing all the way. "Aw, come on, Luke. You made your catch in like four seconds. The rest was me. I'm still getting her timing down, but we're getting better. Yesterday we were almost twelve seconds on some of our first runs."

"Well, it ain't good enough for the NFR," Luke sniffed. "We'll even get laughed out of the jackpots with those times."

"One more go. I was overthinking it, but I've got her dialed now."

"Fine. One more." Luke coiled his rope and trotted toward the chutes. I don't think he realized that I saw when he grabbed his right shoulder and rolled it with a wince of pain. He'd been doing that more often lately, but he hadn't said anything about it. We couldn't keep up these hours-long practices.

I got on and backed Duchess into the chute, and closed my eyes to take a few deep breaths. I had to make this one good. My mare was quivering beneath me, ready to plunge ahead the instant the barrier dropped. If I could just focus, keep my mind clear!

I let my imagination wander to the serene place I'd dreamed up—a high mountain lake with crisp cool waters, and a couple of horses grazing the edges. Snowy peaks in the distance with skies the color of Montana Sapphires, and... I sighed.

She always showed up in this little daydream, too. Jess, with her golden hair drifting softly in the breeze, the collar of her favorite red and blue flannel shirt fluttering at the curve of her graceful neck, and her eyes searching for me. She'd smile just so, and then she'd reach for my arm again, like she did when we were teaching together, and she'd say...

"Go!"

Duchess almost leaped out from under me, jumping so hard I lost my hat. I scurried to regain my balance. Luke was just ahead of me, his rope snaking through the air. Mine was in motion, my elbow high, and my eyes locked on the target. Duchess had me set up just right, and my pulse pounded with the rhythm of her strides. One twirl, two, three…

"Hey, guys!"

That sounded a lot like Jess's voice. My arm jerked, my spine tingled, and I shot my loop before it dropped in stride. It fell harmlessly to the sand as Kelli screamed away with the roping sled.

"Aw, man! What happened?" Luke howled. "Didn't I tell you…" He had that finger in the air again, but then his eyes passed over the gate by the end of the arena to find what my whole body already knew. "Oh. Hi, Jess." He cleared his throat. "And Austen. Whatcha guys doin'?"

Jess's eyes were wide and her hand was covering her mouth. "I'm sorry! I think that was my fault."

Luke glanced over at me, and I gave him a pleading look. If he opened that big mouth of his and embarrassed me…

He winked at me with the eye they couldn't see, then waved a nonchalant hand. "Naw. Just workin' out the kinks with a new horse. If you catch every single throw, they start anticipatin'. He did that a' purpose."

I raised a brow. Where was he getting a story like that?

"Really? I learn something new every time I come up here," Austen said with that cheesy grin of his. "Sorry to interrupt your practice, though."

"We were just finishing," Marshall informed him. He was already coiling up the cords for the electronic timing eye. "What can we do you for?"

"Oh, I called Evan earlier. He said he'd sell me a few of your big one-ton hay bales, so Danny and I brought the semi and the flatbed over. He's out with Evan now getting loaded up."

So, that was what he wanted. And maybe that was why he'd tried to get back on my good side—he needed Walker Ranch to survive the winter. Well, so be it. I wouldn't let a bunch of cows starve over my wounded pride.

I let my gaze drift to Jess. She and Kelli had already found each other and were talking about something, but she must have sensed my eyes on her because she looked over. A smile and a wave, and then Kelli said something that made her laugh and look away.

I got off Duchess, loosened the cinch, and then went back for my hat. Should I stop and talk to Jess? That would be the normal thing to do, right? But when I passed by the gate, Austen walked over to her and put his arm around her. So, I just kept walking. I had a horse to take care of.

I clipped Duchess into the cross ties and pulled my saddle, then returned with a brush to break loose the salt and dirt from our work. She was thin-skinned, and I'd discovered she only liked certain brushes. She also liked it when I hummed to her as I groomed her—she'd go from tense and alert to droop-eared with a foot cocked when I hummed a little tune to help her relax. It helped me, too, because I couldn't hear the voices around the corner quite as well when I was making noise.

Her coat was brushed out soft and dry, and I was bent over to pick the packed dirt out of her hooves when a pair of worn boots stepped into my field of view. I dropped the hoof and straightened.

"Hi, Dusty," Jess said.

I rested my hand on the horse's wither and tried not to look like I was suddenly dizzy. "Hi."

She brushed a lock of hair behind her ear, then stroked Duchess's hip. "How have you been?"

I drew a breath, held it, then tried to let it out carefully. "Just... busy. You?"

Jess smiled. "Same." She bit her lip, her eyes shifting from side to side. "Um, I finally got some regular work. The phone company was looking for a contract mechanic to service their installation vehicles, so that's been keeping me out of trouble."

"Oh, yeah? That's great! Are you still going to White Pines?"

"I wouldn't miss it. Audrey's been helping me, but..." The corner of her mouth tugged shyly, revealing that tiny crease I'd always wanted to soothe away with my thumb. "Neither of us is a real working cowboy. You know Aedyn and Billy. They still talk about 'how Dusty does it' on a daily basis."

I huffed a short laugh. "Tell them I'll be back as soon as I can." I pointed toward the arena with my hoof pick. "As soon as Marshall's really back to work. Won't be much longer now."

Jess nodded. "Good. They'll be glad to have you back." That wisp of hair fell over her eyes again, brushing along her jaw and half concealing her cheek. My chest ached looking at it, and I couldn't help inching just a little closer to her. Would she let me tuck it behind her ear for her? Her chin lifted, and her pupils dilated. And did her breathing deepen?

"Jess?" I asked softly.

She answered with a little sigh, and a fine line appeared between her brows. "Yeah?"

"I…" I swallowed, my hands tingling inside my gloves. And before I could pull them off, reach for her soft cheek and slip that bit of silk between my fingers, she flipped it out of the way herself. I had already rocked forward on the balls of my feet, but I made myself settle again. Well… it was a stupid idea, anyway.

"I'm sorry I haven't been able to come up there," I mumbled.

She exhaled, and her lips thinned in a patient smile. "You've put your time to good use, I'm sure. Duchess is looking fantastic." She ran an admiring hand over my horse's broad back and down her muscular croup. "Sorry for startling you earlier."

I gave a weak laugh. Luke's little fib hadn't fooled her one bit. "Oh, that's okay. I wasn't on my game today, to begin with."

"Oh? I was wondering—"

"Dusty, there you are." Evan was walking toward us down the barn aisle, his broad shoulders bunched under his coat and his eyes hooded by his hat. Austen was right beside him. I could feel my heart sinking like lead, and whatever I might have said to Jess flew right out of my brain.

"What did you tell Austen we were charging for the hay? We've been charging $350 for the one-ton bales this year, but he said you mentioned a discount for neighbors."

I narrowed my eyes. "I don't recall that."

"Oh, well, it's no big deal. I thought I remembered it, and I wanted to make sure I'd heard right, that's all," Austen replied with a shrug.

"Don't worry about it," Evan said, waving his hand. "We can do $320 for you. Dusty can get you all settled up. Are you still planning to come back next week for another load?"

"If I can. I sure appreciate you guys helping me out like this."

Evan smiled shortly and shook Austen's hand. "Sure thing. It's a bad year for hay; shortages starting to stress folks all over the valley. Glad we could keep you stocked. Hey, Dusty, I'm off to check the mama cows." Evan tipped his hat to Jess, then stuffed his hands in his pockets and walked off whistling.

It was all I could do not to glare at Austen. He sure had a way of putting me on the spot, pinning me down with something in such a way that I couldn't deny him without looking like a jerk. I just shot my jaw forward and muttered, "Come on. I've got the invoice forms upstairs."

"Should I put Duchess away while you guys are finishing up?" Jess offered.

I turned back, and for just a second, I felt warm all over. Trust her to think of my horse's comfort. "She'd appreciate that. Her stall's the second on the right. I haven't put new bedding in there for her yet."

"You're just grabbing the invoice, right?" Austen called as I started for the stairs again. "Mind if I stay and give Jess a hand? I can cart the shavings over, save you some work."

I stopped, and my hands flexed inside my gloves. "Yeah," I hissed between clenched teeth. I glanced over my shoulder, leveling such a blistering glare at Austen that even he, bold and presumptuous as he was, turned pale. "She's so lucky to have you."

Jess

"That was nice of the Walkers to give you a discount on the hay." I sipped my soda cup empty and dropped it in one of the dozens of cupholders peppered all over Austen's truck.

"Sure was. They're great guys. I didn't expect Dusty to even remember when we talked about that, it was so long ago."

"It didn't sound like he did remember it," I pointed out, pursing my lips in a question. "You were the one who brought it up."

"Was I? Oh, I don't recall how it all went. Evan and I were talking, and you know how that goes. I'm sure Dusty's just been busy, and it slipped his mind."

"That makes sense. I know he's had his hands full."

"Yeah, but if anyone can juggle a million balls and not drop one, it's Dusty." He shook his head in amazement. "Most unassuming guy you'll ever meet, but he's solid as a rock. You can't even count this because it was probably just a simple case of crossed wires. Not like him, you know? He's a great guy to have as a friend."

"You guys haven't been getting together lately like you were, have you?"

"No, I wish." He pushed his hat up a little, frowning in thought. "It will be good when he gets a bit of a break."

"Huh. Yeah, it will." I chewed the inside of my lip and turned to look out the window. We'd started out following Danny with the hay trailer, but Austen had wanted to stop and grab burgers for all of us before we got to work unloading it. We were now running about twenty minutes behind. I tried to tell Austen that Danny would probably get the whole truck unloaded with the hay squeeze before we got back, but he didn't believe it could happen that fast.

"What about going up to White Pines?" Austen asked. "Did he say if he was going to start coming again?"

I shrugged. "He didn't commit to anything."

"He probably can't. I'm starting to think I wouldn't want a big ranch like theirs, even if someone handed it to me. It owns your every waking minute and half the nights. For me, with my fifty or sixty head, it's a lot easier to try to have a normal-ish life. Wouldn't you say?"

I tilted my head. "Wouldn't I say what?"

"That it's better just to keep things simple. I get a taste of how awesome it is to raise my own animals, live on the land, but I don't have to be a slave to it like the Walkers do. It's the best of both worlds."

"Oh. Yes, I suppose it is." I reached for my cup again, even though it was empty, and fiddled with the straw. I just felt fidgety and on edge, and something Dusty had said right before we left wasn't sitting right with me.

"So, what about you? Are you going to keep going up to White Pines?"

I looked up in surprise. "Me? Why wouldn't I? I have the time, and I enjoy it, and I'm getting to know Audrey and all the kids pretty well. It's been great."

"Well, yeah, but for how long? You'll stop when the weather gets better, right?"

I shook my head slowly. "Nooo, I wasn't planning on it. Morgan's talking about extending the program through the summer if there's enough interest. I'll probably be spending more time there, not less."

He turned back to the road. "Oh. I see." After a minute, he started nodding. "You know what? I think you should go for it, then. You enjoy it, and that's important. Those little kids probably worship you."

"Far from it! They keep me on my toes. I think I learn more from them than they learn from me, but it's great. You should come back sometime. I think you'd have fun."

"I don't see when, but I'll try." He smiled and reached for my hand. "Even if I can't come, I'm proud to be dating the kind of girl who donates her time for that sort of thing. That's cool."

I smiled. "Thanks."

Dad was puttering in the garage when I got home that evening. For once, I didn't really feel like helping. I made a half-hearted offer and didn't object when he waved me off. That was perfect because I wanted nothing more than a long soak in the bubble bath and a hot tea. I really needed to be alone to chew on some things.

What was I doing with Austen? It was almost momentum at this point. I'd started dating him out of curiosity, and he'd never given me a reason to break up with him. He was sometimes a little dense, but he was always kind, always fun to be around.

He seemed to value me for who I was. Yes, he always complimented my looks and sometimes asked me to wear something in particular that he liked. But I had to be careful not to be too sensitive about that. Just because I'd had more than my fill of guys who only wanted me for my appearance didn't mean it was unreasonable for my boyfriend to want me to look good. He didn't like it when I smelled like a grease monkey, but who would? He said he supported the things I wanted to do, and that mattered.

But I didn't think about him when we were apart. That alone was enough to scare me. Why would I waste my time and risk my heart on a man who was just "fine" when we were together and not special enough to daydream about when we weren't?

I'd started to say something about that to Audrey one day, hoping she could advise me, but she'd been distracted with her own problems. "Love takes time, girl. Give that flower a season to bloom." And then she'd had to stop Lizzy from poking someone with a stick. We never got back around to talking about my love life.

Seeing Dusty again today had sent another bell clanging in my mind. I still liked him. A lot.

I'd assumed it was just a matter of proximity, the chemistry of people who work well together. I'd always developed a bit of a thing for co-workers that, while not necessarily romantic, sometimes felt like it. That was why I'd been so rigid in never dating anyone I worked with, because I didn't trust myself to know the difference between an 8-5 friendship and something precious before it was too late.

But today, I knew. He didn't even do anything. Hadn't even noticed me yet, but when I leaned over that arena rail, my heart jumped out of my chest as I watched him charging with his rope flying on that great white beauty. The thought flitted through my mind that he was everything a cowboy should be—tough and quick, strong enough to pull down a half-ton steer, and gentle enough to hold a bolt of lightning on a shoestring rein. The kind of man who knew what it was to be loyal and make sacrifices, who could laugh with a ten-year-old kid who'd roped him over the cowboy hat, and who could wipe the tears off a fourth-grader's cheeks. And I was just now recognizing it.

I was a grade-A idiot.

He didn't even like me! I'd tried to give him a chance to say something, and he didn't take it. For a heartbeat, I'd even thought he might kiss me, but then he just apologized for not coming up to White Pines. Like something a co-worker would say.

Maybe I'd scared him, or maybe he didn't understand that was what I was doing. I would have kept trying, except for that strange thing he said when Austen offered to help me put his horse away. "She's so lucky to have you."

I couldn't see his face when he said it, and I didn't really hear his tone because a horse had whinnied right then. But it could only mean one thing. He thought Austen and I were great together. A guy who liked me as more than a friend would never say that—he'd be trying to find a way to show me that Austen wasn't right for me instead of saying I was lucky to have him.

I closed my eyes and slipped below the foamy suds in the bathtub. At least if my face was already wet, those wouldn't feel like tears gathering in the corners of my eyes.

Chapter 20

Dusty

I hate Valentine's Day.

I've never liked it, just on the principle of the thing. A man was supposed to prove he loved his girlfriend or wife more than the next guy loved his, based on the amount of chocolate he bought or the extravagance of the date he took her on. It was stupid, shallow, and transparent marketing ploy to sell candy and greeting cards.

And also, I'd never had anyone I could call "My Valentine." So it was stupid, as far as I was concerned.

All the restaurants in town would be crowded tonight, with guys taking their ladies out for a dinner they didn't have to cook. Everyone from teenagers to pensioners would be out in their best outfits, smiling dreamily across the table at the one person who made their hearts go pitter-patter.

We Walkers didn't pay much attention, though. Cows have to eat, horses have to be looked after, and life on the ranch doesn't miss a beat. It was just another Tuesday—one more Tuesday I'd stayed home to work instead of seeing Jess. She probably had other plans tonight, anyway.

I stomped the snow off my boots and shook the fresh flakes off my hat at the door of the house. Chores were finished for now, but I'd have to go back outside after dinner to check water tanks. I shivered when I pulled my coat off and hung it up, then something else caught my attention. The house smelled like my mom's chuck stew.

They say the sense of smell is the last thing to linger in your memory—far longer than a person's face or voice. I'd know my mom's stew recipe anywhere. None of the rest of us knew how to make it. It was such a family legend that no one even attempted to copy it. That stew was just kind of sacred. So, who...?

I rounded the corner of the kitchen and found out. There was my dad, his arms around Meryl Justice as she tried to cook, and he was kissing her on the cheek.

"Stop it, you rascal!" she laughed, swatting at him with a wooden spoon. "You're going to get burned."

"That's what happens when you get close to the flame," he joked as he snuck one more kiss. "But if you're going to be that way about it, I suppose I'll bide my time."

I stepped back, feeling a little nauseous. There was the answer to my question: I wasn't ready to see my dad with someone else. They looked so happy and flirty, but... but he was my *dad*. There are just some things a guy doesn't want to see, and his dad getting sweet with his lady friend in the kitchen is one of them. I pivoted on my heel and tried to sneak away.

"Dusty!" Meryl greeted me. "Good evening. I hope you're hungry."

I chewed my lip, then turned around. "Hi, Meryl. What are you making in here?" As if I didn't know.

She dipped out a bit of the stew and brought it over for me to taste. "I hope it's good. Blake says this is a family favorite."

I rolled the rich broth and tender vegetables around my tongue, and I could feel my entire being just melt. "Tastes just like Mom's," I said in a husky voice.

"Not quite," Dad replied as he stole the spoon to take another dip.

I savored the remnants of flavor in my mouth, thought for a second, and had to disagree. "No. That's it, exactly. I'd know those season-ings."

"What I mean is this wasn't your mom's recipe to begin with. Marci got it from Meryl, oh... when was that? Ninety-five or so?"

Meryl frowned and rolled her eyes up. "I thought I brought it over when Luke was born, and you made her get the recipe. Or was it Evan?"

My mouth dropped. I felt like some holy relic had just been tossed out like a fifty-cent golfing trophy. "Mom didn't come up with this? I always thought it was handed down from Grandma, and Mom tweaked it."

"You're thinking of the chicken pot pies. Mm-mm." Dad patted his belly. "Those were the best."

"Oh, yes," Meryl agreed. "She used to bring those to the Aid Society meetings, and we all begged until she told us how to make them. I don't think anyone ever quite duplicated her crust, though."

"But, the stew..."

"Wonderful to have the house smelling like that again, isn't it?" Dad asked. "Meryl offered to cook us all a Valentine's dinner tonight, and I asked for that special. She even baked some home-made biscuits to mop it up with."

I swallowed and something inside me... let go. And I found a smile for Meryl Justice. "It is wonderful. Amazing."

"You look awfully somber this evening."

I'd been daydreaming in the den after dinner and my last round of chores. My belly was full of warm comfort, all the animals were snug and safe, and the den was lit mostly by the glass on the wood stove. It probably wasn't even accurate to say I was daydreaming. I was half asleep. My mind had just slipped into peaceful meanderings, mostly flashes of summertime and Jess's quiet smile.

Meryl's voice called me back to reality, and I shifted the old throw pillow off my lap to straighten. "Somber? Why do you say that?"

"Oh, nothing. You just looked like someone beat your dog." She winked. "Or maybe you're just low on batteries." She eased herself to the opposite side of the couch, and for the first time, I realized the den was empty. Evan had been there earlier, scanning his phone for market prices. Luke would be in the shower about now.

"Where's Dad?"

"Well, he said it was his turn to wash dishes. I tried to help, but he chased me out. I think he drafted Evan to help him."

"I thought you guys were going out for pie or something after dinner. What happened to that?"

"Aw." She waved. "Takes too much energy. I never put much stock into made-up holidays and all that fuss anyway. I'm happy with a bit of roll and jam."

I chuckled. "I can respect that."

She pressed her lips together and nodded. Her eyes got a faraway look for a minute, and I thought she'd just come in to doze, like me. Then she said something that sliced right to my core.

"Dusty, I'm not here to replace your mom."

I shot bolt upright and stared at her. "Uh... Why... why would you say that?"

Meryl lifted her shoulders, her fingers laced over her knee. "I felt like you needed to hear it. I loved Marci Walker for as long as I can remember—way before she married your dad. I'd never want to dishonor her memory or step into her shoes. I couldn't fill them." She gazed at me, her eyes soft and eloquent. "But I love your dad. And I love this family."

The back of my throat burned and tightened, and my eyes tried to sting again. I blinked it back and sniffed casually. "You're welcome in this family, Meryl. Dad loves you, and we all gave our blessing."

"I know that. But you... you were Marci's favorite."

I snorted and grabbed the throw pillow again to clutch it to my chest. I didn't like how vulnerable she made me feel. "Mom didn't play favorites."

"No, she didn't, and that's not how I meant it. I guess what I'm saying is that you were the one who took after her. That tender side of you, the others don't share it. She understood you like she never could with them, and I think you had a special connection with her."

I looked away and had to scratch something off my cheek. "Maybe," I mumbled. "Why are you saying this?"

"Oh, I probably shouldn't, but I think she would, if she were here."

"I don't understand."

Meryl's face was a contortion of doubt. I could see some internal struggle etched in the lines of her jaw, but finally, she brushed it off and plunged ahead. "Marci used to talk to me about you. She was so proud of you, you should know that, but she also worried. She used to say you would hang your heart on the things that were most likely to break you."

I gave her a skeptical look. "Huh?"

"You always picked the runt puppies to train, the lost cause horses to fix. You'd have the money to buy a new truck, but you'd buy an old beater instead."

I shrugged. "What can I say? I like rooting for the underdog."

"Or you don't think you deserve to win."

That was something I couldn't process. My arms sagged around that pillow until it drooped, and I just gazed blankly into the fire for a few minutes, those words hanging between us.

"Can you…" I cleared my throat and took a deep breath. "Can you explain what that means?"

She didn't answer immediately. Instead, she reached for the coffee table to brush through the newspapers and stuff. "I suppose it means that when you want something, it's okay to take a risk for it."

"Like Luke buying stupid-expensive horses on the off-chance they won't be crippled," I grunted.

She grinned. "Yeah, kind of like that. Or like this." She held something up, and my heart skipped a beat. It was the newest issue of *Stockman's*, flipped open to the section in the back.

"Wyatt Chandler," she mused. "Now, there's a guy who knows how to translate feeling into words." She scanned down the page, then lifted her gaze to me. Steady, patient. And absolutely supportive.

My throat closed and all I could do was blink stupidly.

"Does your family know?"

I shook my head. "As far as I know, you're the only one to put it together."

She nodded and cradled the journal in her lap to read it once more. "Marci would have known. She wouldn't have even had to figure out that pen name. She'd just feel it in the way you phrased your words because you're a perfect echo of her."

"I am?"

"Mmm-hmm. She used to write, too, you know."

"I didn't know that, actually."

"We had a little creative writing club after school, founded by Marci, of course. We all had fun with it, but she had a gift."

"And what happened?"

Meryl lifted her shoulders. "She had one date with your dad and decided she was going to be a rancher's wife. I don't know if she ever wrote after that, but it wouldn't surprise me. If you search the attics, you might find lots of dusty old journals. A writer writes; they can't help it. And you, Dusty Walker, are a writer."

A weak smile was forming on my lips. "Thanks. Even if only one person likes it, I guess I am."

"Oh, I guarantee it's more than one person! But the question I have is who inspired this particular poem. It wasn't a horse, was it?"

I sucked my lower lip between my teeth, and my gaze fell. And I shook my head.

Meryl's brows lifted gently, and I could see her eyes scanning my poem again. "She's remarkable."

I huffed. "You don't even know who she is."

"It doesn't matter. You have the eyes of a poet, someone who can read the soul, and what you see in her is priceless."

"Well..." I clutched that pillow again. "Like you said, it doesn't matter. Doesn't matter who she is and it doesn't matter what I see. It's just a poem."

"No." She rose and gently laid the magazine beside me. "It's your dream. Maybe you deserve to win this time, Dusty."

Jess

"Do you and your handsome rancher have plans for tonight?" Audrey asked as she slipped into her coat sleeves. We'd had a fun afternoon with the kids—a muddy afternoon, because the bad weather had held off for a little while, so we took them outside to learn how to identify different kinds of pine trees.

Audrey and I were the only ones who seemed to notice the cold. The kids had had a blast, but we were in the break room now, trying to warm up our frozen fingers under the faucet and dry out the wet hems of our jeans with paper towels. I zipped my fluffy hat into my duffel bag and tied up a fresh ponytail in my hair. "Yeah, I guess."

"You guess? Didn't he plan a nice date for Valentine's Day?"

"Oh, I think so. He said something about Beaufort's." I shrugged. "I should've broken up with him by now, but I'm a big chicken."

"Broken up with him? What for? I thought he was nice."

"That's just the problem. He *is* nice, and whenever I work up the guts to break it off, he shows up with flowers or something. I don't care about the gifts, but I feel bad slapping him in the face when he hasn't done anything wrong."

Audrey slung her Chanel backpack over her shoulder and came close enough to look me in the eye. "It's not about whether he's done something 'wrong.' What has he done *right*? If you feel like you need to cut him loose, then you need to do it before either one of you loses too much. What are you afraid of?"

I looked down at my bag to search for my keys. "I guess I needed to hear someone else say it. I've been worried about hurting him."

"You'll hurt him a lot more, not to mention poison yourself, if you don't do anything. Trust me on this one."

I drew a shaky breath. "Right. So, should I dump him on Valentine's Day or let him pay for dinner first and break up with him over the phone tomorrow?"

Audrey snickered. "No way to win that one. It will work itself out. Here." She wrapped her arms around me in a tight hug. "For luck."

"Thanks. Say hi to Kat for me."

"Will do."

We walked back out to the classroom together so she could collect her niece and I could pick up some books I'd brought about trees. Lizzy was still in there coloring, but so was Aedyn.

"Hey, buddy, your mom hasn't come yet?" I asked.

"Nope. I bet my little brother ran off again." He kept coloring.

"Ran off?"

Aedyn didn't look up. "He hides sometimes. Last time it took an hour to find him."

I met Audrey's eyes, and she shook her head and tapped her watch. "I have to get Kat her meds on time. She's won't do it herself anymore. When do you need to leave for your date?"

I glanced at the clock on my phone. "I can stay with him. No problem."

Audrey blew me a kiss on her way out the door. "Good luck tonight."

"What do you mean you can't make it tonight? We had the whole thing planned." Austen rarely sounded frustrated, but he did now.

"I know, but I can't do much about it," I whispered into the phone. I didn't want Aedyn to overhear and have his feelings hurt. It wasn't his fault. "I'm not allowed to drive him home according to White Pines policy, and..."

"Whoa, whoa, wait. Isn't this Morgan's problem? Shouldn't she be there?"

"I guess, maybe, but I said I'd stay with him. Everyone else has something to do."

"What about you? We have a reservation!"

"I'm sorry. I think I'll have to cancel and..." I swallowed. "Maybe it's... it's for the best. I, uh..."

Austen changed tactics before I could finish what I'd meant to say. "You know, it's okay. Really, it's fine. I get it; you're doing what you need to do, because you're the kind of girl who keeps her promises. I love that about you. How about you text me when you're on your way home? Or we could just meet at the restaurant. I'll push back the reservation. No problem."

I chewed my lower lip. If I didn't just say it now, when *was* I going to? But I didn't feel right about starting something like that when a kid was listening, either. "Okay," I agreed.

"You made it!" Austen stood up from the table with a huge smile. He looked impeccable in pressed Kimes jeans, an Ariat logo shirt, and a new silver belt buckle. Any girl in town would be proud to sit down at his table and gaze into those dark brown eyes.

I gave him a quick hug and reached for my chair. "Sorry to keep you waiting."

Austen was pulling out his own chair again, but his nose was wrinkled. His gaze swept over me from top to bottom, and his brows jumped. He cleared his throat and picked up his menu.

"What is it?" I asked, looking down at myself. I hadn't had time to run home and clean up, but it wasn't like I was in my pajamas.

"Didn't get a shower after work?" he asked, not looking up.

"Uh..." I tipped my nose surreptitiously toward my armpits and took a sniff.

"The engine grease, angel. I'm not sure I like how hard you have to work at that mechanic shop." He lowered his menu, and his eyes traveled to my hair, which was still in the ponytail I'd twisted up without the benefit of a mirror or a brush. "Did you need to freshen up? I'll wait to order."

I grabbed my bag. "Thanks," I mumbled.

In the ladies' room, I turned off the water and stared over the sink at the face in the mirror. The face of a coward. When was I going to grow a spine?

I'd told myself I was through dating men who were wrapped up in my looks, yet here I was, having dinner with a guy who said something whenever I hadn't dolled up to my absolute best. He didn't like my flannel shirt, he didn't like the smell of the mechanic shop or how my hair looked when I pulled it back. He really hated the old handkerchief I wore over my head at work and the fluffy lounge pants I liked to curl up on the couch in. And he did *not* approve of dogs on the furniture.

So, what was I doing with him? Was I just lonely?

I peered closer, noting the fine red streaks in my eyes and the faint dark circles under them. I hadn't slept well for a couple of weeks, and it was starting to show. I pulled the wisps of hair back that fell over my forehead. Were those age lines? I was only twenty-six! But thirty wasn't far away, and after that forty, and after that...

I was scared. That was what it was. Scared of being alone. Scared of becoming my dad, with a long empty road ahead and no one to brighten his life. And I hated myself for it. It would be better to be alone than to spend my time fretting about someone who didn't fit.

If I was honest with myself, I'd been apathetic about my dates with Austen since early January, but the last couple of weeks, I'd actually been irritated every time he called to make plans. And still, I hadn't said anything. *Why?* Why couldn't I speak up with what was on my heart? I'd never been good at that.

Even my dad had mentioned it a few times. I was like my mom, he said. I kept my mouth shut, and people walled out because I didn't like feeling like I lived in a fish bowl. I'd been noticed my whole life, but rarely known. So, instead of showing people who I really was, I just showed them what I thought they wanted to see, and I kept my heart safe behind lock and key. So safe that no one, not even I, knew how to draw it out anymore.

Now, this wouldn't do at all. I was in the bathroom of the busiest restaurant in town on Valentine's Day, and I was crying over the sink. Big, blubbery tears were streaking my face, and I didn't even remember how they got there. All I knew was that I had to hide them.

If that were Dusty Walker out there waiting for me at that table, would things be different? Would I try to put on a brave face, or would I go to him and trust him to hold me through the tears?

If it was Dusty Walker, I scolded myself, *I wouldn't be crying in the first place*. I didn't know what made me so sure of that, but I felt it in my bones.

There was my answer. I was waiting for the kind of man I could trust with my whole self, even when I didn't look pretty. The kind of man who would cradle me against his chest and read to me by firelight. The kind who would get his hands dirty with me and still want to kiss me. I wanted a man who looked at my heart.

But first, I had to clean up my face. Then, I was going to go out there and somehow find the words to say to Austen. It would hurt him, but Audrey was right. I had to do it before it was too late. And once I was free, I was going to call Dusty Walker and ask him out myself, if that was what it took. I had to at least try.

I didn't carry a makeup compact or a brush in my purse, so I made do with a chapstick and some working hands cream. At least my skin felt a little fresher, but I couldn't do much about my hair. It would just look stringy if I left it down, so I piled it up in the most sophisticated-looking bun I could manage with a hair tie and gave myself one last look in the mirror. If Austen didn't think I looked okay and couldn't be a little understanding of the circumstances... well, I just didn't care anymore.

When I got back to the table, there was a box and a card sitting on my plate. Austen was smiling like a Cheshire Cat.

"What's this?" I dropped my bag and eased into the chair, a feeling of dread sinking in my stomach. That box was pretty small.

"You have to read the card and find out," was his innocent reply.

I drew a tight breath. He wasn't making this easy. "Austen, I don't think..."

"Aren't you even going to read the card?" He slapped a hand to his chest with a grin. "I'm hurt."

I stared at the pink envelope. Fine. I'd open it, smile, and say thank you, but no. "Okay." I broke the seal and slipped the card out. It was a cute picture of an Australian Shepherd dog with a heart cut-out in his mouth and big sad puppy-dog eyes. "Aw. That's sweet."

"You have to read the inside."

I flicked my eyes up. He looked confident. Pleased as punch. I breathed out slowly, and opened the card.

There was a poem, hand-written on the inside flap. I gaped at it for a second, frozen. If there was one thing that could make me hesitate, make me hope I had been wrong about Austen, this was it—what I'd been asking for, and what he'd been avoiding. I looked up at him again.

His face was bewildered. "Aren't you going to read it?"

I wetted my lips and caught my breath. Was this what I'd been needing to see? The clue to his inner thoughts I'd given up on finding?

An Angel for the Cowboy

She waits for forever
Stared at, but never seen
Desired by many, but accepted by none
Her heart is like mine—I would beg it for my own
But I cannot find the words to ask
A blessing I cannot give
Her friendship, a gift I must return
I come to her and tell her my secret
"I am in love with your friend."
She looks at me, and asks a question
"Are you the one who saved her?"
"No," I say, and my heart bleeds to hear
My own confession, I would die for her to unravel
"I did not save my angel. It is she who saved me.
And she who taught me to thirst."

She smiles and wishes me luck, but she does not understand.

And so, this cowboy waits. I dream under a blue-roan sky

Of my mountain angel, the one who slips the noose of my embrace.

I lowered the card, my heart pounding in my ears. He'd said it. Somehow, in that quaint, spare lilting style I'd come to know so well, Austen had known exactly how to shatter my resolve and make me want to take another chance on him.

But could I really do that? I had already set my heart on Dusty, on finding out if he could love me. Could I let go of that hope for what I already held in my hand?

"Austen," I whispered, "this is... I don't know what to say."

"Don't say anything yet. Open the box."

My fingers trembled, and I eyed that box with a fear I'd never known. It couldn't be *that*. Surely not. We'd only been dating a couple of months and never talked seriously about anything.

I'd never even said I loved him, and he only said that when he talked *about* me. He loved my hair. He loved the way I rode a horse. He loved how I helped my dad—that sort of thing.

No, this couldn't be what I thought it was. It was probably that pair of silver earrings I'd admired at the western store last week. That *had* to be it. Austen wouldn't dare...

But as the lid creaked open, my eyes were almost blinded by two sparkling carats, princess-cut and set in platinum.

"Huh-huh-wha... what?" I gulped. My voice didn't want to work, to say nothing for my brain. "*Why?*"

Austen had taken the moment to walk around the table and drop to one knee beside me. "*Why?* Because I'm crazy about you, and I hope you feel the same way. Jess Thompkins, will you make me the happiest man alive? Marry me."

I knew what I needed to say. I couldn't possibly accept. I didn't love him—at least not yet. That poem, though, set down in his own hand and speaking from his heart, at last, voicing all the things I needed to hear... I couldn't walk away, either. Not until I *knew*.

"Jess?"

I just stared at him, and a tear slipped down my cheek.

Chapter 21

Dusty

"**Y**ou have a visitor, little brother!"

I was out in the yearling pen, putting Daisy through a few herd work exercises and checking over the cows when Luke's voice called from the barn. I looked back and saw Dustin, the kid who'd gotten lost up at White Pines back at New Year's, walking carefully toward me and carrying a box.

"That'll do," I said to Daisy. "Here." She dropped and slunk under the fence to appear beside me like a little shaggy black apparition. You'd never know she was there unless you happened to look down.

"Hi, Dustin," I called. "What do you have there?"

He waited until he was close to me before he would answer, then he pushed the box toward me and stared at the ground. "It's for you."

"For me?" I smiled, hoping to encourage him to make eye contact, but it didn't work. When he did look up, his eyes settled on the yearlings behind me.

"I made it," he said.

"You made... Oh, wow." I reached into the box and pulled out a wood carving of a horse, about ten inches high and polished to a satin sheen. He'd made it out of some exotic wood with rich color contrasts and natural flaws and knots that highlighted its beauty. The horse itself was posed in a proud gallop, with only one foot on the ground. The rest of the sculpture's weight balanced on what looked like a wave of grass. The neck was slightly bent, the mane and tail whipped out behind, and nostrils flared to the wind.

"Dustin, I don't know what to say. You did this yourself?"

He nodded and pushed his glasses up his nose as he stared at Daisy. "To say thank you."

"Well, that's really nice, Dustin, but what are you thanking me for?"

He acted like he was trying to swallow, and I realized he was struggling with the words. That was something I could understand, so I just waited. "F-for finding me on the mountain wh-when I was cold."

"Aw, Dustin, you didn't have to do that. And anyway, it wasn't all me. Cody and Marshall were out there, too, and Kelli came up with her coat."

He nodded. "They have one too. But theirs are different."

"Ah," I breathed. "How are they different?"

His slim shoulders raised, and his voice tightened with impatience. "They just are. I felt the wood and heard what it should be. This one said it should be yours. It's Duchess."

I examined the carving again, admiring the precision he'd achieved. I thought the legs and the mane would be the hardest, but the detail wrought in that wood was stunning. And when I studied the horse's conformation and stance, I could see what he meant. It did resemble Duchess. "When did you meet Duchess?" I asked in awe.

"M-Miss Morgan showed me her picture. I asked her what your special horse looked like. She said everyone has one, and Duchess is yours."

"I guess she's right. This is incredible. I'm going to keep it on my office desk where I can look at it all the time. Thank you, Dustin." I tucked the box under my arm and put my hand out. Dustin didn't like hugs, but he would fist-bump.

He put his knuckles up and hesitantly rapped mine. "Okay, bye."

I chuckled a little. His mission accomplished, Dustin was ready to leave. "Well, wait, I'll walk you up. I want to put this somewhere safe."

He waited for me, but we didn't talk on the way back to the barn. He did grin at me briefly, then he walked off to his car without looking back. Inside the barn, I found his mom, Meg Truman, talking to Luke and Evan. She waved when I approached, and I took my hat off. "Ma'am. You have a nice kid there."

"Thank you, Dusty. He's been working on those for over a month for you guys."

I held up the carving so my brothers could admire it. "He's got a real gift. I hope he keeps at it."

Meg laughed. "It's getting him to stop that's the problem! You should see the legs on my table and chairs." She turned to smile at each of my brothers, then once more at me. "I really appreciate all of you. Thank you again."

"Our pleasure, ma'am," Evan said, tipping his hat. Luke and I echoed him as she left.

"Lemme see that thing," Luke said after she was gone. He whistled. "Looks like Duchess."

"That's because it is. I didn't know Dustin was into wood carving."

"Yeah, I guess he's pretty good at it. You takin' that to your office?"

"I thought I would."

Luke jerked his head in that direction. "I'll follow you up."

I kept glancing back at him as we walked up the stairs, confused and more than a little amused at the business-like way he was marching after me. He wouldn't make eye contact. "What's with you?" I asked.

"Nothin'." He shoved his hands in his coat pockets and kept climbing.

I sighed and opened the office door when we got to the top. I kept my desk reasonably tidy, so it wasn't hard to find a spot for the carving on the left side of the monitor. Right where my eyes would land on it. "Looks good, doesn't it? That was really thoughtful of him. Did his mom say where he learned to do that?"

Luke was pacing the floor and rubbing his jaw. "Dusty, there's somethin' you oughta know."

"I figured. You're acting weird."

He stopped. "I'm not being weird."

"Okay," I said, rolling my eyes. "Just keep pacing, then. Tell me when you're done."

He sighed out a long breath. "Bro, it's like this. Uh... why don't you sit down?"

"Oh, good grief. Do you think I'm going to faint or something?"

Luke shook his head and dropped into a chair, so I drew mine up. "Are you going to tell me what's got you so spooked?"

"Yeah. Um, so you know Meg took a second job after work, right?"

"I don't even know what her real job is."

"She's a second-grade teacher. She, uh... she used to be Emma's teacher."

"Oh." I closed my eyes briefly. Emma, Evan's daughter who'd died with her mother in that car wreck two years ago, taking the light of my oldest brother's life along with her. "I guess that explains how Evan knew her."

"Uh-huh. Anyway, I guess things have been rough for her and the kid, so she picked up some hours waitressing."

"Really? I'm sorry to hear that. Anything we can do to help?"

"No, and stop interrupting. This sucks enough without you trying to be all nice."

I spread my hands. "What's your deal? I was just asking—"

"Austen asked Jess to marry him," he blurted.

The floor of my office tilted crazily, then swam back the other way. I shook my head. "What?"

"Oh, you heard me!"

"I heard something so implausible and wild that it could only be gossip. I'm not listening." I couldn't listen to anything, even if I'd wanted to, with the blood pounding in my ears like that. It *couldn't* be true. It just couldn't! No one got engaged that fast. Well, except for Marshall and Kelli. But Jess was smarter. Wasn't she?

"It's not gossip. Meg's got more class than that. Just... don't do anything stupid, okay? And stop interrupting so I can tell you what I heard."

I drew a shaky breath and grabbed the edge of my chair. I needed something to hold on to. "Fine. Tell me."

"Okay. So she's working part-time at Beaufort's, right? Busiest night of the year for them, almost, so they call her in, and she goes because the tips are great on Valentine's Day."

"I got that."

"Well, so she's telling Evan and me about how crazy it was at work last night. One girl dropped a tray of wine glasses, somebody gave her a hundred dollar tip, the head cook had to go home early because he got sick all of a sudden, and one guy popped the question to his girlfriend."

I tightened my grip on the chair. "Happens every Valentine's Day, I'm sure. Lots of guys think it's a romantic time to propose."

"Yeah, but not all those guys are named Austen Conrad." He shrugged. "Evan asked Meg if she knew who it was—just making conversation. I 'bout fainted. Hey, are you okay, little brother?"

Fever prickles had broken out all over my face, and bile was surging into the back of my throat. "Yeah," I rasped. "Just fine."

He grabbed the garbage pail to set it in front of me. "If you're going to be sick, do it in there. I'm not cleaning up after you."

"I'm not going to be sick!" I blew out a few stale breaths and rocked forward, my elbows on my knees and my hands plowing through my hair as my head spun. Jess couldn't be engaged! She couldn't be...

"To be fair, Meg couldn't say if she accepted. She was across the room when it happened, but I guess everyone around the table started clapping and stuff when he got down on his knee. You know how it is."

I covered my face with both hands. "Of course, she said yes," I mumbled. For him to put her on the spot like that, he had to know how she'd answer. Even if she wasn't sure, she wouldn't be the first woman to get swept up in the romance and expectations of a proposal, with everyone watching and cheering for the happy couple. She would have said yes, even if she regretted it later.

Luke's hand clasped my shoulder in a gentle shake. "I'm sorry, little brother. Figured I'd better give you a warning so you wouldn't have to hear it around town."

I swallowed, but I didn't lift my head, and I didn't speak.

"Say, how about you and me go into the house and crack open something?"

My body sagged a little lower, and my hands were starting to feel wet. "Just go, Luke. I need... just go."

I heard him sigh, and he patted me on the shoulder again. Then the door clicked, and I was alone.

I was used to being alone.

Jess

"I didn't give him an answer. I didn't even try on the ring. I said I needed to think about it."

My dad's balding head bobbed through the frame of the hotrod, and his ratcheting socket wrench clicked a few times. "What do you need to think about?"

I rocked back on my heels, squatting beside the front tire. "Everything, I guess."

"Do you love him?"

"How can you love someone in such a short time?"

The ratchet twisted and clicked some more, and then he stuck it out under the frame for me to take. "Sounds like there's your answer. Can you hand me the 5/8, please?"

I moved over to the tool box and switched wrenches, then returned with the new one for him. "It's not that simple."

"Tell me what's not simple about it. A guy asks you to marry him, but you don't love him, so it seems pretty clear."

"Yes, but..." I gestured helplessly. "I wonder if I *could* love him."

Dad snorted from under the car. "If you could, you'd already know."

"I'm not so sure. I feel like Austen's the kind of guy you need to take your time with, peeling back all the layers. I see flashes of brilliance in him, things I really admire and could adore. Just... not all the time." I grabbed another wrench from the toolbox and tapped it idly against my palm. Dad would want this one next when he put the skid plate back on.

"Well, that sounds fine, then. If you love him twenty-five percent of the time, that should be good enough."

I rolled my eyes. "Come on, Dad, be serious."

He rolled out from under the car. "I am serious. If you have to talk yourself into caring for this guy, he's not the one."

I gazed steadily into my dad's eyes, reading the intensity of his love for me in every dear nook and crag of his face. "I just don't want to throw something away without being sure," I whispered.

He sighed and sat up off his creeper. "Pass me my soda, will you?"

I reached for the glass bottle of Coke sitting on the toolbox. Dad liked having the vintage pop bottles out here in the garage, maybe because it felt old-fashioned and nostalgic to him. It was the only time he even drank pop. He tipped it back for a long, refreshing swallow, then gasped in satisfaction. "That's good. I like a cold Coke when I'm working."

I tightened my lips and nodded. "I know."

"Reminds me of when I was a kid. My dad would take me to town and give me a quarter, and we'd watch the high school football team practicing. Made me love football." His gaze grew unfocused, and he took another swallow. "Made me love a cold Coke, too."

I huffed a little laugh. "I suppose it would."

Dad set his bottle down. "But it wasn't really football and Coke that I loved. I loved spending time with my dad. The rest was just the association. I still think of him when I pop a bottle top."

I folded up my knees and rested my chin on them. "Kind of like I'll never work on a car without thinking of you."

He chuckled and caressed my cheek with his blackened fingers, probably leaving a dark smear. I didn't even care. He was the reason I'd never object to the smell of engine grease and automotive paint—because the first man I ever loved smelled like them all the time. "You know, honey, I wonder if it's really something *about* Austen that just reminds you of what you're truly looking for. It's not actually him, is it?"

"I don't know."

He tilted his head and gave me that long look that had always made me fess up to my crimes when I was little.

I sniffed and slowly shook my head. "I don't think so."

Dad's chin puckered in one of his gentle half-smiles. "So, what is it? What about him makes you want to see if there's more?"

I clamped my upper lip between my teeth and toyed with the wrench in my hand. "I like it when he opens up and shows me what's underneath. I just wish he would do it more. It's like he's wearing a mask all the time." I wrinkled my brow and stared at the wrench like it was a key to unlock my thoughts. "No, that's not quite it. It's more like he's two different people."

Dad climbed up off his creeper with a grunt for his creaking joints. "Sounds like he needs medication, not a girlfriend."

"Not like that," I giggled. "In person, he's so... I don't know. Full of himself. Cocky. I'd have never given him the time of day if I hadn't had a chance to see the other side of him."

"And that is?"

I shrugged, still looking down. "I like the sensitive man I see once in a while, the one who can make a sunrise sound like a new world and make me feel the cold from a winter's morning with just a few words."

"And why does that appeal to you?"

"I guess..." I frowned at the floor. "I like how he notices things. Little details others miss or gloss over, but to him, even the things that don't seem important to most people are worth lingering over. He's not wrapped up in the loud blaring things, the flashy things."

I flipped the wrench through my fingers, twirling it like a pencil up and down each one. "When he's like that," I murmured softly, "I feel like he really sees who I am. Not just... what everyone else notices."

Dad nodded carefully, leaning on his work bench. "And when do you see this?"

"Well... not often enough."

He sighed and unzipped his work coveralls. "I think you know what you need to do, honey. You can't force an engine to start if you've only got half the parts. Come on, let's call it a night. I'm hungry."

A weight shifted somewhere in my chest, and I felt like I could draw a fresh breath for the first time in weeks. Dad was right—I did know what I had to do. It wouldn't make it any easier, but I'd know it was right. I didn't need to ask for more time to think about it. I'd end things, clean and decisively, and then, I could move on.

"Okay. That's it, then," I said with a nod. I was even able to smile about it.

"Good. I'm glad that's settled." Dad kicked out of his coveralls and tossed them over the hook. "I didn't like him much anyway."

"Oh, come on, Dad," I teased. "You hardly spent any time around him."

"I spent enough. He doesn't know how to work. Maybe I'm old-fashioned, but that makes him a dud in my book." He headed for the door into the house, and I trailed behind.

"And how would you know that?"

Dad turned around with a smug grin. "You don't think I was just asking him to keep me company out here, do you? The guy didn't even know how to set a ladder or put the socket on a wrench."

"There are other kinds of work, you know."

He winked. "But there's only one kind of common sense. If you're looking for some of that, maybe start a little closer to home."

I crossed my arms and eyed him suspiciously. "And where is that?"

My dad's mouth tugged sideways, and he chucked a thumb over his shoulder. "On up the road a ways. Quarter mile past the highway sign, take a right…"

My heart plunged into my feet, and my eyes widened. Had he guessed my little cowboy crush? I'd never told anyone! "W-Walker Ranch? I-I already said I wouldn't date Luke again," I stammered. "Wh…"

"I wasn't talking about Luke." Dad held the door for me and lumbered into the house, rubbing his hands and shivering when the warm air hit us. "Want spaghetti tonight? I'm in the mood for something hearty."

"Wait, wait a second." I ducked in front of him and stared him down. "Do you mean Dusty?"

"Yeah, you didn't know?"

"No, I didn't know! Dusty?"

"Who else would it be? I guess there's Evan, but he's not the one who comes around randomly asking me if I need a hand with stuff."

A shiver went down my spine. "Dusty does that?"

"A couple of times. Not for a while, though. I told you he helped me with the shocks on the hotrod. Also stopped by the shop, and he still texts me once in a while. Are you going to get out of my way so I can get to the pantry?"

"I thought you said it was Blake who helped you!"

Dad's face went blank for a second, then broke into a chortle. "I guess I didn't name him, did I? Well, you had your head full of this Austen character, so..."

"And you didn't say anything? Dad! It's been right in front of my face all along!"

He stepped around me to grab the stock pot and carried it to the sink. "What has?"

"Dusty Walker! My lands, I've been blind!"

Dad turned the faucet on and set the pot under it to fill, then he turned around. "Does that mean you'll give the poor guy a chance?"

All I could do was laugh. I swept forward, patting my sweet father's cheeks and kissing him on the forehead. "No, I'll be the one asking him to give *me* a chance! What a fool I've been!" I slapped my own face in sheer awe.

"So, you like him?"

I had to press both hands to my chest to keep my heart from flying away. It felt like it was spinning a hundred different directions. "I think... yes, I do! I mean, I don't know if he's everything yet, but..." I stopped, my breath heaving and a kaleidoscope of ideas exploding in my brain. "I think he could be. Yes, yes, I like him. A lot!"

"Good. Me too. Now, let's get dinner on, so you can tend to your love life on a full stomach."

Chapter 22

Dusty

We had a full house that night for dinner. Cody and Marshall had heard rumors of Meryl's chuck stew, and Dad talked her into an encore. It was the first time we'd had both of them back with their wives around the table and Meryl sitting beside my dad. I'd forgotten the table would stretch out that far, but it did, with a little room to spare. The last time we'd had all the leaves in it was a couple of years ago, for Emma's seventh birthday party. Did Evan remember that? He was pretty quiet this evening. I sat beside him, and we mostly ate our meal in silence. But we were the only ones.

The house was full of laughter and joy, female voices chorusing with ours for the first time in years. I didn't have an appetite, but I couldn't help admiring how Cody and Morgan held hands under the table and kept smiling at each other or how Marshall and Kelli teased each other until they were laughing. And the way Meryl had slid her chair close to my dad's and was just leaning against his shoulder, enjoying the company with a smile of perfect peace. They were the lucky ones, the few who found someone to hold through life. And I couldn't watch anymore—not tonight, not with my own failure so raw.

I pushed up from the table and asked Evan for his plate. "I'll start washing up. Anyone else done?"

Cody held up a hand. "Oh, hold on, Dusty. I had something to ask everyone."

I dropped slowly into my seat again. Was he going to tell us that he and Morgan were starting a family? Marshall had said something about that. Privately, I hoped they were. Cody would be a terrific dad. But that wasn't what he announced.

"There's a schooling show down in Paso Robles this weekend. I know it's short notice, but I want to take Maserati and a couple of the new three-year-olds down."

"Kind of early, isn't it?" Evan asked. "Show season doesn't start 'til April."

"I know, but Maserati's feeling stale. I have a theory that she's a competition queen, and she'll sharpen up when we get down there. Plus, I'd really like to just haul a couple of the younger horses out, get them some exposure. I have one colt that's a freak of nature, he's so talented, but he's a little on the nervous side, and he needs some experience."

Dad nodded. "Does that mean you're leaving in the morning?"

"Crack of dawn." His gaze slipped to Morgan. "And remember Emily Carson, the girl you hired when Brandon got hurt? I've had her loping some horses for me lately to warm them up, and she's good. Great feel and timing on those colts, and she's eager for an opportunity. I could use a solid assistant, and Morgan has to work."

"I don't like that," Marshall said, crossing his arms. "You're straight as an arrow, Cody, but you gotta think about appearances. You can't take a nineteen-year-old girl down to California, just you and her. That's no good."

"That's why I was hoping someone else could come with me. We'll put Emily up in a hotel, and we can batch it in the trailer. Anyone?"

Everyone looked around at each other, and then Marshall piped up. "I'll go."

"You certainly will not," Kelli objected. "You can barely push a wheelbarrow, and the last time you sat in a car for more than twenty minutes, I had to baby you for the rest of the evening."

Marshall turned red and the rest of us snickered. "Did not," he groused. "Who says I wasn't putting you on?"

"Well, I guess you just can't go out and play with Cody now, can you?" she teased as she kissed him. Luke and Cody hooted and catcalled them, but they were newlyweds. They didn't care about anything but each other, and the louder the guys got, the harder Kelli kissed my brother and the tighter he held on.

That was all I could handle. "I'll go," I said above the din.

The table fell silent. All eyes turned to me, and my stomach tensed. I didn't want to explain. Hopefully, they'd just accept the offer and move on. My gaze wandered the table and locked on Luke, who gave a tiny nod. I let go the breath I was holding.

"Sounds good, Dusty," Cody agreed. "I sorta jumped the gun a little and loaded the trailer already. All the horses still have valid six-month Coggins paperwork, and Emily is packed to go. Nothing left to do but roll out in the morning. I was thinking of being on the road by four."

Four. Which meant I'd have to be up a good hour and a half earlier to muck a few stalls and load the horses. That was even a little earlier than I usually got up. I wouldn't have time to do anything else in the morning. Or talk to anyone.

Perfect.

"How long will you be gone?" Luke was wandering around my room, poking into things, opening drawers, and making a pest of himself.

I tossed a stack of folded shirts into my suitcase. "It's only a one-day show, but Cody said he hooked up with a friend of his down there for some extra cow practice on Sunday and Monday. Sounds like I'll be home Wednesday night."

"So, almost a week." Luke flicked on my desk light. Then turned it off. And back on again.

"Stop that, will you?" I coiled up my favorite belt and tucked it beside the shirts. "We could start seeing calves anytime now. I might be leaving you in a bad spot."

"Nah. Still a little early." Luke reached above my desk to my old guitar, the one I hadn't touched in so long I almost forgot I had it, though it stared me in the face every night. With a metallic "ting," he sent the strings ringing off-key.

"We saw a few early ones last year, and this has been our second easy winter in a row. It wouldn't surprise me if some of them started going sooner rather than later."

Luke tapped the guitar strings one more time. "Well, they ain't started yet, and I haven't seen any of 'em bagging up. Besides, Evan, Dad, and I can handle them until you get back."

"Well, I hope they hold off. Could you hand me that pile of jeans?"

"They will." He passed them across my bed, then started fiddling with the pens on my desk. "Need me to do anything particular while you're gone?"

I straightened and rolled my neck. "I guess you could work Daisy and Duke. They'll get bored and start chewing everyone's boots if they don't have a job."

"Got it. Anything else?" Luke slid some stuff around on my desk, and I looked over just in time to see his hand hovering over my journal.

"Wait, don't—"

I guess even Luke has certain standards because he pushed it aside before I could finish getting the words out. In the process, he accidentally knocked my pen jar over, scattering them all over my desk and the floor. He squatted down to pick them up.

"Oh, come on. Can you stop touching stuff?"

"Sorry. What were you going to say?"

"I don't know, maybe lope Duchess around, keep her exercised. Just don't try to head on her and mess up my horse."

"That's my horse."

"Yeah, yeah." I reached up into the top of my closet for a few lighter-weight neck cloths. If I was going to California for a few days, I might as well clean up a bit and shed a few of the winter layers I'd been bundling in lately. Maybe I'd bring my new silverbelly hat, too—the one I'd bought in Fort Worth last fall. It would be cooler than the dark brown one I wore every day.

"Anything else?"

"I can't think of anything," I mumbled absently as I counted out my neck cloths. "I'd have you do payroll and bills, but you'd get it all messed up. Marshall can handle that."

"Huh." Luke scratched his jaw. "Anything else?"

"Good grief, what am I supposed to say? Why do you keep asking?"

Luke shrugged and stuffed his hands in his jeans pockets. Finally, he was keeping them off my things. "Just wondered if maybe you wanted me to talk to somebody. You know. Find stuff out."

"Oh," I sighed. I turned back to my suitcase and tossed in my socks, then slapped it closed to zip it. "There won't be anything to find out."

"Suppose there is? You don't know anything, 'cept he asked."

"I know enough." I set the suitcase beside the door, where I could grab it in the morning without thinking. "I'm tired, Luke."

He nodded. "Fine, then. I'll let you hit the hay. You've got an early start tomorrow."

"No, that's not what I meant." I dropped onto the mattress and pressed my hands on my knees. "I'm tired of hoping something will change, then it never does. I can't keep doing it."

Luke strode a little closer and leaned against my closet door. "Don't talk like that. You just need a little shut-eye."

"It's more than that." I bowed my head and raked my fingers through my hair. "I'm tired of losing all the time."

"What, losing? You and me are reigning points leaders on the jack-pot circuit these two years running!"

I sat up and gave him a deadpan look.

"Well, I was just sayin'." He shifted restlessly against the closet door, then paced over to plunk down beside me on the bed. "You never even tried any other women. When's the last time you went on a date? High school?"

"That's not true. I took Cassidy White out last year."

"That was year before last, and only 'cause I was seeing her sister, and I set you up."

"I still took her out, and when I asked to take her to the Fourth of July festival, she said no. So, there you are."

"You weren't exactly a ball of fire. She told her sister you hardly said ten words to her all night."

I shrugged. "We were watching a movie."

"Naw, I know what it is. You've been mooning over Jess Thompkins for so long you never even gave anyone else a chance. How do you know you wouldn't win yourself a girl? You haven't tried."

I swallowed the knot in my throat and folded my hands. "I'm not out to just have fun with any random girl. Jess is the only one I've ever wanted."

"And how many times have you asked her out?"

I lifted my eyes to his. "Almost one."

"See, now, there's your problem. You don't have bad luck. You just ain't got any try."

"You're not exactly helping right now. Isn't there someone else you can harass?"

"I harass because I care," he pledged with his right hand over his heart. "Look, what you need is—" He broke off when my phone dinged that a text had arrived.

I reached for it with an apologetic look. "Sorry. It's probably Cody about tomorrow." Not that I didn't look forward to hearing Luke's lecture, but... I didn't look forward to hearing Luke's lecture. I picked up my phone, and heat rushed to my face as I read the message. It was from Austen Conrad, and... my fingers clenched the phone so hard I was surprised I didn't break it.

"Dude, what happened? Did someone get in a wreck? Are the cattle out?"

I chucked my phone across the bedspread and got up. "Oh, nothing. Just the biggest blow-hard this side of the Rockies, texting to gloat about how wonderful his life is."

"Lemme see." Luke sprawled across the bed to grab my phone, and his eyes widened as he read it aloud. "'Hey, Dusty, something big just came up. Love to talk to you about it. Hope there's no hard feelings, really need your help with something.' What the hootin' blazes is this crap? Does this guy always talk like this?"

"Pretty much. Always when he wants something."

"Waaalll," Luke drawled, rubbing his jaw as he read the message again. "I know where I'd tell him to stick it, but you've got better manners than I do."

"Give me that." I scanned the text one more time. "I know what he wants. I'm sure of it. He wants me to help him figure out wedding or honeymoon stuff, and I'd rather tangle with a nest of rattlers wearing nothing but a Speedo."

"Perfect. Tell him that."

I squinted at the phone, then up at Luke. "Well, okay. I'll tidy it up a bit, but..."

"No, really. I dare you. Type that exactly, let him fester a while. Then you can boogie out of town for a few days, and he can't do a dratted thing about it."

I cracked half a grin. "You're a terrible influence."

"Thanks for noticing."

I laughed for the first time all day, but I typed it just like he said. And it felt amazing. My words popped up on the screen, and I drank in a fresh breath of air with a strange sense of satisfaction. "I've never told anyone off in my life, you know that?"

"It's about time, too. Now, shut that thing off and go hit the hay before he can sucker you into a whine fest. He can stew about it till morning."

I shrugged and shut the phone off, then tossed it on my desk. "He'll be pissed. Maybe I should just leave that thing here all week!"

"You've had worse ideas. I got Cody's number if I need you."

"Well, I... really?" I frowned. Could I survive a week without my electronic leash? It would be handy for getting in touch with Cody at the show grounds, but he left the ringer off half the time anyway. And I'd been scrolling on social media way too much lately. The last thing I wanted to come across was Jess posting engagement pictures. I shuddered. I could definitely do without that.

I'd take my journal instead of my phone. It would be good for me to get some things out on paper, spend some quiet non-digital time alone, and refresh my soul. Maybe even throw in my guitar and see if I could remember the chords. The more I thought about it, the more the plan appealed to me.

"You know, that's not a half-bad idea. In fact, it could be just what I need."

Luke slugged me in the shoulder. "That's the spirit, little brother. You go down to California and sow some wild oats. Or tame ones, whatever."

I rolled my eyes and shook my head. "Not exactly what I had in mind."

"Doesn't matter. Just come back here ready to rope like the devil and dance all night with the prettiest girls in seven counties. You go have yourself a nice break and leave the rest to me. I'll get it all hooked up, ya hear?"

I gave my brother a bear hug and pounded my fist on his back. "Right. Thanks, Luke. See you on Wednesday."

Jess

I hate breaking up with someone.

Relationships should last. There should be permanence and dependability in your bond with another person, and shame on you if you're the one who ends it. Yet, here I was, doing that very thing once again.

But hopefully, for the last time ever.

"You're serious?" Austen's face was gray; this was about the third time he'd asked that question.

"I'm really sorry, Austen," I apologized. Again. "You're a terrific guy, and I care a great deal for you. I just don't think we should try to force something that's not right."

"Not right? What's not right about us? We're amazing together!"

I let out a long sigh. "We had a lot of fun, but we aren't very much alike. We want different things in life."

"I didn't think so. We barely gave it a shot, and now you want to call it quits?"

"You were ready to make it forever, so I wouldn't call that 'barely giving it a shot.'"

"Jess, please, let's be reasonable for a minute." He put a hand to his mouth, fisted it, and exhaled sharply. He was blinking fast—were those tears? No, his eyes were dry. "I rushed you, didn't I? It was too soon. Let's just forget the proposal! I'll hold on to the ring, and we give it some time, maybe six months, and—"

"Austen, it's no good," I interrupted. "Time isn't going to change this."

"Time changes everything, angel. Why won't you at least try?"

"Because..." I floundered for the words. All I had was a vague feeling, something I'd never voiced, but for some reason, my dad's words came back to me, and they were perfect. "Dating isn't a recreational sport."

"What is that supposed to mean?"

"It means that I'm not in it for the entertainment. I'm looking for something that will last, and if it can't, I won't risk my heart or my future on it. I'm sorry, Austen."

Austen's shoulders drooped, and he sagged against the door frame. "I suppose there's no use in asking you to come in, talk it over?"

I shook my head.

He turned, so his profile faced me, his feet scuffling on the rug in the entryway. "Is there someone else?"

Every guy I've ever broken up with asked me that question. Always, I could confidently and truthfully say no. But not this time.

When no words came, Austen just laughed and shook his head. "Dusty, Dusty. You quiet, sneaky piece of work, you."

My mouth ran dry. "Hang on, I didn't say—"

"You didn't have to. I saw you watching him when you were together. He knew exactly what he was doing, pretending to be friends with me so he could get close to you. And look how well it worked."

I narrowed my eyes. "That's a pretty rotten thing to say."

Austen's head swung around to look at me. "The truth hurts. I ask the guy for some advice, trust him to be a friend, and he stabs me in the back."

I shook my head. "You don't know Dusty very well, then."

"Maybe it's you who doesn't know him well. He'll sucker you, seeming like the nice, straight-up honest guy, but watch out." He straightened and reached for the door handle. "Don't say I didn't warn you. And don't take too long about changing your mind because I won't wait forever, angel."

Then the door closed.

That was the first time I'd had a door slammed in my face. I'd been met with tears—yes, tears—anger, denial, and even casual acceptance. But this was the first time anyone had actually been rude.

I stood on that porch for about ten more seconds, my mind tumbling with the unjustness of Austen's accusations about Dusty. How dare he claim the nicest guy in town was a fraud and a disloyal friend? Didn't Austen even know who he was talking about? The Walker brothers probably had their picture in the dictionary under the word "Trustworthy"! I wanted to pound on that door and tell him off for saying such terrible things about a great guy.

But what was I thinking? I was free! Without another second's hesitation, I spun on my heel and sprinted for my car. *I was free!*

How had I never noticed that dark cloud that settled in my spirits when I started seeing Austen? Now that it was gone, even the stars in that night sky sparkled brighter. I felt more alive than I had in months, and I knew what to do next.

I thought about calling Dusty right then and there, while my car was still idling in Austen's driveway. Wouldn't that be poetic justice? But I didn't want Austen looking out his window and thinking I was having second thoughts. I wanted nothing more than to be away from there. So, I jammed my car in gear, glanced in the rearview, and enjoyed the spray of snow in my tail lights as I hit the gas.

Then, I spent the rest of the drive home trying to figure out what I would say to Dusty.

"So?" My dad looked up from a magazine when I blazed my triumphant way through the door. "Success?"

I held up my left hand, plain and bare. "Look!"

His face was bewildered. "I don't see anything."

"Exactly!" I bent to kiss him on the cheek and tugged off my coat. "He was upset, but I stood my ground, and it felt terrific. I'm going to try to call Dusty now. You don't think it's too late, do you?"

Dad chuckled and lifted his magazine again. "I think you could wake him at two in the morning, and he wouldn't complain."

I tossed my coat in the closet, and I was hurrying toward my bedroom, but something made me stop. "Dad, you're sure, right?"

His brow furrowed. "About what?"

"About Dusty, that he really..." I chewed my lip. "He really likes me? Because if he does, I missed it for I don't know how long. He didn't exactly come out and confess it."

Dad grinned. "Well, seeing as how he admitted it to me when he gave me that note, I'd say yes, I'm sure."

"Note? What note?"

"The one from when he stopped by the shop. I gave you that, didn't I? I know I did."

I felt like I'd just taken a bucket of cold water to the face. "There was a note in my box at work," I whispered.

"That's the one. I figured you'd take up with him right away, but then Austen came along. I felt bad for Dusty, but—"

"I thought that was from Austen!" I was dizzy. Queasy. I'd given my time and almost my heart to the wrong man! I didn't need to ask Dusty if we could see each other. I needed to ask him to forgive me for being so stupid!

"Hey, are you ok?"

My vision was suddenly flooded, and I tried to blink, to focus. Those were definitely tears. I gasped and tried to breathe. "Not even a little bit. It was him, Dad. All along, Dusty was the one I was looking for." I sniffed and tried to wipe my face, but the flood of regret was coming too fast, the weight of it too much. I crumpled to the couch. "I'm such a fool! He deserves so much more than I could ever give him."

"Hey." Dad got up and came to sit beside me, magazine still in hand. "It's not the end of the world, honey, and it's not too late. Go call that boy."

"Oh, I don't even know where to start! What must I have put him through? He had to watch me dating Austen, when the whole time, it was his note that started it all!"

"Well, he might not know that," Dad offered.

"He's not stupid. He was there in the restaurant when I went to find Austen! I looked right past him and he never said anything! Why wouldn't he at least try to clear up the misunderstanding?"

"Because he shouldn't have."

I craned my head to look at him, resting my hot, teary cheeks on my fist. "Why not? Why couldn't he say anything?"

"It's called respect. You made your choice, and he honored you enough to let you do it. Don't you ever confuse that for weakness because I'm sure it ripped his guts out. Would if it was me."

"And how am I supposed to make it up to him? How could he even trust me now?"

Dad shrugged. "One way to find out."

I sniffed. "Okay." I sucked in a few racking sobs and tried to dry my face with the heels of my hands. "Okay, I'm going to call him right now."

"You do that, sweetheart." Dad patted me on the back and eased to his feet. "I'm going to bed. Oh, before I forget—" He tossed the magazine he was reading onto the cushion beside me. "That came for you. A whole stack of 'em, actually."

I didn't care about any magazine just now, but I flicked some salt from my eye and turned the magazine around to read the title. "Oh, it's *Stockman's*. I heard they had some good articles for youth, and Audrey and I were starting to run out of ideas with the after-school kids. I wrote last week and asked if they'd send me some of their back issues. I'll check these later."

"Good idea. Night, honey."

I already had my phone out, scrolling through my contacts. "Good night, dad." But my dad wasn't the first man on my mind anymore.

There he was. The man who'd been patiently trying to capture my heart and who'd probably watched time and again as I slipped away. Dusty Walker, known only in my phone by the name of his ranch. The guy who sold hay and beef to the neighbors. The guy who gave his time and the sweat of his brow to help a bunch of kids, an injured cow, a friend in need, or even a jerk like Austen who just wanted to use him.

The guy who could steal my breath just by smiling at me.

First things first. I changed that contact name to "Dusty," the way it should have been all along. Dusty, my friend, the one I wanted to hold me for the rest of my life. I didn't even have a picture of him in my photos so I could update the profile, but I'd fix that the next time I saw him. Maybe I'd even get a selfie of us together. Assuming this phone call went the way I prayed it would.

The phone rang once, then went to voice mail.

I hung up out of reflex. I couldn't just leave a message for something like this! I needed to hear his voice, to pour out all my regrets and hope that he could give me one more chance. I drummed my fingers on the arm of the couch.

Should I try again? It was after ten, and those guys at the ranch kept early hours. But if my dad was right, Dusty would want me to call again. I owed it to him to reach out as soon as I possibly could, end whatever suffering I'd put him through.

He still didn't answer, but this time, I didn't hang up when the recorded greeting came on. I just listened to his voice, trying to imagine he was in that room with me. When did Dusty's voice become the one that soothed my raw nerves? I could feel the tension draining from my neck, the blood in my veins slowing down.

There could be no doubt about it. I was in love with Dusty Walker, and I'd never even held his hand. Never kissed him, never whispered into his ear, never felt his heart beating under my cheek. How much had I wasted looking in all the wrong places for the one who was in front of me all along?

When his greeting ended, and the messaging service beeped, I took a breath and made myself say something. He deserved at least that much. "Hello, Dusty, it's Jess. I was hoping to catch you, but I guess it's too late. I'll try again tomorrow, but I just wanted you to know how sorry I am. And... I miss seeing you. There's so much I want to say, but—"

"If you are satisfied with your message, please hang up, or press one now."

I closed my eyes and blew out a sigh of aggravation. Of course, the stupid machine *would* cut me off. But what else did I plan on saying? I punched the off button and clutched my phone like it was my only life line to Dusty. I'd try him again in the morning.

Chapter 23

Dusty

"Wanna ride turnback?"

I almost jumped out of my hide when Cody popped up behind me and tossed a horse's rein over my shoulder as I was cleaning a stall. "Holy smokes! Give a guy a warning, why don't you?"

"I did. Called you three times from the aisle. I thought you must be listening to music or something."

I pointed to my ears. "No earbuds, no phone, remember?"

"That's right, I forgot. 'Woolgathering,' as my wife likes to say?"

I set the pitchfork aside. "I guess."

"Oh, I know that look. Something's eating you inside out, and you're either dead to the world, or you're about to blow. Want to talk about it?"

"No."

"Fine. We need a turnback rider, and that colt needs a little seasoning. Do you mind?"

I shook my head and reeled the colt in by the rein. He was a handsome sorrel stud with four white socks and a blaze; a full brother to our champion stallion Five Iron. Cody thought this might be his Futurity horse this year, providing he could get the colt to settle into his job. That was what this trip was all about.

"Better check your cinch on him. He'll split out from under you," Cody called over his shoulder. "I'm going to look in on Emily in the practice pen."

I patted the colt's neck and slid my hand under the cinch. He dropped his head and twisted his neck as I adjusted the latigo, champing on the snaffle and shuffling his feet. Anxiety nearly poured out of him, but if he was anything like his famous brother, he'd outgrow that and learn to focus his energy once he discovered what this showing thing was all about. For now, though, he looked like he was about to vibrate out from under the saddle.

"You and me both, kid," I murmured as I put my foot in the stirrup. "You and me both."

Riding turnback is a lot harder than it looks. The task seems like it would be simple: sit in the corners of the pen when a rider goes into the herd to cut, and keep the cow in a safe area so it doesn't get out of control and the person working the herd can get his job done. A good turnback rider can set the exhibitor up for a solid run. A bad one can lose the class for them.

But the show was yesterday. Today was just about practice. It was a good thing, too, because I hadn't ridden a cutting horse in over a year. I was used to my big solid rope horses; all steam and power, but they only went one direction. These little cutters could twist out from under the saddle in the blink of an eye, and I always imagined the cartoons where the coyote didn't even start falling until he realized the ground wasn't there anymore. There was probably a metaphor for my life in there somewhere, but I didn't want to think about it too hard. I wiggled into a secure position in the saddle and held on.

Maserati was looking hot. Even stronger than last fall when she'd been crowned the Snaffle Bit Futurity champion. She was the fourth horse to come into the herd while I was working the corners, and I might have been biased, but she was the sharpest-looking thing to step in that pen. She had style, that mare—crouching so low I'm sure Cody's heels were dragging in the dirt, and all I could see of her legs were flashes of white polo wraps as she threw them from one side to the other. Cody had been right. She woke up down here in California, facing some fresh cows and new dirt. She was the type who craved a challenge.

My mind got swallowed up in nostalgia, watching her. I'd been busy yesterday when Cody showed her, and the last time I remembered seeing her work was down in Fort Worth. It was right after Morgan and Cody got engaged, and we were all gathered as a family, cheering together and enjoying that golden moment of victory. It was that evening, back in the hotel room, that I'd written *The Cowboy's Call*; my little ode to the way of life I loved, with all its hardships and triumphs as well as the simple, perfect moments of clarity that went along with it.

I'd been thinking of Jess as I fiddled with my pen between putting down lines. How something about her defined everything I was trying to capture, and how I ached just to touch it. I hadn't even slept that night, because Morgan had been bouncing wedding plan ideas off of me during the show. She was going to ask Jess to be one of her bridesmaids, and I would get to be her escort. Stupid me, I thought it was going to be my big chance. And then, Austen.

The colt jerked beneath me, ducking and diving to head off Cody's cow. It was only by sheer luck that I didn't lose my seat and topple unceremoniously into the dirt. At least the horse was paying attention, even if I wasn't. He trembled with excitement, his feet dancing a staccato as he tried to anticipate the cow's next move. When the black Angus gave up and lumbered away, I felt the colt settle and draw some air.

I leaned back to stroke his hip, praising him for a job well done, and he relaxed enough to play with the bit. His ears swiveled around, listening first to me, then to all the commotion happening in the herd. His eyes were still roving everywhere in eagerness, but he wasn't acting nervous anymore. He'd figured out what he had to do, and now, he was on. That was all this guy needed—time and a little confidence in himself, knowing he was doing what he was put on this earth to do.

If only assurance were so easy to come by for people.

Jess

"I don't understand it. His phone has been going to voice mail for three days."

Audrey's forehead dimpled in a frown. "You're sure you have the right number?"

"Yes, I'm sure. The greeting is his voice, and I've messaged him on there before. Could he be ghosting me?"

"I don't think Dusty would do that, would he? There isn't a mean bone in his body."

"That's my point. What if he's not interested anymore, and he's too embarrassed to tell me?"

"Please, Jess, be serious. How could he *not* be interested?"

"Well, I'm sure I was pretty horrible to him. I wouldn't blame him," I answered miserably.

Audrey shook her head and stretched across the table. We were at my house, going through the *Stockman's* magazines together in hopes that we would find our next brilliant idea for the after-school program. Mostly, it was just an excuse to get together with her. "I'm not buying it," she said flatly. "There's got to be another explanation. Did you ask Morgan on Thursday?"

"I didn't even see her, but what is she supposed to know?"

"Beats me, but I did get a text from her that Cody was going to be out of town this weekend, and she was looking for some barn helpers. I don't know who she thought *I'd* know. I'm surprised she didn't ask you."

I grabbed a fresh magazine, this one the December issue. "Where did Cody go?"

"Some show down in California. Hey, this looks good, doesn't it?" She flipped the magazine back and held up a recipe for corn chili. "I never even liked chili until I moved here."

"Mmm." Cody was gone to a show? Wasn't it too early in the season for that? I sighed, tapping my teeth with my pen.

"Don't do that. Bad for your enamel."

I snorted. "I don't give you a bad time for how you ride the clutch. You shouldn't even have a transmission left by now."

Audrey giggled and turned her magazine over. "Good, I hate that car anyway. Oh, this is cool. There's a reader submissions page in the back. Aw... this girl sent in a picture of her on her horse. Isn't she cute? She's like a peanut up there!"

"Yeah, cute," I agreed distractedly. "Look, if Cody went to a show, he wouldn't have gone alone, would he? He always used to take Blake with him, but I saw Blake's truck at the coffee shop this morning."

"Morgan said he took some assistant. One of her stall cleaners, actually, which is why she needed more help."

"Who was it?"

"Emily, the one with the long blonde hair."

"Really?" That surprised me. Emily was sweet and hard-working, and very, very pretty. Just the kind of girl to turn a cowboy's head without even trying.

"Yeah, I guess she worked for the Walkers for a little while, then Morgan hired her, and she's been riding some with Cody."

"That's... that's great for her." I frowned skeptically. Morgan must have trusted her husband, much more than most women I knew, to send him off on a week-long trip with a beautiful, single young girl. But then I thought of something. "Cody wouldn't take a girl down there by himself. He's too married for that."

"Well, maybe there's your answer. Dusty might have gone with them. Morgan didn't say one way or the other."

I chewed my lower lip and flipped through the magazine. Yes, that made some sense, but it still didn't solve the mystery of why Dusty wasn't answering his phone. Unless it had something to do with Emily—another introverted blonde, just like me.

How many times did a guy have to be rejected and ignored before he finally moved on? If he had any sense, it would only take once, and poor Dusty had hung on a lot longer than that. I didn't even deserve him by this point, and no one could blame him at all if he'd given up on wishy-washy Jess Thompkins, the girl who never even knew he was alive until it was too late. I closed my eyes and buried my face in my hand. It made me sick to even think about it.

"Why don't you just ask Morgan? She'd know something, wouldn't she?"

"If Morgan knew what I needed to know, she'd have already told me. What I need..." I made a face and flipped pages of the magazine just to keep my fingers busy. "I might need to talk to Luke. He and Dusty are pretty close."

Audrey wrinkled her nose. "Isn't that the bull rider brother?"

"Used to be. He can be a little rough around the edges, but he's alright."

"He's a lunatic. I heard he used to pop the caps off fire hydrants and flood the school parking lot."

"And the grocery store, too. Shot the lights out at the football stadium once, but as far as I know, he never got in trouble for that because they were going to put new ones up anyway."

"And you asked why I'm not dating any cowboys. After stories like that? No way."

"Oh, those are just the tame stories. Sometime I'll have to tell you how he broke his knee."

"No, thanks. Way too much crazy for me."

I rested my chin on my hand. "You know, I think I'll call him. He would know something about Dusty. I just hope he'll talk to me."

"He'll probably think you're after *him*."

"We already settled that. Luke and I could never date, but..." I couldn't help smiling wistfully. "I think he'd be an awesome brother."

"So call him, then, and tell me how it turns out." Audrey turned over her wrist to glance at her watch. "Okay, I'd better go. Lizzy was with her dad this weekend, and he was going to drop her off at five."

I nodded absently as she gathered up her purse and pulled her coat on. "See you on Tuesday."

Audrey tied the belt of her coat with a yank, then smiled tenderly and put her arm around my shoulders. "It's going to be fine, Jess. Call me when you find out what's going on."

I grabbed her hand as she withdrew. "Thanks, Audrey. Catch you later."

Should I call Luke? If Dusty was avoiding me, Luke would do the same, just to support his brother. But I couldn't keep doing this. Something had to change. I set my phone on top of the magazine and huffed out a sigh. "Okay. Here goes nothing."

I had his contact pulled up, but my fingers ran cold. I made a fist, willing the nerves in my hand to work, and my eyes left my phone for just long enough to notice something on the magazine behind it. Curious, I blinked and slid my phone aside.

It was a poem. *The* poem, to be precise. The one that had appeared in my pocket that day and kicked off this whole crazy circus to begin with. *My* poem, the one that had spoken to me on a level that resonated with my soul. And here it was, printed in a magazine for everyone to see. *The Cowboy's Call*, written by... I squinted. Who in the world was Wyatt Chandler?

Now, I was really confused.

Dusty

"So, you do remember how to play that thing. I thought it was just for show."

I was crouched on the little sofa that doubled as a fold-out bed in the front of the horse trailer, picking out a few rusty chords on my guitar when Cody opened the door. I set the guitar aside. "I wouldn't call it playing. More like making noise."

He closed the door and hung up his hat. "Didn't sound too bad. Hungry? We still have those frozen burritos in the fridge."

"I already microwaved one. Horses all okay for the night?"

"Yeah." He blew out a weary sigh, untied his neck cloth, and then started unsnapping the cuffs of his shirt sleeves. "It feels weird to be done by a decent time in the evening on one of these trips. Usually, I'm up most of the night waiting for my turn in the practice pen. I'm not sure what to do with myself."

"Go call your wife. I'm sure she's waiting to hear from you."

"What do you think I just did? Do you want to check in with the ranch? Luke's probably going stir crazy without you around to bug." He tugged his phone out of his pocket and offered it to me.

I considered for a moment, then shook my head. "He'll live another two days. It's probably constructive for him to learn a bit of patience. Either that, or he's just moved on to irritating Evan."

Cody laughed as he sat beside me and pulled his boots off. "That won't get him very far. Hey, I've been meaning to ask you about Evan. How's he doing, really?"

"Who knows. He never says anything."

Cody framed his hands on his knees and sighed. "He was always that way when we were younger, but he came out of his shell with Anne and Emma. Now, he's turned the lights off and closed the drapes. Just... shuttered."

I nodded. "Basically, yeah. I don't know if we'll ever see that side of him again."

"Well, here's hoping. Blake found happiness again. It's not impossible." He got up, tugged his arms out of his sleeves, and then pulled a t-shirt.

I grunted softly. "Nothing's impossible." How I wished I could believe that!

"See? I mean, if a screw-up like me can find an amazing woman like Morgan, nothing is too big."

I swallowed. Cody was a lucky man. "How is Morgan, by the way?" Hopefully, he'd change the subject and talk about them—their plans for the property, the therapy program, the show horses, maybe even a family. It sounded better to my ears than my own bleak thoughts.

"She's fine. Busy. I guess someone approached her about hosting a kids' camp this summer. Can you believe that? We haven't even finished building the place yet!"

"Is she interested?"

"Of course, but she isn't sure if she's going to have enough volunteers. A week-long, overnight camp is another level. She was going to call Kelli and Audrey and Jess after she got off the phone with me and see what they all thought."

Something inside me shivered, and I kept my eyes down. "Jess is still volunteering there?"

"Yeah, why wouldn't she be?" Cody hopped up on the bunk, and a minute later, his jeans went flying, then his socks.

"I don't know. I guess I figured she'd have found better things to do by now. Or her boyfriend would have found better things for her to do."

Cody jumped back down, wearing a pair of baggy sweatpants, and set a fist on his hip. "And now the truth comes out. I've been trying to put it together. Jess Thompkins, huh?"

I shook my head and refused to look up. "It doesn't matter."

"Of course, it matters. How long has this been eating you? Six months?"

I lifted one shoulder. "Eleven years. No... twelve."

"Holy Moses! Twelve *years?* Boy, I thought Marshall was bad, but at least he and Kelli tried dating back in high school. I don't remember you and Jess ever going out."

"That's because I never got around to asking her. Look, before you say it, it's probably nothing Luke hasn't already berated me with."

Cody puckered his mouth. "Luke knows? How is it the entire country hasn't heard by now?"

"I know where he sleeps."

Cody's face melted slowly into a chuckle. "Well, I'll be. You've been in love with the Prom Queen since you were a Freshman—"

"Eighth grade," I corrected.

"Eighth grade, sorry, and Luke can keep a secret. Wait till I tell Morgan. She'll faint."

"Please don't tell Morgan. Don't tell anyone. Nothing good can come of it at this point."

"Why's that? Because of Conrad?" Cody hissed and waved dismissively. "She's not serious about him."

A rebellious spark kicked in my chest, and I looked up. "What makes you say that?"

"Because I've seen them together. No chemistry whatsoever. Morgan and I figured it would last three months at best. The only thing we weren't sure of was who would break up first. My money's on her."

"Well, you're wrong there. He proposed on Valentine's Day."

Cody blinked, and his face grayed. He swept a hand over his mouth and lowered himself to a stool. "I hadn't heard that."

"I wish I hadn't."

Cody kicked the rug with his toe. "So, this is why you've been so gloomy. I'm sorry, Dusty. Really."

I leaned forward and folded my hands. "It's my fault. I never asked when I had the chance." My head hung, and I sucked in a long breath, trying not to shudder. "More than anything, I want her to be happy. I just... hoped it wouldn't be with him."

"I bet." Cody slumped and crossed his arms. "You think it's too late to say something to her?"

I snorted. "What do you think?"

"Yeah. Yeah, you're probably right." He shook his head. "Are you sure you don't want me to say something to Morgan? Maybe she could put a word in. I can't imagine Jess could be happy with Austen in the long run."

"Just let it go, Cody." I grabbed my blanket and stretched out on the couch. "Nothing more to do but live with it."

Jess

I feared for a minute that Luke wasn't going to answer his phone, just like Dusty hadn't been. On the fourth ring, however, he picked up. "Hello?"

"Hi, Luke, it's Jess." I flexed my fingers to rid them of the nervous ache and prayed that the most unpredictable Walker brother would cooperate and help me out.

"Yeah, I know. Says so on the caller ID."

"Right. So, I was wondering—"

"I can't get away for the game."

I squinted. "What game?"

"Taco Tuesday at the pub. Sports, peanuts on the floor. Remember, we said we'd catch another one sometime."

"Luke," I sighed, pinching the bridge of my nose. "Football's over for the season."

He was silent for a few seconds. "Hockey. I was talking about hockey."

"Uh-huh."

"I like hockey."

I thought about challenging him to tell me who his favorite team was, but with Luke involved in the equation, that would kick off a downward conversational spiral that would get me nowhere. "Fine," I agreed, rolling my eyes. "You like hockey. That's not why I was calling."

"I still can't get away if that's what you're asking. Knockin' on the door of calving season."

"It's not. I've been trying to reach Dusty, and he's not answering. I was hoping you could tell me—"

"Sorry, can't help you."

I pulled the phone away from my ear and stared at it. "What? Why?"

"Nope. It's the rules. Never rat out a brother."

"Oh, come on." I smacked my head back against the wall behind my bed. "I'm not asking you to rat anyone out or even do anything except tell me if he's okay."

"I guess he is. Haven't seen him all week."

I cut back a sigh of frustration. It was like pulling teeth! "Did he go to California with Cody?"

"And Emily. Yep."

I drummed my fingers. Why would Luke make a point of telling me that? A green, nauseated sensation washed through my stomach. A feeling I'd never been familiar with... *jealousy*. I'd never cared about anything enough to be jealous over it before, and now that I did, I hated it. The insecurity of not knowing was a hideous feeling—and it was exactly what I'd done to Dusty.

But I'd have to cry about that later. My best hope now was getting Luke to talk, and he didn't seem very inclined to do it. "What about Dusty's phone? Haven't you talked to him?"

"Nah, he left it here. Got tired of everyone buggin' him."

He probably got tired of *Luke* bugging him, I thought sourly. At least it explained why Dusty wasn't answering his phone. There was so much more I needed to know, though. "Well, can you tell me when they're going to be back?"

The phone sounded muffled like he'd covered the mouthpiece or dropped it. I thought I heard Evan's voice in the background, but mostly, I heard swooshing and static. "Luke?"

He came back, clearing his throat. "Yeah? What was that?"

"Dusty! When is he going to be back?"

"When he gets back."

"Luke! Please, I'm just asking a simple question! Why are you being so difficult?"

He didn't answer. I could imagine him sitting there, with the phone to his ear and an obstinate look on his face, just waiting me out until I exploded. Well, fine. If he was going to be that way, I'd have to get specific and ask yes or no questions. "Did they start driving home today?"

"No."

"Tomorrow?"

Luke hesitated. "Probably."

"'*Probably?*' Didn't they know their plans?"

"Ah, you know how those cutters are. Twitchy, obsessed bunch. Worse than ropers, if you ask me. If there's a cow, they gotta chase it, schedule be hanged. Cody's just doing his job. He'll head home when he's danged good and ready."

I rubbed my eyes. "Fine. Can you ask Dusty to call me when you see him? Or if you talk to Cody?"

"What for?"

"None of your business, Luke!" I snapped. I probably should have just told him, begged him to share what he knew of Dusty's heart, and pleaded with him to help me win the cowboy I loved. But I swear, Luke prided himself on being a pain in the rear when the mood struck him. He was tweaking my last nerve, and he knew it. He was probably loving every second of it.

"Whatever. I'll tell him when I get around to it." There was a buzzing of voices in the background and Luke muffled the phone again. "Crap. We got a cow down. Gotta go." And he hung up.

Chapter 24

Dusty

The morning sun cut low across the windshield as we rolled through Bakersfield. I was driving this first leg of our trip home, fueled by a full mug of drip coffee and some kind of egg biscuit from the gas station.

Cody was in the passenger's seat, scrolling through his phone feed, and Emily was crashed in the back seat. My eyes slipped to the rearview mirror to look at her—head smashed against the window, arms crossed over her chest, and her feet up on the seat beside her—dead to the world. I think it was the first time the kid had sat down for the whole trip.

She had a lot of potential, Cody said. He liked how dedicated she was. Level-headed, teachable, cheerful attitude, and never quit trying. With a little opportunity, a little luck, she'd make it as a top trainer someday, and Cody was proud that he could be a part of someone else's success. He saw greatness in her, just waiting for its time.

I saw almost a carbon copy of Jess.

She had the same shimmering golden hair, the same sky-lit blue eyes, the same warm smile and casual grace. In a few years, when she matured a little more, her beauty would be a match for Jess's. She had the same cool innocence, too—taking life too seriously and not always understanding when someone was ribbing her. And she was quiet, thoughtful like Jess. Emily and I worked well together because we operated on the same wavelength.

But not once had my heart even fluttered when I was around her.

It never even occurred to me that it could, until just now. But when I considered it, I started to wonder. Why had no other woman, not even the one in front of me who was so much like Jess, ever made me look twice? Who held on to his first teenage crush for his whole life without glancing around a time or two? Apparently, me.

I flexed my fingers on the wheel and frowned in thought. Shouldn't I have noticed anyone else? Take Emily, for one example. On the surface, she was everything I seemed to like. But she was only nineteen—too young for me. Maybe in a few years, that would be fine, but not now. And she worked for us, which meant hands-off, no matter what. Dad had set that rule in stone back when we were teenagers, and not once had any of us come close to violating it.

But those weren't the reasons Emily didn't light some flame in my breast. I flicked another glance at the mirror, then chewed on that for a while. What made a man give his heart to one woman for the rest of his life, even when others came along who were exactly his type? How was it so easy to hold his love's hand and never look back?

Because it was more than attraction. More than fitting a type, or a few good conversations. And maybe it was even more than her reciprocating the feeling because I'd been carrying this stupid torch all alone.

I couldn't define it. It was just a gut feeling I'd had the very first time I set eyes on Jess Thompkins, that we were meant to be something. It was like a seed planted deep in my being that I couldn't stop or control once it took root. And just like the words that had bottled up inside me until they finally found a weak seam to gush out of, my feelings for Jess only grew stronger, the more I tried to repress them. I was my own worst enemy, it seemed.

What was I supposed to do with all this feeling, now that she'd chosen someone else? The only thing I did know was that my love for Jess wouldn't just go away when she slid another man's ring onto her finger. No, just like the urges to write that I'd tried so long to deny, it would get worse. Eventually, it was going to overpower me.

Would I even survive the aftermath?

Jess

This was killing me.

I thought I'd pieced together the parts, fitted all the bits of the story into place, but the more I discovered, the more bewildered I was. The poem in my pocket, the letter at work—those *had* to have come from Dusty, not Austen. The handwriting was the same, the voice of the writer could only be his.

But what about that same poem, published in *Stockman's* under someone else's name? And even worse, after I found that one, I'd started digging through more magazines, and I'd found another—the one Austen had inscribed on that stupid card he gave me on Valentine's Day. Again, it was written by Wyatt Chandler.

I knew Dusty couldn't have had anything to do with that one. He wouldn't have helped Austen propose to me. Had they both just copied them from the magazine? What kind of a ridiculous series of coincidences could that be? Something had to be fake, a lie. And if that was true, what *was* real?

I knew who Dusty was when I was with him, and I loved that man. His was the kind of gentleness that is so often mistaken for weakness because he would rather harm himself than someone else. He would give to others while he did without. That was the sort of man I could love, honor, and cherish for the rest of my life. The rest didn't really even matter. I didn't need a man who could make me melt like caramel with his words. I just wanted Dusty, the faithful, strong one who'd been waiting for me all along.

But I also wanted—*needed*—the truth.

Luke was a dead end. I couldn't figure out why because he could be ornery when he felt like it, but he also liked to talk. And he wasn't talking to me. I must have offended him, but how? I was tempted to call Cody and beg him to put Dusty on, but the next morning, I had a better idea. I took off work, with my "boss's" blessing, and drove up to White Pines.

I found Morgan in the middle of a session for two of their clients; a married couple with mobility problems who liked to have their sessions together. Amber, the lead therapist, was working with the husband on Badger, and Morgan—quite predictably—was across the arena with Biz. They each had a volunteer handling the horses, too, as well as a couple of observers. It was a busy arena.

I lurked in the corner, not wanting to interrupt, but on one of the passes, the volunteer leading Biz looked my way. "Oh, hello, Jess!"

I hadn't even noticed that it was Meryl Justice at the horse's head. Like Morgan, I'd been in her 4-H club for most of my childhood. She held a special place of honor in my heart for all the long, cold practice nights and hot, sweaty Fairs she'd led us through. I uncrossed my arms and stepped over to the fence. "Hi, Meryl."

She waved and smiled, but she couldn't stop and talk in the middle of a session. I just leaned on the rail to watch. It was getting close to the top of the hour, so that should mean this session was almost over. I couldn't count on that, though, because Morgan was known for being a little too flexible with her schedule if she didn't have another appointment right behind this one.

Not this time, though. By just a few minutes after ten, the arena was empty, Morgan and Amber were escorting their clients to the reception area, and the horses were being led back to their stalls. I trailed behind, hoping to make myself useful.

I didn't have long to wait because Meryl passed me a brush. I got to work on the gelding's tawny coat while she bent down to pick his feet. "I thought you weren't on the schedule until this afternoon," she said.

"I'm not. I just wanted to talk to Morgan about something. So, does this mean you're officially retired from the bank now?"

Meryl grinned and reached into the grooming tote for another body brush. "It sure does. I can't twiddle my thumbs at home, so Morgan said she could put me to work whenever I wasn't busy. Originally, I was thinking I'd be up here every day, but plans change."

I tried to smile, but my heart wasn't in it. "Are you talking about Blake?"

She chuckled. "The old bushwhacker. We're a fine pair, aren't we? Too achey to work like we used to, but too restless to be left unsupervised. Don't tell anyone, but he suggested getting his private pilot's license the other day! I tried talking him out if it, but I'm not sure I was successful."

"Heaven help us all. There won't be a safe strip of blacktop in the county."

Meryl pointed her brush emphatically at me. "That's what I said! Then I threatened to send Sheriff Wyatt after him for traffic violations, but I think that only egged him on instead of discouraging him."

I smiled a little more. "Guess we know where Luke gets it."

"You got that right. But, you know..." She stood back to examine her work on Biz. "I see more of Marci in those boys than Blake. Most of them got his eyes, and Luke got that troublesome streak, but they all, even Luke, have that deep 'thinker' side of them that's all their mother." She sighed. "I sure miss her."

"I never really knew her. My mom did."

"Your mom was another one of my favorite people. We used to have a lot of fun together, the three of us." She shook her head, and I wasn't sure, but it looked like her eyes glistened more than usual. "I don't think a single fundraiser or community event went by without at least two of us raising Cain."

"More like holding it together. I remember no one could do anything without one of you guys managing things."

"They just didn't want to," she said tartly. "But we did have some wonderful years, even back to junior high school. I miss those days." She finished with a tight, teary smile. "I miss my friends."

Biz was finished, so I set my brush aside. "Most of my friends aren't even in town anymore. Morgan and Kelli, I guess, but we weren't that close back then. It's like I picked all the wrong ones to be friends with because I don't even miss them. We had nothing in common after high school."

Meryl gave me a sympathetic frown. "Sometimes it's like that. We pick people to be with based on proximity, but there's no real connection. And all the while, the real friends are just waiting for you to find them."

I pulled out a chair that was close to the wall and slumped into it. "It's not just friendships I've done that with. Meryl, I screwed up. Bad."

She tilted her head. "Want to tell me about it?"

How was I supposed to explain that? I didn't even know where to start. My mouth tried to work, but all that came out was, "Dusty."

Meryl's shoulders lifted in a deep breath of understanding. "Ah."

"I have no idea how long I've been overlooking him, but I do know that I'm the biggest idiot alive. How could I miss it?"

"I suppose because you were so busy letting all admirers come your way, you didn't take the time to pick the one *you* liked."

I stiffened. "You make me sound pretty shallow."

"Not shallow. Just oblivious. Even when you were just thirteen or fourteen, you'd have a herd of boys following you around the fairgrounds, and you never noticed them."

I lifted a shoulder. "I noticed. I just couldn't wrap my mind around it, so I ignored it, until I couldn't."

"And you never turned the tables. Tell me when you've ever found someone *you* cared about that didn't chase you down first?"

I swallowed. "Never, I guess. Not until now. I've taught myself to miss what might be the best thing in my life. And now, when I most want to see him and talk to him and ask if he could love me, I can't reach him. What if I missed it for too long?"

Meryl drew up a chair to ease herself down beside me. "Now, what would make you worry about that?"

I pinched my lips and blinked back the sting as my voice broke. "No one will put up with being ignored forever."

"I s'pose it won't make much difference if I remind you that Dusty's a Walker. They're a hard-nosed, pigheaded lot."

I choked on a sudden giggle and sniffed. "I can only hope he's that stubborn. But I have so many questions, things I'm confused about. I'm just not sure of anything anymore."

Meryl patted my knee and sighed. "Oh, Jess, I wouldn't fret. If Dusty was in love with you a week ago or a month ago, or ten years ago, he won't be put off by waitin' around. Gets it from both sides, that one does."

I looked over and managed a hopeful smile. "What do you mean by that?"

"Oh! The Walkers and the Chandlers, they go way back in this town. Ornery cusses. Did you know that Wyatt, Marci's dad, sat around and waited for ten years for his wife's father to give his blessing before he could marry her? And Blake's parents, now—"

"Wait, Meryl." I put up a hand, staring at the concrete under my boots as the connection burst through my brain. "Did you say Marci's father was named Wyatt Chandler?"

Meryl slowly puckered her lips and raised one brow. "I sure did. You've seen that name before, have you?"

I nodded.

"And not, I reckon, on a headstone down at the cemetery?"

"It was..." My voice cracked. "I-I saw it in a m-magazine. On a poem—a couple of poems—that I already knew from... somewhere else. I didn't know who it was, but I thought..."

"Figured it out yet?"

Shivers raced through my body. "It *was* Dusty!" Austen was the fake, presenting himself as the hero. The real man, the one with the heart of a poet and the soul of a lover, was the one who won my love without ever asking for it.

Meryl was nodding. "He may be quiet, but if you sit and listen for a minute, he'll tell you more with a look than most men will with a hundred words."

Butterflies prickled my stomach. It had been Dusty all along, and he loved me. I didn't deserve it, but he cared in spite of the ways I'd ignored him. "Dusty! I thought it was him, but I couldn't get it all to add up. It made me wonder if any of it was actually real. He really wrote that, didn't he? Those beautiful poems—all of it?"

Meryl winked. "Bet your boots. And he wasn't writing it for his horse."

Chapter 25

Dusty

Dusk was already settling over the ranch when Cody pulled in at the gate. I've always loved watching the sun flame out on these winter evenings, with the sky an icy bronze and something surreal about how the shadows played over the frozen grasslands. It was a harsh kind of beauty, a stark sort of glory that I doubted many could appreciate.

But I was ready for spring. Changes happen fast around the ranch, and when February sighs its last, March tends to explode on the scene. Warmer weather never just happens. It always rolls in with fits and rumblings, soothing us with the promise of sunshine one minute, then threatening to send us back to the unforgiving days of winter the next. I peered through the windshield at the dark clouds fading to blackness over the mountains. It was already happening.

"Storm rolling in tonight," Cody said.

We didn't have to say any more. These late winter, early spring storms usually meant cows would start calving to beat the weather. All at once. As soon as that barometer dropped, it was like some unseen hand had laid them all out.

And now appeared to be no exception. No one was lurking around the barn yard, and the house lights were dark. "I gotta find Luke," I muttered, reaching for my hat. "Do you need any help getting the horses settled?"

Cody shut off the truck. "Emily and I can do it. You go ahead."

I stopped off at the house first. It wouldn't do me any good to race out through the cow pastures without bundling up. I'd just slow everyone down as I gradually turned into a cowboy popsicle. I went to my room and threw on a pair of long johns, my heaviest flannel, a warm neck cloth, and my thicker felt hat. I was just rushing out when I remembered my phone.

That would speed things up. I'd call Luke and find out which pastures they had checked. I pushed the on button and stuffed it in my pocket while it started up, and went to the hook for my heavy coat and gloves. Within seconds, the phone started chiming and buzzing with notifications.

I'd figured that. Austen was probably tearing his hair out because I hadn't answered him, and who knows how many others had tried to reach me. Luke was probably one of them, sending me horse ads and forgetting I didn't have my phone to look at them. I bundled up into my coat, then reached for the phone again to call him.

There were about fifty texts, from a few different numbers. I scrolled past most of them. Yep, there were several from Austen, and what I could see of them from the preview on the lock screen didn't sound very happy. I swiped the screen up and ignored them. I'd call Luke first.

When I got to my call screen, it showed a voicemail. Only one, which surprised me. I'd figured people would be leaving all kinds of messages when I didn't answer my texts, but there was just this one. It was probably Austen. I touched over to that screen to just delete it, but when it showed me the transcription of the message, my heart stopped. It was from Jess.

I pulled it up and listened as her voice filled my ears. Was she... was she crying? She sounded broken.

She was sorry. And she was too late. What did she mean by that? She missed seeing me... And she was sorry.

I wasn't breathing anymore. I had heard enough. She knew she had hurt me, let me down. Somehow, she'd figured out that she was the light in my skies, and she was sorry. Jess would never hurt anyone on purpose, but she'd had to make her choice.

And she was sorry.

Sorry didn't cover a lifetime of disappointment. Sorry didn't piece my heart back together, didn't build the kind of future I'd always hoped and dreamed.

But in the end, it wasn't her fault. I was the one to blame for never finding the courage to reach for that future until it was too late.

My ears ringing, my thumb trembled over the delete button. It was the only recording of her voice I would ever have, but if I kept it, listened to it whenever I ached for her, it would drive me into madness. Better to rip off the bandage all at once, right? I made myself push the delete button.

Then I called Luke, still reeling and numb, but there was stuff to do. I still had a family and a ranch to live for. "Where are you?" I asked when he picked up.

"Bro, you picked a bad time to come back. The rest of the gang are getting the big herd in from the flats. I just rode out to the lower eighty. Might have to push the herd back toward the barn, storm coming fast."

"I   saw   that.   I'll   saddle   up   and   head   your way."

Jess

I was pretty useless at work on Wednesday. I dropped things, lost things, forgot what I was doing. Finally, Dad just gave me a long look and sent me home. It didn't seem to matter where I was, though, because my brain was in a constant fog. Dusty should be back today.

I had made Morgan promise to send me a message when her husband got home. That would be my clue to go find Dusty at the ranch. She'd given me a funny look, but agreed to send me a text.

The text had just landed.

I slid into the driver's seat and grabbed the wheel, trying to measure my breaths. It was now or never! If I meant to talk to Dusty, to let him know that he was everything to me, beg him to forgive me for all I had put him through, there was no time like right now.

"Okay," I muttered to myself as I turned the ignition. "Let's do this." My car shuddered to life, and I nosed out onto the highway.

It was long dark, even though it wasn't that late. Spring hadn't yet cracked through those mountains, and heavy black clouds had lingered over the valley all afternoon. The first few drops of rain splattered on my windshield, with the promise of more to follow.

Where would Dusty be? Would he be in the house talking to his father about the trip? Or would he be out in the barns and fields, as usual, picking up his place in the cycle of chores like he had never left?

But when I pulled into the gate at Walker Ranch, it didn't look like chores as usual. About ten men on horseback were milling through the feed yards and shelters near the big barn. Cattle were bawling everywhere, crowding together and setting up such a clamor that I could barely hear the men's voices over the din. The rain was picking up now and starting to turn icy.

I pulled on my hat and coat and got out of my car. It was dark enough that I couldn't see more than silhouettes, save where the lights over the stockyard pierced through the mist and blackness. I wandered over to the cowboys, all working and calling out to the herd, and tried to pick out the one voice I was looking for.

Was he here yet? He had to be here somewhere, since Morgan said Cody had settled the show horses and come home already. But none of them looked up when I walked over to the fence rails. They just kept with her task, milling through the herd, checking each cow, and bringing more in all the time.

Finally, one cowboy noticed me. I stepped on the lower board of the fence and pulled myself up to talk to him as he rode over. But it wasn't Dusty who pushed his hat up off his eyes. It was Blake. "He's out in the fields still."

I blinked. "Dusty is?"

Blake's mouth curved just a bit, a mischievous gleam twinkling in his eye. "Figured you didn't come here to see me. He'll probably be bringing a new group in. Might take them about an hour to get that bunch moving, unless they have a problem or decide to leave them where they are."

I glanced around the pens. "What's going on?"

"Storm's coming. Trying to get all these cows in the shelter so they don't calve out there on the hillsides. But it's a bad deal. I don't like having them calving these pens. Calves get stepped on, get sick, born in the mud and all. But at least we can keep an eye on them and move them to safety a little faster when we need to. Some of these mama cows weren't ready yet, but they're dropping their calves just the same. Hey, Brandon! Get the gate!"

I fell silent, just watching them all. I was in the way. This was Dusty's life, his ranch, and livelihood, and I had intruded at a critical time just so I could tell him I loved him and needed him. I hadn't earned the right to be a part of this.

"Should I just come back?" I asked Blake. "Or wait here? Can I help with anything?"

Blake pushed that hat just a little farther up his forehead and scanned the herds behind him. Of course, there wouldn't be anything for me to do. There wasn't really any point in asking. These guys knew their job, and there were enough of them. But I felt helpless, just waiting, and knowing that Dusty was out trying to save his family's livelihood. He had much bigger things to worry about than me.

"You know, they might could use a hand out there. It was just Luke and Dusty going after that bunch. It's the younger heifers—we had them separated to keep any chance of contamination lower. They have the most trouble, you know."

I nodded as if I understood. I sort of did. Some of the ranchers around here would start splitting their herds up as calving season approached to give the most vulnerable groups, like the smaller cows and the calves that would be born latest in the season, the cleanest fields to rotate through. Clean fields meant lower parasite and disease exposure for those new calves. But a late winter storm could be far more dangerous than a little mud.

"Is there really much I can do? I've never moved a herd, and I don't know my way around the ranch in the dark."

"You can ride a horse, can't you? The horse can see." He pointed over to one of the cowboys I had seen earlier, and I realized that it was Kelli on her big chestnut mare. Her hair was in a dripping braid down her back, and her voice was scratchy and worn, but she was fighting through the icy rainfall and the mud like the rest of them, with just as much energy and courage as any of the cowboys. And then I noticed that the rider on the far side of the same pen was Meryl, up on an old flea-bitten gray and gently moving through the restless group to help them settle.

"You can go grab that sorrel gelding over there and throw a saddle on him," Blake said, gesturing to one of the horse corrals. "But you don't have to if you'd rather not. I'm sure they can handle it."

I looked at Kelli again, working right beside her husband like she had been born to do it, and there was only one answer I could give. "Which field are they in? How do I find them?"

Blake's grin was as wide as his face. "See that ridge?"

I looked over my shoulder where the moon broke through a bank of clouds, and nodded.

"Keep going about another fifty yards. Drop down into the coulee, and you can't miss them. Little warmer down there, cows like at this time of year."

I nodded, my breath catching. Was I really doing this? But for Dusty, I'd do anything. "Okay. I'm on it."

Dusty

Distances in these mountains can be deceiving. You think something will take you five minutes, but it takes you almost an hour. It's worse in the dark.

This is why a good horse will never be replaced by an ATV. And there wasn't a horse in the barn I trusted more than Duchess to get me where I needed to go. Her silvery gray coat against the snow almost disappeared, but as the storm picked up and the sky got darker, it didn't matter what color the horse was anyway. You just felt your way along, trusting the trail you've worn a thousand times.

I heard Luke long before I saw him. The cows were bawling and scrambling around down in that little warm pocket behind the ridge. If they were safe there, we were probably better off leaving them there rather than pushing them over that blustery ridge to the pens. But just the fact that these were the younger heifers and there was a storm coming meant we couldn't leave them alone. We'd probably be out here riding herd all night.

When I heard Luke's voice telling his horse to back up, I had a pretty good idea what was going on. I gave Duchess her head and urged her to follow the sound. The herd broke open before us, and I shone a flashlight on Luke's horse, holding a rope on an unruly cow.

"There you are! About time. Get a rope around her hind legs. She's trying to kill her calf."

Great. That was just the problem we needed right now. Every once in a while, a new mother doesn't know what to do with her baby, and she'll attack it. Usually, if you can get it through that first few hours they'll be all right. But this mama cow was not having Luke's interference. She was swinging her black head around, lunging first at Luke's horse, then at anything else in her way.

I brought Duchess in close, and her training took over. Going to the roping jackpots was fun, but this is where a horse like her really paid off. Her job was, first and foremost, to take care of the stock, and she knew exactly what to do to make it happen. I dropped the loop around the heels of the plunging cow right when she was twisting to make another charge at Luke's horse. Caught now, she could do nothing to hurt herself or us.

"Well, that was fun." Luke got off his horse and pulled out his flashlight to start groping around in the mud. I did the same, and my flashlight crossed the miserable, shivering form of a black calf huddled in the wettest part of the fold. "Is this it?"

Luke's flashlight cut across my feet and fell on the little figure. "That's the one. He's not doing well. We might have to take him in."

I felt the little guy over. He was still wet from birth, and now he was worse off because his mama hadn't licked him dry before the cold set in. He felt like a little ice cube. "He's not gonna make it unless we get him up to the barn and get some colostrum in him. What about the others?"

"Three others born so far. They're all looking good. I don't want to move them across that upper fields through the worst of the weather if I can help it."

I swept my flashlight over Duchess and Luke's horse Dozer, who were both quietly holding their places. A good horse really is worth her weight in gold at times like these. She flipped her ears at me when I came close but never moved a muscle.

"Whoa," I commanded. I pulled another rope off my saddle, then walked the herd perimeter with my flashlight. Luke and I didn't even have to talk. He was doing the same thing, circling in the opposite direction so we would meet at the other end.

"Got one down over there," Luke said when we met up. "Looks like she's doing okay. Any more?"

"Yeah, one. She's not pushing yet, but she's thinking about it. What do you want to do?"

"We got to get that one up to the barn. I can drag his mama behind if you'll throw him over your saddle."

"What about the others? You don't want to keep an eye on them?"

Even as I asked the question, a cow crossed into the beam of my flashlight that I hadn't noticed before. She was standing in the middle of the herd, her head down and her flanks heaving.

Luke spat out a curse. "I saw this one earlier. Thought she was going to be okay."

I passed my light over her again. "She's not okay."

"Lemme get my calf puller."

Luke turned back for his horse, and I heard him speaking softly to Dozer, then the metal clank of the chain. "I can pull this calf," he said when he came back. "You'd better get that other one up to shelter fast, or we're gonna lose him. We'll just leave the mama be for now, unless she'll follow you."

"But if I leave you here and you can't get this calf yourself, we could lose two more." I gestured with my flashlight. "At least check her before I head up."

I got my loop around the cow while Luke stripped off his coat—his only protection from the icy rainfall—and rolled up his sleeve. The cow was too miserable to care what he did, and she just stood there, panting, as Luke checked inside for the position of her calf.

"It's an easy one! Leg back. Not even a big feller. I can get this in a jiffy. Go on, get that other one."

I watched for another minute, but Luke was right. He could handle this. We'd all been pulling calves since we were kids. I trudged back to Duchess and asked her to step forward so I could release my heel rope. Then I did the same with Dozer and got Luke's rope off. The cow had quit thrashing, and she didn't seem all that interested in attacking the horses or me anymore. Unfortunately, she wasn't very interested in her calf, either.

I gathered up the shivering little body and gently laid him across the front of my saddle. "Okay, Duchess. Let's get this one to shelter."

Jess

It was a good thing the horse could see, because I couldn't. How far was this ridge, anyway? It felt like I'd been riding for an hour, but it was probably only about fifteen minutes. My coat wasn't thick enough to handle the wet and the cold together, and my gloves were just little knit things that had soaked through in only a few minutes. My hands were almost warmer without them.

I'd found a head lamp in the barn, as well as an extra hat and a yellow rain slicker. I'd thrown them on, and they were absolute lifesavers. At least I could see the path in front of me, and the rain wasn't falling in my eyes. The horse probably didn't need the light, but I wasn't quite bold enough to turn it off.

Would Dusty even be happy to see me coming? I tried to prepare myself for anything. If he was working—cold, wet, and miserable like I was, and trying to do his job as quickly as possible, he might not appreciate me showing up and trying to hug him. Maybe he would. Or maybe he'd just brush my arms off and bark orders about getting the stock to safety.

But even as I tried to convince myself to expect the worst, some part of me whispered that it would be alright. I was an extra pair of hands if nothing else. I might have to wait for more, but Dusty wouldn't turn me away.

My horse's stride faltered, and he raised his head, then sent up a shrill whinny. I couldn't hear anything over the shrieking wind, but the horse's hearing is never wrong. Someone was coming. I pointed the beam from my headlamp in the same direction the horse was looking. All I could see at first was the dull gleam of old snow, the heavy gray of the sky where the clouds shrouded the moon, and sleet streaking across my vision. But then, a ghost seemed to come into view.

My horse whinnied again, and I let him break into a trot. The figure ahead was faint, silent, and moving so slowly I couldn't be sure it was really there. The fractured rainfall wasn't helping. My breath was fogging the way, and the light bounced off all that mist to blind me. Impatiently, I switched off the head lamp.

What I couldn't see with the light flashed brilliantly clear without it. The clouds had shifted just enough for the moon to break through, piercing through the darkness to shine on a little girl's silly dream come true. The brave knight on his valiant white charger... or just a humble cowboy with a heart of gold, laying himself on the line to save the weakest of the herd.

This was the man I loved.

Chapter 26

Dusty

My eyes had just adjusted to the darkness again when a beam sliced across the field in front of me. I shielded them from the foggy glare with one hand and kept rubbing the shivering calf over my saddle with the other.

"Evan?" *Please be Evan,* or maybe Brandon. Luke needed real help back there, and though he'd never admit it, Marshall wasn't back to his full strength yet.

But he probably couldn't hear me over the rain and wind. His horse neighed, and the beam started coming faster, but with that light in my face, I still couldn't tell who it was. I just kept plodding on, "hurrying slowly," as my mom used to say. It wouldn't do the calf any good if he got beat up on the ride to shelter.

The light switched off, and I lowered my hand. "Evan, is that you? Luke needs some help down in the coulee!"

"Dusty?"

Duchess jerked to a halt beneath me. I hadn't told her to. She just felt me stiffen, and she pulled up on her own. That voice... it sounded like Jess!

I shook my head and urged my horse forward. I was looney, that was the problem. It was just Kelli, coming out to see how we were doing. That was better than nothing. She could take the calf to the barn, and I could go back to help Luke.

She was trotting straight for me, her hat pulled low against the rain. All I could make out was the dim outline of her figure as she came close. But then her horse drew up beside mine, and her face lifted.

A bolt of wonder shook me. *Jess!* I rubbed my eyes. They had to be playing tricks on me—dazzled by the flashlight and a long day on the road. But there was no mistaking her voice.

"Dusty! Are you okay? Please, say something. It's me!"

I could only stare, the pattering rain growing to a deafening roar in my ears. What was she doing there? Shouldn't she be with Austen or something? The calf wriggled beneath my hand, and Duchess snorted, impatient to get back to work, but I couldn't separate the line between reality and hope. Could she have ridden through the storm, blundering around in the night, for *me?*

That was when her hand found mine in the darkness. Where I cradled the calf, she caught me... and I was lost. I turned my hand over and trapped her fingers. Those gloves she wore were so thin I could feel her shivering through them, and instinct took over. I dragged her hand to my lips, cupping it around my mouth so I could breathe some warmth into her even through those pitiful gloves, and kissing the palm of her hand between breaths.

"Oh, Dusty," she whispered. Her hand slid up my jaw, her thumb stroking my cheek, and when I stared down into her face, it glistened in the weak moonlight from the rain. Or were those tears?

The words scrambling around in my head finally broke loose. "Jess! What are you doing here?"

"I came for you. Dusty, I've been such a fool. Please tell me I'm not too late."

My heart heard, but my mind refused to believe. It was too glorious to be true! I couldn't keep riding the wave of crashing hope forever, but I was too reckless, wanted it too much. How many times had I dreamed the woman I loved would come to me, say she wanted me? And here she was in the middle of this storm, risking danger and quaking from the cold, and she said it was all for me.

I jerked off my right glove and reached for her. Her cheeks were wet with warm tears, and she leaned into my hand. I felt her breath, a deep sigh of relief tickling the skin of my wrist, and I let my fingers explore what my eyes already knew so well. The delicate curve of her ear, the fine ridge of her cheekbones, the lushness of her lips. That was enough to thrill my soul for all the ages, but my body craved more.

And Duchess sensed it. Faithful and true, she shifted beneath me and, once more, carried me where I wanted to go. Right into Jess's arms.

Our knees were almost hooked together now, and my arm fell to loop around her waist. This *was* real! She was truly there, asking for nothing less than my whole heart, the thing that had been hers from long ago. I tipped my hat down to gaze into her eyes, and a splash of water ran off, drenching her even more than she already was. "Oh, Jess, I'm sorry." I needed to get her to safety, get her warm and dry.

But Jess had other ideas. She laughed and pushed my hat away from my face. "I don't mind a little rain so long as I'm with you."

And she found me, there under that stormy moon. Her lips tasted like honey, the warmth of her skin against mine was a homecoming to my battered spirits. I kissed my Jess until her shivering stopped, and I'd dried every last raindrop and tear from her cheeks, and then I kissed her a little more.

"I love you, Dusty Walker," she whispered against my lips. "And if you'll let me, I want to stay here forever."

The storm was starting to let up a little. The rain had slowed, and the clouds were shifting to the east. I pulled back just enough to admire how a fresh shaft of moonlight splintered over her face, illuminating those glorious eyes and that smile that was just for me. "I'm sorry, but I can't let you do that."

The hurt in her eyes was immediate. A crease formed on her brow, and her throat bobbed in a restrained sob. "Oh." She sucked in a short breath and nodded jerkily. "I... I see. I've waited too long. I know I—"

I touched a finger to her lips and chuckled. "Jess Thompkins, I'd have waited forever for you. But I'd really like to get you and this calf warm and dry. After that, if you don't mind, I'm hoping to kiss you some more, and maybe talk about holding you for the rest of my life."

A smile formed under my finger, and she softly pressed her lips to it. "Okay, cowboy. I'll follow you wherever you go."

Jess

A blanket draped around my shoulders, and a steaming mug of tea appeared before me. I grabbed the hot mug and looked up, expecting Kelli or Meryl. But it was my cowboy, easing onto a straw bale beside me. He spared a glance at the calf I was guarding, sleeping under a heat lamp in fresh straw, but then his attention was all for me. His cheeks were bright red with the cold, but his smile was as warm as the sunrise.

"How's the calf doing?"

I sipped my tea. Rich and sweet, just like I liked it. How did he know? "I'm no expert, but he's not shivering anymore. Meryl helped me get a bottle of milk into him, and he took it really well."

He nodded. "Good. I brought his mama up with me. We can try reintroducing them after she's eaten and settled a bit. Mind if I share that blanket?"

I set down the tea mug and spread the blanket he had given me over his shoulders. Then I nestled into the crook of his arm. He was far more comforting than any old hot mug, and I pressed my cheek into the warm flannel at his throat as a sigh soaked through my being. My cowboy was here, he was real, and he hadn't turned me away when I'd finally come to my senses. He'd had work to do because I'd come to him at the very worst time. But he had carried out his duty, faithful and true, and was already back with me sooner than I'd dared to hope. "I thought you'd still be out helping Luke."

"Evan and Brandon came out to spell us. Luke went to the house to warm up, but I had something more important to do." Dusty turned his face to nuzzle my hair, and my insides turned to butter when I realized he wasn't just pressing a quick kiss to my head. He was drinking me in, just reveling in holding me, and heedless of the fact that I probably looked like a wet mop and smelled like a musty old cowboy hat. I felt his breaths deepen and slow, and his arm tightened around me.

"And what was that?" I whispered into his ear. I just wanted to hear him say it.

"Watching over the calf, of course," he said casually.

I elbowed him lightly in the ribs. "I know you've got better lines than that, you big tease."

"I have no idea what you mean by that."

I turned my face into his and let my forehead rest on his cheek. "Do you know why I dated Austen?"

He swallowed, and his breathing dipped. "It really wasn't my business, Jess."

"Yes, it was. I thought he was you."

Dusty stiffened. "I don't understand."

"The poem in my pocket. The note at work. And the journal! I can't believe I thought Austen could have written that. Even the poem he copied out of that magazine and gave me in that stupid Valentine's Day card. I was looking for *that* man, but instead, I looked right past him and found the wrong one."

He was silent for a few seconds, his eyes low. Then, he lifted them to me—clear and blue as the summer skies and gentle as a spring mist. "That was it? Really?"

"You stole my heart, cowboy. I just didn't know where to find you, and I trusted the wrong person. I believed him when you were the one I wanted all along."

He blinked, and his shoulders sagged. "I thought you just weren't interested in that sort of thing. I've tried to figure out how to talk to you for years, and that was my best idea. When it didn't work, I figured it meant that was it. I'd missed all my chances."

My lower lip trembled. What had I put this poor man through? "Did you say *'years'*?"

He grinned shyly. "Yeah. Half my life."

"Oh, Dusty! And I was that blind, that stupid!"

"Jess, love, don't ever say that. You couldn't know what I never told you. The blame is mine alone." He caught my hand and caressed my fingers like I was his finest treasure. And just like in all the romance books, and all the silly movies, my body and spirit sparked with electricity. Hunger. I didn't just love this man for his goodness. I wanted him with every fiber of my being like I'd never wanted anything in my life. And I'd already waited too long to show it.

"I'm going to make it up to you," I promised. "Starting right now."

He straightened, that crooked Walker smile growing as his brow quirked playfully. "I'm listening."

"I don't need you to listen. Just feel." I slid my hand around his neck and pulled him close. All those words I loved didn't matter when the reality of the dream was here in my arms. And he was waiting for me to show him.

I kissed the little cleft of his chin, then the sweet corner of his mouth that turned up in a bashful grin. I kissed that strong jaw and scruffy cheek, the chilled tip of his nose, and the thoughtful furrows of his brow. I threaded my fingers into his damp, wavy hair and gloried in the smell of fresh rain on his clothes and his skin, and all the while, I found new places I'd never kissed before.

And still, he waited, just letting me discover him at long last. His eyes were closed, his breath ragged, and some unspoken pain lined the corners of his eyes. I held his face and tried to soothe that ache away with my lips, and a warm tear slipped between my fingers.

He sucked in a breath, his eyes still closed. "Oh, Jess," he whispered. "Is this real?"

"I hope so." I pressed my face into the cleft of his neck, letting his arms fold around me and his body warm mine. "I'm going to tell you something I've never told anyone else."

His breath tickled the hair at my temples as he rested his cheek on my forehead. "What's that?"

"I love you. You, and only you, and I want to spend the rest of my days right here."

He drew back slightly, those bright blue eyes wide. "You've never..."

"Never loved before you? Not even close. I've never said those words to any man. Well..." I grinned. "Except for my dad."

Dusty's mouth twitched, first in awe and disbelief, then a slow smile blossomed. "I guess second place isn't so bad."

"I wouldn't call that second. You're the first in my heart, forever. I'm just sorry I wasted so much time figuring it out."

He kissed my hair. "We have all the time in the world, love. A minute, an hour, a year—I'd rather spend one with you than a lifetime anywhere else."

"But why?"

He lifted his head, his gaze puzzled as those clear eyes wandered over my face. "Why what?"

"Why would you love me? I've been so awful, so ignorant."

Dusty's smile warmed, and he tucked a wisp of hair behind my ear. "You were never awful. I can't blame you for not seeing what I never had the courage to show you. But I fell in love with your heart years ago. You kept yourself above all the petty things, and you lived on your own terms. You were always kind, always gentle, and I felt like you were someone I could trust in—be at peace with. You were kind of like my own personal angel."

I couldn't help a little laugh. "It used to annoy me when Austen called me that. But I think I could hear it from you every day and never grow tired of it."

"Good, because that's what I was going to ask for. Every day. Marry me, my love, my angel?"

I didn't answer with words. Words were beautiful; they fed my soul and led my heart to its perfect home, but they weren't enough now. I cupped his face and kissed him, tugging his lower lip and giving him everything I had until he opened his whole self to me. I was going to marry my cowboy, my friend, the one in whom my heart trusted.

Dusty pulled back, his face alight with joy. He was laughing.

"What?"

"I was just thinking how Marshall is never going to let me live this down."

I wove my fingers through his and rested my head on his shoulder. "And why is that?"

"Because I gave him the hardest time for rushing to the altar after only dating Kelli for two months. I think two minutes is slightly more shocking."

I giggled and pulled his hand to my heart. "It's more than long enough for me. I've been waiting all my life for you."

Chapter 27

Dusty

My phone wouldn't stop buzzing, but I never even pulled it out of my pocket. In fact, I was thinking seriously about getting rid of it. The only thing preventing me from getting up and chucking it in the can was the woman who'd spent the wee hours before dawn with her head pillowed on my chest, keeping watch with me over a newborn calf and his reluctant mother.

Well... she wasn't keeping watch. Not now. I looked down and loved her all over again for the way her golden hair tangled over her face, and her dark lashes twitched in her dreams. The prom queen, every guy's high school fantasy, was my real, flesh-and-blood woman. Flawed and humbled, exhausted and disheveled—I had never seen her look more beautiful than now, with her cheek wrinkled from resting on my flannel shirt and her lips moving softly.

She talked in her sleep. Nothing that made much sense, but she said my name. A lot. I trailed a finger over her chin, and she sighed, stirred, and then settled on my chest once more.

Mine.

Somewhere around two in the morning, we'd managed to get that unhappy mama cow to let her calf nurse. It took some doing, but Jess and I got the job done together. We stayed to make sure everything went smoothly, but Mama and calf were going to be just fine now. We really didn't need to be here any longer, but it was that or head back to the house. Or back to work.

I figured if anyone really needed me, they could come get me. I wasn't going to wake Jess for anything less than an earthquake or a hay barn on fire. Quick footsteps sounded behind me, but I froze. Maybe they'd think I was asleep and go away.

No such luck. "Dude, did you turn your phone off aga... Oh."

I craned my neck around to see Luke backing away with his hands up. "Sorry. I didn't know you had a... uh... What exactly do you have there?"

I turned back to smile down at my love. "The rest of my life, brother. That's what I have here."

Luke gave a low whistle. "They say it's always the quiet ones. Turn you loose, and you work even faster than Marshall."

I chuckled and snaked my fingers into Jess's hair, then kissed her forehead. "And now I know why. He was only ever fixated on one woman, and once he got her in his arms, he didn't let go. I'm no different."

"'Cept you and Jess won't fight like cats and dogs. I bet you'll both be so easy-going that your kids will walk all over you."

Kids. I grinned at that thought. My imagination hadn't even gotten there yet. "I guess that remains to be seen. Did you need something? Because, if not..."

"Hmm? Oh! Right." He held up his phone. "Got a call from an old friend of yours."

"So? Is it a crisis? Is someone bleeding? Broken bones?"

Luke's face blossomed in a wicked grin. "You're not gonna believe this, but yes. All that and probably more."

I straightened. "You sound awfully tickled about it. Is someone actually hurt, or are you pulling my leg?"

"Oh, he's hurt alright. But unfortunately, he'll probably pull through."

I narrowed my eyes.

Luke jiggled his phone with a smirk. "You really need to check your messages."

Jess

I was having the best dream. I couldn't remember any details later—just that I had felt so warm and safe. And Dusty was there, protecting me and loving me just as I was—muddy boots, dirty face and all. I didn't ever want to leave that lovely place, but he was kissing my temple so temptingly. Then my cheeks, my forehead, and finally, he brushed soft kisses over my closed eyes. I was smiling by the time he stopped.

"Are you awake?" he asked gently.

"No. Can you keep doing that?"

"Gladly." He bent down again, and this time, he kissed my mouth. I caught him by the shirt collar, so he couldn't stop.

"We need to get up," he said with a low chuckle. "Something's happened."

I shot upright, my bleary eyes searching the little warming pen. The cow and calf were both gone. "Where are they? Oh, please tell me he's okay!"

"He's fine. Luke and I let them out in the big pen a few minutes ago. But we need to go to the hospital now. Here." He gave me his hand to stand up, then started picking the straw out of my hair.

I was still rubbing my eyes and more than a little confused. "Hospital? Why?" Then, cold horror seized my stomach. "It's not my dad, is it?"

"No. Austen Conrad got trampled by his bull last night. I guess he's pretty beat up, and he's been trying to reach me."

I froze, staring at Dusty as he held up my coat. "He's what? Is he okay?"

Dusty walked behind me to slip my coat over my shoulders since I wasn't getting it done myself. "He will be, from what Luke heard, but apparently, he's been trying to reach me since yesterday. Something about his cows, but I didn't make out most of the message." Dusty caught my hand and invited me to step over the straw bale toward him, but my feet were stuck.

He stopped and rubbed his jaw. "Uh, look, you don't have to come if it makes you uncomfortable."

"I thought *you* would be the one who didn't want to go. I don't know everything that happened, but from what I do know, he was a lousy 'friend' to you."

A shy grin hid behind his hand, and his eyes twinkled. "Yeah. Yeah, he was."

"So, why are you running to help him out now? What can you possibly do but let him try to use you again?"

"Well..." He tugged my hand again, and this time, I followed him. "You know how it is. With him all banged up, he'll need help. Animals won't feed themselves, and I won't let animals suffer."

I tilted my head and arched my eyebrow. "And?"

He shrugged and looked down, but the edge of his mouth curved. "And it kind of feels good. You know... not getting the short end of the stick for once."

I laughed. "He deserved to be decked for the stunts he pulled. He was awful to you, and he told me so many lies he almost had me fooled into thinking he was the right guy. I'm surprised you never gave him a black eye yourself."

"Oh, I wanted to. Especially when I thought he was going to have all the happiness I'd ever dreamed of! Yeah, I would have cheerfully knocked his teeth out, but now... I'm glad I never got the opportunity."

I slid my hands up Dusty's chest and nuzzled the underside of his chin. I loved how he smelled, and I loved the possessive way he dug his hands into the back pockets of my jeans to pull me closer. "Really? You're sure that's how you feel about it?"

"Well..." Dusty winked. "Let's just say I'm feeling especially generous today."

Dusty

Austen didn't say much when Jess walked into that hospital room beside me, her hand locked firmly in mine. His gaze just skipped over us, and his shoulders sagged.

"How are you feeling?" I asked.

"Like I got stomped on by a ton of angry hamburger." His face was swollen from a dozen bruises, his lip decorously adorned with a neat row of stitches, and his arm was in a cast.

"Is it serious? How long will you be down?"

Austen glanced at Jess, then stared at his lap. "Broken arm. It was bad enough they had to put a plate in, which is why I'm still here, but the rest is just sprains and a heck of a lot of bruises."

"How did it happen?"

He shrugged. And still wouldn't look up. "Danny quit the other day. I was out by myself yesterday afternoon, trying to move stock into shelter before the storm hit. I didn't think I had anything to worry about since that bull had been so friendly."

"It's almost spring," I reminded him. "Bulls get a little frisky when the season changes."

"Yeah. I figured that out." He gestured to some papers beside his bed. "Anyway, I was hoping I could ask you for one last favor. I know you probably don't want to, but..."

"I'll make sure your cows get fed and checked. We'll stop by there on the way home and see what needs to be done."

Austen shook his head. "I'm done." He finally met my gaze. "I'm selling out. Not the life for me."

Jess's fingers tightened in mine, and I heard a soft sigh of relief. I hated to confess it, but I agreed with the sentiment. Austen was really terrible at ranching, and I didn't like seeing a place and a herd go downhill because they weren't getting the right care.

Plus, I was kind of tired of seeing him around town.

Jess and I traded glances, and then I looked back at Austen. "Anything I can do?"

"You can buy my place."

Could I? It would give Jess and me a place of our own to begin our new life together. We'd figured on starting out in the bunk house while we built a house on my portion of Walker Ranch, but this would mean our own house, a lot sooner. His ranch wasn't big, and it was still in need of a lot of work, but it was large enough to keep us fed, give us something to grow with.

But it wasn't just my decision. I looked down, and Jess's starry blue eyes found mine. And, ever so slightly, she shook her head. She didn't want anything to do with that ranch.

That was good enough for me. "Sorry, Austen. We're not interested."

Austen let his gaze rest on Jess. She stiffened beside me, and from the corner of my eye, I saw her chin lift. She was staring him down, asserting the iron I'd always known was in her blood. She was usually so sweet and gentle that most people didn't realize that she could also be fierce when she had to be.

Austen looked down, and he never looked at her again. "Fine. At least take Shep back. You trained him. He won't listen to me."

I nodded. "I'll pick him up on the way home. And I'll send some help to run your place until you sell it. Did you want to pay for the labor in cash or trade some of your cows?"

His cheek flinched. "Guess you know how to play hardball, after all."

"When I have to. Usually, I'll just take a man's word and give him the benefit of the doubt. Unless I get burned."

He rolled his eyes. "Whatever. I'll cut you a check when the place sells."

"Good enough." I tightened my hand around Jess's and started to turn away but stopped. "I hope you heal up soon."

Austen's gaze tightened, and his head tilted. "Why would you even care?"

"Because that's what decent folks do around here." I replaced my hat and tipped the brim. "Take care of yourself."

We walked out of that room together, my love and I, leaving all the hurts of the past behind us. Jess laced her fingers through mine and wrapped her free hand around my elbow. I had a feeling she'd have more to say to me once we got out to the truck.

But the hospital room door opened before we touched it, and a tall woman with a dark brown Brazilian blowout stepped inside. She spared us little more than a swift glance, then marched toward the bed. "Well, well. I finally found you, Michael."

Jess and I jerked to a halt together and spun around. "Michael" was about the color of his sheets, and his eyes were round as dinner plates. "Rachel!" He cleared his throat. "Uh... what are you doing here?"

"Wondering where my child support check is. You're six months behind, and I have a lawyer."

"I sent the check! What, did you and your boy toy lose your apartment and move again?"

She stuck her finger in his face. "We bought the house a year ago, and he's not my boy toy. Ryan and I have been married for two years!"

"Only after you left me for my best friend."

"And you know what? If I'd been thinking clearly, I'd never married you in the first place. I'd have picked him first. I can't *believe* I fell for your crap!"

They kept bickering, and I couldn't help rubbing my eyes. Was I really seeing this? Jess leaned close and whispered, "I think I dodged a bullet."

I couldn't make any response. I just gaped as Austen... Michael... grabbed the papers on the hospital tray, the ones he'd tried to give me, and flung them in his... ex-wife's? face. And I knew I'd never get paid for keeping his cows fed until his place sold.

But I'd do it anyway, because it wasn't about Austen... or whatever his name was. It was about doing what was right; sometimes, you just stick your neck out there and let the chips fall where they may.

Jess tugged at my arm. "You know? I think we should leave. Now."

I nodded, but I'm sure my mouth was still hanging open. "Good idea."

Jess
Two weeks later

I leaned on the door frame of the garage and closed my eyes. I could listen to those voices forever. But five minutes would do. Five minutes to just soak it all in, and then I'd walk in and interrupt.

"So, how do you plan get your horsepower up? Bore the engine, or are you going to put a pipe on it?" Dusty's head was under the hood, while my dad's feet were sticking out from behind the tire.

Dad laughed. "Are you kidding? Both! But first, I think we ought to put a lowering kit on it." The creeper rolled out, and Dad sat up. "Add some low-profile tires and custom rims. What do you think?"

"I'm not the person to ask. Everything I drive has to be able to cover potholes and muddy back roads."

"Well, you gotta have at least one car just for fun, right?" I heard Dad getting up, and one of them cracked the top off a bottle of soda. "Hey, don't tell Jess, but I've been thinking of painting it yellow."

"Why? The red is beautiful!"

"Sure, but yellow is different. I hear it's cool now."

Dusty chuckled. "You're never going to finish this thing if you keep changing stuff."

"Of course not. What, do you think the goal of working on a hot rod is to finish it?" Another bottle of soda popped. "You've got a lot to learn, son."

I bit back a giggle. Dad had never been in a hurry to finish his car, but since Dusty had been coming around, they'd spent a lot of hours out in that garage. I doubt they actually got much work done, but they always came in laughing together. And that made my heart happy.

"Yellow sounds perfect, then," Dusty agreed. They were quiet for a minute, probably drinking their sodas. I hated to break things up, but Dusty had left his phone on the kitchen counter, and it had been exploding with texts. From Luke, naturally.

I stepped around the corner, holding the phone, and my dad and Dusty lowered their bottles. "Uh, oh," Dad said. He winked at Dusty and gave him a friendly nudge with his elbow. "Duty calls, eh?"

Dusty set his soda aside and came toward me, his smile enough to light my sky. He slipped a hand around my waist and kissed my cheek. "Let me guess. My brother?"

"Yeah. I think you'd better get back to the ranch."

Dusty took the phone and glanced through his messages. A smile tugged at his lips now and then, and finally, he shook his head and sent a quick reply.

"Calving season?" Dad guessed. "They need you back up there, huh? When is that over for you guys?"

"Oh, another month at least, but that's not what Luke was texting about."

I looped an arm around Dusty's shoulder, and he tucked me closer to his side. I loved holding this man, and I'd never even felt awkward about it in front of my dad. He was just part of me, and being in his arms was as natural as breathing. "I'll bite. If it's not about work, then he's horse shopping again."

Dusty held up the phone. "There's one horse ad. Wouldn't expect any less, but the rest are pictures of string lights and big wooden spools."

Dad squinted. "What would you use something like that for?"

"Tables. Decor. He found ideas online for a rustic barn wedding, and he's got all these crazy ideas." Dusty turned down to me and kissed my temple. "What would you think of getting married up at the ranch? I know it's not very elegant. I can tell Luke to stop."

"At the ranch?" I hadn't even thought of that. I'd already booked the church, and we'd agreed we didn't want a fancy wedding. Just something simple, authentic, and *us*. "You know, I love that idea!"

"You do? I want you to have the wedding you deserve. We don't have to rush or settle on anything."

I shook my head and framed his face with my hands. "It's perfect. Big and airy and we can spend all the time we want, just celebrating with our friends. What do you think, Dad?"

But my dad wasn't there. He'd slipped out again, letting us have a few minutes of privacy. That was one of the hundreds of little ways he had of letting me know how much he liked Dusty.

I'd always felt deep in my soul that I could never be content in loving a man who didn't have my dad's approval. Dusty had more than that. They were close, like family already. I would have married Dusty no matter what because he was the one my heart treasured. But it was a blessing beyond what I could have ever hoped that he and my dad enjoyed and respected each other.

I wrapped my arms around my cowboy's neck and smiled up at him. "Two more weeks. Can we get everything done in that much time?"

Dusty's arms slipped behind me, his hands resting lightly at my waist, and he leaned his forehead on mine. A deep sigh of pleasure lifted his shoulders, then another. "I don't even care if we get everything done. I just want yours to be the last face I see before I drift off to dream each night and the first to greet me with the sunrise each day."

I wove my fingers into his hair and just held him. It didn't matter what we were doing or if we were even doing anything at all. My heart rate actually slowed when I was holding Dusty, like my soul was at peace at last. "When do you think we can break ground on our house?"

"As soon as things dry out a little more. I've ordered the gravel to start the driveway, and I talked to Cody's guy about lumber and trusses." He cupped my cheek. "This is really happening, love!"

"I can hardly believe it! How did I get so lucky?" I stroked his cheek with my thumb and kissed the dimple of his chin.

"It's not luck. We were meant to be, Jess Thompkins. I don't know how or why, but I'm sure of it, deep in my marrow. In fact..." He held up a finger and tugged something from his pocket. I laughed when I recognized that worn leather journal, the one I used to think belonged to Austen... Michael... whatever his name was. Dusty flipped it open, which was no easy feat because he had one hand locked around my waist and wasn't letting go.

"I wrote this for you yesterday. Well, actually, I've been working on it for a couple of weeks. *Stockman's* wants me to send something in, but... I wanted to show you this first."

I took it and read. And in his easy, rhythmic, free verse, I found the words I'd been trying to express since the first time he kissed me. How I was home now, and how our hearts were singing harmony and melody of the same beautiful, haunting song. And there was more than just ourselves—we were part of something bigger, richer, something that would grow and change and endure long after we were no longer of this earth. I would plant myself, plunge my roots down deep into good soil, and flourish alongside my cowboy.

And that was all I ever wanted.

"Can I be selfish about this one?" I nibbled my lip and held the journal close to my heart.

"You don't want me to send it in?"

I shook my head. "Please, no. I want to keep this one just for us if you don't mind."

Dusty smiled. "That was how I felt about it, too. I love sharing my words with people who will understand them, but I was only thinking of you with this one. Let's keep it that way—yours and mine. Something we don't share with anyone else."

"Good. Because I'm not in a sharing mood right now. I just want you, and all of you, cowboy."

"That makes two of us." Dusty cradled my face again, those brilliant blue eyes drinking me in. He had a way of looking at me that made me feel *seen*. Understood. Valued and cherished and adored, and not for my hair or my eyes or my skin or my figure. But for who I was, with all my faults and mistakes; when I was tired and sore, when I was covered in dirt or grease from hard work, when I was bundled in my comfy lounge pants and just wanted to rest my head on his shoulder. He loved me through all of it, and I was blessed.

I stood on my toes and captured his mouth. I could kiss this sweet man all day—the way he let me show him what I wanted, then teased me toward the kind of desire I'd only ever experienced with him—I couldn't get enough of the tender feeling of his lips against mine, the strong, patient hands caressing up and down my spine and the shy, crooked smile he always gave me when I pulled back just to gaze at him.

He was beautiful, from the inside out, and he was mine.

Dive into Luke and Audrey's story next, and keep up with the rest of the Walker family in *Taming the Cowboy*.

From our hearts to yours

Thank you for spending a little time with the family at Walker Ranch.

I hope you've enjoyed getting to know everyone. I'd love it if you would share this family with your friends so they can experience life on the ranch with these swoony cowboys and sassy cowgirls. As with all my books, I have enabled lending to make it easier to share. If you leave a review for ***An Angel for the Cowboy*** on Amazon, Goodreads, Book Bub, or your own blog, I would love to read it! Email me the link at **TheCowgirlWrites@TessThornton.com**

Would you like to read Blake Walker's romance? Dive into Blake and Meryl's story, and stay up to date on upcoming releases and sales by joining my newsletter: https://dashboard.mailerlite.com/forms/ 249660/75244350638917199/share

And now, keep reading for a sneak preview of Luke and Audrey's story!

Epilogue

Luke

Two weeks later

Well, that was it. My little brother and his new wife turned around, hand in hand, and beamed at the rest of us. Mr. and Mrs. Walker. Giddy and excited and about as sure of themselves as a pair of frisky young colts. They weren't even looking at anyone but each other, and I only said what they were probably thinking.

I cupped my hands around my mouth. "Kiss her again, Dusty!"

They were both pink with embarrassment and giggling, but Dusty grabbed Jess and dipped her back for a kiss that made every cowboy in the room whoop and toss his hat in the air. Morgan was standing beside me, crying. Kelli was on the other side of me, bouncing up and down and taking pictures. But when the new couple finally came up for air and walked down the aisle—practically in each other's shoes, not sure how they could have gotten closer—Morgan and Kelli turned to their own husbands.

That left me in the middle, the odd man out. Everyone in the room was talking over each other, laughing about how cute it was that Dusty had almost forgotten to repeat his vows since he'd been just staring at his bride with stars in his eyes. A few were wiping tears over the sentimental lines Jess had written to pledge to Dusty, and I overheard some comments about how the string lights I'd ordered online made our big old drafty barn feel like a swanky, upscale event center.

But no one was talking to me.

Served me right for sitting between two married couples. I ought to have plunked down next to Evan when all the fuss started, but I'd been ushing... is that the right word? Anyway, the seat I ended up with was right in the front row, between Morgan and Kelli.

I was probably supposed to help dismiss people after the new couple walked up the aisle, but there wasn't any point by now. It was like a mob of wandering heifers, everyone converging into one spot and then just standing there talking and occasionally shuffling their feet toward the door.

I looked around and wandered out through another way. But nowhere was safe from the herd of chatty folks. It was a barn, not a cathedral with private halls. Not that I minded people. I like getting out on the town, and I'll shoot the breeze with anyone, but when it's a bunch of crying and gushing, I'm out. I headed for the stable and rolled aside the big door.

Confound it! I wasn't the only one here. A bunch of kids ran up and down the barn aisle, blowing bubbles and shooting Nerf darts. Who on God's green earth bought those stupid things?

Oh, wait. Those were my idea. But they were supposed to be popping them off at Dusty's truck when he left, not spooking the horses! Darned kids.

"Hey, you!" I bellowed. Only one of them stopped. He stared at me, his mouth agape, and his Nerf gun dropped from lifeless fingers.

"You, kid! What's your name?" I'd seen him before. He was that kid who'd brought Dusty the wooden sculpture of Duchess, but I'd never talked to him. And he wasn't talking now, either. Just petrified to his spot like a lump of clay.

"I got you, Dustin!" shrieked a girl in a frilly pink dress. She raced by and pinged the kid on the side of the head about three times before she took off toward the tack room. Pretty good aim, actually.

Dustin finally blinked and put his hand to his cheek. He looked down and didn't move again.

"Hey, you alright?" I asked. I remembered a little more about this kid now. This was the one Cody had pulled off the mountain, the one they said didn't talk much. Scary things would overwhelm him. Scary things like girls with Nerf guns who shot him in the side of the face.

This was way above my pay grade.

But no one else was around, and I couldn't just leave the kid glued to the center of the barn aisle. "Dustin? Hey, snap out of it. You want some punch? Cake? There's going to be cake. Come on, let's go find your mom."

He swiped roughly at his cheek and finally looked up, his eyes glittering. "Just leave me alone!" He aimed a savage kick at the Nerf gun, and it went sailing over one of the barred doors, right into Duchess's stall. That gol durn kid! I'd whoop him if he hit the horse in the head!

But I didn't have time for anything like that because he was running off. For Pete's sake, I didn't know how to talk to him. But Morgan knew the kid pretty well, so maybe I'd message her to go check on him. I was pulling my phone out to do just that when I heard Evan's voice across the courtyard, calling Dustin back. I poked my head out just long enough to see that someone was handling things, then I walked back to check on Duchess.

I slid the door of her stall open, and she lifted her head with the Nerf gun trapped between her teeth. "Hey, Sugar. That thing didn't hit you, did it?"

The toy dropped and she sneezed, then rubbed her face on my shoulder. "Cut it out, now. What'll Dusty say if you get all spoiled rotten while he's on his honeymoon?" But I didn't stop scratching her ears. She liked that. The mare was a queen, really, and it still tore me up that she wasn't the horse for me. She had champion written all over her. I'd just have to keep looking for something that was the same, but different.

"Well, old girl, I'm supposed to be back at the party. You stay out of trouble now, you hear?" I picked up the plastic gun and was backing out of the stall, sliding the door closed, when something stung my backside with two quick blasts.

"Gotcha, Aedyn!"

I turned around, and that same girl was charging out from the haystack, still brandishing her Nerf gun, but she stopped dead when she saw me.

I pointed at the gun, almost quaking with rage. That little hooligan actually shot me in the butt! Her mouth fell open, and she froze. "*Drop. It.*" I hissed. "Or I'll break it over my knee!"

Her nostrils were fluttering, and her eyes filled with big, syrupy tears. "I-I th-thought you were Aedyn."

"Do I look like a twelve-year-old?" I thundered. "And what are you thinking, anyway, shooting those darn things in the barn? Don't you know animals can choke on those stupid darts?"

Her lip started to tremble, and a puddle big enough to do a crocodile proud slipped down her cheek. "I didn't know," she whispered. "Please don't tell my aunt."

Oh, dad gum it. I couldn't lecture a little girl who was crying any more than I could yell at a horse for making a mistake. What good would it do? I just pinched the bridge of my nose. "Tell you what. You go around and pick up all these darts, and I'll forget you were in here causing trouble."

She sniffed and carefully offered me her Nerf gun. "Can I still shoot it at the newlyweds when they leave?"

I shrugged and threw my hands up. "Sure. You can shoot at his windshield for all I care. Now, get going." I took the toy gun. "Hey, just so I know whose mom to look for if I catch you out here again, what's your name?"

"Lizzy." She bit her bottom lip. "Lizzy Tracy. Only my mom's not here. You can't talk to her."

Something tickled my brain and I narrowed my eyes. "You James Tracy's daughter?"

She nodded, her wide brown eyes fixed earnestly on mine, and her throat bobbed. I sighed and pushed my hat up. I knew a little about James Tracy, and none of it was awesome. He'd been in Evan's class, married right after school, and divorced just a few years later. He was still around, pulling odd jobs and stuff. But Lizzy's eyes begged me not to ask more about her father.

For some reason I couldn't explain, something about that little girl clicked in my head. I used to be the wild kid like that. And I'd had my own reasons, just like I was sure she had hers. I wasn't going to fix her by going and tattling to her mom, her aunt, or whoever was in charge of her. Maybe what the kid needed was an outlet. Something that felt amazing and powerful but wouldn't hurt anything.

"Well, tell you what. You pick these up quick-like, and I'll set you up with the water canon instead of one of these silly foam dart guns."

Her face blanched in awe. "Water canon?" she whispered.

I winked and made a shushing motion. "Little surprise for my brother. You keep a secret, now?"

She nodded, her eyes moving up and down in their sockets because they never left mine.

"Good. I'm going to go look in on the party, and when I come back in twenty minutes, I want this barn put to rights. There's a broom right over there. Understand?"

This time, she smiled when she nodded.

I have a thing for chocolate. I always have. My mom used to hide it in a locked case whenever she got some, but I always found the key. And I don't care for fancy chocolate. Hershey's is just fine. Generic is okay. As long as it's sweet and smooth, it hits the spot.

Dusty knew that, and he'd bought bucket loads of chocolate kisses for the wedding guests... but mostly for me because he figured I'd be the one taking care of the leftovers. And right now, I was filling the pockets of my vest with big handfuls.

They weren't dancing at this wedding because Dusty and Jess weren't into it. It was just cake and toasts and some of Dad's famous smoked brisket served buffet style. I'd already missed the main course, but I did my duty, held up my glass, and said the nicest things I could think to say about my kid brother and my new sister. Jess was going to be a killer sister—fun to watch football with, and she could soup up my truck for me. People laughed when I said that, but I was serious.

Then I filled a plate of leftover brisket, pocketed my goodies and headed outside. I had the after-party to prep. I found Lizzy still in the barn, just sweeping up the last pile of dirt. I set the plate down and looked around. "I didn't say you had to detail the place. Just pick up the darts. This looks great."

She set the broom aside. "Did you really say water canon?"

I chuckled. "Yep, I sure did. We have a big water truck out back. See, Cody and Marshall thought it would be funny to paint a bunch of pink hearts and stuff all over Dusty's truck before they leave for their honeymoon, but Dusty will die of embarrassment to have smooching signs all over his rig. I figure we'll give them a sendoff to talk about for years to come, and wash some of that stuff off the truck into the bargain."

Lizzy came close, sly and smooth as a little cat. "And I can hold the water hose? Is it strong, like a fire truck?"

"Not quite, but that's a good thing. A fire hose would take Evan and Marshall and me just to hold it. But it's bigger than a garden hose. Trust me, you'll love it. Hey, you hungry?" I offered her the plate of brisket. "I didn't grab a fork, but we're in a barn. Pretty sure bare fingers are legal."

She giggled and dove in. The kid could put it away, and she liked the same pieces I did—the crusty edge pieces with all the flavorful bark to savor. We cleaned the plate slick, and I tossed it in the trash.

"Okay, one last thing. We're missing out on the cake, so I brought some dessert." I dug into my pocket and produced a handful of silver-wrapped deliciousness.

Lizzy's whole face lit up. "Those are my favorites! My aunt won't let me have them."

"Well, your aunt don't need to know. You got pockets in that dress? No? Here, gobble quick, then we'll run out back and drive the truck around before everyone comes outside."

Lizzy unwrapped about five chocolate kisses and shoved them all in her mouth at once. There were so many she couldn't close her mouth to chew them, and we both laughed at how she jawed her chocolate like a cow. Her teeth were bathed in brown syrup, and her lips were covered with sticky goo. Oh, her aunt would know she'd had candy, all right, but who cared? We were at a wedding, and it was chocolate.

She was still smacking her lips, trying to sweep all the chocolate off her gums, and her face was glowing with happiness. "Dis is da bes' wedding ever!"

"And it's going to get better. Need some more?" I gave her another handful, then grabbed my hat off the bench beside me. "Let's go make this a wedding no one will ever forget."

Audrey

I always cry at weddings. I don't even have to know the couple. It's just the idea of two people plunging into the unknown forever, and swearing to do it side-by-side and hand-in-hand. I don't know; it just gets me every time. Usually, by the time the groom takes the bride's hand and looks utterly breath-taken, I'm dabbing tears. And when the bride lifts her sure, but trembling voice to pledge her heart to the man she adores, I'm a blubbering mess. I've learned not to wear mascara to these things.

But today, I was in worse shape than usual. I'd gotten to be pretty good friends with Jess. We'd spent many hours together over the past few months, mostly volunteering at White Pines. I had met a lot of great people there, but she was the only person I'd made much time for after hours. It wasn't like I didn't enjoy other people. I used to be a social butterfly, with such a full engagement calendar that I'd hired a virtual assistant just to keep it all sorted.

These days, I had my hands full taking care of my sister Kat, who was in the final stages of kidney failure, and her precocious, energetic daughter Lizzy. Social life? That was a thing of the past. I was surviving, putting one foot in front of the other, trying to keep everyone's spirits up, and praying against the inevitable.

Jess was the one person I'd gotten comfortable enough with to let her in behind closed doors on those days when I just needed someone to talk to who didn't try to solve the unsolvable. She just listened. She smiled. She held my hand, brought over some books to read, and she picked up Lizzy from school a few times when I'd been swamped at work. And now, she was moving to Walker Ranch.

What was it about these Walker cowboys? All my friends were dropping like flies for them! First, Morgan—although, I guess Cody was adopted, but that still counts in my book. Then Kelli, who'd snapped up maybe the most handsome of the bunch. From what I could see, she and Marshall spent as much time "bickering" as they did kissing, and they seemed to thrive on it.

Even Meryl Justice, the retired bank manager who'd approved my loan to buy the dental practice, was engaged to the patriarch of the Walker family. Blake was a good guy. They all were, everyone said. But what was the deal? I honestly didn't understand the obsession with cowboys.

Especially *that* one. I rolled my eyes and counted to three when Luke Walker, the wild one of the family, yelled out for Dusty to kiss Jess again in front of everybody. The man was a yokel.

I was embarrassed for Jess, but she didn't seem to mind kissing her new husband again. Everyone else erupted in applause and laughter.

It *was* cute, the way Dusty draped his blushing bride over his arm and shielded their faces with his hat.

I had to admit that Jess had done pretty well for herself. Dusty was one of the sweetest men alive, but that didn't mean I had any intentions of following in her footsteps. The only cowboy to make me swoon was Cowboy Bill, who owned Beaufort's steak house. He made a pretty delicious chili, and, wonder of wonders, it was now one of my favorite comfort foods to pick up in a carry-out box after a long day.

But other cowboys? Nope. I had a type already, and my type didn't include a dusty hat and worn-out boots.

Everyone was wandering toward the backyard of the house, where a dozen picnic tables had been set out under shade tents in case it started raining again. Blake promised everyone a plate of smoked brisket, baked beans, cheesy potatoes and corn bread, and nobody minded a little rain with that kind of inducement. Hardly standard wedding fare where I'm from, but it *was* amazing. If anyone knew how to smoke a brisket, it was the Walkers.

I waited in line for my turn to fill my plate and glanced around. My niece was nowhere to be seen. I stood nervously on my toes and swept the wedding party with a worried glance. Lizzy had a bad habit of getting into trouble.

She wasn't a bad kid. She was book-smart and sharp as a whip at the same time—a dangerous mixture combined with the boredom that was her life. A kid with a terminally ill mother did a lot of waiting around.

I'd been taking care of Lizzy for over a year now, and I'd watched with dismay the slow unraveling of her behavior. She got in trouble at school for making too much noise and not turning in her homework, even when I'd checked it the night before. She got dropped from the girls' volleyball team for showing up late to practices, even though she was at school by the proper time.

And she had trouble making friends because nobody quite knew how to take her. The more she was left to her own devices, the worse things got. And I hadn't seen her since the last vows were spoken.

"Hey, Morgan," I asked, sidling over to her at a table, "have you seen Lizzy? She promised not to run off this time."

Morgan winced and gave a guilty smile. "Sorry, Audrey. Luke bought a bunch of Nerf guns for the kids to shoot at the newlyweds' truck when they drive away, and I told them they could all go get ready."

I felt my entire face drop. "He bought *what?* Who does that?"

Morgan chuckled. "Luke does. Come on, they can't hurt anything, and they'll have a ton of fun with it."

I closed my eyes and shook my head, searching for that calm center that would keep me from doing or saying something unreasonable. I tried... honestly, I was trying. I counted in my head a lot these days. "You're not kidding. They're really going to fire a bunch of darts at the truck as it drives away?"

She shrugged with a helpless grin. "Guess so. But keep it quiet, please. The surprise is part of the fun."

"Oh, I just bet it is."

Lizzy would love it. I wasn't personally crazy about the idea, but Morgan was right. Where was the harm? It wasn't what I was used to, and I wouldn't want someone pulling a surprise like that at *my* wedding.

Weddings should be classy, beautiful affairs. The new couple had just sworn to love each other for their whole lives! That deserved a little respect, a little decorum. But here we were, eating brisket and baked beans on paper plates in the backyard and waiting for a bunch of kids to pepper the honeymoon vehicle with Nerf Darts.

Yeah. Not at all what I was used to.

I wasn't as sociable as I should have been at dinner. The food was incredible, and people were going back for seconds and thirds. Everyone was having a great time, laughing and talking nonstop. But I was more worried about what Lizzy had gotten up to. I hadn't seen her in over an hour. When we were at home, and things got quiet, I got nervous. She was an imaginative, mischievous kid who had a lot to deal with, and sometimes things... happened.

The worst of it was that most people didn't realize why she acted out. Instead of guidance and understanding, Lizzy's behavior was usually met with frustration and punishment. I spent a lot of time trying to shield her from the typical corrections meted out by the school because they would only make things worse. But I couldn't let her just run wild, so I tended to be a protective mama bear to her in public, but I overcompensated with more correction at home. Which wasn't working, either.

My fears came to a head when I saw Evan Walker escorting Dustin Truman up from the barns in search of Meg, his mother. He was crying. And somehow, I knew before I even walked over to find out what had happened.

Lizzy.

"She shot him in the side of the head with the Nerf darts," Meg whispered. "But I don't think she meant to. It was just a game."

"Lizzy knows better, especially when it comes to Dustin. Either she wasn't watching where she was pointing, which is bad enough, or she *was*, and she hit him on purpose."

"He's okay. I'll just keep him with me until he's able to calm down. I'm just impressed that he was playing with the other kids at all. Really, Audrey, I think they were just having fun, and it got out of hand."

I blew out a breath. Meg Truman was one of the few people who *did* get it. Of course, she got it. She faced some of the same challenges raising a bright, autistic son on her own. "Thanks, Meg, but she still needs a consequence for that one. I'm going to have to tell her she can't shoot at the truck as it's leaving. Any idea where the kids are?"

Meg shook her head with a laugh. "There are so many barns and outbuildings here. They've probably already moved from the last place I heard about! I'm sure they'll turn up for cake and ice cream."

Oh, great. Sugar. Because that was *exactly* what Lizzy needed. Every time she visited her dad, she came home bouncing off the walls. I'd spend the week getting her detoxed from all the junk food he fed her, and then the weekend would roll around, and she'd come home berserk again. "Yeah. I'm sure she'll turn up for that. Thanks, Meg."

But Lizzy didn't appear when Dusty and Jess cut their cake. And I was starting to actually worry. I didn't even stay for the toasts but headed for the last places I'd heard the kids playing. The problem was, this place was huge. I was crossing the lawn again to try somewhere else, when someone called me.

"Audrey, there you are!"

I turned around to find Kelli Walker, carrying a serving tray of coffee cups. She lifted it toward me. "You look like you need a pick-me-up. I have a super dark roast for the guys who want to put some hair on their chests and a medium-roast crema blend for the rest of us humans. Care for a cup?"

I reached for one of the lighter-colored cups. "I can't resist a good crema. Thank you."

"Of course. I noticed Kat didn't come today. Jess wasn't sure if she'd make it or not."

I shook my head. "This would be too much for her. I actually need to get back soon. We're doing all her dialysis treatments at home now, and she gets a treatment almost every afternoon."

Kelli blinked. "Every day?"

I shrugged and sipped my coffee. Kelli really did know how to make a proper brew. "Almost. It's easier on her than going to the hospital twice a week. It's three hours or so every time, though. I have a respite nurse sitting with her right now, but she can't run the treatments."

Kelli's forehead wrinkled, and she stuck her lip out in sympathy. I used to think she was pouting and being overly dramatic when she made that expression, but it was just what her face did when she hurt for someone. "That's really hard for you, though. Isn't there anyone else who can help? I thought she had some skilled in-home nursing."

"Sure, but Katherine gets upset when I'm gone for very long." I stared down into my cup and let go just a morsel of the awful truth. "It's... it's not good."

Kelli turned and shoved the tray of coffee cups onto a convenient oak barrel that had been set up as a standing tabletop. She came back and rested a hand on my shoulder. "I'm sorry to hear that. Morgan and I were wondering about her. She seemed to think Kat might pull through."

I looked up, met Kelli's deep brown eyes, and bit my lips together.

"Oh, Audrey. I didn't know it was that bad," she whispered. "How long?"

I shook my head and sipped some more coffee. "I don't know. The doctors say a few months, but what do they know?"

Kelli's mouth trembled, and she swallowed. "Does Lizzy know?"

I huffed, blinked away the mist from my eyes, and looked to the corner of the room. "Oh, I'm sure she knows, deep down. But Kat doesn't want me to tell her anything yet. I think it's wrong, because the poor girl's confused, and nobody's giving her any answers. But what can I do? I'm just her aunt."

"You're all she's got. That's what you are."

I rested my gaze on Kelli and wished I had something of the charming flintiness she could brandish whenever it suited her. "Yeah," I agreed softly. "I guess I am."

"Speaking of which…" Kelli pointed to the driveway, where the newlyweds were commencing their farewell march away from the party. "Looks like it's time. Is Lizzy joining the Nerf battle?"

Too late to stop it now. I sighed. "I'm sure she wouldn't miss it."

"Come on!" Kelli dragged my hand from my face and pulled me along with the crowd. "This is going to be fun, Audrey Livingstone, and you deserve five minutes of fun. Look!"

Jess was twirling around, swaying her bouquet to a chorus of cheers. Most of the single girls were clustering around her, hopping, excited, and playfully jostling each other.

"Why aren't you going up there, Audrey?" Kelli demanded. She actually pushed me forward! I was so astonished I let my feet move before I could turn and gape at her. I wanted nothing to do with catching that bouquet. But it didn't matter anyway, because after Jess acted like she was going to throw it, she turned and handed it to Meryl Justice. And nobody could object to that.

Meryl kissed Jess on the cheek, dabbed her eyes, and then the newlyweds walked toward Dusty's truck. Dusty opened the door for his new wife and knelt in the gravel so she could step on his knee instead of jumping. And even my stodgy old heart gave a little thump at that. Maybe cowboys could be pretty great, after all.

"And... now!" a voice shouted.

I didn't even have to look to know which cowboy *that* was.

Jess had barely got her door shut when Luke Walker, leading a mob of short savages, charged the truck, pelting it and Dusty with green and blue foam darts. Dusty laughed, pointed at Luke like he was going to make him pay for that little stunt, then ducked inside the cab. Even then, they weren't safe because an army of monsters rushed after him for about twenty yards, firing an avalanche of darts.

But the mayhem was just getting started. "Fire in the hole!" Luke cried. I couldn't see him anymore, but there was no mistaking that cowboy drawl. And that was when I realized my niece hadn't been one of the kids wielding a plastic dart gun.

I had a bad feeling about this.

The kids all drew back to the sound of a heavy old truck rumbling around the corner of the nearest barn. It was a water truck, and it turned down the drive to follow Dusty's pickup. And sitting right on top was Luke Walker with my niece, wearing her best party dress.

"Oh, no," I whispered. "What is that girl up to now?"

But it was pretty obvious. Lizzy was holding a huge hose, and when Luke flipped a lever, she reared back with the force of the water and proceeded to douse Dusty and Jess's truck as it tried to escape.

That thing had some power, too, and my heart stopped. It had almost flipped Lizzy over backward! The only reason she didn't fly off was because Luke made a quick grab for her shoulders to steady her and then had to keep a hand braced behind her.

Yeah, he saved her from falling, but he was the idiot who had put her up there in the first place. That didn't make him a hero.

I followed to the edge of the slope, where I could watch the water truck's progress down the long driveway. There was nowhere to turn around until it got down to the bottom of the hill, and there was nothing for me to do but wait until it got back. And so, I waited.

Seething.

When it did finally roll up the hill to a smattering of cheers and shouts, I was waiting for it. Luke and Lizzy were still sitting on top, laughing like a couple of crazy people. Luke barely glanced over my head—I doubted he even knew who I was. But he'd know in a few seconds, the rascal.

When I got around the corner of the truck, Luke was helping Lizzy down, and she straightened to face me. She wasn't laughing anymore. "I'm sorry, Aunt Audrey," she said. Oh, her voice was perfectly respectable, but there was a rebellious twinkle in her eye. And chocolate all over her face.

I just stared. "What in Heaven's name? What did you do, drink syrup from a trough?"

Lizzy gave me a weak smile, and I reeled in dizzy horror when I saw that even her teeth hadn't been spared. Her entire mouth was stained brown. "How much did you eat?" I asked in alarm.

Chocolate was the very worst thing for her. Not only was it the onslaught of mass quantities of sugar, which was like a nuclear bomb to her system, but I'd started to suspect Lizzy was lactose intolerant. She was going to spend the night sick to her stomach again, I just knew it. My head exploded with visions of me, running between Kat's dialysis treatment and Lizzy doubled over the toilet. This was just too much.

That was when a tall cowboy jumped down from the truck, his booted feet landing beside Lizzy. I looked up... and up... and into the darkest violet-blue eyes I'd ever seen on a man. I'd never been this close to Luke Walker, and... uh... he wasn't... too bad. To look at. Just to look at, mind you.

"Just a couple handfuls of Hershey's Kisses," he said. "It won't kill her."

"A couple of *handfuls?* That's more than she should have in a month!"

"Hey, come on, sweet thing. It's a wedding! Let the kid have a little fun."

My eyelid started to twitch. "Did you just call me *sweet thing?* Is this a joke to you? Lizzy, go wash your face. It's time to go home."

Luke Walker stuck a flannel-clad arm in front of Lizzy, barring her from doing what I'd told her to. "Now, just wait a second. We were in a hurry, that's all. She didn't get any cake or ice cream because she was helping me, so I gave her some chocolate. What's the big deal?"

"Helping you *what?* You fed her enough chocolate to kill an elephant and then put her up on top of that water truck where she could fall and break her neck!"

He lowered his arm and got a cheesy grin. "Overprotective. I get it. You must be the aunt."

I rolled my eyes. Maybe I *was* overprotective, but raising Lizzy was like running around putting out fires everywhere she went. And he wasn't helping. "Audrey Livingstone. *Doctor* Livingstone to you. And you're Luke Walker, the lunatic."

"Lunatic?" He cocked his head thoughtfully. "I kind of like the sound of that."

"Of course you would, but trust me, it wasn't a compliment. What on earth were you thinking?"

Luke Walker's cheek flinched, and he stuffed his hands in his pockets. "I was thinking it'd be fun, that's what I was thinking. Dusty was laughing."

"I don't really care if Dusty was laughing. You didn't even check with me before you let Lizzy do all that stuff. That's not okay. What is wrong with you?"

He winked and shot me a grin. "You're the doctor. You tell me."

I narrowed my eyes. "The only kind of doctoring you're going to get from me is a dentist's drill with no Novocaine. Come on, Lizzy. We're leaving." I put my arm around Lizzy and marched her toward the car.

"Promise?" Luke called after me.

I turned and glared daggers at him, but he just grinned wider.

"Guess I'll make an appointment for next week, then?"

I straightened. You didn't get anywhere with this kind of guy by rolling your eyes and walking away. You had to challenge them, head-on. "Fine. Next week. I'll sharpen my drill."

Read the rest of *Taming the Cowboy!*

More from Tess Thornton

<u>The Walker Ranch Series</u>

A Home for the Cowboy

Cody and Morgan's Story

A Second Chance for the Cowboy

Marshall and Kelli's Story

A Winter Surprise for the Cowboy

*Blake and Meryl's Story

An Angel for the Cowboy

Dusty and Jess's Story

Taming the Cowboy

Luke and Audrey's Story

A Heart for the Cowboy

Evan and Meg's Story

*_A Winter Surprise for the Cowboy_ is a Free Novella available only to newsletter subscribers

<u>The Ridgeview Brothers Ranch Series</u>
Coming in 2024...

A Rival for the Cowboy

Cole and Emily's Story

A Crossroads for the Cowboy

Chase & Kate's Story

A Christmas Wish for the Cowboy

Trent & Lauren's Story

A Match for the Cowboy

Gage & Amber's Story

A Partner for the Cowboy

A Cowboy Buddy Book featuring Luke Walker and Gage Langton